THE SUMMER OF
DEAD TOYS

The Summer of Dead Toys

A THRILLER

ANTONIO HILL

CROWN PUBLISHERS
New York

Translation copyright © 2012 by Laura McGloughlin

All rights reserved.
Published in the United States by Crown Publishers,
an imprint of the Crown Publishing Group,
a division of Random House, Inc., New York.
www.crownpublishing.com

Originally published in Spain as *El verano de los juguetes muertos*
by Grijalbo, an imprint of Random House Mondadori, Barcelona, in 2011.
This translation originally published in hardcover in the UK by Doubleday,
an imprint of Transworld Publishers, London, in 2012.
Copyright © 2012 by Antonio Hill.

CROWN and the Crown colophon are registered trademarks
of Random House, Inc.

Library of Congress Cataloging-in-Publication Data
Hill Gumbao, Toni.
[Verano de los juguetes muertos. English]
The summer of dead toys : a thriller / Antonio Hill. — 1st ed.
1. Murder—Investigation—Fiction. 2. Barcelona (Spain)—Fiction. 3. Mystery
fiction. I. Ttile.

PQ6708.I45V4713 2013
863'.7—dc23
2012034335

ISBN 978-0-7704-3587-5
eISBN 978-0-7704-3588-2

PRINTED IN THE UNITED STATES OF AMERICA

Book design by Jaclyn Reyes
Jacket design by Roberto De Vicq De Cumptich
Jacket photograph: Jorge Delgado
Author photograph: James Recoder

1   3   5   7   9   10   8   6   4   2

First United States Edition

To my mother, for everything

It's been a long time since I thought of Iris or the summer she died. I suppose I tried to forget it all, in the same way I overcame nightmares and childhood fears. And now, when I want to remember her, all that comes to mind is the last day, as if these images have erased all the previous ones. I close my eyes and bring myself to that big old house, this dormitory of deserted beds awaiting the arrival of the next group of children. I'm six years old, I'm at camp and I can't sleep because I'm scared. No, I lie. That very early morning I behaved like a brave boy: I disobeyed my uncle's rules and faced the darkness just to see Iris. But I found her drowned, floating in the pool, surrounded by a cortège of dead dolls.

WEDNESDAY

1

He turned off the alarm clock at the first buzz. Eight a.m. Although he'd been awake for hours a sudden heaviness overcame his limbs and he had to force himself to get out of bed and go to the shower. The stream of water cleared his sluggishness and along with it some of the effects of jet lag. He had arrived only hours before, after an interminable Buenos Aires-Barcelona flight which was prolonged further in the Lost Luggage office at the airport. The assistant, who had definitely been one of those sadistic British schoolmistresses in a previous life, consumed his last shred of patience, looking at him as if the suitcase were a being with free will and had opted to trade in this owner for one less moody-looking.

He dried himself vigorously and noticed with annoyance that sweat was already appearing on his brow: that was summer in Barcelona. Humid and sticky as a melted ice-cream. With the towel wrapped round his waist he looked at himself in the mirror. He should shave. Fuck it. He went back to the bedroom and rummaged in the half-empty wardrobe for some underwear. Luckily the clothes in the lost suitcase were winter ones, so he had no problems finding a short-sleeved shirt and trousers. Barefoot, he sat on the bed. He took a deep breath. The long journey was taking its toll and he was tempted to lie back down, close his eyes and forget about the meeting he had at ten o'clock sharp, although deep down he knew he was incapable of doing so. Héctor Salgado never missed a meeting. Even if it might be with his executioner, he said to himself and smiled ironically.

His right hand searched for his mobile phone on the nightstand. Very little battery life remained and he remembered that the charger was in the damn suitcase. The day before he'd felt too wrecked to speak to anyone. He looked up Ruth's number in the phonebook and stayed looking at the screen for a few seconds before pressing the green button. He always called her on her mobile, surely in an attempt to ignore the fact that she had another landline. Another house. Another partner. Her voice, somewhat hoarse, just awake, whispered in his ear:

"Héctor . . ."

"Did I wake you?"

"No . . . Well, a bit." He heard a stifled laugh in the background. "But I had to get up anyway. When did you get back?"

"Sorry. I arrived yesterday morning, but those idiots lost my bag and I was in the airport for half the day. My mobile is about to run out of battery. I just wanted you to know that I'd arrived safely."

Suddenly he felt stupid. Like a child talking too much.

"How was the flight?"

"Calm," he lied. "Listen, is Guillermo asleep?"

Ruth laughed.

"Your accent always changes when you come back from Buenos Aires. Guillermo's not here, didn't I tell you? He's spending a few days at the beach, at a friend's house. But I'm sure he'll be sleeping at this time," she added immediately.

"Yeah." A pause; lately their conversations stalled continually. "And how's it going?"

"He's good, but I swear if pre-adolescence lasts much longer I'm sending him back to you, postage paid." Ruth smiled. He remembered the shape of her smile and that sudden light in her eyes. Her tone changed. "Héctor? Hey, have you heard about your thing?"

"I have to see Savall at ten."

"OK, let me know how it goes afterward."

Another pause.

"We could have lunch together?" Héctor had lowered his voice. She took a little longer than necessary to answer.

"Sorry, I already have plans." For a moment he thought the battery had run out completely, although finally the voice continued. "But we'll talk later. We could have a coffee . . ."

Then it did. Before he could respond, the phone had become a lump of dead metal. He looked at it with hatred. Then his eyes went toward his bare feet. And with a jump, as if the brief chat had given him the necessary impulse, he rose and walked once again toward that accusatory wardrobe full of empty hangers.

Héctor lived in a three-story building, on the third floor. Nothing special, one of many such buildings in Poblenou, close to the metro station and a couple of blocks from the other *rambla* that didn't appear in tourist guidebooks. The only notable features of his flat were the rent, which hadn't risen when the area took on the airs of a privileged place near the beach, and a flat roof, which, for all practical purposes, had become his private terrace. The second floor was vacant, awaiting a tenant who never arrived, and the landlady lived on the first floor, a woman of almost seventy who hadn't the least interest in climbing two flights of stairs. He and Ruth had fixed up the old roof, covering part of it and installing various potted plants, now withered, as well as a table and chairs for eating outside on summer nights. He'd hardly gone back up there since Ruth left.

The door of the first-floor apartment opened just as he was passing and Carmen, the owner of the building, came out to greet him.

"Héctor." She was smiling. As always, he told himself that when he was old he wanted to be like this good woman. Even better, to have one like her by his side. He stopped and gave her a kiss on the cheek, a little awkwardly. Affectionate gestures had never been his strong point. "Yesterday I heard noises upstairs, but I thought you'd be tired. Want a coffee? I've just made some."

"Are you spoiling me?"

"Nonsense," she replied decidedly. "Men must go out well fed. Come to the kitchen."

Héctor followed her obediently. The house smelled of freshly made coffee.

"I missed your coffee, Carmen."

She observed him with a frown as he helped himself to a generous cup of coffee, then added a drop of milk.

"Well fed and well shaved," the woman added pointedly.

"Don't be hard on me, Carmen, I've only just arrived," he pleaded.

"Don't you play the victim. How are you?" She looked at him affectionately. "How did it go in your native land? Ah, smoke a cigarette, I know you want one."

"You're the best, Carmen." He took out a packet of cigarettes and lit one. "I don't understand how you haven't been snared by some granddad made of money."

"Because I don't like granddads! When I turned sixty-five, I looked around and said to myself, Carmen, enough's enough—close up shop. Spend your time watching films at home . . . By the way, the ones you lent me are over there. I've watched them all," she said proudly.

Héctor's film collection would have turned more than one cinephile green with envy: from Hollywood classics—Carmen's favorites—to the latest releases. All placed on wall-to-wall shelves, with no apparent order. One of his greatest pleasures on sleepless nights was to pull out a few and lie down on the sofa to watch them.

"Marvelous," continued Carmen. She was an avid fan of Grace Kelly, whom she was said to have resembled when she was young. "But don't try to distract me. How are you?"

He exhaled slowly and finished his coffee. The woman's gaze didn't falter: those blue eyes must have been true man-eaters. Carmen wasn't one of those old women who enjoy evoking the past, but thanks to Ruth, Héctor knew there had been at least two husbands ("easily forgotten, poor things," in Carmen's own words) and a lover ("a swine of the kind you don't forget"). But in the end there'd been one last one, who had secured her old age by leaving her that three-story building, in which she could live even better were she not saving one of the apartments for a son who'd left years before and never returned.

Héctor poured himself a little more coffee before answering.

"I can't deceive you, Carmen." He tried to smile, but his exhausted expression and sad eyes ruined the effort. "Everything is shit. I beg your pardon. For a long time everything has seemed like shit."

Investigation 1231-R
H. Salgado
Resolution Pending

Three short lines noted in black felt-tip pen on a yellow post-it note attached to a file of the same color. So as not to see them, Superintendent Savall opened the file and looked over its contents. As if he didn't already know them by heart. Statements. Affidavit. Medical reports. Police brutality. Photographs of that scumbag's injuries. Photographs of that unfortunate young Nigerian girl. Photographs of the flat in the Raval where they had the girls corralled. Even various newspaper cuttings, some—very few, thank God—deliberately narrating their own version of the facts, emphasizing concepts like injustice, racism and abuse of power. He slammed the file shut and looked at the clock on his desk. Ten past nine. Fifty minutes. He was moving his chair back to stretch out his legs when someone knocked on the door and opened it almost simultaneously.

"Is he here?" he asked.

The woman entering the office shook her head without asking to whom the question referred and, very quietly, leaned both hands on the back of the chair facing the desk. She looked him in the eyes and spoke.

"What will you say to him?" The question sounded like an accusation, a burst of gunfire in six words.

Savall shrugged his shoulders, almost imperceptibly.

"What I have to. What do you want me to say to him?"

"Fine. Great."

"Martina . . ." He tried to be brusque, but he was too fond

of her to get truly angry. He lowered his voice. "Fuck it, my hands are tied."

She didn't give up. She moved the chair back a little, sat down and drew it back up to the desk.

"What else do they need? That guy is out of hospital. He's at home, cool as can be, reorganizing his business while—"

"Give it a rest, Martina!" Sweat broke out on his forehead and for once he lost his temper. He'd promised himself he wouldn't when he got up that morning. But he was human. He opened the yellow file and took out the photos; he scattered them across the desk like uncovered playing cards showing a poker of aces. "Broken jaw. Two fractured ribs. Contusions to the skull and abdomen. A face like a fucking map. All because Héctor lost his head and planted himself in this shit's house. The guy was lucky not to have internal injuries. He beat him half to death." She knew all this. She also knew that had she been sitting in the chair opposite, she would have said exactly the same. But if there was something that defined Sergeant Martina Andreu it was her unswerving loyalty to her own: her family, her colleagues and her friends. For her the world was split into two distinct groups: her people, and everyone else, and without doubt Héctor Salgado fell into the first. So, in a loud and deliberately disdainful voice, one that irritated her boss more than seeing those photos, she counterattacked.

"Why don't you take out the others? The ones of the girl. Why don't we see what that evil black quack did to that poor young girl?"

Savall took a deep breath. "Watch it with that black stuff." Martina gestured impatiently. "That's all we need. And the thing with the girl doesn't justify aggression. You know it, I know it, Héctor knows it. And what's worse, so does that asshole's lawyer." He lowered his voice: he'd worked with Andreu for years and trusted her more than any of his other subordinates. "He was here the day before yesterday." Martina raised an eyebrow.

"Yes, What'shisname's lawyer. I put things very clearly to him. Withdraw the charges against Salgado or his client will have a cop following him until he goes to his fucking grave."

"And?" she asked, looking at her boss with renewed respect.

"He said he had to consult him. I pushed him as much as I could. Off the record. We left it that he'd ring me this morning before ten."

"And if he agrees? What did you promise him in return?"

Savall didn't have time to respond. The telephone on the desk rang like an alarm. He asked the sergeant to be quiet with a finger to his lips, then picked up.

"Yes?" For a moment his face was expectant, but instantly his expression became one of simple irritation. "No. No! I'm busy now. I'll call her later." Rather than hang up, he slammed the receiver down and, directing himself to the sergeant, added: "Joana Vidal."

She snorted.

"Again?"

The superintendent shrugged.

"Nothing new in her case, is there?"

"Nothing. Did you see the report? It's as clear as water. The boy got distracted and fell from the window. Pure bad luck."

Savall nodded.

"Good report, by the way. Very thorough. It was the new girl's, right?"

"Yes. I made her do it again, but in the end it was good." Martina smiled. "The girl seems clever."

Any praise coming from Andreu had to be taken seriously.

"Her record is impeccable," the superintendent said. "First

in her class, unbeatable references from her superiors, courses abroad. Even Rosa, who's merciless with the newbies, wrote a complimentary report. If I remember correctly, she mentions 'a natural talent' for investigation."

Just as Martina was preparing to give one of her sarcastically feminist commentaries on the gap in talent and average IQ between the men and women of the force, the phone rang again.

At that moment, in the station's front office, the young investigator Leire Castro was using that natural talent to satisfy one of the most striking features of her character: curiosity. She'd proposed having a coffee to one of the agents who'd spent weeks giving her discreet yet friendly smiles. He seemed a good guy, she told herself, and giving him what he wanted made her feel somewhat guilty. But since her arrival at the central police station in Plaça Espanya, the enigma that was Héctor Salgado had been challenging her thirst for knowledge, and today, when she was expecting to see him appear at any moment, she couldn't take it anymore.

So it was that, after a brief preamble of small-talk, with a black coffee in her hands, controlling the desire to smoke, wearing her best smile, Leire got straight to the point. She couldn't spend half an hour gossiping in the office.

"What's he like? Inspector Salgado, I mean."

"You don't know him? Oh yeah, you arrived just as he started his 'holiday.'"

She nodded.

"Well, I don't know what to tell you," he continued. "A normal guy, or so he seemed." He smiled. "You never know with Argentines."

Leire did her best to hide her disappointment. She hated

generalizations and the individual with the friendly smile automatically lost points. He must have noticed, because he made an effort to expand on his explanation.

"A couple of days before it all happened I'd have said he was a calm man. Never raised his voice. Efficient. Stubborn but patient. A good cop . . . Thorough, sleuth-style. But suddenly, boom, his mind clouds over and he goes wild. Left us all dumbfounded, to tell the truth. We've enough bad press without an inspector losing his head like that."

He was right about that, Leire said to herself. She took advantage of her companion's silence to ask: "What happened? I know the gist, I read something in the papers, but—"

"What happened was he lost it. No more, no less." In this respect the guy seemed to have a firm opinion with no hesitation. "No one says it out loud because he's the inspector and all that, and the super is very fond of him, but it's true. He beat that guy half to death. They say he turned in his resignation but the super threw it back in his face. He did order him on a month's 'holiday' until the air cleared. And you know the press haven't fed on the subject. It could have been much worse."

Leire took another sip of coffee. It tasted strange. She'd kill for a cigarette but she'd decided not to smoke her first one until after lunch, at least another four hours away. She breathed deeply, to see if filling her lungs with air killed the nicotine cravings. The trick half worked. Her companion threw his plastic cup in the recycling bin.

"I'll deny everything I've said if need be," he said, smiling. "You know, all for one and one for all, like the musketeers. But there are things that aren't right. Now I've got to go: duty calls."

"Of course," she nodded, distracted. "See you later."

She stayed a few moments, remembering what she'd read

on the subject of Inspector Salgado. In March, barely four months previously, Héctor Salgado had coordinated an operation against the trafficking of women. His team spent a year tracking a criminal gang that made a living bringing in young African girls, principally Nigerians, to fill various brothels in Vallés and Garraf. The younger the better, of course. Those from the East and South America had gone out of fashion: too clever and too demanding. Clients were requesting young, frightened, black girls to satisfy their basest instincts, and the traffickers found themselves more able to control these illiterate, disoriented girls, taken out of extreme poverty with the vague promise of a future that couldn't be worse than the present. But it was. Sometimes Leire asked herself how they could be so blind. Had they ever seen one of their predecessors come back, having become a rich woman, capable of lifting her family out of misery? No: it was a flight forward, a desperate route down which many were pushed by their own parents and husbands with no choice. A journey, certainly tinged with a mixture of excitement and suspicion, which ended in a nauseating room where the girls learned that hope was something they couldn't afford. No longer was it about aspiring to a better life; it was about survival. And the pigs manipulating them—a network of criminals and former prostitutes who had ascended in the ranks—used all means available to make them understand why they were there and what their new, repugnant obligations were.

She felt a vibration in her trouser pocket and took out her private mobile. A red light flashed, signalling a message. On seeing the name of the sender a smile crossed her face. Javier. Five foot eleven, dark eyes, the right quantity of hair on his bronzed torso and a puma tattooed diagonally just below the abs. And to top it all, a nice guy, Leire said to herself, as she opened that little envelope. "Hey, I just woke up and you're already gone. Why do u always disappear without saying anything? We'll see each other tonite and tomorrow you make me breakfast? Miss you. Kisses."

Leire stared at her mobile for a moment. That was that with Javier. The boy was charming, no doubt, although he wasn't exactly a spelling whiz. Nor very mature, she thought, looking at her watch. What's more, something about that message had set off an inner alarm she recognized and had learned to respect, a twinkling flash that went off when certain members of the opposite sex, after a couple of nights of good sex, started asking for explanations and saying they felt like "taking hot chocolate to bed." Luckily there weren't many of them. The majority accepted her game without problems, the healthy no-strings sex that she laid out openly. But there was always someone like Javier who didn't get it. A pity, Leire told herself, as she tapped out an answer at top speed, that he belonged to that small group of men. "Can't tonight. I'll call you. By the way, tonight has a 'g' and 'h' and no 'e,' remember that. See you soon!" She re-read the message and in a fit of compassion she deleted the second part before sending it. An unnecessary cruelty, she reproached herself. The small sealed envelope flew through space and she hoped that Javier would know to read between the lines, but just in case she put the mobile on silent before finishing her coffee.

The last gulp, already half cold, turned her stomach. A cold sweat soaked her forehead. She breathed deeply a second time, while thinking she couldn't delay any longer. This morning nausea had to have an explanation. This very day you'll drop into the pharmacy, she ordered herself firmly, although deep down she knew perfectly well there was no need. The answer to her questions lay in a glorious weekend a month before.

She came back to herself slowly and some minutes later she felt strong enough to return to her desk. She sat down in front of her computer, ready to concentrate on her work, just as the door of Superintendent Savall's office was closing.

The third man in the office might intend to earn his living as a lawyer, but if he were to be judged by his eloquence and capacity for expression, the future before him was a little gloomy. In his defense, he wasn't in a comfortable position, and neither the superintendent nor Héctor Salgado was making it any easier for him.

For the fourth time in ten minutes, Damián Fernández wiped away sweat with the same wrinkled tissue before answering a question.

"I already told you. I saw Dr. Omar the night before last, around nine."

"And did you communicate the proposal that I made to him?"

Héctor didn't know what proposal Savall was speaking of, but he could imagine it. He threw an appreciative glance at his boss, although anger shone in the depth of his eyes. Any deal in that bastard's favor, even in return for saving his neck, left his stomach feeling hollow.

Fernández nodded. He loosened the knot of his tie as if it were strangling him.

"Every word." He cleared his throat. "I told him . . . I told him he didn't have to accept it. That you had very little on him anyway." He must have noticed the rage rising in the superintendent's face but he justified himself immediately. "It's the truth. With that girl dead, nothing links him to the trafficking . . . They can't even accuse you of malpractice when you don't pretend to be a doctor. If they locked you up for that, they'd have to lock up all the fortune-tellers, quacks and holy men in Barcelona . . . the prison couldn't hold them all. But," he hastened to say, "I emphasized that the police could be very in- sistent and, since he was already recovering from the assault," and saying that word he directed a rapid and nervous glance toward Inspector Salgado, who didn't turn a hair, "maybe the best thing would be to forget the whole thing . . ."

The superintendent inhaled deeply.

"And did you convince him?"

"I think so . . . Well," he corrected himself, "the truth is that he just said he'd think it over. And he'd call me the following day to give me an answer."

"But he didn't."

"No. I called his clinic yesterday, various times, but no one answered. That didn't surprise me. The doctor doesn't take calls while he's working."

"So you decided to go to see him first thing this morning?"

"Yes. I had to have an answer for you, and well . . ." he hesi- tated, "it's not as if I have much to do these days."

Not for the foreseeable future either, Savall and Salgado thought in unison, but they said nothing.

"And you went. About nine."

Fernández nodded. He swallowed. "Pallor" was too poetic a word to describe the color of his face.

"Do you have any water?"

The superintendent exhaled.

"Not in here. We're almost finished. Continue, Señor Fernán- dez, please."

"It wasn't even nine. The bus came immediately and—"

"Get to the point, please!"

"Yes. Yes. What I was saying was that, although it was a bit early, I went up anyway and when I went to knock on the door, I saw it was ajar." He stopped. "Well, I thought I could go in; at the end of the day, maybe something had happened to him." He swallowed once more; the tissue came apart in his hands when he tried to use it again. "It smelled . . . it smelled strange. Rotten. I called him as I went toward his office, at the end of the corridor . . . That door was ajar as well and . . . I pushed it. Christ!"

The rest he'd already described at the beginning, his face distorted, before Héctor arrived. The pig's head on the desk. Blood everywhere. And not a trace of the doctor.

"Just what we needed," muttered the super as soon as the nervous lawyer had left the office. "We'll go back to having the press biting us like vultures."

Héctor thought the vultures were hardly biting, but he stopped himself commenting. In any case, he wouldn't have had time because Savall picked up the receiver and called an extension. Half a minute later, Sergeant Andreu was coming into the office. Martina didn't know what was happening, but she guessed by her boss's face it was nothing good, so after winking at Héctor by way of a greeting, she got ready to listen. If the news Savall gave her surprised her as much as it had them, she hid it well. She listened attentively, asked a couple of pertinent questions, and left to carry out her orders. Héctor's eyes followed her. He almost started on hearing his name.

"Héctor. Listen carefully because I'm only saying this once. I've risked my neck for you. I've defended you to the press and the brass. I've pulled out all the stops to bury this business. And I'm on the verge of convincing that guy to drop the charges. But if you go near that flat, if you intervene in this investigation even for one minute, I won't be able to do anything. Understood?"

Héctor crossed one leg over the other. His intense concentration showed in his face.

"It's my head on the chopping-block," he finally said. "Don't you think I've a right to know why they are cutting it off?"

"You lost it, Héctor. The same day you came to blows with that swine you gave up your rights. Now you're facing the consequences."

The thing was, Héctor knew all this but at that moment he didn't care. He couldn't even manage to repent: the blows he'd showered on Omar seemed to him just and deserved. It was as if the serious Inspector Salgado had regressed to his youth in a Buenos Aires *barrio*, when disagreements were resolved by punching each other to shit at the school gates. When you'd go home with a split lip but say you'd been hit in the face playing football. A burst of rebellion was still pricking him in the chest: an absurd, break-my-balls thing, decidedly immature for a cop just turned forty-three.

"And no one remembers the girl?" asked Héctor bitterly. A poor defense, but it was the only one he had.

"Let's see if you get this into your head, Salgado." To his regret, Savall had raised his voice. "As far as we know, there wasn't the least contact between Dr. Omar and the girl in question after the flat where the girls were kept was taken apart. We couldn't even show there was any beforehand without the girl's word. She was in the center for minors. Somehow they managed to do . . . that . . . to them."

Héctor nodded.

"I know the facts, chief."

But the facts didn't manage to convey the horror. The intensely panicked face of a little girl, even in death. Kira wasn't fifteen, didn't speak a word of Spanish or of any language other than her own and yet she'd managed to make herself heard. She was slight, very slim and in her smooth, doll-like face her eyes shone, a color somewhere between amber and chestnut that he'd never seen before. Like the others, Kira had taken part in a ceremony before leaving her country in search of a better future. They called them ju-ju rites, in which, after drinking water used to wash a corpse, the young girls offered pubic hair or menstrual blood, which was collected before an altar. They then promised never to report their traffickers, to pay the supposed debts incurred by their journey and generally to obey without question. The punishment for whoever did not comply with these promises was a horrible death, for her or for the relatives she'd left behind. Kira suffered it herself: nobody would have said so fragile a body could contain so much blood. Héctor tried to block the image from his mind, that same vision that at the time had made him lose his head and go in search of Dr. Omar to extract every bone from his body. That individual's name had come up during the investigation: in theory his only function had been to attend to the girls' health. But the fear betrayed by the girls on hearing his name indicated that the doctor's duties went further than purely medical attention. Not one had dared speak of him. He took precautions and the girls were brought to his clinic individually or in pairs. The most he could be accused of was of not asking questions, and that was a very weak accusation for a witch doctor who ran a squalid clinic and tended to illegal immigrants. But that wasn't enough for Héctor; he'd chosen to lean on the youngest, the most frightened, with the help of an interpreter. All it had achieved was that Kira said, in a very quiet voice, that the doctor had examined her to check whether she was still a virgin and in passing he'd reminded her that she must do what those men said. Nothing else. The following day, her child's hand took up a pair of scissors and made her body a fountain of blood. In Héctor's eighteen years in the police force he'd never seen anything like it, and he'd seen a lot: from junkies without a healthy piece of skin to inject into, to victims of every type of violence. But nothing like this. A macabre, perverse sensation emanated from Kira's mutilated body, something unreal which he couldn't put into words. Something belonging to the realm of nightmares.

"Another thing," Savall continued, as if the previous point had already been agreed without argument. "Before being reinstated, you have to attend some sessions with a force psychologist. It's mandatory. Your first appointment is tomorrow at eleven. So do what you can to appear sane. Starting with a shave."

Héctor didn't protest; in fact, he already knew. Suddenly, and in spite of all the good resolutions he'd made on the long flight back, he didn't give a shit about any of it. Any of it except the bloody pig's head.

"Can I go?"

"One moment. I don't want statements to the press, not even a hint of one. As far as you're concerned, all of this is ongoing and you have no comment. Have I made myself clear?"

Seeing Héctor nod, Savall exhaled and smiled. Salgado got up, ready to leave, but the superintendent didn't seem disposed to let him go yet.

"How was Buenos Aires?"

"Well, you know . . . it's like the Perito Moreno glacier: from time to time it looks like it's going to fall to pieces but the block stays firm."

"It's a fantastic city. And you've put on weight!"

"Too many barbecues. Each Sunday I had one in a different friend's house. It's difficult to resist." The phone on Savall's desk rang again and Héctor wanted to take advantage of the moment to get out of that office once and for all.

"Wait, don't go. Yes? Fuck! Tell her I'll call her back. Then tell her again!"

"Problems?" asked Héctor when his boss had hung up.

"What would life be without them?" Savall fell silent for a few seconds. This usually happened when an idea suddenly seized him and he needed time to translate it into words. "Listen," he said very slowly. "I think there's something you can do for me. Unofficially."

"Do you want me to beat someone up? Fine with me."

"What?" Savall was still absorbed in his deliberations, which exploded like bubbles in an instant. "Sit down." He inhaled, nodding and smiling with satisfaction, as if he were convincing himself of his brilliant idea. "The person who called was Joana Vidal."

"I'm sorry, but I don't know who you're talking about."

"Yeah, you were away when it all happened. It was the night of San Juan." Savall opened one or two files on the desk until he found what he was looking for. "Marc Castells Vidal, nineteen. He was celebrating the festival in his house, just him and two friends. At some point during the night, the boy fell through the window in his room. He died instantly."

"A Superman complex after a couple of lines?"

"There were no drugs in his blood. Alcohol yes, but not in great quantities. It seems he had the habit of smoking a cigarette sitting on the windowsill. Maybe he lost his balance and fell, maybe he jumped . . . He was a strange boy."

"Everyone's strange at nineteen."

"But they don't fall from windows," replied Savall. "The thing is that Marc Castells was the son of Enric Castells. That name ring a bell?"

Héctor meditated for a few seconds before answering.

"Vaguely . . . Business? Politics?"

"Both. He used to run his own company with over a hundred employees. Then he invested in the property market, and he was one of the few who knew to get out before the bubble burst. And recently his name has cropped up repeatedly as the possible number two of a party. There's quite a lot of movement in the lists for the next local elections and they say new faces are needed. At the moment nothing's confirmed, but it's clear that a couple of right-wing parties would like to have him in their ranks."

"Successful businessmen always sell."

"Even more at times of crisis. Well, the case is that the boy fell, or jumped from the window. Full stop. We have nothing else."

"But?"

"His mother won't accept it. It was she who called just now." Savall looked at Héctor with the friendly attitude he did so well from time to time. "She's Castells' ex-wife . . . Bit of a murky story. Joana abandoned her husband and son when the boy was one or two years old. She only saw him again at the funeral."

"Holy shit."

"Yes. I knew her. Joana, I mean. Before she left. We were friends."

"Oh yeah. The Barcelona old guard. Polo companions? I always forget how much you stand by each other."

Savall made a disparaging gesture with his hand.

"Same everywhere. Look, like I said, officially we have nothing. I can't put anyone on it to investigate, and I'm not so flush with inspectors that I can keep them busy with something that definitely won't go anywhere. But . . ."

"But I'm free."

"Exactly. Just take a look at the case: speak to the parents, the kids who were at the party. Give her a definitive answer." Savall lowered his head. "You have a son too. Joana is only asking that someone dedicate more time to the boy's death. Please."

Héctor didn't know if his boss was asking a favor of him, or if he'd guessed what he intended to do and was preventing it before it happened.

Savall passed him the file with a pained smile.

"We'll sit down with Andreu tomorrow. She opened the case with the new girl."

"We have a new girl?"

"Yeah, I put her with Andreu. A little bit green, but on paper she's very clever. First in all the tests, a meteoric rise. You know how the young push."

Héctor took the file and got up.

"I'm delighted to have you back with us." Here was the solemn moment. Savall had numerous registers. At these times, his face reminded Héctor of Robert Duvall's. Paternal, hard, condescending, a little bit slick. "I want you to keep me posted on how it goes with that shrink." All that was missing was a "Behave yourself," an "I hope I don't regret this."

They shook hands.

"And remember." Savall squeezed his subordinate's hand lightly. "The Castells case is unofficial."

Héctor let go, but the echo of the phrase stuck in his mind, like one of those bluebottles that insist on bumping their heads against the glass.

2

For the first time in days Joana Vidal felt something akin to peace. Even satisfaction, or at least relief. Someone had responded to her call, someone had assured her that they'd continue investigating until they reached a conclusive answer. "We'll get to the bottom of it, Joana, I promise you," Savall had assured her. And that was all she wanted, the reason she'd stayed in Barcelona, the city she'd fled and to which she'd returned to attend the funeral of a son whom, to all practical purposes, she didn't know.

Now it was a matter of waiting, she told herself as she wandered around the high-ceilinged flat, which had been her grandmother's and had been closed for years. Ancient—that is, old—furniture, covered with sheets that in their day had been white, gave an overall ghostly air. She'd taken them off in the bedroom and dining room, but she knew that on the other side of the long wide corridor other rooms remained full of immobile, off-white shapes. Her steps led her to the balcony where a half-broken green blind was shielding a row of flowerpots containing only dry soil from the sun. She leaned out, and the midday sun made her half-close her eyes. This balcony was the border between two worlds: on one side Astúries, the heart of the *barrio* of Gràcia, now converted into a pedestrian street where boisterous people dressed in vivid colors—red, green, sky-blue—were walking; on the other, the flat, faded by the years, with walls once an ivory color now appearing grayish. She had only to raise the blind, allow the light to flood the interior, mix the living with the dead. But it wasn't the time. Not yet. First she had to decide which was the place for her.

The heat made her return inside and head toward the kitchen in search of something to drink. Although she'd never been religious, she felt at peace in her grandmother's apartment. It was her private church. In fact, at the age of fifty, it was all she could call her own. Her grandmother had left it to her when she died, against everyone else's wishes, probably because her mind was confused and she'd forgotten in her later years that Joana had committed the ultimate sin: the one which earned her the unanimous condemnation of her whole family. She took the plastic jug from the fridge and poured herself a glass of water. "Maybe they were right," she thought, sitting on the Formica chair with the glass in both hands; maybe there was something cruel or even unnatural in her. "Not even animals abandon their babies," her mother had said to her, unable to control herself. "Leave your husband if you want. But the little one?"

The little one. Marc. The last time she'd seen him was sleeping in a cradle and now she was seeing him in a box of oak. And on both occasions all she'd felt was an appalling fear at her own lack of emotion. The baby she'd created and given birth to meant as little to her as the young man with very short hair, ridiculously dressed in a black suit, lying on the other side of the mortuary glass.

"Hey, you came." She'd recognized the voice at her shoulder instantly, but it took a few seconds for her to dare to turn around.

"Fèlix told me," she replied, almost as an excuse.

A tense silence hung in the mortuary, which shortly afterward would unleash a torrent of whispers. She'd come in without anyone paying much attention—another middle-aged woman, dressed discreetly in dark gray—but now she felt everyone's gaze fixed on her back. Surprise, curiosity, reproach. The sudden leading lady in a funeral that wasn't hers.

"Enric." Another male voice, Fèlix's, which gave her the required strength to face the man before her, one step too close, invading that space one wishes to keep free.

"I wanted to see him," she said simply. "I'm going."

Enric looked at her with surprise, but moved aside as if inviting her to leave. The same expression she'd read on his face the last time she saw him, six months after leaving, when he came to Paris to ask her to return home. There were more wrinkles around those eyes, but the mix of incredulity and disdain was the same. Both times Joana asked herself how he could look so immaculate: well shaved, suit without a wrinkle, the knot in his tie perfect, his shoes shining. An irreproachable appearance that aroused an instinctive aversion in her.

"Come on, Joana," Fèlix intervened. "I'll walk you out."

From the corner of her eye she saw the ironic smile on her ex-husband's lips and he shrugged almost imperceptibly. As if twenty years hadn't passed. Enric waited a few seconds before speaking, the time required for them to have a little distance between them, and he had to raise his voice slightly.

"The funeral is tomorrow at eleven. If you're free and feel like coming. No obligation, you know."

She guessed the look Fèlix was giving his brother, but kept walking toward the door: half a dozen paces that seemed unending to her, surrounded by a rising tide of disdainful whispers. At the threshold she stopped abruptly, turned back toward the room and had the satisfaction of hearing the murmur suddenly cease.

She gave the old fridge a thump to silence the annoying purr, but on this occasion she was less successful. The silence lasted only a moment and then the noise began again, defiant. She went toward her laptop slowly, giving thanks for the wireless connection which allowed her to stay in contact with her world. She sat at the table and opened her mail. Four messages. Two from colleagues at the university where she gave classes in Catalan literature, the third from Philippe, and the fourth from an unknown sender: alwaysiris@hotmail.com. Just as she opened it, she heard the doorbell, a musical sound from another era.

"Fèlix!" There he was, at the threshold, with one hand leaning on the doorjamb, panting from climbing the steep staircase. Suddenly, she realized she was still in her dressing-gown and was embarrassed. "What are you doing here?"

He stayed quiet, still recovering from the five flights of stairs.

"I'm so sorry, please come in. I'm not used to having visitors," she excused herself with a fleeting smile. "I'm going to get dressed; sit down wherever you can . . . The flat was closed up, you already know that."

When she returned he was waiting for her opposite the balcony, facing the street. He'd always been a big man, but the years had added extra kilos to his corpulence, visible around the waist. He took a handkerchief from his pocket to wipe away sweat, and Joana thought he must be the only person still using cotton handkerchiefs.

"Would you like something to drink?"

He turned round, smiling.

"I'd be grateful for a glass of water."

"Of course."

He followed her to the kitchen.

"Are you all right here?" he asked her.

She nodded as she took a glass from the cupboard and rinsed it before pouring him water from the jug.

"The flat's a little abandoned, but it's comfortable," she said, and handed him the glass. He drained it in one gulp. He clearly wasn't fit. Priests mustn't get much exercise, thought Joana.

"Why have you come, Fèlix?" The question was brusque, and this time she didn't bother to soften it.

"I wanted to see how you were." He smiled, unconvincingly. "I worry about people."

She leaned against the wall. The small white tiles, more like those of a hospital than a kitchen, were cold.

"I'm fine." And she couldn't help adding, "You can tell Enric that I plan to stay as long as necessary."

"I didn't come on my brother's behalf. I already told you: I worry about people; I worry about you."

She knew it was true. Even at the worst times, she'd always been able to count on Fèlix. It was curious that, in spite of his priestly vocation and the collar he no longer wore in the street but that was still in his wardrobe, he'd been the only one who seemed to understand her.

"And there's something I wanted to ask you. Did Marc get in contact with you? In the last year?"

She closed her eyes and nodded. She breathed in and held her gaze on a corner of the floor before answering. The noise of the fridge started up again.

"He sent me some emails. Oh, stop!" She gave the white wall a powerful thump; this time the noise stopped immediately. "Sorry. It's driving me crazy."

He sat down on one of the kitchen chairs and Joana feared for a moment the old piece of junk wouldn't bear his weight.

"I gave him your email," he explained. "He asked me for it from Ireland. I was very unsure about doing it, but in the end I couldn't say no. Marc wasn't a child any longer and he had the right to know certain things."

She said nothing. She knew Fèlix hadn't finished.

"A week later he wrote to me again, saying he hadn't received an answer. Is that true?"

Joana fought back her tears.

"What did you want me to tell him?" she asked, her voice hoarse. "His email came out of nowhere. At the beginning I didn't know how to answer." She brushed her hand across her face, taking a stray tear with her. "I was thinking it over. I wrote messages without ever sending them. He kept insisting. Finally I answered and we maintained a sort of contact until he suggested coming to Paris in one of his emails."

"You didn't get to see him?"

She shook her head.

"You know I've always been a coward," she said, with a hint of a bitter smile. "I suppose I failed him again."

Fèlix lowered his head.

"Why are you still here? You're only hurting yourself. You need to reclaim your life. Go back to Paris."

"Don't tell me what I need to do." She didn't move and for the first time she looked the priest in the eye, without hesitation. "I'm staying here until I know what happened that night. This vague explanation—maybe he fell, maybe he jumped— means nothing. Maybe he was pushed . . ."

"It was an accident, Joana. Don't torture yourself with this."

She didn't listen to him: she continued speaking as if she couldn't stop.

"And I don't understand how Enric accepts it. Doesn't he want to know what happened?"

"He already knows. It's a tragedy, but you have to move on. Wallowing in sorrow is morbid."

"The truth isn't morbid, Fèlix! It's necessary. At least, I need it."

"For what?" He sensed they were reaching the heart of the matter. He got up and went toward his ex-sister-in-law. Her knees buckled under her and she would have fallen to the floor if he hadn't held her up.

"To know how much I am to blame," murmured Joana. "And the price I have to pay."

"This isn't the way to atone for blame, Joana."

"Atone for blame?" She raised a hand to her forehead; she was sweating again. "Your jargon doesn't change, Fèlix. Blame isn't atoned for; it's carried!"

The phrase echoed for a few moments of terse silence. Fèlix tried for the last time, although he was conscious that the battle was lost.

"You will hurt many people who are trying to get over this. Enric, his wife, his daughter. Me. I loved Marc a lot too: he was more than a nephew. I watched him grow up."

Suddenly she straightened up. She took Fèlix's hand and squeezed it. "Sometimes pain is inevitable, Fèlix." She flashed a sad smile at him before turning round and walking to the door of the flat. She opened it and stood there, waiting for him to go. As he came nearer, she added, "You have to learn to live with it." Her tone changed and she pronounced her next words with a cold, formal air, free of emotion. "I spoke to Savall this morning. He's assigned the case to an inspector. Tell Enric. This isn't finished, Fèlix."

He nodded, and gave her a kiss on the cheek before leaving. Out on the landing, before starting his descent, he turned back to her.

"There are things better left unfinished."

Joana pretended not to hear him and closed the door. Then she remembered she'd left her email open and sat down to read it.

3

It was half past twelve by the time a taxi left Héctor in front of the Post Office building. That ancient, solid mass protected a network of labyrinthine alleys that had remained immune to the wave of design that was battering nearby *barrios*, like the Born. These were streets where people hung out clothes on the balconies and you could almost steal them from your neighbor opposite; façades that would be difficult to renovate because there was no space for scaffolding; ground floors, previously abandoned, where now Pakistani grocers, ethnic clothes shops and a bar with tiled walls had sprung up. There, on Milans, on the second floor of a narrow, dirty building, Dr. Omar had his "clinic." When Héctor arrived at the corner, he instinctively searched for his mobile and then remembered he'd left it dead at home that morning. Shit . . . His intention had been to call Andreu and ask her if there were Moors abroad, or if the coast was clear. He smiled at the thought that such phrases had become politically incorrect, and advanced slowly toward the building in question. Contrary to what he'd imagined, the street was empty. But that wasn't surprising. The visit of the *Mossos*, Catalonia's police force, had made many of the area's inhabitants, who had no papers, opt for staying at home. There was indeed an agent at the door, a relatively young guy whom Héctor knew by sight, making sure that only residents could access the building.

"Inspector Salgado." The agent seemed nervous. "Sergeant Andreu told me you might come."

Héctor raised an eyebrow and the boy nodded.

"Go on up. And I haven't seen you. Sergeant's orders."

The stairwell smelled of damp, of urban poverty. He met a black woman who didn't raise her eyes from the floor. On the second-floor landing there were two doors, each of a different wood. The darker was the one he was looking for. It was closed and he had to touch the bell twice before it decided to ring. When he remembered the events of that fateful evening, everything came back to him in the form of flashes: the destroyed body of the little black girl and a dense, bitter rage that could be neither swallowed nor spat out; then his closed fist, pitilessly striking a guy he'd only seen in the interrogation room once. Hazy images he'd have preferred not to remember.

Stationed at the corner, Héctor waits for the fourth cigarette he's lit in the last half an hour to be consumed. He feels a pain in his chest and the taste of tobacco is starting to make him sick.

He goes up to the second floor. He pushes the office door. At first he doesn't see him. The room is so dark that instinctively he's on his guard. He stays still, alert, until a noise indicates that there is someone seated on the other side of the desk. Someone who lights a lamp.

"Come in, Inspector."

He recognizes the voice. Slow, with an indefinable foreign accent.

"Sit down. Please."

He does. They are separated by an antique wooden desk, which must be the best thing in that run-down, slightly stuffy flat.

"I was expecting you."

The shadow moves forward and the light from the floor lamp fully covers him. On seeing him Héctor is surprised: he's older than he remembered from that day he'd interrogated him at the station. Black, thin, an almost fragile appearance, and the eyes of a beaten dog who has learned that there is a daily ration of blows and waits resignedly for the moment to arrive.

"How did you do it?"

The doctor smiles, but Héctor could swear that deep down there is something like fear. Good. He has good reason to fear him.

"How did I do what?"

Héctor contains the desire to grab him by the neck and slam his face against the desk. Instead he clenches his fist and simply says:

"Kira is dead."

He feels a chill on saying her name. The sweet smell is beginning to make him nauseated.

"A pity, isn't it? Such a pretty girl," the other says, as if he's speaking of a gift, an object. "You know something? Her parents gave her that absurd name to prepare her for a life in Europe. Or in America. They sold her without the least remorse, convinced that anything was better than what she could expect in their village. They were brainwashing her from birth. A pity they did not teach her to keep her mouth shut as well."

Héctor swallows. Suddenly the walls advance toward them, reducing the already small room to the size of a cell. The cold light falls on the doctor's hands then: fine, with long fingers like serpents.

"How did you do it?" he repeats. His voice sounds hoarse, as if he has spent hours without speaking to anyone.

"Do you really think I could do anything?" He guffaws and leans forward again so the light focuses on his face. "You pleasantly surprise me, Inspector. The Western world usually makes fun of our old superstitions. What cannot be seen or touched does not exist. They have closed the door to a whole universe and live happily beyond it. Feeling superior. Poor fools."

The oppressive feeling grows. Héctor cannot take his eyes from the other man's hands, which are relaxed now, lying still on the desk. Offensively languid.

"You are a very interesting man, Inspector. Much more so than most police officers. In fact, you never thought you would end up as an officer of the law. I am sure of that."

"Cut the crap. I came looking for answers, not to listen to your nonsense."

"Answers, answers . . . Deep down you already know them, although you do not believe them. I am afraid I cannot help you in that."

"How did you threaten her?" He struggles to stay calm. "How did you scare her so much that she did that to herself?" He can't even describe it.

The other man leans back, hides in the shadows, but his voice continues, coming out of nowhere.

"Do you believe in dreams, Inspector? No, I suppose not. Curious how all of you are capable of believing in things as abstract as atoms and then dismiss something that happens every night. Because we all dream, do we not?"

Héctor bites his lip so as not to interrupt. It's clear that this bastard is going to tell it in his own time; the doctor lowers his voice so he has to strain to hear him.

"Children are clever. They have nightmares and fear them. But as they grow up they are taught that they should not be scared. Did you have nightmares, Inspector? I can already see that you did. Night terrors, perhaps? I see you have not thought about them for a while. Although you still do not sleep well, correct? But tell me something, how else could I have put myself in her head and told her what she had to do? Take the scissors, caress your stomach with them. Up to those little breasts and stick them in . . ."

And that's where his memories stop. Next thing he remembers is his fist ceaselessly punching the face of that son-of-a-bitch.

"What the fuck are you doing here?"

Martina's dry voice brought him back to the present. Disconcerted, he didn't have time to respond.

"Doesn't matter, no need to answer. I knew you'd come. This is disgusting."

Héctor advanced down the corridor.

"Don't come in here, you'll have to look from the door."

It was the same office, but in daylight it looked like a squalid room, not at all ghostly.

"I've seen nicer piggies, to tell the truth," the sergeant said at his shoulder.

What was on the table, presented like a sculpture, wasn't the head of a piglet, but that of a good-sized boar. They had already put it into a black bag, from which a piece of the face poked out, bloated, as if boiled, the wrinkled ears and fleshy snout a repugnant pink.

"Oh, and the blood isn't the pig's. Look, it hasn't bled anywhere."

It was true. There was no blood on the desk, but there was on the walls and the floor.

"I think that's it. I won't be eating ham for the next month," Andreu said, turning to the man inside the office equipped with gloves. "Take that and bring it to . . ."

For a moment she was quiet, as if she didn't know where a pig's head should be taken.

"Yes, Sergeant. Don't worry."

"And we haven't seen Inspector Salgado, have we?"

The man smiled.

"I don't even know who he is."

They went to eat at a nearby bar. A set menu for eleven euros, including dessert or coffee and paper napkins matching the tablecloths. Withered salad, cuttlefish in a sea of oil and a sad fruit salad.

"How has it been the last month?" he asked.

"Awful." The answer was sharp. "Savall's been unbearable and taken his bad mood out on everyone."

"Because of me?"

"Well, because of you, because of that asshole's lawyer, because of the minister, because of the press . . . Truth is you left us in the shit, Salgado."

"Yeah," he nodded. "It pisses me off that you've had to deal with this. Truly."

"I know." She shrugged. "There was nothing you could have done. Better this way. Anyway, Savall has been brilliant. Anyone else would have thrown you to the wolves. And you know it."

She knew Héctor hated owing favors, but she told herself it was right that he knew the truth.

"Fortunately," Andreu continued, "for once almost everyone is happy to bury the subject: the press preferred the photos of the mutilated girl, the minister didn't want anything to endanger an operation that up to then had gone well, and the lawyer only wanted to use it to save his client from the pending charges against him. If he was being bugged too much, then there wouldn't be a way of dropping the charges against you in exchange for . . . Well, you get me, one favor for another. You know how these things work."

There was a brief silence. Héctor could tell that his colleague hadn't finished. He awaited the question with his eyes half-closed, like someone waiting for the firework he's seen lit to explode. And, as usual, Andreu got straight to the point.

"What the fuck happened to you, Salgado? Everything was going brilliantly! We had the principals, we'd dismantled the network's brothels. A European-scale operation where we'd all worked ourselves into the ground . . . And just when everything is tied up, when the news has appeared in every paper, when the minister is drooling with satisfaction, you go and start whacking the only one we haven't managed to nab yet."

Héctor didn't answer. He took a gulp of water and shrugged his shoulders. He was beginning to get sick of that question, so he changed the subject.

"Listen, did you find anything? Inside there."

She shook her head.

"Andreu. Please," he pleaded, lowering his voice.

"Very little, to tell the truth. Maybe the strangest thing was a hidden camera. It seems Dr. Omar liked to keep recordings of his appointments. And then there's the blood. I'd say it's human. I've sent it to be analyzed and we'll have the results tomorrow. And the pig's head was clearly a message. What I don't know is who it's for and what it means." She poured her coffee over the ice in her glass without spilling a single drop. "I'm going to tell you something else, but promise me you'll stay out of it."

Héctor nodded mechanically.

"No. I'm serious, Héctor. I give you my word that I'll keep you informed if you promise not to interfere. Whatever I tell you. Understood?"

He raised his hand to his chest and put on a solemn face.

"I swear."

"The heart's on the other side, idiot." She almost laughed. "Listen, this doctor had a filing cabinet. It was empty. Well, almost. There was a file with your name on it."

He stared at her in surprise.

"Containing what?"

"Nothing."

"Nothing?" He didn't believe her. "Who's lying now?"

Martina exhaled.

"There were just two photos. A recent one of you. The other . . . of Ruth with Guillermo, from years ago. When he was little. Nothing else."

"Fucking bastard!"

"Héctor, there's something I need to ask you." Andreu's eyes expressed slight sorrow and great determination. "Where were you yesterday?"

He backed away, as if something had just exploded on his plate.

"It's routine, Héctor . . . don't make it more difficult for me," she almost begged.

"Let's see . . . The plane touched down just after four. I spent a good while waiting for my bag to come out and when it didn't arrive I had to go to Lost Luggage, where I was for at least an hour. Then I took a taxi and went home. I was wrecked."

Martina nodded.

"You didn't go out again?"

"I stayed home alone, half asleep. You'll have to take my word for that."

She looked at him gravely.

"Your word's enough for me. And you know it."

4

The heat had decided to concede a truce that evening and some low clouds had covered the sun. Because of that, and because he couldn't keep going over what Andreu had told him, Héctor put on tracksuit bottoms and went out running. Physical exercise was the only therapy that worked for him when his brain was too exhausted to operate efficiently. As he ran along the seafront, Héctor contemplated the sea. At this time only a few stragglers remained, small groups wanting to take maximum advantage of the summer, and one or two bathers with the sea almost completely to themselves. Urban beaches were different, he said to himself, trying to ignore the nagging pain in his left calf: they weren't at all heavenly or relaxing, but catwalks with disco music on which wannabe models shone an intense bronze, with bouncing boobs and gymnastic abs. Sometimes he got the impression that they held casting calls before allowing them access to the beach. Or maybe it was more a thing of self-exclusion: whoever didn't comply with the stereotype found some other more distant sand on which to exhibit their soft flesh. But if at dusk the beach was half empty, the same couldn't be said for the esplanade: couples with children, boys and girls on bikes, runners like him who came out whenever the sun permitted, vendors on foot who came back each year with the same stuff, seeming not to have heard the maxim "adapt or die." Round here, the city in the summer acquired the air of a Californian television series, with the *manteros*—blanket-sellers—providing an ethnic touch. There were even those who tried to surf in a sea without waves.

Little by little, Héctor accelerated the rhythm as his legs adapted to the exercise. He hadn't done anything for almost two months: the Buenos Aires winter wasn't conducive to running, and in fact he'd grown accustomed to running with that marine depth on one side and the two tall towers as a reference. The sea wasn't one of turquoise waters, or anything like it, but it was there: immense, tranquilizing, the promise of endless space in which to submerge his thoughts, let them leave with the waves. A slight twinge in his calf made him slow his pace and he was overtaken by a kid with a cap, dressed entirely in black clothes two sizes too big, riding a noisy skateboard. The image reminded him suddenly of the file Savall had given him of that boy who'd fallen from the window, and the sea seemed to bring him back different worries from those it had carried away. They stayed with him. The photos of Marc Castells: some taken the previous summer, when he wore his hair longer and curly, and he was riding some inline skates on this very esplanade; the next from the spring, his hair closely shaven, more serious and no skates. And the last: forensic photos of a body that appeared tense, even when dead. He hadn't had a peaceful death at all, though it was instantaneous, according to the file. He'd fallen sideways, from a height of at least forty feet, and the nape of his neck had slammed against the flagstones on the ground. A silly accident. A fall born of the lapse of concentration alcohol causes. A second's distraction and everything goes to shit. According to this very file, Marc and two of his friends, a boy and a girl, friends of the victim since childhood, had had a little party in the Castells' house, situated in the most uptown area, in every sense of the word, of Barcelona, taking advantage of the fact that the owners—Señor Enric Castells, his second wife and their adopted daughter—had gone to spend the long San Juan bank holiday in the chalet they had in Collbató, celebrating with friends. Around two-thirty in the morning, the boy, Marc's neighbor, had decided to go home; the girl, one Gina Martí, had "stayed over." According to the file, she declared, practically on the verge of hysteria, that she had lain down in Marc's bed "a little while after Aleix left." The girl didn't remember very much, and it wasn't surprising: she'd been, by her own admission, the one who'd drunk the most. It seemed that she and Marc had had an argument when Aleix left, and, offended, she went to his bed, hoping he would follow her. She didn't remember anything else: she must have fallen asleep shortly afterward and was woken by the cries of the cleaning lady, who found Marc's body first thing on the floor of the courtyard around 8 a.m. the following day. It was supposed that, as he did most nights, the youth had opened the window and sat on the sill to smoke a cigarette. Some habit. As stated, he fell or jumped from there between three and four in the morning, while his girlfriend slept it off in the room below without hearing anything at all. Rather pathetic, but not very suspicious. Like Savall had said, no thread to unravel. Only one detail seemed to stand out from the scene: one of the panes in the back door was broken, and that—which on any other night might have been seen as an indication of something—

had, in the absence of any other evidence, been regarded as just a typical occurrence on a night like San Juan, when kids throw fireworks and convert the city into something resembling a battlefield.

The esplanade was becoming emptier as Héctor moved away from the most popular beaches. His body was already beginning to show signs of fatigue, so he turned around and began the route back. It was after half past eight. He sped up in a long, painful sprint. He was out of breath when he arrived at his house, soaked in sweat. Someone seemed to be sticking an awl into his left calf, and he limped the last few meters separating him from the door of that old building on Pujades, the façade of which was crying out for urgent redecoration. Panting, he leaned against the door and took his keys from his tracksuit pocket.

He heard someone calling him and then he saw her. Serious, with the car keys in her hand and walking toward him. Héctor smiled despite himself, but the pain in his leg made the smile a grimace.

"I guessed you'd gone out running."

He looked at her, uncomprehending.

"You gave my number to Lost Luggage. Your suitcase has arrived. They were trying to get hold of you but you didn't answer your mobile, so they called mine."

"Oh, I'm sorry." He continued panting. "They asked me for a second number . . . my mobile is dead."

"I thought so. Go and shower and change. I'll take you."

He nodded and Ruth smiled for the first time.

"I'll wait here," she said before he could invite her up.

He came down shortly afterward with a plastic bag containing a box of caramel cakes and a graphic design book Ruth had requested before he left. She thanked him with a smile and a "Damn you, bringing me these calorie bombs in the middle of summer when you know I can't resist them." Surprisingly, there wasn't much traffic and they arrived at the airport in half an hour. They spoke little during the journey, and Guillermo took up most of the conversation. He was always safe territory, a subject they had to tackle out of necessity and which arose between them naturally. The separation had happened almost a year before and if there was something of which they could be proud it was the way they'd handled the thorny issue of their son, a boy of thirteen who'd had to adjust to a different reality and seemed to have managed it without any major problems. At least at first glance.

With the luggage—a badly treated suitcase with a broken lock which appeared to have survived a war rather than a plane journey—in the trunk, Ruth drove slowly. The city lights were shining at the end of the motorway.

"How'd it go today with Savall?" she asked finally, turning to him for a moment.

He exhaled.

"Well, I suppose it went OK. I still have graft . . . work. It seems they're not throwing me out, which is something. The guy's dropped the charges," he lied. "I suppose he thought it suited him better not to get on the wrong side of the forces of law and order. But I have to see a shrink. Ironic, isn't it? An Argentine visiting a shrink."

Ruth nodded silently. A long tailback had formed at the traffic lights at the entrance to the city.

"Why did you do it?"

She looked at him without blinking, with those big chestnut

eyes that had always managed to get under his skin. A look that had managed to unmask small white lies, and others not so small, as soon as he'd put them forward.

"Drop it, Ruth. He deserved it." He corrected himself. "It happened. I messed up. I never pretended to be perfect."

"Don't go off on a tangent, Héctor. The morning . . . the day you attacked that man was just after . . ."

"Yeah. Can I smoke in this car?" he asked, rolling down the window. A gush of warm air slipped inside.

"You already know you can't." She made a gesture of fatigue. "But smoke if you want to. Carefully."

He lit a cigarette and took a long drag.

"Give me one?" she murmured.

Héctor laughed.

"Fuck . . . here." When he lit it for her, the flame of the lighter illuminated her face. "I'm a bad influence on you," he added in a light-hearted tone.

"You always were. My parents used to tell me so . . . Of course they're not exactly delighted now either." They both smiled, with the complicity given by shared rancours. Smoking gave them something to do without having to talk. Héctor contemplated the city through the smoke. He threw away the butt and turned toward Ruth. They were already arriving. They could have filled a much longer journey with all the things they still had to say to each other. She slowed down to turn and parked in an unloading space.

"One last cigarette?" he said.

"Sure. But we'll get out of the car."

There wasn't a breath of air. The street was empty; however, televisions could be heard. It was the news hour. The weatherman was predicting a new heatwave for the next few days and the possibility of storms for the weekend.

"You look tired. Are you sleeping any better?"

"I do what I can. It's been a full-on day," he said.

"Héctor, I'm sorry . . ."

"Don't apologize. You don't have to." He looked at her, knowing full well he was exhausted and in this condition the best thing he could do was to stay quiet. He tried to make light of it. "We slept together, that's all. The wine, the memories, habit. I think that at one time or another eighty percent of ex-couples do it. See, deep down, we're typical."

She didn't smile. Maybe he'd lost the ability to make her laugh, he thought. Maybe they no longer laughed at the same things.

"Yeah, but—"

He cut her off.

"Yeah but nothing. The following day I split the guy's face but that had nothing to do with you." He continued in a more bitter tone that he couldn't help. "So you can relieve your conscience, sleep soundly." He was going to add something else, but stopped himself in time. "And forget about it."

Ruth was about to answer when her mobile rang. He hadn't even seen her take it from the car.

"It's for you," he pointed, suddenly exhausted.

She walked a few paces away to answer. During the brief conversation he took the opportunity to open the trunk and take out his luggage. He dragged it to his house.

"I'm going," she said and he nodded. "Guillermo comes back Sunday night. I . . . I'm happy that everything's been sorted. At the station, I mean."

"Did you doubt it?" He winked at her. "Thanks for taking me. Listen," he didn't know how to ask her without alarming her, "have you noticed anything strange at your place lately?"

"Strange how?"

"Nothing . . . don't listen to me. There have been a few bur-
glaries in your area. Just stay alert, OK?"

The good-byes were uncomfortable; neither of them had yet
learned how to handle them smoothly. A kiss on the cheek, a
farewell nod of the head . . . how did you say good-bye to someone you lived with for seventeen years, who had another home,
another partner, another life now? Maybe that was why they
ended up in bed the last time, thought Héctor. Because they
didn't know how to say good-bye.

It had been inevitable. Something they both knew was going
to happen as soon as Ruth agreed to come up to the flat after
dinner, planned for a discussion of their son's next exams, and
Héctor uncorked a bottle of red that had been in the kitchen
cupboard since before she left, nine months before, after announcing that there was a part of her sexuality which she
wanted, and needed, to explore. At any rate, both pretended
that it was a matter of a nightcap, celebrating the fact that
they were a civilized couple who managed to get on reasonably
well after a sudden separation. Sitting on the same sofa where
they'd embraced so many nights, where Ruth had waited, so
many hours awake, for her husband, and where Héctor had
struggled to sleep since half the bed lay empty, they downed
one glass of wine after another, perhaps to find the courage to
do what they desired, or maybe to be able to attribute to alcohol what they knew they were going to do. They sought something that might cloud their minds, send their feigned sense
to hell. It doesn't matter who started it, who opened the game,
because the other joined in with an impatient, accelerated
greed. They slid smoothly from the sofa to the rug while they
removed their clothes, separating their lips only for as long
as was absolutely necessary, and coming back to seek the

other's tongue as if they were extracting oxygen from it. Their bodies were burning and her hands, seeking familiar corners, pieces of warm skin which became perfectly elastic under her touch, served only to revive the flames. Lying on the carpet, pinned down by Héctor's hands, she thought for an instant how different it was to make love to a woman: the feeling, the smell of skin, the rhythm of movements. The complicity. The moment's reflection dispelled the effects of the alcohol, just seconds before he fell on her, spent and satisfied. Ruth stifled a moan, more of pain than pleasure; she looked away and saw her wine-stained shirt and an overturned glass on the floor. She tried to separate herself from Héctor gracefully, giving him a last perfunctory kiss, nothing like those previous ones, as she moved away lightly to one side. He took a few seconds to move; she felt trapped. He finally sat up and Ruth tried to get up, a little too quickly, like someone attempting to flee after a landslide. The same urgency that had carried her from the sofa to the rug was now pushing her toward the door. She didn't want to see his face, nor had she anything to say to him. She felt ridiculous as she pulled up her underwear. She picked up her clothes from the floor and dressed with her back turned. She had a feeling Héctor was asking her something, but getting out had become her priority.

When he saw her leave he knew his marriage was dead. If up to then the possibility had remained that their relationship might emerge from its coma, that Ruth's escapade with someone of her own sex was only that, a fleeting adventure, he knew now without doubt that they'd just buried it. He groped in the dark for a cigarette and smoked it alone, sitting on the floor, leaning back against the sofa, contemplating the upturned glass and the definitively empty bottle.

———————

This time the good-bye was easier. She half-turned and got into the car as he was putting the key in the door. Through the rearview mirror she saw him limping with the bag in his hand. Inexplicably, she felt something toward him that seemed very much like tenderness.

5

He should have gone to bed some time ago, but age insisted on robbing him of hours of sleep and reading was the only thing that helped him get through those long evenings. However, despite having a book he liked in his hands, that night Father Fèlix Castells couldn't concentrate. Comfortable in his favorite armchair, in the silent flat in Passeig Sant Joan which had been his home since infancy, his eyes, tired for years, seemed incapable of following the lines of the novel by Iris Murdoch, an author he'd discovered not very long ago, whose entire oeuvre he was reading. Finally, sick of trying, he rose and walked toward the bar where he kept the brandy; he poured himself a generous glass and, after taking a gulp, returned to the armchair. The only light in the room came from the lamp, and contemplating the book's white cover, he couldn't help shuddering. Iris. Always Iris. He half-closed his eyes and saw the message on Joana's computer that he'd read while she was dressing, hardly able to believe it. He'd had to struggle to contain himself, to not erase it. Iris couldn't write messages. Iris was dead.

It was he who entered the pool, who turned her over and saw her little face, blue with cold, who futilely tried to blow a little air through frozen lips that had already closed forever. When he turned around, with a shaken face and the little girl in his arms, he met the terrified gaze of his nephew. He wanted someone to take him out of there, save him from that horrifying sight, but Marc seemed rooted to the ground. Only then did he notice something surrounding his body and, almost unable to believe it, saw that there were numerous dolls floating in the same blue water.

He groped for the glass of brandy and took another gulp, but couldn't chase away that chill which knows no seasons. Iris's drenched little body, her blue lips. The dolls lying around her, like a macabre court. Images he thought he'd forgotten, but now, since San Juan, since that other recent tragedy, plagued him more than ever. Nothing could be done to combat them: he tried to evoke pleasant thoughts, of happy moments . . . Marc alive, Marc safe and sound, though with that distant, eternally sad expression. He'd done what he could, but the well of melancholy remained, immune to his efforts, ready to overflow at the smallest sarcastic comment on Enric's part. How many times had he told his brother that irony wasn't the way to bring up a child? It made no difference: Enric didn't seem to understand that sarcasm could hurt more than a slap. That home needed a woman. A mother. If Joana had been with them things would have been different. And Glòria had come too late: her arrival had contributed to softening Enric's bitterness, but the damage, to Marc, was already done. The subsequent adoption of Natàlia served to seal the new family circle, excluding that timid and sullen, solitary and unaffectionate boy. His sister-in-law had tried, although perhaps more out of a sense of duty than from genuine affection for Marc. It wasn't fair to criticize Glòria, he thought: she'd done what she could in those years, which hadn't been easy for her either. Her inability to conceive naturally had meant a torment of medical tests culminating in a lengthy adoption process. These things moved slowly, and although Eric's position had managed to speed up part of the application, for Glòria the wait had been interminable. She was so happy after she brought the little girl home. In Fèlix's opinion, she was the perfect mother. When he saw her with her daughter, Fèlix felt at peace with the world. It was a fleeting sensation, but one so comforting he sought it out whenever possible. Its effect on him lasted for hours, dispelling other ghosts: it was thanks to moments like these he could continue forgiving the sins of the world. He could even forgive himself . . . But not now: that effect had vanished after Marc's death, as if now nothing could console him. The image of his nephew, lying motionless on the patio flagstones, came to mind every time he tried to relax. One night he even saw him fall, arms outspread, trying to find something in the air to grasp, and he felt his fear as he neared the hard ground. Other nights he would see him at the window and glimpse the shadow of a girl with long blonde hair; he would try to warn him from below, he would shout his name but not get there in time. The shadow would push the boy and he'd shoot out with an almost superhuman force before falling at his feet with a dull thud, an unmistakable and fatal crunch, followed by a guffaw. He lifted his head and there she was: as drenched as when she was taken out of the water, laughing, finally getting her revenge.

THURSDAY

6

Héctor had never much trusted those who presume to know how to treat human neuroses. Not that he considered them frauds or irresponsible: he simply believed it improbable that an individual, equally subject to emotions, prejudices and manias, might have the capacity to delve into the winding paths of the minds of others. And that idea, rooted inside him for as long as he could remember, wasn't breaking down in the least now that for the first time in his life he was attending the clinic of one of them as a patient.

He observed the youth sitting on the other side of the desk, trying to control his skepticism so as not to seem rude, although at the same time it seemed strange that this kid—yes, kid—fresh from university and dressed informally in jeans and a white checked shirt, should have in his hands the file of a forty-three-year-old inspector, who, if he'd had an unlucky break in adolescence, could even be his father. The notion made him think of Guillermo and his son's reaction years before when his tutor at school suggested that it wouldn't be amiss for them to take him to a psychologist who—his exact words—"might help him open up to others." Ruth wasn't a big fan of shrinks either, but they decided they'd nothing to lose, although they certainly both knew Guillermo socialized with whoever he felt like and didn't bother with anyone who didn't arouse his interest. He and Ruth laughed for weeks at the outcome. The psychologist had asked their son to draw a house, a tree and a family; Guille, who at the age of six was going through a phase of adoring comics and was already demonstrating the same skill for graphic art as his mother, threw himself enthusiastically into the task, albeit with his usual selective disposition: he didn't like trees so didn't bother with that one, but instead drew a medieval castle as the house, and Batman, Catwoman and The Penguin as the family. Héctor didn't want to imagine what conclusions the poor woman drew on seeing the supposed mother imagined in a leather suit with a whip in her hand, but they were both sure that she'd kept the drawing for her thesis on the dysfunctional modern family, or something like that.

He'd smiled without noticing; he saw it in the inquiring look the psychologist was giving him through metal-rimmed glasses. Héctor cleared his throat and decided to feign seriousness; he was almost sure, however, that the boy opposite him still read comics in his spare time.

"Well, Inspector, I'm glad you feel at your ease."

"Sorry, I suddenly remembered something. An anecdote about my son." He regretted it instantly, sure that this wasn't the most opportune moment to bring it up.

"Ah-ha. You don't have much faith in psychology, right?"

There was no hostility in the phrase, but an honest curiosity.

"I haven't formed an opinion of it."

"But you mistrust it from the outset. Fine. Of course most people feel the same about the police, wouldn't you say?"

Héctor had to admit that was true, but he qualified it.

"Things have changed a lot. The police aren't seen as the enemy anymore."

"Exactly. They've stopped being the body that strikes fear into a citizen, at least an honest one. Although in this country it took time to change that image."

In spite of the neutral, impartial tone, Héctor knew that they were sliding down a rocky slope.

"What do you mean by that?" he asked. He was no longer smiling.

"What do you think I mean?"

"Let's get to the point . . ." He couldn't help a certain impatience, which usually translated into a lapse into his childhood accent. "We both know what I'm doing here and what you have to find out. Let's not beat about the bush."

Silence. Salgado knew the technique, although this time he found himself on the receiving end.

"Fine. Look, I shouldn't have done it. If that's what you want to hear, then there you have it."

"Why shouldn't you have done it?"

He tried to stay calm. This was the game: questions, answers . . . He'd seen enough Woody Allen films to know that.

"Come on, you know. Because it's not good, because the police don't do that, because I should've stayed calm."

The psychologist jotted down a note.

"What were you feeling at the time? Do you remember?"

"Rage, I suppose."

"Is that a regular thing? Do you usually feel rage?"

"No. Not up to that point."

"Do you remember any other moment in your life when you lost control in that way?"

"Maybe." He paused. "When I was younger."

"Younger." Another note. "How long ago . . . five years, ten, twenty, more than twenty?"

"Very young," stressed Héctor. "Adolescent."

"Did you get into fights?"

"What?"

"Did you usually get into fights? When you were a teenager."

"No. Not as a regular thing."

"But you lost control one time."

"You said it. One time."

"Which time?"

"I don't remember," he lied. "None in particular. I suppose I went through an out-of-control phase, like all boys."

A new note. Another pause.

"When did you arrive in Spain?"

"Pardon?" For a moment he was on the verge of answering that he'd arrived a few days previously. "Ah, you mean the first time. Nineteen years ago."

"Were you still in this out-of-control adolescent phase?"

Héctor smiled.

"Well, I suppose my father thought so."

"Hmmm. It was your father's decision, then?"

"More or less. He was Galician . . . Spanish; he always wanted to return to his native country but couldn't. So he sent me here."

"And how did you feel?"

The inspector made a gesture of indifference, as if that wasn't the pertinent question.

"Excuse me, but I can see you're young . . . My father decided I had to continue studying in Spain and that was it. No one asked me." He cleared his throat a little. "Things were like that then."

"You didn't have any opinion on the matter? At the end of the day you were made to leave your family, your friends and your life there behind. Didn't it matter to you?"

"Of course. But I never thought it would be permanent. Besides, I repeat: they didn't ask me."

"Ah-ha. Do you have siblings, Inspector?"

"Yes, one brother. Older than me."

"And he didn't come to Spain to study?"

"No."

The silence following his answer was denser than before. There was a question working its way to the surface. Héctor crossed his legs and looked away. The "kid" seemed in doubt and, finally, decided to change the subject.

"In your file it says you separated from your wife less than a year ago. Was she the reason you stayed in Spain?"

"Among others." He corrected himself. "Yes. I stayed here for Ruth. With Ruth. But . . ." Héctor looked at him, surprised he didn't know: these details would also be in the files. The feeling that his whole life, at least the most recent facts, could be in a dossier within reach of anyone who had the authority to examine it bothered him. "Sorry." He uncrossed his legs and leaned forward. "I don't want to be rude, but can you tell me where this is going? Look, I'm perfectly aware that I made a mistake and that it could—can—cost me my job. If it means anything, I don't think I did a good thing, and I'm not proud of it, but . . . But I'm not going to discuss all the details of my private life, nor do I believe you have a right to meddle in it."

The other man listened to his speech without turning a hair and took his time before adding anything. When he did, there

wasn't the least condescension in his tone: he spoke with composure and without the slightest hesitation.

"I think I should make some things clear. Perhaps I should
have done so at the beginning. Look, Inspector, I'm not here
to judge you for what you did, or to decide whether or not you
should continue working. That's a matter for your superiors.
My interest lies solely in you finding out what it was that provoked this loss of control, learning to recognize it and react in
time in another similar situation. And for that I need your cooperation, or the task will be impossible. Do you understand?"

Of course he understood. Liking it was another matter altogether. But he had no option but to agree.

"If you say so." He leaned back and stretched his legs out a
little. "In answer to your previous question, I will say yes. We
separated less than a year ago. And before you continue, no, I
don't feel an uncontrollable hatred or wild anger toward my
wife," he added.

The psychologist allowed himself a smile.

"Your ex-wife."

"Pardon. It was subconscious . . . you know . . ."

"Then I take it that it was a mutual separation."

It was Héctor who laughed this time.

"With respect, what you just described is practically nonexistent. There's always someone who leaves someone. The
mutual aspect consists of the other person accepting it and
shutting up."

"And in your case?"

"In my case, it was Ruth who left me. Don't you have that
information in your papers?"

"No." He looked at the clock. "We have very little time
left, Inspector. But for the next session, I'd like you to do
something."

"Are you giving me homework?"

"Something like that. I want you to think about the rage you felt the day of the assault, and try to remember other times you experienced a similar emotion. As a child, as an adolescent, as an adult."

"Fine. Can I go now?"

"We have a few minutes. Is there anything you want to ask me? Any query?"

"Yes." He looked him directly in the eyes. "Do you not think there are occasions when rage is the appropriate reaction? That feeling something else would be unnatural when facing a . . . demon?" Even he was surprised by the word, and his questioner seemed interested in it.

"I'll answer you in a moment, but let me ask you something first. Do you believe in God?"

"The truth is, no. But I do believe in evil. I've seen a lot of bad people. Like all police officers, I suppose. Would you mind answering my question?"

The "kid" thought for a few moments.

"That would lead us to a lengthy debate. But in short, yes, there are times when the natural response to a stimulus is rage. Equally fear. Or aversion. It's about managing that emotion, containing it so as not to provoke a greater evil. Fury can be acceptable in this society; to act motivated by it is more arguable. We'd end up justifying anything, don't you think?"

There was no way of rebutting that argument, so Héctor got up, said good-bye and left. While he was going down in the lift, cigarette packet in hand, he told himself that the shrink might be young and read comics, but he wasn't a complete fool. Which, truly, at that moment seemed to him more inconvenient than helpful.

7

"I believe we're boring Agent Castro." It was Superintendent Savall's tone of voice, dry and ironic, accompanied by a direct gaze, that made Leire Castro aware he was speaking to her. More accurately, it got her attention. "I'm very sorry to pull you away from your passionate inner life for a matter so irrelevant as the one we're discussing, but we need your opinion. Whenever you think it convenient, of course."

Leire blushed up to her hairline and tried to find an apology. It would be difficult to come up with a coherent answer to a question she hadn't heard because she was immersed in her worries.

"I'm sorry, sir. I was, I was thinking . . ."

Savall realized, as did Salgado and Andreu, that his question, still hanging in the air, had gone unnoticed by Agent Castro. All four were in the superintendent's office, behind closed doors, with the Marc Castells case file on the desk. Leire desperately forced herself to find something adequate to say.

The super had described the autopsy report, which she knew well. Alcohol levels slightly over the limit; the guy wouldn't have passed a breathalyzer test, but he wasn't so drunk that he couldn't stand upright. The medical analysis hadn't shown the smallest trace of any drugs in his blood which would allow them to deduce a delirium that might have made him fall into the void. The phrase "medical analysis" had thrown up a whirl of resolved doubts which led to others more difficult to resolve, a mental storm from which she awoke abruptly.

"We were discussing the matter of the broken door," said Inspector Salgado, and she turned toward him brimming with gratitude.

"Yes," she breathed, relieved. There she was on safe ground: her voice took on a concise, formal tone. "The problem is that no one was very clear on when it broke. The cleaner thought she'd seen it already broken when she left that evening, but she wasn't sure. In any case, there were numerous fireworks in the rear part of the house, in all probability originating in the neighboring garden. Its owners have four sons, and the boys admitted they'd been throwing them part of the evening and the night."

"Yeah. At the end of the day, it was San Juan," interjected the superintendent. "God! I hate that night. At one time it used to be fun, but now those little monsters throw small bombs."

Leire continued, "What is certain is that nothing in the house was missing and there was no meaningful sign that might indicate anyone having entered there. What's more—"

"What's more, the supposed burglar would've had to go up to the attic to push the boy. And for what? No, it doesn't make sense." The super made an irritated gesture.

"With all due respect," said Andreu, who'd kept quiet until then, "this boy fell. Or at worst, he jumped. Alcohol affects people differently."

"Is there something that makes you think suicide?" asked Héctor.

"Nothing significant," answered Leire instantly. Then she realized the question wasn't directed at her. "Pardon."

"Since you're so sure, explain why," barked the super.

"Well," she took a few seconds to organize her thoughts, "Marc Castells had come home a while ago after spending six months in Dublin, learning English. According to his father, the trip had done him good. Before leaving, he'd had problems at school: not attending, negative attitude, even a three-day suspension from the center. He managed to pass Second Baccalaureate, but he didn't obtain the necessary marks to study what he wanted. It seems he wasn't very sure of what he wanted to study really, so he deferred beginning a degree for a year."

"Yeah. And he was sent to Ireland to study English. In my time, he would've been put to work." The superintendent couldn't help a sarcastic tone. He closed the file. "That's enough. This is like a school board. Go and talk to the parents and the girl who slept in the house that night, and close the case. If necessary, question the other boy, but watch it with the Roviras. Dr. Rovira made it very clear that, given that his son had left before the tragedy happened, he wasn't inclined to have anyone disrupt his life. And taking into account that he attended the births of various ministers' children, including our own minister's, it's best not to get up his nose. In fact, I don't think any of them are hugely interested, I'm telling you now. Enric Castells made it clear that if the investigation has finished, he wants us to leave them in peace, and in a way I can't blame him for it." His attention focused for an instant on the photo of his daughters. "It must be hard enough to bury a son, and then on top of that to have to put up with the press and the police poking their noses in every minute. I'll see Joana next week and try to placate her. Anything else to add, Castro?"

Leire started. She had certainly been thinking of contributing a detail he hadn't mentioned.

"I'm not sure," she said, although her tone suggested otherwise. "Maybe it's just my impression, but the reaction of the girl, Gina Martí, was . . . unexpected."

"Unexpected? She's eighteen, she goes to bed a bit drunk and on waking up she finds out her boyfriend has killed himself. I think 'on the verge of hysteria,' as you describe her in your report, is a more than expected reaction."

"Of course. But . . ." She recovered her assuredness when she found the right words. "The hysteria was logical, sir. But Gina Martí wasn't sad. She seemed more frightened."

The superintendent remained silent for a few moments.

"All right," he said finally. "Go to see her this afternoon, Héctor. Unofficially—not too much pressure. I don't want problems with the Castells and their friends," he stressed. "Agent Castro will accompany you. The girl already knows her and adolescents tend to confide more in women. Castro, call the Martís and tell them you're coming." The commissioner turned to Andreu. "Wait a minute. We have to talk about these self-defense courses for women at risk of domestic violence. I already know that they're delighted, but can you really continue giving them?"

Salgado and Castro looked at each other before leaving: they had no doubt that Martina Andreu not only could but wanted to continue teaching these courses.

You there?
Aleix, man, you there?

The little screen of the computer indicated that < Aleix is off-line and may not answer your messages >. The girl bit her lower lip, nervous; she already had her mobile in her hand when the other person's status changed from absent to busy. Gina dropped her phone and went to the keyboard.

I have to talk to you! answer.

Finally the answer appeared. A hello, accompanied by a smiley face winking at her. The sound of the door handle startled her. She just had time to minimize the screen before the scent of her mother's perfume filled the air.

"Gina, sweetheart, I'm off." The woman didn't cross the threshold. She was carrying an open white bag, in which she was rummaging as she continued speaking. "Where the hell is the damn remote car key? Could they make them any smaller?" Finally she found it and flashed a triumphant smile. "Angel, are you sure you don't want to come?" Her smile faded a little on seeing the rings under Gina's eyes. "You can't shut yourself up in here all summer, angel. It's not good. Look what a lovely day it is! You need fresh air."

"You're going to L'Illa, Mama, ten minutes away," grumbled Gina. "By car. Not running in the country." If any doubt remained that the countryside didn't feature in her mother's plans, a look at her attire was all that was required: a white dress cinched at the waist with a belt of the same fabric; white sandals with a heel high enough to elevate her five-foot-five stature to a respectable five foot seven; hair, naturally blonde, shining, brushing her shoulders. Against a background of palm trees she would have been the perfect image for a shampoo ad.

Regina Ballester ignored the sarcasm. It had already been a while since she'd become hardened to the biting comments of this daughter, who, in pajamas at half one in the afternoon, looked more like a little girl than ever. She went over and gave her a kiss on the head.

"You can't go on like this, sweetheart. I'm not leaving with an easy mind . . ."

"Mama!" She didn't want to start another fight: these days her mother barely left her alone and she had to talk to Aleix. Urgently. So, overcoming how that intense fragrance bothered her, she let herself be hugged, and even smiled. To think that there'd been a time when she sought those arms spontaneously; now she felt they were smothering her. Her mother had even put perfume on her breasts! She smiled, with more malice than inclination. "Are you going to the swimwear shop?" It didn't fail: giving her mother something to do that included the words "shop" and "buy" was usually a sure route to peace. And although she couldn't swear to it, the perfumed breasts indicated that the shopping center was a secondary destination in her mother's plans. "Get me the one we saw in the window." Taking into account that she wasn't planning on going to the beach all summer and the fucking swimsuit didn't matter to her at all, she managed to give a fairly convincing ring to the request. She even pleaded in a spoiled-little-girl voice that she herself hated with all her heart. "Go on—please."

"The other day you didn't seem so enthusiastic. When we were both outside the shop," replied Regina.

"I was bummed, Mama, . . . " "Bummed" was a word Regina Ballester hated deeply, because as well as sounding rather vulgar, it described any of her daughter's moods: sad, worried, grouchy, bored . . . "Bummed" seemed to encompass them all, without distinction.

Gina fiddled with the computer mouse. Would she never go?

She extricated herself smoothly from the embrace and played her trump card.

"Fine, don't buy it for me. It's not like I feel much like going to the beach this year—"

"Of course you're going to the beach. Your father gets back from his promotional tour tomorrow and next week we're going to Llafranc. Not for nothing have I taken holiday this month." This was something Regina usually did: implicit reminders of how much she did for others. "I can't stand Barcelona anymore this summer! The heat is unbearable." Regina looked discreetly at her silver watch: it was getting late. "I'm going or I won't have time to do everything," she said with a smile. "I'll be back before five. If the *Mossos* get here before me, don't say anything to them."

"Can I open the door to them? Or would you prefer me to leave them out in the street?" asked Gina, with feigned innocence. She couldn't help it: these days her mother drove her crazy.

"There'll be no need. I'll be here. I promise."

The tap of her heels echoed on the stairs. Gina was about to maximize the Messenger screen when those same footsteps came back toward her, hurriedly.

"Have I left—?"

"Here's the remote, Mama." She picked it up from the table where Regina had left it to hug her, and threw it smoothly, without moving from the chair. Her mother caught it. "You should wear it around your neck." And, when she was sure her mother could no longer hear her, she murmured, "Of course it would scramble in that stench."

Click. The little screen shone before her once again.

gi, what's up?
u there???

okaaaay, im bored
see u babe, chat l8r!!!! :-)

No, no, no, no . . .

My mother was here, I couldn't talk.

Fuck, answer, Aleix, please.

heyyyyy!!! thought so. still droning away then?

Gina exhaled. Minor relief. She launched herself at the keyboard at top speed. And not to criticize her mother.

Have the cops called you?
cops? no, y?
Shit, they're coming to see me this afternoon. I don't know
what they want, seriously . . .

A pause of a few seconds.

definitely nothing. same as always. dont u worry.
I'm scared . . . and what if they ask me about . . .
they're not going to ask anything, they dont have a clue.
How do you know?
i just know. anyway, we didnt do it in the end, remember?

Gina's frown signaled an intense mental effort.

What do you mean?

Gina could almost see Aleix's annoyed face, the one he put
on when he was forced to explain things that seemed obvious

to him. An expression which, at times—sometimes—irritated her, and usually calmed her down. He was cleverer. That no one doubted. Having the school prodigy as a friend meant putting up with certain condescending looks.

> we thought about doing something but we didnt do it. not the same thing, right? doesnt matter what we planned, in d end we backed out.
> Marc didn't back out.

The cursor was blinking as if it were waiting for her to continue writing.

> gi, WE DIDNT DO ANYTHING.

The capitals rang out like an accusation.

> Yeah, you stopped it . . .
> and i was right. or was i not? you and i spoke about it and we agreed. it had to be stopped.

Gina nodded as if he could see her. But deep down she knew she had no fixed opinion on the matter. Realizing it like this, so crudely, filled her with a profound self-loathing. Aleix had convinced her that afternoon, but in her heart of hearts she knew she'd failed Marc in something that had been very important to him.

> u def have the USB, right?
> Yes.
> ok. listen, want me to come to ur house this afternoon? for the cops thing.

Gina did want him to, but a stab of pride stopped her admitting it.

> No, no need, I'll call you.
> weird they're coming to your house . . .

She changed the subject.

> By the way, my mother put perfume on to go out ;-)
> hahaha . . . and my father's not coming home for lunch!

Gina smiled. The supposed affair between her mother and Aleix's father was something they'd come up with out of boredom one afternoon, while Marc was in Dublin. They'd never bothered to confirm it, but over time, on the strength of repeating it, the hypothesis had become an absolute certainty for them. It amused them to think that her mother and Miquel Rovira, the serious, ultra-Catholic Dr. Rovira, were at that moment fucking furtively in a hotel room.

> im gonna have something to eat, gi! talk soon, ok? Kisses

He didn't wait for her to answer. His icon suddenly went gray and left her alone in front of the screen. Gina looked around: the unmade bed, the clothes dumped on one of the chairs, the shelves still full of teddies. It's a little girl's room, she said to herself scornfully. She bit her lower lip until it bled, and she passed the back of her hand over the injury. Then she got up, took an enormous empty cardboard box from the wardrobe, which until recently had contained all her schoolbooks— all of them, kept out of feigned affection for years—and put it in the center of the room. Then she went along grabbing the teddies one by one and throwing them face down into the box, almost without looking at them. It didn't take long. Barely fifteen minutes later the sealed box rested in a corner and the walls looked strangely empty. Naked. Sad. Soulless, her father would say.

8

As the car climbed toward the upmarket area of the city, the streets seemed to empty. From the dense, noisy traffic around Plaça Espanya, plagued by motorbikes taking advantage of the smallest gap to slip between the cars and taxis moving slowly forward like zombies awaiting a potential victim, they'd come in barely fifteen minutes to the wide expanses of Avinquda Sarrià: they crossed the city in the direction of the Ronda de Dalt. On a day like this, of blinding sun and suffocating temperatures, the sky gave the impression of having been whitewashed and the mountain, scarcely visible at the end of the long avenue, hinted at the promise of a cool oasis which contrasted with the scorching asphalt of three in the afternoon.

Sitting on the passenger side, Héctor contemplated the city without seeing it. By his sad expression and slight frown, one would say his thoughts were far away from those streets, roaming some shadier but not at all pleasant place. He hadn't uttered a single word since they got into the car and Leire took the wheel. The silence might have been uncomfortable had she not also been lost in her own world. In fact, she was even grateful for those minutes of peace: the station had been hectic that morning and she wasn't very proud of her performance in front of the superintendent. But the image of the "Predictor" confirming her fears with an intense purple color came into her mind at the most unexpected moments.

Héctor half-closed his eyes in an effort to re-order his thoughts: he hadn't spoken to Andreu in private and he was dying to ask her if there was anything new in the case of the doctor. He also remembered that he'd called his son in the morning after coming out of the psychologist's and he hadn't returned his call. He looked at his mobile again, as if he could will it to ring.

A sudden braking jolted him back to his senses and he turned to his colleague, not knowing what had happened. He understood instantly on seeing an urban cyclist, a member of that reckless tribe that had recently invaded the streets, who turned toward them more offended than scared.

"I'm sorry," Leire apologized. "That bike crossed suddenly." He didn't respond but nodded with a distracted air. Leire exhaled slowly: the bike hadn't come out of nowhere; she'd simply become too distracted. Fuck, enough! She breathed deeply and decided that the silence was overwhelming, so she opted to strike up a conversation with the inspector before he got submerged in thought again.

"Thanks for before. In Superintendent Savall's office," she clarified. "My head was in the clouds."

"Yeah," he said. "It was obvious, to be honest." He made an effort to follow the conversation: he was also sick of thinking. "But don't worry: Savall barks a lot and bites very little."

"I know I deserved the barks," she replied, with a smile on her lips.

Héctor continued speaking without looking at her, his eyes straight ahead.

"How did the Castells family seem to you?" he asked out of the blue.

She took a few seconds to answer.

"It's strange . . . I thought it would be harder. Interrogating them about the death of a son only nineteen years old."

"And it wasn't?" His voice was still tense, rapid, but this time he deigned to turn toward her. Leire had the feeling of being in an oral exam and concentrated on finding the right answer.

"It wasn't pleasant, that's for sure. But not"—she searched for the word—"dramatic, either. I suppose they're too reserved to make a scene, and after all she's not his mother . . . Although that doesn't mean they don't give free rein to their emotions when they're alone."

Héctor said nothing and the lack of comment made Leire expand on her answer.

"What's more," she continued, "I suppose religion helps its faithful in these cases. I've always envied that. Although at the same time I can't quite swallow it."

For the second time that day, the concept of God had come up. And when Héctor answered his companion, a little before they reached their destination, he did so with an explanation she didn't fully understand.

"Believers have an advantage over us. They have someone to confide in, someone who protects or consoles them. A superior power that clears up their doubts and dictates their conduct. We, on the other hand, have only demons to fear."

Leire noticed that he was speaking more to himself than

to her. Fortunately, on her right she saw the modern façade of the building to which they were heading and, given that it was summer, the surrounding area was practically empty. She parked on the opposite corner, in the shade, without a problem.

Héctor got out of the car immediately; he needed a cigarette. He lit one without offering one to his colleague and smoked greedily, his eyes on the school Marc Castells had attended until the year before his death. While he smoked, she moved toward the railings that marked out the landscaped area: another consequence of this new condition her body was experiencing was that, although she felt like smoking, she couldn't tolerate passive smoke. That place was as similar to the small-town school in which she had studied as the White House is to a whitewashed shack. The rich still live in a different world, she said to herself. However much more equal things had become, the building in front of her—surrounded by gardens, with grass spread out like a green carpet, and with a gymnasium and an adjacent auditorium—strictly speaking looked more like a university campus than a school, and it marked the profound difference, from infancy, between a select group of students who enjoyed all these facilities as the most normal thing in the world, and all the other kids who only saw places like this in American sitcoms. By the time she realized this, the inspector had already put out his cigarette and was entering the open gate. Somewhat annoyed, feeling as if he were treating her like a chauffeur who should wait at the door, she followed him. In fact, the visit to the school was an impromptu, last-minute idea. Most likely, she said to herself, they'd find no one there at that hour, but he hadn't asked her opinion. Typical boss, she thought as she walked a pace behind the inspector. At least this one has a nice ass.

They both moved down the wide, irregularly paved path that

crossed the garden to the main building. The door was closed, as Leire expected, but opened with a metallic hum after Héctor rang the bell. A spacious corridor stretched before them, with a glass-walled office, no doubt the school secretary's office. A middle-aged woman with a tired expression received them from the other side of the glass.

"I'm sorry, but we're already closed." She glanced toward a notice which clearly stated that the summer opening hours of the office were from nine until half past one. "If you want information on enrollment or about the center you will have to come back tomorrow."

"No, we're not interested in enrollment," said Héctor, showing her his badge. "I'm Inspector Salgado and this is Agent Castro. We wanted information about a pupil of this center, Marc Castells."

A glow of interest flickered in the woman's eyes. No doubt this was the most exciting thing that had happened to her for a while.

"I suppose you are aware of what has happened," continued Héctor in a formal tone.

"Of course! I myself took charge of sending a wreath to his funeral on behalf of the school." She said it as if any doubt might offend. "A terrible thing! But I don't know what I can tell you. It would be better to speak to one of the teachers, but I don't know who is here. In summer they don't keep a fixed schedule: they come in the mornings until the fifteenth to do paperwork and curriculum planning, but at lunchtime almost all of them disappear."

However, at that moment footsteps resonated in the enormous corridor and a man of around thirty-five approached the office with various yellow files in his hand. The woman flashed a radiant smile.

"You're in luck. Alfonso," she said, turning to the new arrival, "this is Inspector . . ."

"Salgado," finished Héctor.

"Alfonso Esteve was Marc's tutor in his last year here," clarified the secretary, deeply satisfied.

The said Alfonso didn't seem quite so satisfied and looked
the visitors over, eyes reticent.

"Can I help you?" he asked after a moment or two's hesitation. He was a man of short stature, no more than five foot
seven, dressed in jeans, a short-sleeved, white-and-green
checked shirt and trainers. Tortoiseshell glasses bestowed
an overall air of seriousness. Before Salgado could answer,
he put the yellow files on the counter. "Mercè, can you file
them, please? They're the September exams." The secretary
took them but didn't move from the window.

"Could we talk somewhere?" Héctor asked. "Just for a few
minutes."

The teacher threw a sidelong glance at the secretary and she
seemed to nod, not too convinced.

"I don't know if the principal would approve," he said even-
tually. "Our pupils' files are private, you know."

Héctor Salgado didn't move a millimeter and his eyes
seemed fixed on the teacher.

"All right," he gave in, "we'll go to the teachers' lounge. It's
empty."

The secretary looked disillusioned, but said nothing. Salgado
and Castro followed Alfonso Esteve, who was walking rapidly
toward one of the rooms at the other end of the corridor.

"Please, take a seat," he said to them on entering, and closed
the door. "Would you like a coffee?"

Leire saw a shining red coffee machine situated above a little fridge. Héctor answered before her.

"Yes, please." His tone had changed and became much more approachable. "Holidays about to start?"

"Yes, they have already. And you?" The teacher smiled at Agent Castro while he put the capsule in the coffeemaker.

"No, thank you," she said.

"A little milk for me, please," Salgado interjected. "No sugar."

Alfonso brought the two coffees to the table. As soon as he sat down, a worried expression clouded his face. Before he could express his reservations, Inspector Salgado took the initiative.

"Listen, this is in no way an official visit. We just want to close this boy's case, and there are certain things the family and friends can't tell us. Details of his personality, his character. I'm sure you know your pupils well and have formed opinions of them. What was Marc Castells like? I'm not talking about academic results, more his conduct, his friends. You know what I mean."

The teacher seemed visibly flattered and answered without hesitating.

"Well, strictly speaking, Marc was no longer my student. But he was a while back, for the last year of Secondary and the two years of Baccalaureate."

"What do you teach?"

"Geography and history. It depends on the year."

"And you were his tutor for the second year of Baccalaureate."

"Yes. It wasn't a good year for Marc. Let's be clear, he was never a brilliant student or anything like it. In fact, he just finished Secondary and had to repeat first year, but up to then he'd never had any problems with conduct."

Leire looked at the teacher with an expression of frank interest.

"And this changed?"

"He changed a lot," confirmed Alfonso. "Although at the beginning we were happy about it. You see, Marc had always been a very timid, introverted boy, not much of a talker. One of those that go unnoticed in the classroom and, I'm afraid, out of it. I believe throughout all of Secondary I never heard his voice unless it was to answer a direct question. So it was a relief when he began to come out of his shell, in the first year of Baccalaureate. He was more active, less silent . . . I suppose being at Aleix Rovira's side woke him up."

Héctor nodded. The name was familiar.

"They became friends?"

"I think the families already knew each other, but when Marc repeated and was in the same class they became insepa- rable. That's normal in adolescence, and it's clear this friend- ship favored Marc, at least academically speaking. Aleix is, without doubt, the most brilliant student this school has had in recent years." He spoke with confidence and yet an ironic echo resonated in the phrase, a note of rancour.

"You didn't get on with him?"

The teacher fidgeted with the coffee spoon, obviously un- sure. Leire was going to repeat the reassuring murmur about the conversation being unofficial but Alfonso Esteve didn't give her the time to do it.

"Aleix Rovira is one of the most complicated students I've ever had." He noted that his comment required an explanation and so he continued. "Very intelligent, of course, and, accord- ing to the girls, quite attractive. Not at all the typical swot: he was as good at sports as he was at mathematics. A born leader. I suppose it's not surprising: he's the youngest of five siblings, all boys, all strictly educated in what we might call 'Chris- tian values.'" He paused. "In his case, a serious problem in his childhood has to be factored in: he had leukemia, or something like it. So it's even more commendable that once recovered he was always top of the class."

"But?" Héctor smiled.

"But," Alfonso stopped again, "but there was something cold in Aleix. As if he'd seen it all before, as if his intelligence and the experience of his illness had given him a . . . cynical maturity. He had the group wrapped around his little finger, and some teachers as well. Being top of the class, the best in the history of the school, and the memory of his battle against cancer gave him a type of insensitivity to everything."

"Are you talking about bullying?" asked Leire.

"That would be stating it too strongly, although there was some. Biting comments directed toward the less clever or less attractive; nothing you could accuse him of, but it was clear the whole year did what he wanted. If he was rude to one of the teachers, they all copied him; if he decided one must be respected the rest did the same. Anyway, this is only my opinion; most people think he is a charming boy."

"You seem quite convinced of this opinion, Señor Esteve," pressed Castro. She sensed there was something else and didn't want the teacher to leave it unspoken.

"Listen, me being sure is one thing; it being the truth is something very different." He lowered his voice, as if he were going to tell them a secret. "A school is a rumor factory and it's difficult to establish their origin; they emerge, they spread, they're discussed. They start in a whisper, hidden from the person concerned; then they become louder until in the end they explode like a bomb."

Both Salgado and Castro still stared at him, willing him to continue.

"There was a teacher, not so young, forty-something. She arrived when Aleix and Marc were doing First Bacc together. For some reason, she and Aleix didn't get on. It's strange, because he usually made an effort to have a rapport with the female teachers. The rumors began immediately, of every kind. No one knows much about what happened, but she didn't last the year."

"And you believe those rumors came from Aleix?"

"I'd swear they did. One day she didn't come to work and I subbed for her. Aleix had an expression of cruel satisfaction, I'm sure."

"And Marc?"

"Well, poor Marc was his number-one fan. His father had remarried and I think his wife couldn't have children, so they adopted a little Chinese girl. That meant trips, absences . . . Marc needed someone in his corner, and that someone was Aleix Rovira."

"They ended up expelling him for a few days," added Héctor. This had been the main reason for their visit: in places like this, crawling with pupils from good families, expulsions were rare. However, if he was hoping the teacher would clarify the matter, he immediately became aware that that wasn't going to happen: suddenly regretting his previous indiscretion, the man chose to dig his heels in on that subject.

"That happened the following year, but I'm afraid it's part of the student's private file. And it's confidential. If you want to know more, you'll have to speak to the principal."

Leire cleared her throat, expecting Inspector Salgado to insist, but he didn't.

"Of course. Tell me, did Marc come to see you after coming back from Dublin?"

The question made Professor Esteve relax: he found himself back on safe ground and he answered quickly, as if he wished to make up for his lack of cooperation on the previous question.

"Yes. I found him much more grounded. We talked about his future: he told me he'd decided to repeat his exams to get higher marks and enroll in Media Studies. He was very excited."

Héctor nodded.

"Thank you very much. You've been very helpful." He rose from his chair, considering the interview finished, but, already on his feet, he added a question, as if it had just occurred to him that he was forgetting something. "And the girl? What's her name?"

"Gina Martí," Leire pointed out.

The teacher's expression softened.

"Gina is charming. Very insecure, overprotected, but cleverer than she thinks. She has a great talent for writing. Inherited from her father, I suppose."

"Her father?" He tried to remember if the file said anything.

"She's Salvador Martí's daughter. The writer."

Héctor nodded, although in fact he hadn't the least idea who Salvador Martí was, or what he wrote.

"Was she also a friend of Marc and Aleix?"

"I think she'd been a friend of Marc's since they were kids, although she's a year younger. She came to do Bacc here when he repeated First Bacc. And yes, Aleix included her in his circle as well, to please his new friend. Truth is, this girl was following Marc like a puppy for two years. This last year, with no Aleix or Marc, she's been much more grounded: it was good for her to repeat Second Bacc, as her final exam results show. She was so happy when we gave them to her . . . Now she must be in pieces: she's a very sensitive girl."

9

Gina opened her eyes when the bell rang. Befuddled, lying on the sheets, she took a few seconds to react. Twenty past four. Hadn't her mother said something about five o'clock? More rings, short and in quick succession. She remembered that the cleaner left at three and she was alone in the house, so she went barefoot down the stairs and almost ran toward the hall. She looked at herself in the foyer mirror before opening the door. God, she was horrible. Still looking at her reflection with an expression of intense disgust on her face, she opened the door.

"Beautiful, were you sleeping?"

"Aleix! What are you doing here?" She didn't move, momentarily thrown by this unexpected visit.

"You didn't think I was going to leave you here alone with the fuzz, did you?"

He was smiling and his brow gleamed with sweat. He took off his sunglasses and winked at her. "You going to let me in or what?"

Gina stood aside and he strode across the threshold. He was wearing a faded blue T-shirt and loose, checked Bermuda shorts. He was perfectly bronzed. Beside him, Gina's pale skin seemed like a consumptive's.

"You should get dressed, shouldn't you?" Not waiting for a response, he strolled toward the kitchen. "Hey, I'm going to get a drink. I came on my bike and I'm parched. What time are they coming?"

She didn't answer. Slowly, she went upstairs. Before he could follow her, she closed her bedroom door, though she knew that wouldn't stop him. Sure enough, she was still deciding what to wear when he appeared at the door. He was still smiling and had a can of Coke in his hand.

"Are you in a bad mood?" He went toward her and started tickling her. He smelled faintly of sweat and she moved away.

"Leave me alone . . ."

"Leave me alone," he repeated, mocking. He gave her a kiss on the lips. "Do you really want me to leave you alone? Shall I go?"

"No." The answer came out much faster than she'd expected. No, she didn't want him to leave. "But wait outside while I get dressed."

He raised both hands, like a robber caught with his fingers in the dough. He closed his eyes and kept smiling.

"I promise not to peek . . . Although I can't help remembering!"

"Do what you want," she replied, turning to the clothes folded on the chair. She grabbed a pair of denim shorts and a black, low-cut T-shirt with very short sleeves. Rapidly she took off her pajamas, but before she could dress herself he came up behind her.

"I'm still not looking, I swear." He kissed her again, this

time on the neck. As he did so, without meaning to, he brushed Gina's skin with the still-cold can and she flinched. "OK, OK, I'll leave you alone. I'll be good! By the way, have you got rid of the teddies? About time . . ."

Gina got dressed. He sat down in front of her computer and started typing. She watched him, annoyed: she hated him using her things without even asking, as if they belonged to him.

"Let's go downstairs," she said to him. "My mother will be here any minute."

"One second, I'm just looking at Facebook."

She went over and positioned herself at his shoulder. Then she saw the same message she'd received less than an hour before. "Alwaysiris wants to be friends on Facebook." The blurred photo of a blonde little girl, squinting in the sunlight.

"You too?" she asked.

"Screw them," he replied. Without hesitating, he hit the "Delete Request" button.

"I did the same a little while ago." Suddenly, without knowing why, she realized tears were running down her cheeks. She tried to control herself but she couldn't.

"Gina . . ." He rose and hugged her. "Sweetheart, that's enough. That's enough."

She leaned against his chest. Hard, smooth, a strong and unyielding washboard. She sobbed like a little girl, ashamed of herself.

"Enough, enough, enough. It's all over." He moved away a little and brushed away her tears with his fingertips. She tried to laugh.

"I'm stupid."

"No. No." He looked at her tenderly, with a kind of older-brother affection. "But we have to forget about all this. It was Marc's business, we have nothing to do with it."

"I miss him so much."

"Me too." But she knew he was lying. The thought made her uneasy and she moved away from him. "By the way, give me the USB stick. Better that I have it."

She didn't ask why. She opened a drawer and gave it to him. Aleix delayed a second in putting it in his pocket and smiled at her.

"Come on, let's go downstairs. See if they've arrived yet and finish with this once and for all. And remember, not a word. About anything."

Gina saw it in his eyes. A flash of fear. A gentle threat. This was why he'd come: not because he wanted to keep her company, not because he was worried about her, but because he didn't trust what a girl like Gina would say if the police pressured her. The memory of Marc's face came to her, a shadow over it, and she heard his quivering voice, almost inaudible, "You're a motherfucker, a real motherfucker," while fireworks exploded in the sky on the other side of the window. She felt a hand forcefully grasping her arm. He was still looking at her intently.

"This is important, Gina. No messing around."

He let go and she rubbed her wrist.

"Did I hurt you?" It was he who rubbed it then. "Sorry. Really."

"No." Why did she say no when she wanted to say the opposite? Why did she let him kiss her again, on the forehead, when his sweaty smell made her feel sick?

The buzz of the intercom interrupted her seeking an answer she didn't wish to find anyway.

The porter of the building, situated in Via Augusta, just before Plaça Molina, showed no sign of being shocked that two agents of the law were coming to visit one of the building's inhabitants. He rose from his chair as if doing so were an inconceivable effort, an indecent thing to ask of a man at ten to five on one of the hottest days of the summer, while he was honorably working by leafing through the sports pages with his headphones on. It appeared that the person who answered the intercom from the flat had given them permission to go up, because, with a lethargic gesture, the porter pointed them toward the lift and mumbled, "Top floor, second door," before falling back into his chair.

Héctor and Leire went toward the lift, which was slow and gloomy like the porter. She looked at herself in the dark mirror and saw that her face was starting to show signs of a definite bad mood. However curious she'd felt about Inspector Salgado before meeting him, working at his side was rather uncomfortable. After leaving the school she'd tried to discuss what the teacher had told them, but to no avail. Apart from answering in monosyllables, Salgado had spent the journey—not very long, it must be said—looking out of the window, in a posture that clearly showed that he'd prefer to be left in peace. And still the same: politely he'd let her go ahead of him into the foyer and the lift, but his face, which she was watching out of the corner of her eye, still had the same impenetrable, worried expression. Like a civil servant obliged to stay late at work.

Gina Martí met them at the door, and one didn't have to be a master of observation to see that she'd been crying not long before: the red nose, the glazed eyes. Behind her was a boy with a serious, respectful expression whom Leire instantly recognized as Aleix Rovira.

"My mother will be back soon," said the girl after Héctor introduced himself. She seemed to hesitate as to whether it was right to bring them into the lounge or remain standing in the hall. Aleix decided for her and invited them in, as if it were his home and not Gina's.

"I came to see Gina," he commented, as if to justify his presence. "If you want to speak to her alone, I'll go," he added. His tone was protective, affectionate. But the girl remained serious, tense.

Once seated in the lounge, Salgado looked at Gina Martí and for the first time all afternoon Leire saw a glimmer of empathy in the inspector's eyes. While he explained in a calming voice that they were just there to ask some questions and Aleix was nodding, standing at Gina's side with a hand on her shoulder, Leire contemplated the Martís' lounge and decided she didn't like it at all. The walls were lined with bookshelves crammed with books, the table and the rest of the furniture were dark wood and the armchairs were upholstered in a deep green. The whole place—finished off by dense still-lifes in huge gilt frames and walls painted in a clear ochre—gave off a slightly antiquated, claustrophobic air. Dusty, although she was sure that if she ran her finger across the table she wouldn't pick up even a speck of dirt. The curtains, thick and the same green as the chairs, were drawn, which added to the feeling of semi-darkness and lack of air. Just then she heard the inspector's last words.

"We'll wait for your mother if you'd prefer."

Gina shrugged her shoulders. She avoided looking directly at her questioner. Might be simply shyness, Leire said to herself, or the desire to hide something.

"You both knew Marc for a long time, didn't you?"

Aleix spoke before Gina could do so.

"Gina most of all. We were just talking about that. This summer's been so strange without him. And also, I can't get it out of my head that we parted half angry. I went home earlier than I meant to, and I didn't see him again."

"Why did you argue?"

Aleix shrugged.

"Something stupid. I can barely remember how it started." He looked at his friend seeking confirmation, but she didn't open her mouth. "Marc came back from Dublin different, much more serious, irritable. He'd get angry over anything, and that night I was sick of it. It was San Juan and I didn't feel like putting up with it. It sounds awful now, doesn't it?"

"According to your previous statement, you went straight home."

"Yes. My brother was awake and he's confirmed it. I was in a bad mood because of the argument, and a bit drunk as well, so I went to bed straight away."

Salgado nodded and waited for the girl to say something, but she didn't. Her eyes were fixed on a point on the floor and were only raised when she heard the key turning in the lock and someone calling from the hall.

"Gina, angel . . . Are they already here?" Rapid footsteps preceded Regina Ballester's entrance. "God, what are you doing here in the dark? This young lady wants us to live in a tomb." Not paying them the least attention, the blonde apparition walked rapidly toward the curtains and pulled them. Light streamed into the room. "Now it's completely different."

And it was, but not only because of the light. There are people who fill spaces, people whose presence changes the atmosphere. Regina Ballester, in less than a minute, had transformed a stale library into a light-filled catwalk, on which she was the principal—and only—model.

Salgado had risen to extend his hand to Señora Ballester, and in her eyes Leire saw an appreciative yet cautious expression.

"I believe you already know Agent Castro."

Regina gave a quick nod, indifferent. Agent Castro, it was clear, didn't hold much interest for her. However, her coldest greeting was without doubt for the visitor she hadn't expected to see. Aleix was still beside Gina, whispering something in her ear.

"Well, then, I'll go. I only came to see Gina."

"Thanks, Aleix." It was clear that the boy's departure didn't upset Regina Ballester in the slightest.

"We'll talk, OK?" he said to his friend. He went toward the door, but before leaving he turned. "Inspector, I don't know if I can help you in anything, but if so . . . I'm at your disposal." From any other boy the phrase would have sounded hollow, excessively formal. But from him it was respectful, friendly without being obliging.

"I don't think it will be necessary, but thank you," replied Salgado.

As Professor Esteve had said, Aleix Rovira could be a charming boy.

10

The lights of a parked car swept over him when he turned the corner of his street on his bike. Old, with a dent in its side, the car attracted attention in this peaceful neighborhood of houses with gardens and private garages. For a moment he was tempted to turn around or to speed past, but he knew that only meant postponing the inevitable. Also, it wouldn't do at all for someone from home to see him with a chav like Rubén. So, trying to appear calm, he approached the window and got off his bike.

"Hey, you appear at last, man," said the guy in the driver's seat. "I was about to go looking for you at home."

Aleix forced a smile.

"I was thinking of calling you just now. Listen, I need—"

The other shook his head.

"We have to talk. Get into the car."

"I'm going in to leave my bike. I'll be back in a second."

He didn't wait for him to answer: he crossed the street,

opened the white garden gate and pushed the bicycle inside. In less than a minute he was sitting in the car: he turned to check if anyone at home had seen him going in and out.

"Hit it," he said.

The other didn't say anything. He started the car and moved slowly along the road.

Aleix fastened his seatbelt and inhaled deeply. It didn't help much; when he spoke his voice still sounded nervous.

"Listen, you have to give me more time . . . Fuck, Rubén, I'm doing what I can."

Rubén remained silent. Strangely quiet. Like a driver instead of a colleague. He wasn't much older than Aleix, and in fact his thinness made him seem even younger. Despite the tattoo descending his arm and the sunglasses, he had a childish air, accentuated by his tracksuit bottoms and white T-shirt. No one would have said he'd been grafting for years, first as a waiter then on a building site, until first the bar closed and then so did the scaffolding. He didn't turn to his companion until he had to stop at a traffic light.

"You fucked it up, man."

"Fuck it, I know. What do you want me to do now? Do you think I can get the dough just like that, in a couple of days?"

The other shook his head again, glum.

"By the way, where are we going?" asked Aleix.

Again, Rubén didn't answer.

In the Martís' salon, Héctor attentively observed the little girl in front of him. Despite her eighteen years, Gina had the air of a defenseless child. And for a while now, seemed uneasy. He told himself the best thing to do was ask her direct questions, at least at the beginning; direct the questioning with neutral inquiries until she felt more comfortable.

"Listen," he repeated, aiming to reassure her, "we're only here to talk to you. I know you don't feel like remembering what happened that night, so we'll try to be brief. Just answer my questions, OK?"

She nodded.

"What time did you arrive at Marc's house?"

"Around eight. Well," she rectified, "I arrived at eight. Aleix came later. I don't know what time it was. Nine or something like that . . ."

"OK." He kept his friendly expression as he looked at her. "And what was the plan?"

She shrugged.

"Nothing in particular . . ."

"But you planned to stay the night, yes?"

The question made her nervous. She looked at her mother, who until then had remained silent, attentive to the questions and answers.

"Yes."

"And what happened then? You drank, put on music? Had some food?"

Gina half-closed her eyes. Her knee began to tremble.

"Inspector, please," Regina intervened. "She was already asked all this the day after." She looked at Agent Castro, seeking confirmation of her words. "It's been really horrible for her. Marc and Gina knew each other for years; they were like brother and sister."

"No." Gina suddenly opened her eyes and her bitter tone surprised them all. "I'm sick of hearing that, Mama! We weren't brother and sister. I . . . I . . . loved him." Her mother tried to take her hand but she shook her off and turned to the inspector more decisively. "And yes, we drank, we put on music. We made pizzas in the kitchen. It's not that we did anything special, but we were together. That was what was special."

He let her speak without interrupting and gestured to his companion not to say anything.

"Then Aleix arrived. And we had dinner. And we drank more. And we listened to more music. Like we had so many times. We talked about exams, Dublin, the notches on Aleix's bedpost. It had been a while since all three of us had been together. Like before."

Regina's gesture of surprise didn't pass Héctor unnoticed. It was momentary, a simple arching of the eyebrows, but it was there. Gina continued, ever faster.

"Then a song came on that we liked and we started dancing like crazy, and singing loudly. At least Aleix and I did, because Marc stopped immediately and sat back down. But we kept dancing. It was a party, wasn't it? We told him so, but he wasn't in the mood . . . Aleix and I turned up the volume, I don't remember what was playing. We were dancing for a while until suddenly Marc turned off the music."

"Was he worried about something?"

"I don't know . . . He'd become very strange. More serious. I almost hadn't seen him in the two months he'd been back. I was studying and everything, but he hardly called."

"But—" Regina interrupted. Her daughter cut her off:

"And then Aleix said that if the party was over, he was going. They argued. And it pissed me off, because I was having a good time, like before. So when Aleix left I asked Marc what was going on."

She paused and looked on the verge of breaking into tears. "He said, 'You've drunk a lot, you'll feel awful tomorrow' or something like that, and it was true, I suppose, but I got angry and I went to his bed and I waited there for a while . . . and, well, I vomited in the bathroom but I cleaned it all up and I felt cold all of a sudden and got into bed because the room was spinning and I was shivering." Tears rolled down her cheeks but she didn't brush them away. Her mother put her arm around her and this time Gina didn't shy away from her touch. "And that was it. When I woke up, it had already happened."

The girl took refuge in her mother's arms, like a baby bird. Regina held her in her embrace and, turning to the inspector, said severely:

"I think that's enough, don't you? As you can see, my daughter has been badly affected by all this. I don't want her to have to repeat the same story again and again."

Héctor nodded and gave Leire a sideways glance. She didn't know what he meant by that look, but she was sure that at that moment, protected by her mother, Gina wouldn't tell them anything else. And although the girl's tears appeared sincere, she'd noticed a certain relaxation in Gina's posture after her mother's last words. Leire was going to say something, but Regina beat her to it.

"I still remember how terrible the following morning was." The spotlights were back on the principal actress, who was demanding to act her role.

Héctor kept up the game.

"How did you hear about what happened?"

"Glòria called me first thing in the morning to tell me. God! I couldn't believe it . . . And although she told me straight away that Gina was fine, that it was poor Marc who had . . . Well, I wasn't happy until I saw her." She hugged her daughter even tighter.

"Of course," agreed the inspector. "Had you been having a party at the Castells' chalet?"

The woman smiled ironically.

"Calling it a party is an exaggeration, Inspector. Let's leave it at a simple dinner with friends. Glòria is charming, and one of the most organized women I know, but parties aren't exactly her thing."

"Who was there?"

"There were seven of us: the Roviras, the Castells, my husband and I, and Enric's brother, the monsignor. Well, and Natàlia, of course. The Castells' adopted daughter," she clarified.

"Did it end early?"

If Regina was surprised by the question, she showed no sign of it.

"Early? I don't know what to tell you; to me the night went on forever. I haven't been so bored since the last Turkish film Salvador took me to see. Imagine, the Roviras, who dedicate more time to blessing the meal than eating, because they believe enjoying food is a sin of gluttony or greed or something. And Glòria, who spent the whole dinner getting up to see if the fireworks were bothering the little one. I told her the Chinese have spent centuries playing with powder but she looked at me as if I were an idiot."

Gina sighed with annoyance.

"Mama, don't be nasty. Glòria isn't that hysterical. And Natàlia is a darling. When I babysit she always goes to sleep straight away." Turning to the inspector, she added, "My mother can't bear Glòria because she's still a size eight, and because she's studying for a degree."

"Gina, don't talk rubbish. I'm very fond of Glòria; she's been the best thing that could have happened to Enric: finding a wife." If the comment was meant to be complimentary, her tone clearly expressed a certain scorn. "And I admire her organizational ability, but that doesn't change the fact that the 'party' was a bore: my husband, Enric and the priest spoke at length and in detail about Catalonia's disastrous position at present, the crisis, the lack of values . . . To top it all, one can't even have a drink with the controls they put on the road during the night of San Juan." She said it as if this were Inspector Salgado's direct responsibility.

"What time did you return?"

"It would have been around two when we arrived home. Salvador returns from a trip tomorrow. I'll ask him; he pays much more attention to time than I do."

While her mother was speaking, Gina rose and went looking for a tissue. Leire's eyes followed her. The tears had stopped and in their place, for a moment, was something like satisfaction. Driven by an impulse, Leire rose and went over to the girl.

"Excuse me," she said to her, "I have to take a tablet. Would you mind giving me a glass of water? I'll go with you, no need to bring it."

He feels a slap in his mouth, given with the back of the hand by the guy in front of him. It's more humiliating than painful. A trickle of salty blood stains his lip.

"See what passes for answering?" the bald one says to him, moving away a little. "Come on, be a good boy and try another answer."

The bald guy is so close to him that he feels his breath on his face. Warm air flecked with saliva. The other is behind him and has his vice-like arm around his shoulders. Rubén, sitting in the corner of the room, looks away.

It's not the first time Aleix has been in this place: an old garage in Zona Franca where he's been many times to score cocaine. Because of this, he's let Rubén bring him here, never imagining that the other two would be inside waiting for him. He doesn't even know their names: only that they are pissed off. And with reason. Aleix is sweating, and not only because of the heat. The first punch in the stomach leaves him breathless. Truly surprised, he opens his eyes. When he tries to explain himself he feels another blow, and another. And another.

He doesn't even try to escape the fat one; he tries to make his mind go blank. They don't know that from an early age he had to tolerate so much pain that it doesn't frighten him anymore. He repeats to himself: this is a warning, a threat. They want the money, not to kill him or anything like that. But when the bald one stops after beating him for just enough time, he sees his face. The fucker is enjoying himself. And it's then he panics: seeing those eyes injected with satisfaction, a hand resting on his cock like he's going to masturbate. He guesses what he's thinking as if his brow were transparent glass with his intentions written on the other side. He fixes his gaze on the lump that has formed in the bald one's crotch and tries to transform the terror he feels into an ironic grimace. When the fat man gives him two more punches, he knows he's succeeded and also welcomes the pain. It's better than other things.

"That's enough!" Rubén has risen from the chair and comes over to the others.

Baldy's fist stays suspended in the air and the pliers slacken. Enough that Aleix slides like a liquid stain down a wall to fall to his knees. Amid a mist of pain he hears Rubén's footsteps coming closer. Baldy kneels by his side and speaks to him in a voice so low he can't even hear what he's saying.

"You're lucky that this one's here." Baldy looks at his watch. "Four days: next Tuesday we're coming to collect."

Aleix nods because he can't do anything else. He feels a hand resting on his shoulder and it helps him get up. He leans on Rubén, who looks wounded.

"Sorry, man," he whispers in his ear. And Aleix realizes that he means it. Despite having to drive him to this trap, he's worried about him.

"Take him home," Baldy tells him. "He already knows what he has to do."

Rubén grabs hold of his shoulders and brings him to the car.
Outside, Aleix has to stop: his stomach is churning, his eyes
streaming. And what's worse, he's weighed down by the fear of
not knowing how to get out of this.

In the kitchen, Leire drank the glass of water slowly while she
wondered how to broach the subject. Gina watched her with a
blank expression. There was something behind it, something
Leire discerned as much in the bitter tears from before as in
her apathetic expression now.

"Do you have a photo of Marc?" she asked in a friendly tone.
"I'd like to see what he looked like." It was a shot in the dark,
but it worked. Gina relaxed and nodded.

"Yes, I have them in my room."

They went upstairs to the room and Gina closed the door.
She sat down at the computer and typed rapidly.

"I have lots on Facebook," she said. "But these are from San
Juan. I didn't remember I'd taken them."

They were improvised photos. The pizzas, the drinks, the
traditional pine-nut cake. There were a couple of Aleix, but
the majority were of Marc. Hair closely shaven, a sea-blue
shirt with white numbers, and faded jeans. A normal boy,
handsome-ish, but too serious for being at a party. Leire looked
at Gina's face as much as at the photos, and if she had harbored
any doubt that the girl was in love, it dissolved immediately.

"You looked beautiful." And it was true. It was evident
that the girl had dressed up for that night. Leire imagined her
dressing to please him. And she'd ended up drunk and alone,
after vomiting in the bathroom. The question rose to her lips
without thinking: "He'd met another girl, hadn't he? In Dublin, maybe."

Gina instantly tensed up and minimized the screen. But her
face betrayed the answer.

"Wait." A sudden memory came to Leire: Marc's corpse on the ground of the patio, dried blood on the back of his head, jeans, trainers . . . And yes, she was sure, a light green polo shirt, nothing like the blue T-shirt. "Did he change his clothes?"

Aleix had told her, "If all of a sudden you don't know how to answer, say you don't remember." Gina tried to feign confusion.

"Why do you ask?"

"The clothes he was found in weren't the same as the ones he's wearing in these photos."

"No? To be honest, I don't remember." Her knee was trembling; she couldn't stop it. She stood up and went toward the door. The gesture was unmistakable: the conversation was over.

The old Citroën stopped on the same corner where it had picked Aleix up a few hours before. They hadn't spoken throughout the whole journey: Aleix because he could barely pronounce a word, Rubén because he had nothing to say.

"Wait a minute," stammered Aleix.

The driver turned off the engine. He stayed silent.

Rubén lit a cigarette.

"These guys are serious," he said, not looking at him. "This time there's a lot of money at stake, man. You have to get the money somehow."

"You think I don't know that? Shit, Rubén!"

"Get the dough, man. Ask your folks, your friends, your girlfriend . . . She's well off, isn't she? If one of my friends needed four thousand euros, I'd scrape it from under a stone. I swear."

Aleix sighed. How could he explain to Rubén that it was exactly those who had the most money who were the most reluctant to let it go?

The smoke was drifting out of the open window, but it left a faint odor in the car. Aleix thought he was going to vomit.

"Are you OK?"

"I don't know." He stuck his head out in search of air, a pointless gesture in this heat. He inhaled deeply anyway.

"Listen." Rubén had thrown the butt into the street. "I want you to know something: my head is on the line. If these people come to believe that you've kept . . . you know . . . They're in a different league, man. I told you."

True. The deals between Aleix and Rubén went back a year, and they'd started almost as a game: the possibility of getting some free lines in exchange for moving part of the merchandise in circles Rubén couldn't access. Aleix had enjoyed doing it: it was a way of breaking the rules, taking a small step on the other side. And when, weeks back, in light of the fact that business was booming, Rubén had proposed increasing the volume of sales courtesy of these new colleagues, he hadn't given it a second thought. On the night of San Juan he was carrying enough to liven up half the city's parties.

"Fuck, how many times do I have to tell you? Marc got pissed off with me and threw it down the toilet. I couldn't do anything. D'you think I'd be putting up with all this if I could help it?"

"Why did you push him?"

The pause was too tense: like a rubber band stretched to its limit.

"What?"

Rubén looked away.

"I went looking for you, man. San Juan night. I knew where you were, so when I got tired of calling you I took the motorbike and I stood outside your friend's house."

Aleix looked at him, astonished.

"It was late, but the attic light was on. You could see it from the other side of the railings. Your friend was at the window, smoking. I called your mobile again and I was leaving when . . ."

"What?"

"Well, from where I was I'd swear someone pushed him. He was still and suddenly he catapulted forwards . . . And I seemed to see a shadow behind. I didn't stay around to check. I grabbed the bike and got the hell out of there. Then, the following day, when you told me what had happened, I thought maybe it was you."

Aleix shook his head.

"My friend fell from the window. And if you saw anything else it's because you were out of your mind that night. Or weren't you?"

"Well, it was San Juan . . ."

"Whatever, best you don't say you were around here."

"Fine."

"Listen, do you have . . . ?"

Rubén exhaled.

"If those idiots hear that I've given you some they'll kill me."

Rubén rapidly prepared two lines on an empty plastic CD case. He passed it to Aleix, who snorted the first greedily. He looked at him sideways before giving it back.

"Take the other one as well," Rubén told him as he lit another cigarette. "I have to drive. And today you need it."

11

Last visit of the day, thought Héctor as the car stopped just in front of the Castells' house. One more and he could go home and forget all about it. Shelve this absurd favor and focus on what really mattered. What's more, Savall would be happy for once; he would arrange a meeting with the boy's mother, tell her it had all been an unfortunate accident and they'd move on. During the journey, his companion had told him the detail of the T-shirt and her reinforced belief that Gina Martí wasn't telling them the whole truth. He'd made signs of agreeing, although he thought, without saying it aloud, that lying wasn't the same as pushing a childhood friend out the attic window. A window which was visible now, above the creeper-covered railings. Héctor looked toward it and squinted: from that point to the ground was a good thirty-five or thirty-six feet. Where on earth did this custom of kids doing dangerous stunts come from? Was it out of boredom, a desire for risk, or simple irresponsibility? Maybe an equal amount of all three.

He shook his head, thinking of his son entering adolescence, that awkward age plagued by stereotypes, during which he, as a father, could only arm himself with patience and hope that everything he had tried to impart in the past might have some effect in offsetting the hormonal turmoil and congenital stupidity of those years. Marc Castells was almost twenty when he fell from that window. Héctor kept his eyes fixed on it and realized he was overwhelmed by the sudden fear he'd felt at other times when confronted by absurd deaths: accidents that could have been avoided, tragedies that should never have happened.

A middle-aged woman with South American features accompanied them to the lounge. The contrast between the house they'd just visited and this one was so huge that even Héctor, for whom interior design was as abstract a discipline as quantum physics, couldn't help noticing it. White walls and low furniture, a painting in warm tones and Bach smoothly wafting through the air. Regina Ballester had made it very clear that Glòria Vergès seemed rather dull to her, but the atmosphere she'd created in her house was one of harmony, of peace. The type of house that a man like Enric Castells wants to come home to: calm and beautiful, with large windows and bright spaces, not too modern or too classic, in which every detail exudes money and good taste. Without wanting to, he noticed that the table runner flaunted a black-and-white geometric pattern, which he recognized as one of Ruth's designs. Maybe that was what made him feel a stab of sadness, rapidly mixing with an ill-at-ease feeling, a bitter pang he recognized as unfair. Someone had died there less than two weeks before, and yet the house seemed to have recovered completely: the tragedy had been neutralized, everything had gone back to normal.

"Inspector Salgado? My husband told me you were coming. He should be here any minute." Héctor understood instantly why Glòria Vergès and Regina Ballester couldn't move beyond a superficial friendship. "We should wait for him," she added, with a note of uncertainty in her voice.

"Mama! Look!"

A little girl of four or five claimed Glòria's attention and she didn't hesitate in giving it to her immediately.

"It's a castle!" announced the little one, waving a drawing in the air.

"Wow, the castle where the princess lives?" asked her mother.

Seated at a small yellow table, the little girl looked at the drawing and thought about the answer.

"Yes!" she exclaimed at last.

"Why don't you draw the princess? Walking in the garden."

Glòria had crouched down beside her and from there she came back toward Salgado and Castro. "Would you like something to drink?"

"If you don't mind, we would prefer to go up to the attic," said Salgado.

Glòria hesitated again: it was obvious her husband had given her precise instructions and she didn't feel comfortable disobeying them. Luckily, at that moment someone entered the lounge. Salgado and Castro turned toward the door.

"Fèlix," said Glòria, surprised but relieved. "This is my husband's brother, Father Fèlix Castells."

"Inspector." The man, very tall and rather stout, extended his hand to greet them. "Enric just rang me: something has come up unexpectedly and he'll be a little late. If you need anything in the meantime, I've come to be of use to you in any way I can."

Before Héctor could say anything, Glòria approached them.

"I beg your pardon, would you mind talking somewhere else?" She gave a sidelong glance at the little girl. "Natàlia has had a very bad time recently; she's had some appalling nightmares." She exhaled. "I don't know if it's best, but I'm trying to bring everything back to normal," she added, almost as an excuse. "I don't want to remind her of it again."

"Of course." Fèlix looked at her affectionately. "Let's go upstairs, shall we?"

"I'll go up with you," said Héctor. "Would you mind if Agent Castro had a look at Marc's room?" He lowered his voice on saying the boy's name, but even so the little girl turned toward them. Evidently she was following the conversation although she seemed absorbed in her drawing. How much of what was going on around them did children understand? It must be very difficult to explain a tragedy like this to a little girl of her age. Maybe her mother's choice was the best: returning to normal, as if nothing had happened. That is, if that were even possible.

Enric Castells' unwelcome thing that has come up unexpectedly is at this moment observing him from the other side of the table with a mixture of curiosity and scorn. It's a tranquil bar, above all in summer, because the soft armchairs and tables of dark wood give off a feeling of heat that the air-conditioning can't quite dispel. Waiters are dressed in uniforms of an old-fashioned formality, and a pair of old-timers sitting at the bar clearly spend every afternoon there since their health is the topic of conversation. And them, of course, sitting in the back, almost crouching, as if they are hiding from anyone who might come in by chance. On the table there are two cups of coffee with their respective saucers and a little white jug.

Seen from the other side of the glass, their gestures are

those of a couple in crisis facing an imminent and unavoidable break-up. Although their words can't be heard, there is something in the posture of the woman which suggests extreme tension: she spreads her arms and shakes her head, as if the man opposite her is disappointing her once again. He, for the most part, seems immune to anything the woman may say to him: he looks at her with irony, with an ill-concealed indifference. His rigid posture, however, contradicts this indifference. The scene continues thus for a few minutes. She insists, asks, demands, pulls out a piece of paper with something printed on it and throws it on the table; he looks away and answers in monosyllables. Until suddenly something she says makes its mark: it is immediately obvious in his darkened expression, in the fist he makes before clasping both hands, tense, on the table; in his manner of getting up, as if he's no longer prepared to endure anymore. She looks out of the window, pensive, turns to add something but he's already gone. The piece of paper is still on the table. She picks it up, re-reads it. Then she folds it carefully and puts it back in her bag. She suppresses a bitter smile. And, as if doing so is a great effort, Joana Vidal gets up from her seat and walks slowly toward the door.

The word "attic" brings to mind sloping roofs, wooden rafters and old rocking chairs, forgotten toys and dusty chests: an intimate space, a refuge. The one in the Castells' house must be the pasteurized version: spotless, with white walls, in perfect order. Héctor didn't know how the room had looked when Marc was alive, but now, two weeks after his death, it was a perfect extension of the harmonious atmosphere of the floor below. Nothing old, nothing out of place, nothing personal. An empty table of pale wood, arranged at a right angle to the window to take advantage of the light; a modern, almost office-

like chair; shelves full of books and CDs, slightly illuminated
by the evening light coming through the window, situated at
waist height. A large, impersonal room, nothing standing out.
The only thing that evoked real attics was a large box leaning
against the wall opposite the table.

Héctor went toward the only window, opened it and leaned
out. He closed his eyes and tried to visualize the victim's movements: seated on the windowsill, legs hanging, cigarette in
hand. A little drunk, just enough for his reflexes to be less
quick than usual, probably thinking about the girl awaiting
him in his room, although, it seems, without too much enthu-
siasm for following her to bed. Maybe he is mustering up the
courage to turn her down, or the reverse, taking in air to give
her what she wants. It is his moment of peace: a few minutes
in which he puts the world in order. And, when he finishes
his cigarette, he puts one leg inside, intending to turn around.
Then the alcohol has its effect; a momentary but fatal dizzi-
ness. He falls backward, his arms moving through space; the
foot on the floor slips.

Fèlix Castells had stayed on the threshold, observing him
in silence. Not until Héctor had moved away from the window
again did he close the door and turn to him.

"You have to understand Glòria, Inspector. All this has been
very hard for Enric and the little one."

Héctor nodded. What had Leire said before? "After all, she's
not his mother." It was true: Glòria Vergès might mourn her
stepson's death—and no doubt she did—but her priorities were
her daughter and her husband. Nobody could reproach her
for that.

"How did they get on?"

"As well as could be expected. Marc was at a difficult age
and he tended to retreat into himself. He was never a very

talkative boy: he spent hours in here, or in his room, or roller-blading. Glòria understood him and in general left Enric to worry about his son. That's not hard: my brother tends to take charge of almost everything."

"And Marc and your brother?"

"Well, Enric has a strong personality. Some would describe him as old-fashioned. But he loved his son very much, of course, and worried about him." He paused as if he had to expand on his answer and didn't know how. "Family life isn't easy these days, Inspector. I'm not so reactionary as to be nostalgic for other times, but it's clear that ruptures and separations pro-voke . . . a certain imbalance. In all those affected."

Héctor said nothing and went toward the box. He guessed its contents, but was surprised: Marc's mobile, his laptop, various chargers, a camera, cables and a torn teddy bear, completely out of place among the other objects. He took it out and showed it to Father Castells.

"Was it Marc's?"

"I really don't remember. I suppose so."

Well-guarded possessions, placed in a box like their owner.

"Do you need anything else?"

Truthfully no, thought Héctor. Even so, the question came out without thinking:

"Why was he suspended from school?"

"That was a long time ago. I don't see what good remember-ing it now could possibly serve."

Héctor said nothing: as he hoped, the silence spurred the de-sire to speak. It made even a man of Fèlix's age, an expert in blame and absolution, uncomfortable.

"It was a stupid thing. A joke in bad taste. Very bad taste." He leaned on the table and looked Héctor in the eye. "I don't know how such a thing occurred to him, if I'm honest. It seemed so . . . out of character for Marc. He was always a rather sensitive boy, not cruel at all."

If Father Castells wanted to intrigue him, he was doing a good job, thought Héctor.

"There was a boy in Marc's class. Óscar Vaquero. Fat, not bright, and . . ." he searched for the word, which clearly made him uncomfortable, ". . . a little . . . effeminate."

He inhaled and continued talking, now without pausing. "It seems Marc recorded him naked in the showers and put the video on the internet. The boy was . . . well, you know, excited, it seems."

"He was masturbating in the changing room?"

Father Castells nodded.

"Some joke."

"The only thing that can be said in my nephew's defense is that he owned up straightaway to being the one who did it. He apologized to the other boy and took the video down only a few hours after putting it up. Because of that the center decided to only suspend him temporarily."

Héctor was about to answer when Agent Castro knocked at the door and entered without waiting for a response. She was carrying a blue T-shirt in her hand.

"It's been washed, but it's the one in the photo. Definitely."

Father Castells watched them both, ill at ease. Something in his bearing changed and he stood up from the table. He was a big man—four inches taller than Héctor, who at five foot ten wasn't exactly short—and no doubt thirty kilos heavier.

"Listen, Inspector, Lluís . . . . Savall told us that this was an unofficial visit . . . to reassure Joana more than anything."

"So it is," replied Héctor, somewhat surprised at hearing the superintendent's name. "But we want to be sure to tie up all loose ends."

"Inspector, look here, at the top of the T-shirt, just below the collar."

Some reddish stains. They could be many things, but Salgado had seen too many bloodstains not to recognize them. His tone also changed.

"We'll take it. And," pointing to the box, "that too."

The voice from the door surprised them all.

"What are you taking?"

"Enric," said Fèlix, addressing the recent arrival, "this is Inspector Salgado and Agent Castro . . ."

Enric Castells was in no mood for formal introductions.

"I thought I'd made it clear that we didn't want to be disturbed anymore. You were already here and rummaged through everything you wanted. Now you're back and expect to take Marc's things. May I simply ask why?"

"This is the T-shirt Marc was wearing on San Juan. But not the one he had on when he was found. For some reason he changed his clothes. Probably because this one was stained. And if I'm not mistaken they are bloodstains."

Both Enric and his brother received the news in silence.

"But what does that mean?" asked Fèlix.

"I don't know. Probably nothing. Perhaps he cut himself by accident and changed his clothes. Or perhaps something happened that night that the kids haven't told us. Either way, the first thing is to have the T-shirt analyzed. And speak to Aleix Rovira and Gina Martí again."

Enric Castells' attitude suddenly changed.

"Are you telling me something happened that night that we don't know about? Something to do with my son's death?" He spoke steadily, but it was clear the phrase had pained him.

"It's too early to say. But I think we all want to get to the bottom of this matter." He said it as delicately as he could.

Enric Castells lowered his eyes. His face clearly indicated that he was thinking about something, deciding what to do. Seconds later he seemed to come to a decision and, not looking at anyone, he said in a clear voice:

"Fèlix, Agent Castro, I'd like to speak to Inspector Salgado. Alone. Please."

12

Aleix contemplated the food on his plate with a feeling of help-lessness, but even so he forced himself to begin. Slowly. He felt like his stomach would expel any food as if it were a foreign body. Dinner at the Rovira home was served at half past eight, winter or summer, and his father required that everyone—namely him—should be seated at the table at that hour. These days, however, his older brother had returned from Nicaragua, so at least his parents had someone to entertain them during dinner. He watched in silence, not really listening to what they were saying, thinking how stunned they'd be if they knew where he'd been, what they'd done to him. The idea amused him so much he had to make an effort to suppress a roar of laughter. Wasn't that what his father always said? Family is for sharing problems: a motto floating in the atmosphere of this house for as long as he could remember. And at that moment he realized that, despite his longing for rebellion, that phrase had marked him more than he thought. It didn't matter what might happen behind closed doors: from the outside the Roviras had to be a unit, an army of ranks closed against the world. Maybe he should interrupt his father and say it right there, out loud: "Know what, Papa? I'm not hungry because I was beaten up an hour ago. Yes, well, it's just that I was carrying a few grams of coke around to sell, you know, and I lost it. Well to be honest, that idiot Marc took it off me and flushed it down the toilet, and now I need a little dough so they don't beat me again. Nothing excessive, about four thousand euros . . . a little more to make sure they don't scar my face. But don't worry, I've learned my lesson: I won't do it again. Also, it's certain the person who took it from me will never do it again. Will you help me? After all, as you always say, family comes first." Imagining his father's face, the temptation to laugh was so strong that he grabbed the glass of water and drained it in one gulp. His mother rapidly refilled it, with a smile as mechanical as her action. His father was still talking and in a moment of lucidity, surely due to the effect of the cocaine, Aleix realized he wasn't the only one not paying attention: his mother was mentally somewhere else, he could read it in her expression, and his brother . . . Well, who knew what Edu was thinking? He watched him out of the corner of his eye: he was nodding at what their father was saying, attentive to the words of Dr. Miquel Rovira, reputable gynecologist, devout Catholic and fierce defender of values like family, life, Christianity and honor. Suddenly, Aleix felt as if he were traveling in an inexorably accelerating train carriage. A cold sweat broke out on his forehead. His hand was shaking and he had to clench his fist to stop it. A profound desire to cry came over him, something he hadn't felt since he was a little boy in his hospital bed: that fear that the door would open to admit the doctor; nurses who treated him with a refined cheerfulness that even he at

his young age recognized as false; the treatment as painful as
it was inevitable. He'd been lucky that he could count on Edu.
He didn't ask him to be brave, or pretend that what was happening to him wasn't terrifying: he sat beside him all of the af-
ternoons, many of the nights, and read him stories or told him
things, or simply gave him his hand to show he was there, that
he could always, always, count on him. He didn't doubt that his
parents had been there in those long months in hospital, but it
was Edu he remembered most. It was with him that he'd forged
a bond that proved his father's phrase: family comes first. He
raised his hand to his pocket and checked that the USB Gina
had given him was still in its place. He exhaled slowly on feeling that it was.

The breath must have been louder than he'd thought because
all eyes at the table were fixed on him. Aleix tried to turn his
exhale into a cough with even worse results. The parental eyes
went from surprise to distaste. And then, only then, he noticed
a sour smell that seemed to be coming from him, and seconds
later he saw that he'd just vomited up the little he'd eaten.

> hey gi, you there?
> Yeah
> howd it go with the cops?
> OK, good, I suppose. they left a while ago.
> whatd you tell them?
> Nothing, don't you trust me?
> yes, of course.
> . . .
> . . .
> gi, love you a lot really.
> :-)
> really . . . youre the only girlfriend i have. and i feel bad . . . im
> bad.

Are you still taking? You're still taking, right?

im going to bed. kisses

Fuck, aleix, what's wrong? It's only nine!

nothing, dinner didnt go down well. shit, its my brother. gotta go, talk tmrw.

Eduard enters his room with a serious expression, closes the door and sits on the edge of the bed.

"Feeling better? Mama was worried."

"Yes. Just stomach cramp from the heat."

His brother's silence is obvious proof of his disbelief. Aleix knows it and for a moment he is tempted to unburden himself.

"You know you can trust me, don't you?"

No, Aleix screams inside. I can't.

Edu gets up from the bed and puts a hand on his shoulder. And all of a sudden Aleix is that frightened little boy again, waiting for the doctors in his hospital bed. The tears flow down his cheeks but he can't do anything to stop them. He's ashamed to be sobbing like a child but it's too late. Eduard repeats in a whisper: "You can trust me. I'm your brother." And his embrace is so warm, so comforting, that Aleix can't hold back any longer and cries openly, without the least shame.

Gina kept staring at the screen for a few more seconds, asking herself why Aleix only spoke like that when he was doing it through a keyboard. Was it just him, or did it apply to all guys? Of course people didn't go around saying how much they loved each other—it was embarrassing. That was something only her mother did, not realizing that repeating the phrase made it lose its value. It wasn't possible to love a daughter who didn't stand out in any way. People had to be loved for something. Marc, for example: he was tender, affectionate and he really smiled, with his whole face, and he explained math problems,

which for her were indecipherable hieroglyphs, with infinite
patience. Or Aleix, who was handsome, clever, brilliant. Even
when he was stoned. But her? She had no special gift, good or
bad. She wasn't pretty or ugly, tall or short; thin, yes, but not
with the sensual slimness of a model, just thin: flat with no
curves. For the second time that day she opened the photos she
had uploaded to Facebook on San Juan. They were from the beginning of the night. From when they were still friends. From
before the fight. But something strange was already in the air.
In the afternoon, she and Aleix had agreed definitively not to
go ahead with Marc's plan. Now she couldn't even remember
the arguments Aleix had used to convince her, but at the time
they had seemed reasonable. And she'd believed, naïvely, that
this same reasoning would work to persuade Marc as well. But
nothing had gone right. Marc had been furious. Really furious.
As if they were betraying him. Gina closed her eyes. What had
that nosy police officer said? "He'd met another girl, hadn't
he? In Dublin, maybe?" Gina hadn't known what jealousy was
until Marc returned. It was an emotion unfamiliar to her and
nothing had prepared her for its force. It poisoned everything.
It made you wicked, twisted. It made you say things that never
would have occurred to you, do things that had never crossed
your mind. She'd never thought of herself as a passionate girl:
that was for films, novels, songs . . . women capable of stabbing
their boyfriends because they cheated on them. Ridiculous.
Almost laughable. And in this case she didn't even have the
consolation of being the betrayed girlfriend: not in the strict
sense of the word. It wasn't his fault. Gina had spent months
making believe they were boyfriend and girlfriend and telling
herself over and over that some day, soon, he'd realize affection had turned into something more. How could she have been
so stupid? So she'd had no choice but to swallow her jealousy,

pretend it didn't exist, force a smile disguising hatred as admiration. *She's pretty, isn't she?* Of course she was. Pretty, and blonde, and languid. A fucking Renaissance madonna. But the worst thing about this photo—the one Marc had shown her the day after he arrived, just after she confessed that she'd missed him very much, to which he responded, "Yeah, Gi, me too," not looking at her, not making the phrase any more meaningful while he searched the file for said photo—wasn't that the girl in question was pretty. The worst, most painful thing was seeing Marc's eyes as he looked at it. Like he wanted to learn her by heart, like he felt the softness of her hair by touching the paper, like he discovered something new and marvelous in that face every time he looked at it.

Lucky she'd taken that photo. Surprisingly, it was the first thing she'd done after seeing Marc broken on the patio floor. So no meddler would find it, like that cop who was pretending to be nice and to whom it would confirm what she was already guessing. That Gina wasn't good enough for Marc. That there was another girl. That on San Juan she'd asked her mother to help her choose a dress and put on makeup for the first time in years. Why not? This Iris might be beautiful, but she was just a photo. She wasn't real. She wasn't there. In a way, she wasn't even alive. But Gina was.

She took the photo from her drawer and leaned it against the keyboard. She'd have liked to burn it, but she had nothing with which to do so in her room, so she settled for cutting it with scissors: first through the middle at nose height, and then she continued cutting it into pieces until it was reduced to one of those jigsaws with hundreds and hundreds of pieces, each so diminutive that they are unrecognizable in themselves.

13

If a man's study is a reflection of his personality, Enric Castells was a sober and organized individual like few others. His study could have been the set of a legal thriller starring Michael Douglas, thought Héctor, as he sat on the stiff yet comfortable black leather chair and waited for his host to decide to tell him why exactly he'd wanted to speak to him. Castells took his time: he lowered the blind carefully, pulled back the chair on the other side of the glass-topped aluminium desk, and after sitting down he moved a shiny black antique telephone at one end slightly, barely millimeters. Héctor wondered if it was a calculated choreography to unnerve or exasperate his interlocutor, but Castells' face showed intense concentration, a worry difficult to feign. He must have been an attractive man before the years and responsibilities left him with that bitter sneer on his thin, slightly turned-down lips, and an expression of perpetual dissatisfaction which spoiled his appearance. His eyes were small and a faded, tired blue, tending to gray. Suddenly, Enric Castells exhaled slowly and leaned back. For a moment, his wrinkles relaxed and showed the face of someone younger and more insecure: definitely more like young Marc.

"This afternoon I spoke to my ex-wife." The irritated expression had once again taken over his appearance. "It upsets me to say it, but I think she's mad. On the other hand, it was to be expected."

"Oh?" Héctor stuck to his technique of saying as little as possible. Apart from which he didn't really know what to say to something like that.

"Inspector Salgado," continued Castells in a dry tone, "I know things seem to have changed a lot in recent times, but there are actions that simply go against human nature. Abandoning a son before he has even begun to walk is one of them. And nobody will convince me that actions such as these won't have a price to pay, sooner or later. Above all when tragedies like the one we've just gone through happen."

Héctor was surprised by the rancor exuding from these words, both from what was said and from how it was said. He asked himself if this grudge had always been there or if it had resurfaced now, after the death of the son the couple had in common. Castells seemed to find comfort in giving free rein to a hatred he hadn't fully overcome.

"What I mean by that is that I'm not going to allow the suspicions of a neurotic to hurt my family. To inflict more damage than it has already suffered."

"I understand, Señor Castells. And I promise you we will respect your grief as much as possible. But at the same time," Héctor looked the man opposite in the eyes, gravely, "we have to do our job. In good conscience."

Castells held his gaze. He was evaluating him. At that moment Héctor felt annoyed: his patience was running out. However, before he could say anything else, Castells asked:

"Do you have children, Inspector?"

"One boy."

"Then it will be easier for you to understand me." No, it isn't, thought Héctor. "I raised mine the best way I knew. But in life one has to accept failures."   .

"Marc was a failure?"

"Not him; me as a father. I let myself be persuaded by modern theories, assumed the absence of his mother was a difficult obstacle to overcome, something that justified his apathy . . . his mediocrity."

Héctor felt almost offended in a way he didn't fully understand.

"You're looking at me as if I'm a monster, Inspector. But believe me when I say I loved my son, as much as you love yours. I have nothing to reproach him for, only myself. I should have been able to prevent something like this happening. Yes, I know you think accidents happen by chance, and I'm not denying it. But I won't fall into the trap of everyone absolving themselves of their responsibilities: young people drink, young people do stupid things, adolescence means tolerating your son doing whatever he wants and waiting for the cure, as if he has the flu. No, Inspector: our generation made many mistakes and now we have to bear the consequences. For ourselves and our children."

Salgado saw the sorrow then. A real sorrow, as genuine as that of a devastated mother in tears. Enric Castells wasn't crying, but that didn't mean he suffered any less.

"What do you think happened, Señor Castells?" he asked quietly.

He took his time answering. As if extracting the words was an effort.

"He could have fallen. I don't deny it. But sometimes in accidents there is an element of carelessness, indifference."

Héctor nodded.

"I don't think Marc had the audacity or motive to commit suicide, if that's what you're thinking. And, although she doesn't say it, what Joana seems to fear. However, I think he was irresponsible enough, rash enough to do something stupid. Just to have done it. To impress that little girl or feel more of a man. Or simply because it was all the same to him. Almost twenty and they're still playing like children, as if there are no limits. Nothing matters, it's all good, think about yourself: this is the message we've passed on to them. Or that we've let them absorb."

"I understand what you mean, but it seems Marc returned more adult from Dublin . . . or didn't he?"

Castells nodded.

"I thought so too. He seemed to have matured. To have a clear goal in life. Or at least so he said. I learned that, with him, I had to wait to see actions, not words."

"He'd lie?"

"Not the way most would, but yes. For example, the school expulsion, that story of the video posted on the internet."

"Yes?"

"At the beginning I thought it was both aspects: the boy masturbating in a public place and the boy who records it and shares it with the whole world. Disgusting from start to finish."

Although he saw qualitative differences between the two acts, Salgado said nothing and waited: Castells hadn't finished.

"However, once it was over, and the matter seemed forgotten, one day Marc came to see me here, in my study. He sat down on that very chair where you are now and asked me how I could have believed him capable of a thing like that."

"He'd confessed to it."

"So I told him." He smiled bitterly. "But he insisted, almost with tears in his eyes. Do you really think I did it? he asked. And I didn't know how to respond. When he left, I thought it over. And the worst thing is I didn't come to any conclusion. Look, Inspector: I've not misled you with respect to Marc. He was lazy, apathetic, spoiled. But at the same time, because of all that, I sometimes think he was incapable of doing something so cruel. He might have mocked that boy, or rather, allowed him to be mocked, but I don't think he'd ever have humiliated someone in cold blood. That wasn't typical of him."

"Do you mean he took the blame for someone else?"

"Something like that. Don't ask me why. I tried to talk to him but he refused to listen. And you know something? While we were burying him, I cursed myself again and again for not giving him the satisfaction of knowing that no, in reality I didn't believe he could have committed such a dishonorable act."

A silence descended which Héctor maintained. He couldn't agree with this man, but a part of him understood him. For Enric Castells there was someone responsible for everything, and he'd taken on himself the role of guilty party for his son's death. For that reason he was rejecting any kind of investigation: to him it was pointless.

"You know something, Inspector?" continued Castells, in an even lower voice. "When we got the call first thing in the morning on San Juan, I knew something terrible had happened. I think it's what every father fears: the call in the middle of the night that splits your life in two. And in one way or another I'd been expecting this to happen, praying that it wouldn't." Héctor could barely hear him by then, but suddenly his interlocutor returned to his normal tone. "Now I must decide what to do with this new half of my life. I have a wonderful wife and a daughter I must care for and protect. So it is time to reconsider many things."

"Are you going into politics?" asked Salgado, remembering what Savall had said to him.

"Possibly. I don't like this world we're living in, Inspector. People may consider certain values outdated, but what is definite is we haven't managed to replace them with others. Perhaps they're not so bad after all. Are you religious?"

"I'm afraid not. Although you know what they say: 'In the trenches there are no atheists.'"

"It's a good saying. Very descriptive. Atheists think we never doubt, that faith is like a helmet that prevents us seeing further. They're deluded. But it's at moments like these that believing acquires its true meaning, the feeling that there is a plank to cling to so as to keep swimming instead of giving up and being carried by the current. That would be easier. But I don't expect you to understand."

His last phrase held a note of contempt which Héctor decided to overlook. He hadn't the least intention of arguing about religion with a resolute believer who had just lost his son. Enric Castells waited for a moment, and seeing that the inspector wasn't saying anything, moved on.

"Can you tell me why you wish to take Marc's belongings? Is there something that might be useful?"

"Honestly, I don't know, Señor Castells." He elaborated a little about the bloodstained T-shirt and his hunch that something had occurred between the boys that night. He didn't want to place too much importance on it, but at the same time he knew the victim's father had a right to be informed. "With regard to the laptop, mobile and other things . . . I don't think we'll get anything useful out of them but it will help us complete the investigation. They are diaries nowadays: emails, messages, calls. I doubt they'll clarify what happened but it's worth giving them a look."

"I'm afraid you won't get much information from his laptop. It looked broken."

"Broken?"

"Yes. I suppose it might have been dropped. I didn't notice until four or five days afterward."

Somehow, Enric Castells suddenly felt uncomfortable, so he rose from his chair, signalling that the interview was over. Already at the door, however, he came back to the inspector.

"Take my son's things if you want. I doubt they'll give you any answers, but take them."

"We'll return them to you as soon as possible. I give you my word."

Castells' expression was slightly indignant.

"They're just things, Inspector," he said coldly. "In any case, I ask that if you need anything else you contact me at my office. Glòria is very worried about the little one. Natàlia is small, but she notices everything: she's been asking for her brother and it's very hard to explain what has happened in a way she can understand."

Héctor made a gesture of assent and followed him to the corridor. Castells was moving forward, shoulders upright and back ramrod straight. Any trace of weakness had evaporated on crossing the threshold. He was back to being the man of the house: firm, balanced, self-assured. A role, Héctor was certain, that had to be exhausting.

Meanwhile, Leire had remained seated in the lounge, watching how Natàlia finished drawing after drawing before her mother's tireless admiration. Father Castells had left shortly after Enric and the inspector had shut themselves in his study, and once she'd confiscated the bloodstained T-shirt, she'd sat down on a chair, waiting for them to emerge. For a moment she imagined herself like this, stuck at home on a summer afternoon, contemplating the artistic progress of a little boy or girl, and the idea horrified her. For the umpteenth time since the night before she did the fateful test, she tried to imagine herself with a baby in her arms, but her brain didn't succeed in forming the image. No. People like her didn't have children. That—and financial independence—was the basis of her life, of how she conceived it. How she liked it. And now her whole future was tottering because of one careless slip-up. At least, she told herself with a certain satisfaction, the guy had been worth it . . . Unfortunately, he wasn't one of the hot-chocolate boys and he valued his freedom as much as she did. Relative freedom, she thought, since he was a slave to a job that took him all over the continent.

"Look." The little girl had come over to her and was showing her latest drawing, an indecipherable smudge, to Leire. "It's you," she explained.

"Ah. Is it for me?"

Then Natàlia hesitated and her mother spoke for her.

"Of course. You are giving it to her, aren't you?"

Leire put out her hand, but the little girl hadn't decided to give up the drawing.

"No," she said at last. "A different one." And she ran to the table in search of another of her works of art. "This one."

"Thank you. And what is it?" asked Leire, although in this one it was more obvious.

"A window. Bad dodo."

Glòria Vergès went to her daughter. She looked deeply worried.

"She's taken to calling upstairs that now," she whispered,

turning to the agent. "I suppose she feels it's bad because he's not there."

"Bad," repeated Natàlia. "Bad dodo."

"OK, sweetheart." Her mother crouched down and stroked her straight, shiny hair. "Why don't you fetch your doll? I'm sure that . . ."

"Leire."

". . . Leire would love to see her." She threw Agent Castro an apologetic smile and the little girl hastened to obey.

"I'm sorry," said the agent. "I suppose it's very complicated for her. For everyone."

"It's horrible. And the worst is you don't really know how to explain it. Enric is in favor of telling her the truth, but I can't . . ."

"Was she very attached to her brother?"

Glòria hesitated.

"I would like to say yes, but I'm afraid the age gap was too wide. Marc basically ignored her, and I suppose that's normal. But lately, since he came back from Dublin, he seemed to have more affection for her. And now she misses—"

Before she could finish, Natàlia came running in. Somehow that childish noise, so normal in any other house where a child lives, sounded strange. As if the perfect set was tottering.

"Natàlia, sweetheart . . ."

But the little girl didn't pay her the least attention, and turned to the table where she was drawing to pick up the bits of paper.

"How tidy!" commented Leire.

"Don't you believe it . . . Now she'll put them all over my studio." She smiled. "Since I also 'go to school,' as she says, she likes to leave her things on my desk. I'll go and see what she's doing before it's too late."

Leire, for whom that scene of devout motherhood was becoming unbearable, decided to get up from her chair and wait
for the inspector in the car.

There Héctor found her, when he came out weighed down with
the box containing Marc's belongings. Oblivious to his appearance, lost in thought, she was looking at the screen of her mobile as if it were a foreign object, something that had just fallen
into her power by magic and was completely indecipherable.
He had to attract her attention so she would open the trunk.
The girl stammered an apology, unnecessary apart from anything else, and put her phone in her pocket.

"Are you feeling all right?" he asked her.

"Of course. I see you managed to convince Castells."

The desire to change the subject was so obvious Héctor
didn't persist. He looked at his own mobile before getting into
the car: three missed calls. Two from Andreu and one from his
son. At last. He didn't want to respond to any of them in front
of Castro, and so he decided to go as far as Plaça Bonanova and
then go his own way.

"Bring all this to the station. I have some stuff to do," he
said as he got into the vehicle. "By the way, the laptop is broken. You didn't see it the day you were there?"

Leire was doubtful. She'd spent most of the time below, wit-
nessing the removal of the corpse.

"In fact," she said finally, "we didn't see any laptop. There
was the desktop in the attic and it was examined to see if Marc
had left any message on it, something that could be interpreted
as a suicide note. There was nothing. And at no time did anyone mention that he had another computer."

Héctor nodded.

"Well, he had one. In his room, I suppose." He didn't say anything else, and the notion that they hadn't done a thorough job hung in the car's interior. The inspector noticed it, so before he got out, he commented, "I don't think it will give us anything. It's still most probable that the boy fell accidentally. We'll analyze the T-shirt and see what comes from that. Oh, and when we have something we'll have to speak to the other boy, this Aleix Rovira. But at the station. I'm sick of visiting these brats at home."

"Good. Sure you want me to leave you here?"

"Yes, I'll take the opportunity to run some errands," he lied. And given that it was already almost nine o'clock, it was obvious there were few errands that could be run. "I'll see you tomorrow." He was going to ask her again if she was all right, but stopped himself. Castro's affairs weren't any business of his. "Good night."

The car moved off, and Héctor waited a few seconds before taking out his mobile again and returning Martina Andreu's calls. She answered immediately, although the conversation was brief, the sergeant's trademark. There was nothing new regarding Dr. Omar's disappearance, but on the subject of the pig's head, it had been delivered by a nearby butcher. It seemed he regularly brought him entrails for his sinister tricks. With regard to the fake doctor, he seemed to have vanished off the face of the earth leaving only a few traces of blood. Yes—the results hadn't yet arrived but it was most probable that it was his. A hasty flight or a settling of accounts by someone who had taken all his papers and left only part of Salgado's file. Which, in truth, was rather strange. Andreu said a brusque good-bye and Héctor immediately called his son, who, not wanting to break a habit, didn't answer his mobile. I need to talk to him, Héctor thought. After a whole day with the parents of spoiled adolescents he wanted to hear Guillermo's voice and reassure himself that everything was OK. He left a new message, and after doing so found himself on Bonanova with nothing to do and decided to walk for a while.

It had been some time since he strolled through this part of the city and, seeing it again, he was amazed at how little it had altered. More or less all of Barcelona's *barrios* had undergone some sort of change in recent years, but it was clear that the exclusive areas remained immune to most of it. No tourists en masse or immigrants, except those who worked cleaning the houses of the area. He asked himself if this happened in other cities: the existence of impermeable old-fashioned areas, protected from modernizing breezes in an effective yet not hostile way. The metro didn't reach that part of the city; its inhabitants took the trains, which to them seemed a completely different class of transport. A snobbish detail that Ruth, for example, had struggled to overcome. He smiled remembering how horrified her parents were when their only daughter abandoned the tranquil *barrio* of Sarrià, a few blocks away from where he was now, and went to live with an Argentine—the slur *sudaca* wasn't used then—first to Gràcia, and then, horror!, down there, near the sea. However much they had changed after the Olympics, the beaches of Barcelona and their surroundings were still fourth-rate destinations to them. "The humidity will kill you," had been their comment. And he knew for certain that his mother-in-law took a taxi every time she came to see her daughter and grandson alone.

Of course Ruth's capacity for scandalizing her family hadn't faded . . . Now separated, beginning a new life with another woman, she'd rented a loft not far from the flat she'd shared with Héctor, where she had room for her studio as well as living space. "This way you'll still be close to Guillermo," it had been her idea, shattering the stereotype of the vindictive ex-wife. Ruth had asked for what was fair, and he had conceded it without hesitation. In this, as in everything, they had been most civilized. I should have said that to the shrink, he thought with a smile. "Look, doctor, my wife left me for another bird . . . Yes, you heard right. How do I feel? Well look, it's a kick in the nuts. Like they might disintegrate from the blow. And you keep this so-stupid-you-can't-even-imagine face on, because for seventeen years you've been proud of how good it's been in bed for you both (proud of being almost her first and in theory only man—there's always some casual boyfriend from before with whom 'we hardly did anything, don't be stupid') and however much she insists that things changed little by little, and she swears that she discovered orgasms with you and that she has really enjoyed herself at your side, and she tells you, with disarming sincerity, that this is something 'new she needs to explore,' you look at her like a zombie, more bewildered than incredulous, because if she says it it must be true, and if it's true then part of your life, of both of your lives, but mostly of yours, has been a lie. Like on *The Truman Show*, remember, doctor? This guy who believes that he is living his life but in fact he is surrounded by actors who play their part and his reality is nothing more than a fiction invented and represented by others. Well, that's how you're left, doctor, with a Jim Carrey face." He laughed at himself with no bitterness as he waited to cross. Although lately he hadn't been doing it too much, inventing semi-ridiculous monologues about himself, or sometimes others, had always served as therapy for him.

He was walking slowly, advancing toward the center of this city that had been his home for so many years. It was a long way, but he felt like walking a little, putting off the arrival at his empty flat. Also, there was something about the streets of l'Eixample, that geometric grid of parallel and perpendicular roads, and those regal old façades that gave him peace and a certain feeling of nostalgia. He'd explored these streets, and many others, with Ruth; with her he'd seen as many monuments as bars. For him, Barcelona was Ruth: beautiful without harshness, superficially tranquil yet with dark corners, and with that touch of classy elegance that was as charming as it was exasperating. Both were aware of their natural charm, of having that indescribable something that many others wanted to achieve and could only admire or envy.

He arrived home wrecked after walking for almost two hours and flopped down onto the sofa. The recovered suitcase awaited him in a corner and he avoided looking at it. He should've eaten something en route, but the thought of dining alone in public depressed him. He smoked to kill his hunger through nicotine and felt guilty for it. He'd left the films Carmen had returned to him on the coffee table: a selection of classics starring her favorite actress. How long had it been since he'd watched *Rear Window*? It wasn't one of his favorites; he liked the worrying atmosphere of *The Birds* or the obsessive passion of *Vertigo* much better, but it was the one closest to hand and, without thinking about it, he put it in the DVD player. While it was starting up he went to the kitchen to find a beer, at least: he thought he'd seen something that morning in the fridge. With it in his hand he returned to the dining room and looked at the dark screen. The disk was playing, he could see on the little green screen of the machine, but there were no images. However, finally a light appeared on the screen: weak, crude, strange, shining in the middle of a blurred background. Astonished, he watched as the cloud dissipated and the light gained ground. And then, not able to take his eyes off the television, he

saw what he'd never wanted to see: himself, his face contorted
with rage, ceaselessly hitting an old man sitting in a chair. A
shiver ran down his spine. The phone ringing startled him so
much he dropped his beer. He picked up apprehensively, eyes
still fixed on that other him he hardly recognized, and heard a
woman's voice, hoarse with rage, screaming at him: "You're a
bastard, you fucking Argentine. Motherfucker."

FRIDAY

14

"I'm in Barça this weekend and want to see you. T." That was the message Leire had read as soon as she came out of the Castells' house. She'd answered the message positively, without hesitating, almost without thinking, carried away by the desire to see him. Something that now, after a long conversation with her best friend, she regretted with all her heart; something that, combined with the stifling summer weather and the terrible yowling of a cat in heat crossing the nearby roofs, wouldn't let her sleep.

María was a dark beauty, with a Barcelonian father and Italian mother, and she wreaked havoc in the male population. Five foot ten inches of perfect curves, she had a smiling face, a huge sense of humor and a trucker's mouth.

"Holy shit!" she burst out in the middle of a restaurant as soon as Leire explained her intention of telling Tomás, the T of the message, that their last encounter had left behind a gift in the shape of an embryo. "What, has pregnancy affected your brain or something? Must be the baby hormones that make people stupid."

"Don't be nasty." Leire finished off the tiramisu, which she'd devoured after a generous plate of spaghetti carbonara. "Are you going to finish the lemon mousse?"

"No! And you shouldn't either . . . You're like a piranha." But she pushed the dish toward her. "Listen, I'm serious. What do you gain by telling him?"

Leire held the spoon in mid-air before attacking the mousse. "It's not what I gain or don't gain. It's that he's the father. I think he has a right to know there's a child with his genes in the world."

"So, where is this child now? Who's carrying it in their womb for nine months? Who is going to give birth to it, screaming like a madwoman? He just dropped four swimmers and went off traveling, for fuck's sake! And if he hadn't been left with no plans for the weekend, you'd never have heard from him again."

Leire smiled.

"Say what you want, but he wrote me a message."

"One second, what do you mean by that? No, don't blush—answer me."

"Nothing." She put a spoonful of mousse in her mouth. It was delicious. "Leave it. Maybe you're right. When I see him, I'll decide."

"When I see him, I'll decide," repeated María in a mocking tone. "Eh, earth calling Leire Castro. Houston, we have a problem. Anyone know where Leire 'One-Date-Only' Castro is? Is this the person who always tells me love is a perverse invention of Hollywood's to subjugate the women of the world?"

"All right. Give me a break, please." Leire snorted. "It's the first time in my life I've been pregnant. Excuse me if I don't know how to behave."

María looked at her affectionately.

"Listen, one more thing and we'll change the subject. I have things to tell you as well." She stopped before asking, "Are you sure you want to have it?"

"Yes." She hesitated. "No. Well . . . I'm sure it's in there," pointing to her stomach, "and that it's going to be born in less than seven months." She finished the mousse and licked the spoon. "What about you? What's happening with Santi?"

"We're going on holiday!" exclaimed María, radiant.

"But wasn't he going to work for an NGO? To build a clinic in Africa?"

"Yes. And I'm going with him."

Leire could barely suppress a snort. The vision of María building anything, let alone a clinic in an African village, seemed even more ludicrous than her getting baby clothes ready.

"I'm only going for a few days."

"How many?"

"Twelve," she lied. "Well, maybe more, I don't know yet. But it will be nice: we'll be doing something together. Look, I'm sick of boys who only talk about football, their bosses, and how their last girlfriend hurt them; sick of metrosexuals who steal your moisturizer and sick of separated guys who want you to entertain the kids on the weekend. Santi is different."

"Yeah." Their taste in men was an inexhaustible source of disagreement, but a fundamental part of their friendship. They had never liked the same type of man. To Leire, Santi was a boring pedant who needed a good stick of deodorant. And María, she was sure, would have thought Tomás was cocky, thinking he was George Clooney by wearing a suit with a white shirt and having perfect teeth. She raised her glass of water and said out loud: "A toast to sexual tourist solidarity!"

María imitated her with her glass of red wine.

"To sexual tourist solidarity! And to the little swimmers that make their mark!"

"Bitch!"

The sheet was wrinkled from so much tossing and turning. Leire closed her eyes and tried to relax in the darkness. A warm darkness, because there wasn't the slightest breeze: the open window just inundated the room with the wailings of the cat. She'd only been in that apartment for a few months and during the first few weeks she'd been startled awake by those squeals, which sounded like a baby crying; she'd ventured out onto the tiny terrace in search of the source of the pitiful sob, not able to ascertain where it came from until one night she met the eyes of that insomniac cat, as immobile as a statue, watching her impassively to the beat of the feline yowl. Now she was used to it, although deep down that animal scream still bothered her, that pure instinct demanding sex without the least decency. At this moment, however, she thought closing the window would only muffle the wails and on the other hand increase the heat.

She lit a cigarette, although she'd already consumed her usual five that day, and went out onto the diminutive terrace, barely a meter square, with two window boxes hanging from the railing and a little round wooden table. She looked around for the cat and there she was, suddenly quiet now, watching her like a small buddha with whiskers. The first drags calmed her a little—a false peace, she knew, but peace all the same. As if wishing to remind her of her existence, the animal wailed again from the opposite roof and Leire looked at her with more affection than before. She finished her cigarette and threw it to the ground, reproaching herself but lacking the will to go searching for the ashtray. The cat watched her and cocked her head, with a gesture of frank disapproval. "Hungry?" Leire asked her in a low voice, and for the first time since she'd lived there the idea of putting a little milk in a bowl occurred to her. She did so and returned inside, sure the animal wouldn't approach if she saw her outside. She waited by the door for a few minutes, with the light on inside, hoping the cat might overcome her fear and jump onto the terrace, but she didn't make the slightest move. Suddenly Leire felt exhausted and decided to go back to bed: it was twenty past four in the morning, and with a bit of luck she might still sleep for at least two and a half hours. Once in bed, she stretched out her hand and picked up her mobile. Two new messages from Tomás. "Arriving tomorrow, Sants station, express, 17.00. Dying to see you. T." "Oh, I've something to propose to you. Kisses."

She rested her head against the already cool pillow and closed her eyes, determined to sleep. In that sweet moment before losing consciousness she thought of Tomás's smile, her pregnancy test, solidarity for sexual tourists and the bowl of milk on the terrace, until abruptly a discordant detail, a note out of place, kept her from falling asleep. Suddenly alert, she sat up in bed and tried to remember. Yes, she was sure. She visualized the attic from which young Marc Castells fell, the window, the sill, the body on the ground. And she knew something didn't fit, that the sequence of events couldn't have been as it was reconstructed. Something jarred in that scene, something as simple as an ashtray in the wrong place.

15

Breakfast was one of Ruth's favorite times. She had it in the kitchen, sitting on a high stool, and gave it the necessary time. She liked the ritual of preparing the toast and orange juice for herself, the combination of the aroma of coffee and that of warm bread. It was a pleasure she'd never managed to share with either of her partners: Héctor could barely touch a piece of toast in the morning, and it seemed the same was happening with Carol. What's more, given that they usually looked surprised or incredulous at the attention she paid to every detail, she enjoyed it much more when she was alone.

Sometimes she wondered if this solitary morning pleasure was a sign of what awaited her in the future; ever more frequently she saw herself as a person inclined to independence—strange for someone who had actually never been without company. Her parents, her husband, her son and now Carol . . . She frowned, thinking she hadn't succeeded in giving her a title other than her own: "lover" sounded vulgar, "girlfriend" was

THE SUMMER OF DEAD TOYS

something she hadn't yet managed to say, "companion" seemed false, a prudish euphemism to disguise the truth. While she smeared butter on the toast with exquisite care, and spread a thin layer of homemade apricot jam over it, she asked herself what Carol really was. It was the same question put to her by that same person the night before, after the argument with Héctor, and Ruth hadn't been able to give a satisfactory answer, so the dinner for two had gone uneaten and Carol, her lover, her girlfriend, her companion or whatever she was, had left for her flat enveloped in a sullen silence without Ruth making the least attempt to stop her. She knew one word would have been enough, a simple squeeze of her hand to dispel her fit of impatience or jealousy, but she simply lacked the will to do so. And although they'd then spoken on the phone for almost an hour—fifty-three long minutes to be exact—and though Carol had a change of heart and apologized for her brusque departure and reiterated her understanding and unconditional love, the feeling of fatigue hadn't diminished in the slightest. On the contrary, the whole scene had awoken a mad longing in her to escape, to go away for a weekend, this weekend, no hanging around, to somewhere she could be calm: no pressure, no apologies, no promises of love.

What a damn night, Ruth said to herself. She'd arrived home in a good mood, ready to enjoy a lovely evening with Carol, and found her hysterical, shouting down the phone, insulting Héctor like a lunatic. Her expression demanded explanations and she'd finally managed to get her to hang up the phone and tell her how this surreal scene had come about. Carol only said: "Look at it yourself. This was inside the box your bastard of an ex gave you yesterday." And after those words, she pressed a button on the remote. The screen had filled with images of her and Carol taken some days back: both of them on a nudist beach in Sant Pol, naked as night fell. Ruth remembered the day well, but seeing it in that way, seeing their kisses turned into a cheap and crude recording, generated a profound feeling of disgust in her. Their bodies caressing each other on that solitary beach aroused a sudden feeling of shame in her. From there, everything went from bad to worse. She'd tried to reason with Carol, tell her that Héctor was in Argentina when those images were recorded; and that, even if he had been here, he'd never have committed so . . . obscene an act. Carol had finally given up, although she kept arguing that there were private detectives to whom these things were entrusted, asking how that fucking DVD had arrived in that box of cakes that Héctor had given her, asking why she defended her ex-husband more than her, finally putting the key question to her: What the hell am I in your life? Questions with no answers, which had plunged Ruth into an exhausting vertigo. She just wanted to throw that film in the bin and forget all about it. But before she did so she thought she should call Héctor to speak to him, a short conversation to calm him, which of course Carol didn't understand at all. When she hung up, she'd already gone, and all of a sudden Ruth felt relieved to be completely alone.

She kept going over the same idea, although she was fully aware that Carol wouldn't be happy, and not without reason: they'd planned things to do that weekend, taking advantage of the fact that Guillermo wasn't coming back until Sunday night. According to Carol, they needed to spend more time together. Waking up, eating, having dinner and sleeping together like a real couple. Ruth had been left staring at her, not knowing how to explain herself: she couldn't tell her that that string of common actions, stated in a tone more imperious than af-

fectionate, sounded more like a sentence than anything else. I
should have more patience with Carol, she told herself, while
she attacked the second piece of toast. She was young, fierce
and tended to be demanding when she wanted to show affection. That attitude, the extreme frankness that had managed
to break down Ruth's defenses when they'd met the year before, turned out to be exhausting day to day. Carol had the
blackest eyes Ruth had ever seen, and a perfect body, strong
yet still feminine, sculpted through hours of Pilates and strict
dieting. She was without question a beautiful woman: not just
good-looking but gorgeous. And on the other hand, her insecurity, her fear of the possibility that Ruth might renege on this
new sexuality discovered at the age of thirty-seven, gave her
a fragile air which, combined with her extreme characteris-
tics, was irresistible. Nothing was calm with Carol, reflected
Ruth: she exploded and regretted; she went from cool jealousy
to unbridled passion; she roared with laughter or sobbed like a
little girl at any tearjerker. A delight, but a delight that could
be overwhelming.

By her second coffee, she'd made a decision. She would call her
parents, and if they weren't going, she would spend the weekend at the apartment in Sitges. She didn't usually go in summer
because the crowds drove her crazy, but she needed a close, familiar refuge and this was better than nothing. All of a sudden
the prospect of spending three days alone, doing whatever she
felt like, sounded marvelous and in spite of it being early she
rang her mother to find out if the apartment was free, crossing
her fingers in the hope that the answer would be yes. It was,
so without wasting a moment she sent Carol a message describ-
ing her plan—a short, succinct text that wouldn't prompt a
reply. However, she hesitated a moment before doing the same

to Héctor: she didn't have to inform him of her comings and goings, but the night before she'd noticed he was worried. His tone of voice was anxious and Héctor, for all his faults, wasn't a man easily perturbed. She fiddled with her mobile until she finally decided to speak to him.

"Hello?" he answered, almost before the phone rang. "Everything all right?"

"Yes, yes," she rushed to reassure him. "Listen, you had me worried last night. You have to tell me what's going on."

He took a deep breath.

"The truth is I have no idea." Héctor told her more calmly what he'd said to her the previous night: that veiled threat that seemed to be hovering over him, and perhaps over his family. "I don't think anything will happen, maybe they just want to make me nervous, create problems, but just in case . . . stay alert, OK? If you see anything strange or suspicious, tell me straight away."

"Of course. In fact I was ringing to tell you I'm going to Sitges this weekend. To my parents' place. I'll come back via Calafell and pick Guillermo up on Sunday night."

"Are you going alone?" He asked more for reasons of safety than anything else, but he immediately regretted it and Ruth's tone confirmed it had been an ill-timed intrusion.

"That's none of your business."

"Sorry. I don't . . . didn't want to interfere in your life."

"Yeah." Ruth bit her tongue so as not to be unpleasant. "Well, it sounded like it. Good-bye, Héctor, speak to you Monday."

"Yes, enjoy yourself. And Ruth . . ." He realized he didn't know how to say it. "Like I said, if you see anything strange, call me immediately, OK?"

"Bye, Héctor." Ruth hung up straight away, and saw that she had two missed calls from Carol. The last thing she felt like doing was arguing, so she opted to ignore them and began to prepare the couple of things she wanted to take with her.

Héctor didn't waste any time either. He had slept very little and very badly as usual, but that morning the lack of sleep translated into hyperactivity. Apart from what he had said to Ruth, he was worried. Above all because, although he sensed the threat, he didn't know from where it would come or what was really going on. Something told him it wasn't just he who was at risk from this vague danger; the revenge, if that's what it was, would extend to those around him. When he had finally managed to reach his son the night before, he'd let out a sigh of relief. Guillermo was loving it at his friend's house and for a moment Héctor was tempted to tell him to stay a few more days if possible, but he didn't: he wanted to see him too badly. Between the event before his departure for Buenos Aires and the trip itself, it had been a month since the last time. And he missed him, more than he would ever have believed. In a way, his relationship with his son was stretching as he grew. Héctor couldn't pretend to have been a model father: excessive working hours on one hand, and the inability to get excited by childish games on the other had made him an affectionate but vaguely absent father. However, recently he'd been surprised by the maturity with which Guillermo accepted the changes in his life. He was a rather introverted, yet not unsociable boy, who'd inherited his mother's talent for drawing and his father's ironic air, which made him seem older. Héctor had found himself thinking not only did he love his son, no doubt about that, but he also got on well with the boy and a relationship had begun to be established between them that was, if not one of friendship—which seemed absurd to him—then one that certainly had undertones of camaraderie. The separation and

having to spend some full weekends alone together had contributed to improving the relationship between father and son
instead of hindering it.

But the night before, Héctor hadn't only checked that his
family was safe and sound. He'd worked on the case of the Nigerian girls. He'd made an appointment to meet Álvaro Santacruz, doctor of theology specializing in African religions who
gave classes in the Faculty of History. His name had emerged
as an expert in the subject during his previous inquiries but
he hadn't managed to speak to him. Now he felt the pressing
need to obtain the help of someone who could shed a little light
on the matter, someone who might be able to give a degree of
clarity to his suspicions. Dr. Santacruz was expecting him and
Martina Andreu at half past ten in his office at the History
Faculty, and he headed there. He'd met Andreu a little beforehand so he could be brought up to date with the news, if there
was any.

There were still more questions than anything else. Sergeant Andreu, whose dark-circled eyes suggested she hadn't
slept well that night either, informed him of what they knew
while they had breakfast in a café close to the faculty.

"There's definitely something weird about this Dr. Omar,"
said Andreu. "Or at least, what little there is is quite strange.
Let's see, our dear Dr. Omar arrived in Spain eight years ago
and settled in Barcelona five years ago. Before that he was in
the south, although it's not very clear what he was doing. We
do know he arrived here with enough cash to buy that flat and
start up his thing. And he either kept his money in a drawer at
home or the businesses he was involved in didn't pay much. His
banking movements are few and he didn't live in luxury, as
you've seen. There's always the possibility he sent the money
abroad, but at the moment we have nothing. To all appear-

ances, Dr. Omar, whose real name is Ibraim Okoronkwo by the way, lived modestly from his appointments. If it wasn't for what that girl said—and she could have been confused—we've got nothing that connects him to the trafficking ring, or to any other crime apart from selling holy water to cure gastritis and banish evil spirits."

Héctor nodded.

"And what about his disappearance?"

"Nothing. The last person to see him was that lawyer of his, Damián Fernández. The blood on the wall and the floor points to a kidnapping, or worse. And the damn pig's head seems to be a message, but directed at whom? Us? Omar?"

Héctor got up to pay and Andreu joined him at the bar. They crossed the street and together they looked for Dr. Santacruz's office.

The history department was an ugly, unwelcoming building, and the wide corridors, half-empty in the middle of July, didn't help either. Doctors of theology were somewhat intimidating for a confirmed atheist like Héctor, but Dr. Santacruz was a man with little resemblance to a mystic, closer to sixty than fifty, and his knowledge was based on a broad foundation of research. His books on culture and African religions were classics studied in anthropology departments all over Europe. Despite his age, Santacruz seemed to keep himself in good shape, which contributed to his six-foot-two figure, with shoulders like a Basque *jai-alai* player. He was the least likely looking theologian Héctor could imagine, and that made him feel more comfortable.

Santacruz listened to what they put to him attentively and with absolute seriousness. Héctor went over the operation against the traffickers and Kira's death, and went on to tell him the latest events, although he withheld the beating he'd doled out to Omar, as he did those mysterious DVDs that had appeared the night before and of which even Andreu didn't know a thing. He spoke of the disappearance, the pig's head and the file with his name. When he'd finished, the theologian remained quiet for a moment, pensive, as if something he'd heard didn't quite convince him. He shook his head slightly before speaking.

"I'm sorry." Uncomfortable, he shifted in his chair. "Everything you've told me surprises me greatly. And worries me, to be honest."

"Something in particular?" asked Andreu.

"Yes. Various things. Well, the part with the prostitutes is nothing new. Voodoo in its worst sense has been used as a tool of control. These rituals you've heard of are absolutely real and, for those who believe in them, greatly effective. These girls are convinced that their lives and those of their families are at risk and, in fact, in a way they are. I could describe various cases I witnessed during my studies in Africa and in certain parts of the South Caribbean. The condemned spends days plunged into the most profound terror, and it is this terror that causes death."

"Well?" asked Héctor, somewhat impatient.

"Absolute terror is a difficult emotion to explain, Inspector. It doesn't obey logic, nor can it be cured with reasoning. It's more a case, as certainly happened in this instance, of the victim choosing an expedient way to die, to relieve panic and in doing so save her family. Don't doubt that the poor girl sacrificed herself, to put it like that, convinced that it was the only way out. And, although it may seem absurd to you, for her it was."

"That I understand. At least, I think I understand it," replied Héctor, "but what is it that surprises you?"

"Everything that has happened since. This individual's dis-appearance, the grotesque episode of the pig's head, your pho-tos in a file . . . This has nothing to do with voodoo in its purest form. It seems rather like a set. A *mise en scène* dedicated to someone." He paused and looked closely at both of them. "I'm guessing there's something you don't want to tell me, but if you want me to help you, you must answer a question. Does this man have a score to settle with either of you?"

There was a moment of hesitation before Salgado answered.

"Maybe. No," he corrected himself, "he has."

Dr. Santacruz could have smiled out of pure satisfaction, but his expression changed to express clear, frank worry.

"That's what I was afraid of. Look, you have to understand something. However powerful his magic—as they sometimes call it—is, it remains totally innocuous to those who don't believe in it. Am I mistaken in thinking that you are rather skeptical, Inspector? Not only toward this subject, but toward anything related to the occult? No, I thought not. But you fear for your family, for the safety of your loved ones . . ."

"Might they be in danger?"

"I daren't say so, and I don't wish to alarm you. It's just . . . how would I put it? They want you to feel afraid, unsettle you. Remove you from your rational, Western thinking and draw you toward theirs: more atavistic, subject to supernatural ele-ments. And therefore they are using paraphernalia that any-one could understand." He turned to Andreu. "Your colleague told me you searched this Omar's clinic. Did you find anything that backs up what I'm saying?"

Martina looked down, obviously uneasy.

"He already said it. Some photos of Héctor and his family."

"Nothing else?"

"Yes. Sorry, Héctor, I didn't tell you because it seemed ri-diculous: something had been burned in a corner of the room.

And the ashes were placed in an envelope, along with one of those grotesque dolls made of rope. All of it was inside the file with your photos, the ones of Ruth and Guillermo. I took it out before you arrived."

Dr. Santacruz intervened before Héctor could say anything.

"I thought it strange you hadn't found it, simply because it's the most well-known ritual of voodoo: something we've all heard of." He looked at Salgado and said frankly, "They want to scare you, Inspector. If there is no fear, their power is nil. But I'll tell you something else: from what I can see they seem determined to awaken that fear in you, scaring you with things you do fear. Your family's safety, the sanctity of your home. Even that of your close friends. If you play their game, if you start to believe that their threats can become real danger, then you are in their hands. Like that girl."

16

As soon as they got to the station Héctor noticed that Leire had something to tell him, but before he had a chance to go over to her, Savall called him into his office. By his face, the meeting behind closed doors didn't bode well, and Héctor mustered all his patience to get through the sermon, which he guessed related to Dr. Omar. However, he realized it wasn't going in that direction on seeing that there was another person sitting in front of the super's desk: a fair-haired woman, about fifty, who turned toward him and gazed at him intently. Héctor wasn't surprised when Savall introduced them: he was sure she had to be Joana Vidal. She greeted him with a slight movement of her head and remained seated. Tense.

"Héctor, I've been informing Señora Vidal of your inquiries." Savall's tone was smooth, conciliatory, with a hint of warning. "But I think it's better for you to tell her yourself."

Héctor took a few seconds before speaking. He knew what the superintendent was asking of him: a neutral, friendly tale, and at the same time persuasive, which might convince this woman that her son had fallen from the window. The same argument a teacher would use with a pupil who has failed by one point: you can walk with your head held high, it is a worthy failure, come back in September and I'm sure you'll pass. In Joana Vidal's case, better to go and not come back. But at the same time, something told him that this woman, legs still crossed and clutching the arms of the chair tightly, was keeping an ace up her sleeve. A bomb she'd drop at the opportune moment, which would catch them all unawares, not knowing what to say.

"Of course," he said at last, and fell silent again to weigh his words. "But first perhaps Señora Vidal has something to tell us as well."

The woman's quick glance told him he'd hit the nail on the head. Savall raised his eyebrows.

"Is that so, Joana?" he asked.

"I'm not sure. Perhaps. But first I want to hear what Inspector Salgado has to tell me."

"Fine." Now yes, thought Héctor, noting that the woman sitting beside him was relaxing a little. He moved his chair to see her face and spoke to her directly, as if the super wasn't in the room. "From what we know, the night of the festival of San Juan your son and two of his friends, Aleix Rovira and Gina Martí, had a little party in Marc's attic. The kids' stories generally match: the party seemed to develop normally, until for some reason Marc's mood changed, he turned off the music and argued with Aleix when he accused him of coming back very much changed from Dublin. Aleix went home, but Gina, who was rather drunk, stayed over in Marc's room. His anger had affected her as well, and as soon as Aleix left he sent her to bed, telling her she was drunk, which annoyed the girl. Then she lay down and fell asleep immediately. For his part, Marc stayed alone in the attic and did as he usually did: smoked a last cigarette sitting on the window sill."

He stopped there, although this woman's face showed only concentration. Not sorrow or pain. There was something Nordic about Joana Vidal's features, an apparent coldness that might or might not be a mask. It was, thought Héctor; but it was a mask that had been in place for a long time and was beginning to merge with the original features. Only her eyes, an even dark chestnut color, seemed to contradict it; they hid a sparkle that, in the right circumstances, could be dangerous. Unable to help it, he mentally compared Joana to Enric Castells' second wife and told himself there was a superficial likeness, a pallor common to both women; however, the similarities ended there. In Glòria's eyes there was doubt, insecurity, even obedience; Joana's hinted at rebellion and challenge. There was no doubt that Castells hadn't wanted to run the same risk twice and had chosen a softer, more docile woman. More manageable. Héctor Salgado told himself that the woman in front of him deserved to know the truth and went on in the same tone, ignoring the expression of impatience coming over the super's face.

"But the kids are lying, at least partly. I'm not saying they had anything to do with what happened," he clarified. "Only that there's a part of the story they've smoothed over, if I might put it that way." He went on to refer to what Castro had discovered on seeing the photos on Gina's Facebook page, as well as the finding of the T-shirt Marc was wearing during the party: clean but with some stains that might well be blood. "So the next step is to question Aleix Rovira closely"—he said this without looking at Savall—"because the alleged fight they've told us about may have been somewhat more violent than the story suggests. And speak to Aleix's brother to confirm once again that the boy arrived home and didn't go back out. Honestly, I think that is the most likely thing. Perhaps that's all that happened, a fight between friends, nothing too serious but enough for Marc to stain his T-shirt and change his clothes. A fight that maybe caused Marc's laptop to fall to the floor and break . . ."

He remained thoughtful. Why hadn't Gina said anything about the broken laptop? Even if it was a matter of a simple argument, as she said, it was less suspicious to tell them something they would find out anyway. He forced himself to slow down: his thoughts were moving too quickly and he should continue. "It doesn't change what happened afterward," he said, but his voice didn't sound too convincing. "Only that we need some pieces to complete the picture. For the moment we've taken Marc's laptop and mobile to see what we can extract from them. And we should question Aleix Rovira again." Then he did look at the super. He was pleased to see he was nodding, although with a bad grace. "And now, is there something you wish to tell us, Señora Vidal?"

Joana uncrossed her legs and searched in her bag until she pulled out some folded pages. She kept them in her hand as she spoke, as if she didn't want to part with them.

"A few months ago, Marc got in contact with me by email." It was difficult for her to say it. She cleared her throat and threw her head back: she had a long, white neck. "As you must already know, we hadn't seen each other since I left, eighteen years ago. So it was a complete surprise when I received his first message."

"How did he get your address?" asked the super.

"Fèlix, Enric's brother, gave it to him. It may seem strange to you, but we've kept in touch all this time. With my ex-brother-in-law, I mean. Do you know him?" she asked, turning to Héctor.

"Yes, I saw him yesterday at your ex's house. He seemed to love his nephew very much."

She nodded.

"Well, Enric is a busy man." She shook her head. "No, I have no right to criticize him. I'm sure he did everything he could . . . but Fèlix has no family other than that of his brother and he's always worried a lot about Marc. Either way, the fact is I received an email at the beginning of the year. From . . . my son." It was the first time she'd said it and it hadn't been easy for her. "I was very surprised. Of course something like that could have happened at any time, but the truth is I wasn't expecting it. You never expect it."

Silence fell, which Savall and Héctor dared not break. She did.

"At the beginning I didn't know how to answer him, but he persisted. He sent me two or three more emails and I couldn't refuse any longer, so we started to write to each other. I know it sounds strange, I can't deny it. A mother and her son, who have practically never seen each other, communicating by email." She flashed a bitter smile at them, as if she were challenging them to make the smallest comment. Neither of them opened their mouth. She continued: "I was afraid of the questions, reproaches even, but there were none. Marc just told me things about his life in Dublin, his plans. It was as if we'd just met, as if I wasn't his mother. The correspondence continued for about three months, until . . ." She was quiet for a few moments and looked away. "Until he suggested coming to see me in Paris."

She lowered her eyes to the pages she had in her hand.

"The idea terrified me," she said simply. "I don't know why. I said I had to think about it."

"And he got angry?" asked Héctor.

She shrugged her shoulders.

"I suppose it was a rude awakening. From then on his emails became less and less frequent until he almost stopped writing. But toward the end of his stay in Ireland he sent me this email."

She unfolded the pages, chose one and gave it to Savall. He read it and then passed the sheet to Héctor. The text read:

> Hello, I know it's been a long time since I gave any signs of life, and I won't insist on us seeing each other, at least for the moment. In fact, I have to return to Barcelona to sort out some unfinished business. I don't even know how to do it, but I know I have to try. When all this is over, I'd like us to meet. In Paris or Barcelona, wherever you like.
>
> A kiss,
>
>   Marc

Héctor lifted his eyes from the page and Joana answered his question before he had even formed it.

"No, I have no idea to what business he's referring. At the time, I thought it must be something to do with studying, focusing on a degree or something like that. The truth is, I didn't place that much importance on it until yesterday afternoon. I started reading all the emails, one after the other, like it was a real conversation. This is the last one I received from him." Héctor and Superintendent Savall exchanged glances. There was little to say. That message could refer to anything, and nothing.

"I know this may seem a little far-fetched, but I don't know . . . maybe it's something else, maybe it has something to do with his death." Her hands moved restlessly, more out of impatience than sorrow, and she stood up. "Well, I suppose it's just foolishness on my part."

"Joana." Savall stood up as well and walked around the table to her. "Nothing is foolish in an investigation. I told you we'd get to the bottom of this and so we will. But you must understand, accept, that perhaps the obvious explanation is what really happened. Accidents are difficult to come to terms with, and yet they happen."

Joana nodded, although Héctor had the feeling that wasn't what was worrying her. Or at least not only that. She must have been a very pretty woman, and she still was in a way, he thought. Elegant and stylish, although her face showed a glimpse of the passing of the years which she did nothing to disguise. No makeup, or operations. Joana Vidal accepted maturity in a natural way and the result was a dignity lacking in other faces of her age. He watched her, taking advantage of the fact that she seemed absorbed in what the super was saying to her.

"We'll keep you informed. Personally. Inspector Salgado or myself, I promise you. Try to relax."

Savall offered to see her to the door, but she refused, with the same impatient gesture that Héctor had noticed a few minutes before. She couldn't be an easy woman, of that he was sure, and as he watched her walk away the image of Meryl Streep came to mind. The figure of Leire Castro, who'd approached as soon as Joana Vidal emerged, brought him back to reality.

"Do you have a moment, Inspector?"

"Yes, but if I'm honest I need a cigarette. Do you smoke?" he asked her for the first time.

"More than I should and less than I feel like."

He smiled.

"Well, now you will on your superior's order."

Without knowing why, Leire continued the game.

"I've been asked to do worse."

He raised his hands in a gesture of mock innocence.

"I don't believe you . . . Let's go and contaminate the air in the street and you can tell me about it."

They managed to find a corner in the shade, although shade in Barcelona is a false refuge. The midday sun was beating down on the city and the humidity increased the temperature to African levels.

"That was Marc's mother, wasn't it?" she asked.

"Yes." He took a long drag and blew the smoke out, slowly. "Tell me, was there anything on the laptop or mobile?"

She nodded.

"We're investigating the numbers, although the majority of calls and texts in the days before his death are to Gina Martí and Aleix Rovira. And some Iris, although in her case they are basically WhatsApps." He showed his discomfort, and she explained what she was talking about. "It's free, and by the prefix we know this girl was in Ireland. In Dublin, I suppose. They spoke very little English—the girl must be Spanish—and from what I've read, Marc was crazy about her. I've transcribed all the messages to see if there's anything, but at first glance they seem normal: I miss you, wish you were here. I think they were planning to see each other because there's some reference to 'soon this will all be over.'" She smiled. "All with very un-romantic abbreviations, to tell the truth. With regard to the laptop, they're trying to repair it but they told me it's pretty wrecked. As if it was broken on purpose."

"Yeah." The laptop worried him. He was going to voice his doubts out loud, but Leire didn't let him.

"There's something else I realized last night at home." Her

eyes shone, and Héctor noticed for the first time that they were dark green, at least in the sun. "There's no way to sleep in this heat, so I went out onto the terrace to smoke a cigarette. I forgot the ashtray and ended up stubbing it out on the terrace, thinking I'd pick it up later. I know, it's not very hygienic. Then, when I was in bed it occurred to me. What would you do if you were going to smoke a cigarette sitting at the window?"

He thought for a second.

"Well, I'd either flick the ash into the air or I'd bring an ashtray and have it nearby: beside me or even in my hand."

"Exactly. And from what the cleaner told me, Glòria Vergès is obsessive about cleaning. She can't stand smoke, or cigarette butts. I suppose that's why the boy smoked at the window." She paused briefly before continuing. "The butt wasn't on the ground, at least not below the window, when we processed the scene. Yes, he could have thrown it farther, but I can't imagine Marc dirtying the garden in any way. The most logical thing was that he brought the ashtray to the window to save him the bother. But it wasn't there. It was inside, I remember perfectly, on the shelf beside the window. I think it even appears in some of the photos we took."

Héctor's brain was working at full speed, despite the heat.

"It means Marc put out his cigarette and came back in."

"I thought that. I've been mulling it over and it's nothing definitive. He could easily have smoked, come in and then returned to the window. But according to what we've been told, it wasn't something he usually did. I mean the idea we've been sold is that Marc used to sit at the window to smoke. That's it. Not to think, not to kill time."

"There's another possibility," he rebutted. "Someone might have brought in the ashtray from the window."

"Yes, I thought of that as well. But the cleaner had to take care of Gina Martí, who had a nervous fit when she woke up; she didn't go up to the attic before we got there. Señor Castells arrived with his brother, the priest, at the same time as us; his wife and daughter came down afterward; Glòria Vergès didn't want her daughter to see the body, which is logical, so she stayed in the Collbató chalet until the afternoon."

"Are you sure Gina didn't go back into the attic in the morning?"

"According to her statement, she didn't. The cleaner's screams woke her and she ran downstairs to the door. Seeing Marc dead brought on a nervous fit and the woman had to make her an herbal tea, which she didn't drink. Then we arrived. And I can't see her taking the ashtray from the window and putting it in its place."

"Let's see." Héctor half-closed his eyes. "Let's imagine the scene: Marc has been hanging out with his friends and the night ends badly. They've fought. Badly enough that his T-shirt is bloodstained. Aleix leaves and he sends Gina to bed. It's almost three a.m. and it's hot. He changes his dirty T-shirt and before going to bed he does what he always does: smokes a cigarette sitting at the window. We'll assume that he brought the ashtray—I'm sure he did it out of habit. So he smokes peacefully, stubs out the cigarette, and goes back into the attic: he leaves the ashtray . . ."

"See?" insisted Castro. "It doesn't fit with the idea that he was drunk and fell accidentally. And also, if he was dizzy, he would have noticed and in that case, why go out?"

Héctor thought of the fear he'd read in Joana Vidal's eyes just a moment before, of Enric Castells' words, denying with excessive vehemence that his son might have thrown himself into the void voluntarily. Could it have been a suicide? A desperate outburst, because of something that had happened that night perhaps? Or had someone come in, argued with him and ended up pushing him out of the window? It had to be a relatively strong person, which discounted Gina. Aleix? Had they fought, and the broken computer was the result? Leire seemed to follow his reasoning, as her eyes were sparkling.

"I did something else," she said. "This morning I called the Faculty of Computer Science, where Aleix Rovira studies. It wasn't easy, but in the end they told me: he hasn't passed a single subject; in fact he's practically not attended classes since Easter."

"Wasn't he some kind of child prodigy?"

"Well, it seems he lost his superpowers when he went to university."

"Check his calls. I want to know everything about Rovira: who he calls, where he goes, what he usually says, what he does in his spare time, which must be plentiful if he's not attending class. I get the impression these two brats are playing with us. I'll call him into the station on Monday so he'll have to sweat a little. Any problem?"

Leire shook her head, although her expression wasn't nearly as certain. In fact, that evening she had to collect Tomás from Sants station, and in theory she was off this weekend. She was going to say so out loud when she thought having something to do might not be a bad idea.

"No problem, Inspector."

"Great. Another thing: Marc wrote to his mother saying he had something he had to sort out here. I don't think it's important but—"

"But in this case we're going along blindly, don't you think?"

"Completely blind." He remembered what Savall had said to him and added, unable to avoid a slightly ironic tone, "And don't forget all this is 'unofficial.' I'll talk to the superinten-

dent. I want to get all possible information on Aleix Rovira
together before Monday. Take care of it; I'll look after interrogating Óscar Vaquero."

She seemed taken aback.

"The fatty they played the trick on. Yes, I know it was a couple of years ago, but sometimes grudges don't disappear with
time, more like the opposite." A cynical smile spread over his
face. "I assure you."

17

The air conditioning in that sorry room made an infernal noise. With the curtains—stiff pieces of a moss-green fabric—pulled to block out the blazing sun falling on the city at that hour, the drone of the machine resembled the labored roar of a beast from the underworld. It could have been a roadside motel, one of those establishments that, despite their sordidness, radiate romance or at least sensuality. Rooms that smell of sweaty sheets and intertwined bodies, of furtive but inevitable sex, of desires never fully satiated, of quick showers and cheap cologne. In reality, it wasn't a motel but a pensión near Plaça Universitat, discreet and even clean if you looked at it with a favorable eye—or, better still, didn't look at it too much at all—specializing in renting rooms by the hour. Given the proximity to the Gayxample, the gay area par excellence of Barcelona, the majority of the clientele were homosexual, something that in a way was reassuring to Regina. In the seven months of this year so far she'd come more or less regularly to this pensión without ever bumping into anyone she knew. The worst was going in and coming out, but up to now she'd been lucky. Certainly because deep down she couldn't care less. Not that she and Salvador had an explicitly open relationship, but it had to be more or less obvious to her husband that if he wasn't making love to her, someone else would have to take his place in bed at least once in a while.

If she was honest with herself, Regina had to admit that when she married Salvador, sixteen years her senior, it wasn't because the man was an animal in the sexual realm, although in the early years she'd had no cause for complaint in that respect. No, Regina wasn't an especially passionate woman, but she was proud. She'd been married for twenty-one years and for the first half of that time she had been tremendously happy. Salvador adored her, with a devotion that seemed unswerving, eternal. And she blossomed in his flattery, in those glances that caressed her like a tight mesh enhancing her curves, but not too tight. The only thing she didn't allow for when she married this gentleman, unconventionally attractive, tall and already gray in the wedding photo, was that this well-known intellectual's tastes wouldn't change over time. If at forty-five Salvador noticed twentysomething girls, at sixty-five his interests were still centered on the same young bodies, the same insultingly smooth faces. The kind that need only soap and water to shine. And those young girls, even sillier than Regina had been years ago, found him distinguished, charming, intelligent. Even romantic. They excitedly read his love stories—urban fairytales with titles like *The Sweet Taste of First Dates* or *Overlooking Sadness*, which he started to write when his profound books with experimental aspirations bored even the most pretentious critics—and attended his lectures in which words like desire, skin, taste and melancholy were repeated ad nauseam.

It was a hard blow to Regina, realizing that his constant admiration was fading little by little. Or rather it was subtly shifting in other directions. At thirty-eight Regina was no longer the coveted white ball of the billiards game, the center of her husband's attentions; and by forty-five she'd definitely become the black ball, the one whose turn comes only at the end of the game when there's no other option. Now, turning fifty, after various facial touch-ups that hadn't received more than a glimmer of recognition from Salvador, she'd decided to change her game. One day logic had prevailed over self-esteem: she had realized that she was fighting against an enemy as brutal as it was implacable, one she could hold back but not defeat. It had been her New Year's resolution of the previous year: raise her self-esteem whatever the cost. And looking around her, she discovered that the glances her husband no longer gave her could come, surprisingly, from unexpected corners. In one sense, she thought, infidelity restored order and balanced her marriage. And although at the beginning she wasn't really seeking sex, more to heal a battered ego which didn't respond to anti-wrinkle treatments or the incisions of a scalpel, the avalanche of feelings she experienced from those strong muscular arms, hard smooth buttocks like blunt rocks, clumsy kisses and that restless tongue, which reached the most remote corners of her sex, was a real surprise. This new-generation lover was capable of fucking her to exhaustion and never losing his smile, of biting her neck like a playful puppy, even of slapping her when the pleasure was so intense his eyes closed without wanting them to. Like her, like everyone, he wanted to be seen and admired, but involuntarily unlike others, the big opinion he had of himself stayed in the street; in bed he was generous and tireless, demanding and affectionate. Some days a real bastard; some days a scared kid who asks for hugs. She wouldn't have known how to say which she preferred; she did know that week by week she'd become hooked on those games behind closed doors, and the idea of going a month without seeing him, exiled on the Costa Brava with a sexagenarian husband she found repulsive now— the image of Salvador in trunks had become a nightmare she couldn't escape—and a daughter in a full-on emotional storm was frankly disagreeable. Thank God, she wasn't "in love" with someone who could be her son; in fact for a while now she had doubted the existence of this love with a capital "L" of which her husband never tired of writing, to the delight of women who wanted to live in such books. It was, simply, the inescapable lure of weeks that without him would have had no core. Although at times, alone in her room, she enjoyed remembering these encounters so much, nevertheless she thought she could go without them . . . That day would come, she was sure, but in the meantime she would hoard explicit gruesome details in her memory to which her body responded without hesitation.

"What are you thinking?" Aleix whispered in her ear.

"I thought you were asleep," she said and kissed him on the forehead. She shifted a little so he could put his arm around her. Their hands intertwined. The force radiating from those strong fingers gave her life.

"Only a little. But it's your fault," he purred obscenely. "You wear me out."

She laughed, satisfied, and his other hand sneaked under the sheets and brushed her thighs.

"Stop," she protested, moving away a little. "We have to go."

"No." He pinned her down with his whole body. "I want to stay here."

"Ah, come on, get up. Lazy . . . It's too hot to have you on top of me." She used a mock-severe tone; like a rebellious child, he held her even more tightly in his arms. At last Regina succeeded in freeing herself; she sat on the edge of the bed and turned on the harsh light on the nightstand.

Aleix lay spread out in the shape of a cross, occupying practically the whole space. She couldn't help being surprised once again by the beauty of that naked body. It was a bittersweet feeling: a mixture of admiration and embarrassment. Without getting up, she stretched out her arm to grab her bra and blouse, thrown on a nearby chair.

"You can stay in bed if you want," she said, as she dressed, her back to him.

"Don't go yet. I have to talk to you."

Something in his tone of voice alarmed her suddenly and she turned, her blouse half buttoned.

"Does it have to be now?" She finished buttoning the blouse and picked up her watch from the nightstand. "It's really late."

He moved to kneel on the sheets and kissed her on the neck.

"Stop . . . If you hadn't stood me up yesterday, we'd have had more time. Salvador arrives in less than an hour and I have to go to the airport to collect him."

"I did it for Gina, I already told you . . . And it's partly your fault: no mobile messages, no contact outside of here. I couldn't tell you."

She nodded rapidly, impatient.

"That's how it has to be. OK, make the most of it while I'm dressing. What do you have to tell me?" She rose from the bed and began to put on her underwear and then her skirt. She didn't even have time to go home and shower. She'd go straight to collect the Old Man.

"I'm in trouble. Bad trouble."

Silence.

"I need money."

"Money?" Regina didn't know what to say. She turned red and stopped dressing.

He realized he'd offended her; he jumped out of bed, still naked, and came toward her. Regina looked away.

"Hey, hey . . . Look at me," he said to her. She did so, and then, seeing his face, she understood that he was really serious. "I wouldn't be asking you if it wasn't essential. But I've fucked up and I need it. Really."

"You have parents, Aleix. Surely they'll help you."

"Don't be absurd. I can't go to them."

Regina exhaled.

"What's going on? Have you got some college girl pregnant or something like that?"

His expression changed and he grabbed her hand.

"Let go!" He didn't. He grasped it more firmly and drew her toward him.

"This isn't a joke, Regina. If I don't get three thousand euros before Tuesday—"

She didn't let him finish. She interrupted him with a dry, ironic laugh.

"Three thousand euros? You're mad!"

Aleix squeezed her hand harder, but then dropped it. They were face to face, measuring each other up.

"I'll pay you back."

"Listen, no way. It's not about whether you'd return it or not. Do you think I can take three thousand euros out of the account without Salvador noticing? And what would I say to him? That the fucking has been a little expensive this time?"

She was offended: it was what he'd been afraid of, making her feel like someone who has to pay for sex. He tried to explain.

"Listen, I'm not asking you as a lover, I'm asking you as

a friend. I'm asking you because if I don't give it back, these guys will kill me."

"What are you talking about?" It was getting late. She wanted to finish this conversation and get out of there. "What guys?"

He lowered his head. He couldn't tell her the whole thing.

"I wouldn't be saying this to you if it wasn't important."

Regina didn't want to give him any more options: she sat down on the chair to put on her white sandals, but the weight of silence, broken only by the sound of the air conditioning, was too much for her.

"Aleix, I'll be straight with you. If you really are in trouble, you have to turn to your parents. I can't solve your problems. Understand?"

"Don't come over all protective on me. Not when I just fucked you twice."

She half smiled.

"Leave it, Aleix. I don't want to fight with you."

It was his last card: he played it in desperation, with a pang of regret. He fell back on the bed and fixed his eyes on her.

"I don't want to fight either." He tried to make his voice sound cold, suddenly unconcerned. "But I think you're going to help me in the end. Even if it's only for your daughter's sake."

"Don't you dare bring Gina into this."

"Don't worry, I don't plan on telling her that I screw her mother once a week. I'll leave that to you." He lowered his voice: once he'd started, there was no way back. "What I will do is tell that Argentine inspector that I saw frightened, innocent Gina push Marc out of the window."

"What the hell are you saying?"

"The cold hard truth. Why do you think Gina's like she is? Why do you think I went to your house yesterday? So she wouldn't be alone with the police, because your little girl is terrified of what she did."

"You're making it up." Her voice was trembling. Fragmented images of the last few days flashed through her head. She tried to dispel them before continuing. This was a bluff; it had to be this bastard brat's fucking bluff. She became indignant.

Aleix kept talking.

"She'd been dying of jealousy since Marc told us he'd met a girl in Dublin. And on San Juan she couldn't take it anymore. She put on that dress to hook up with him, but he wasn't interested."

Regina got up and went toward Aleix. She had to control her voice, control herself so as not to lose her temper and slap him across the face. Control herself so as to leave no doubts that she was serious.

"You left . . . you stated so to the police and Gina said so as well."

He smiled. Regina hesitated. Right now all he needed was to sow doubt in her mind.

"Of course. It's what you do for a friend, isn't it? In spite of Marc being my friend too. It's in your hands, Regina. Simple: one favor for another. You help me, I help you and Gina."

Just then Aleix's mobile, which he'd left on the nightstand, rang. He stretched out his arm to see who it was and frowned. He answered under Regina's glare.

"Edu? Something up?" His brother rarely called him, and never without a reason.

While he listened to what Edu had to tell him, Regina slowly picked up her bag. The conversation lasted barely a minute. Aleix said thank you and good-bye and hung up.

He looked at her, smiling. He was still naked, aware of the attractiveness of his body. She knew he had something to say:

she saw it in his satisfied face, in that smile expressing more arrogance than any kind of happiness.

"What a coincidence. It seems the cop wants to see me. Monday afternoon. Just enough time for you and me to resolve this matter between ourselves."

For a moment Regina hesitated. A cold mask came over her face. A part of her, the part belonging to the disappointed woman, wanted to slap that cocky brat's face, but her maternal side finally prevailed. The first thing was to speak to Gina. She decided the slap could wait.

"I'll call you," she said, then turned around.

"What?"

Regina smiled to herself.

"Just that. I'll let you know." She turned back toward him, trying to make her expression as contemptuous as possible. "Oh, and if you really need that money, keep looking for it. If I were you, I wouldn't count on me giving it to you."

He held her gaze. Bitch, he mouthed.

"You know what you're doing," Aleix said instead. He desperately sought a phrase to settle this wrangle in his favor, but found none, so he just smiled at her again. "You have until Monday to save your little girl from this mess. Think about it."

She waited a few seconds before opening the door and escaping.

18

Martina Andreu looked at her watch. Her shift finished in less than half an hour and she had just enough time to go to the gym before picking up the kids. She needed some good stretches; her back was killing her these days and she knew it was partly due to lack of exercise. She tried to be organized, but sometimes it was simply too much. Work, husband, house, two little children overflowing with after-school activities . . . She placed the papers from the Dr. Omar case in the file with a sigh of frustration. If there was anything that drove her crazy, it was cases that were going nowhere. She began to think this guy had taken off with his macabre music for somewhere else. It wasn't a ridiculous idea at all: if the women-trafficking network had been his main source of income, now he had to find another way of earning a living. The blood on the wall and the stunt with the pig's head could have been just a smokescreen, a way of disappearing in triumph, so to speak. Although, on the other hand, the guy wasn't young. In Barcelona he had his con-

tacts and that repugnant clinic. Maybe he wouldn't earn enough
to make him a millionaire, but certainly more than he'd make
somewhere else, where he'd have to start from scratch.

The man's personality was a mystery. The people of the *barrio* hadn't contributed much information. She herself had gone
door to door all morning, trying to find out anything, and the
only thing clear was that the name of the "doctor" inspired
distrust at the very least; in some cases, genuine fear. One of
the women she'd spoken to, a young Colombian who lived on
the same floor, had distinctly said: "He is a strange guy . . . I
used to cross myself when I passed him. He did bad things in
there." She had pushed her a little more and had obtained only
a vague "They say he takes the devil out of the body, but if
you ask me I say he is the devil in person." And from then on
she was as silent as the grave. It wasn't that strange, thought
Martina: however surprising it might seem, a number of "exor-
cisms" took place regularly in cities like Barcelona, and given
that now the City of Counts' priests didn't get involved in these
affairs, believers in such things had to find alternative exor-
cists. She was sure that Dr. Omar was one of them. Searching
his clinic had contributed very little but none the less significant evidence: a multitude of crosses and crucifixes, books on
satanism, *santería* and other similar stories, written in French
and Spanish. His banking transactions were ridiculous: he'd
bought the flat for cash years before; he had no friends; and if
he had clients, they wouldn't go to the station to make a statement. Martina shivered at the thought that these things could
still be happening in a city like Barcelona. Modernist façades
and modern shops, hordes of tourists ravaging the city, camera
in hand . . . and underneath all that, protected by anonymity,
individuals like Dr. Omar: no roots, no family, devoting himself to aberrant rituals without anyone knowing. Enough, she

told herself. I'll continue on Monday. She left the closed file on top of the desk and was already getting up when the phone rang. Shit, she thought: last-minute phone calls always lead to problems.

"Yes?"

A woman's voice, trembling with nerves and with a marked South American accent, stammered on the other end:

"Are you covering the doctor case?"

"Yes. Your name, please?"

"No, no . . . Call me Rosa. I have something to tell you. If you like we can meet in person."

"How did you get my number?"

"A neighbor you questioned gave it to me."

Martina looked at her watch. The gym was fading into the horizon.

"And you want us to meet right now?"

"Yes, straight away. Before my husband gets back . . ."

I hope this is worth it, thought Martina, resignedly.

"Where can we meet?"

"Go to the Ciutadella. I'll be behind the fountain. Do you know where I mean?"

"Yes," answered Martina. Taking the kids to the zoo in the park so much had its advantages.

"I'll wait for you there, within the next half-hour. Be punctual, I don't have much time . . ."

The sergeant was going to say something, but the call was ended before she could do so. She grabbed her bag and left the station. With a bit of luck, she'd at least get to pick up the kids.

The afternoon was also proving fruitful for Leire Castro. Before her, she had a record of Aleix Rovira's telephone activity for the last two months, and the list was interesting, not solely because of the extremely high number of calls. With the list on the table she was noting the numbers that occurred most often, which, given the intensity of this mobile's communications, was no easy task. The most curious were those on the weekend: throughout the day, and for a large part of the night, Aleix's mobile received brief calls, barely seconds long. There were other numbers that occurred quite frequently. Leire wrote them down, ready to find out to whom they belonged. One of them had called various times, ten to be exact, on the night of June 23. Aleix hadn't answered any of them, but he did contact that number the following day. A four-minute conversation. It was the only call he bothered to return, after leaving numerous others unanswered. She counted: six different numbers had called repeatedly, and Aleix had answered the first. No more.

She tried to put the scattered data in order while she mentally went over the story Gina and Aleix himself had given in previous statements. A story that wasn't wholly true. Why had he and Marc Castells argued? An argument bad enough to leave Marc's T-shirt bloodstained. To whom did the number that had persistently called that night, and that Aleix had bothered to answer the next day, belong? That, at least, would be easy to discover. In fact, after some quick checks, she obtained the user's name: Rubén Ramos García. She sighed. The name meant nothing to her. She then entered another of the numbers that appeared most in the list. Regina Ballester. Gina Martí's mother . . . They were certainly going to have things to ask Aleix on Monday.

She looked at her watch. Yes, she still had time. She put the name Rubén Ramos García into the computer. Seconds later, thanks to the magic of information technology, a photo of a young, sallow man appeared on the screen. Leire, completely

bewildered, read the details. What the hell was a young guy
from a good family, as the superintendent would say, doing
mixing with this kid who clearly didn't belong in his social
circle? Rubén Ramos García, twenty-four years old, cited in
January of the year before and again in November for possession of cocaine. Suspected of drug dealing, unproven. Another
note: questioned in relation to a skinhead assault on some immigrants who ended up dropping the charges.

Leire made a quick report of all this and left it on the table,
just as she'd agreed with the inspector. Then, not wanting to
stop to think about anything, she picked up her helmet and
went for her motorbike.

Martina Andreu entered the gates of the Parc de la Ciutadella
at exactly twenty past five. Some dark clouds were beginning
to appear from the sea and a wind, warm but strong, was shaking the branches of the trees. In the flowerbeds, somewhat
dry from the lack of rain, groups of youngsters were playing
the guitar or simply enjoying a beer. Summer in the city. She
moved with quick steps over the ground until she reached the
fountain, and the sound of the water gave her a fleeting sensation of coolness. She walked around it, making her way toward
a corner of the park beyond where there were two scattered
benches. She looked around the space until she located a short,
dark-haired woman with her back to her, playing with a little
girl. The woman turned just as she was approaching and gave
a slight nod.

"Rosa?"

"Yes." She was nervous: dark shadows under her eyes revealed a fatigue that was the result of a lifetime. "My love,
Mama is going to speak to this lady about work. Play by yourself over there for a minute, OK?"

The little girl looked at the new arrival gravely. She'd inherited her mother's shadows, but in exchange she had beautiful black eyes.

"We'll be on that bench," added Rosa, and pointed to the nearest. "Don't go too far, my love."

Martina went toward the bench and Rosa followed her; both sat down. The wind was becoming stronger, boding a night of rain. About time, thought the sergeant.

"It's going to rain," said Rosa, who didn't take her eyes off her daughter, or stop twisting her hands: short, sturdy fingers, hardened from cleaning strangers' houses.

"How old is she?"

"Six."

Martina smiled.

"A year younger than mine. They're twins," she clarified.

Rosa smiled at her, somewhat less nervous, although her hands were still tense. Complicity between mothers, thought the sergeant.

"What did you have to tell me, Rosa?" She didn't want to seem impatient, but her time was running out. Seeing the woman wasn't responding, she persisted. "Something about Dr. Omar?"

"I don't know if I'm doing the right thing, Sergeant. I don't want to get into trouble." She lowered her head and clutched a medallion she wore around her neck.

"Calm down, Rosa. You thought you should call me, so it must be something important. You can trust me."

The woman looked around and breathed: "It's . . ."

"Yes?"

"I . . ." Finally she found the strength and decided to speak. "Promise me you won't come looking for me, and I won't have to make a statement at the station."

Martina hated making promises she didn't know she could keep, but this type of lie was part of her work.

"I promise you."

"Good . . . I knew the doctor. He cured my little girl." Her voice began to tremble. "I . . . I know you don't believe in these things. But I saw it, day after day. The little one was getting worse every day."

"What did she have?"

Rosa glanced at her sideways and held the medallion tightly.

"I swear by the Virgin, Señora. My little girl was bewitched. My husband didn't even want to hear about it. He even raised his hand to me when I said so . . . but I knew."

Martina suddenly felt cold, as if the woman by her side had brought it with her.

"And you took her to Dr. Omar's clinic?"

"Yes. A friend recommended him to me, and we don't live too far. So I took her and he cured her for me, Señora. He put his holy hands on her chest and banished the evil spirit."

She crossed herself as she said it. Martina couldn't help her icy tone when she asked: "Have you brought me here to tell me this?"

"No! No, I wanted you to know the doctor is a good man. A saint, Señora. But there's something else. I didn't have the money to pay him all at once and so I had to go back . . . I think I saw him the day he disappeared."

The sergeant became alert.

"At what time?"

"In the evening, Señora, around eight. I went to pay him, and when I came out of the clinic I saw him."

"Who did you see?"

"A man waiting at the front door, smoking, as if he hadn't decided to go in."

"What did he look like?" Martina took out her notepad, completely alert.

"There's no need to describe him." The woman almost broke down crying. "You . . . you know him. The following day I saw him again, with you, eating in a nearby restaurant."

"Do you mean Inspector Salgado?"

"I don't know his name. He was eating with you, like you were friends."

"Are you sure?"

"I wouldn't have called you if I wasn't, Señora. But promise me no one will come to my house. If my husband finds out I took my daughter to that doctor . . ."

"Don't worry," whispered Martina. "Don't say anything about this to anyone. But I need to be able to reach you. Give me a mobile number, or—"

"No! I come here every afternoon with the little one. If you need anything you already know where to find me."

"Good." Martina looked at her gravely. "I repeat, Rosa: don't say a word about any of this."

"I swear by the Virgin, Señora." Rosa kissed the medallion before rising from the bench. "Now I have to go."

The little girl, who had stayed away from the conversation, turned on hearing her mother coming toward her. She still didn't smile.

Martina Andreu watched them walk away. She should be going too, but her legs refused to move from the bench. The fountain's gilded horses seemed to be rearing up against the wind still whipping the trees, and in the distance the echo of thunder could be heard. A summer storm, she said to herself. All this will be nothing more than a fucking summer storm.

19

The high-speed train from Madrid arrived at the scheduled time, defying years of delays in the country's railway service. At this time in the evening, on a Friday in summer, the foyer of the station was replete with people hoping to exchange the suffocating city for the crowds of the beaches, even though that might mean a journey on a crammed train. Sitting on one of the benches in the large foyer, Leire watched people coming and going: hikers with backpacks who spoke in shouts, mothers with immense bags on their shoulders dragging little kids who insisted on clumsily putting the ticket in the slot, exhausted immigrants after a day of work which had almost certainly begun at dawn, tourists studying the departures board as if it were the tables of the law and not keeping an eye on their wallets. Leire's careful gaze picked out two boys who were walking around the building without deciding to take a single train. Pickpockets, she said on seeing a look of complicity between them: an even bigger summer plague than mosquitoes and of course more difficult to combat. Petty robberies, nonexistent sentences, bitter tourists and triumphant thieves: and this was only a best-case scenario. She was watching one of them going into the toilets after a middle-aged lady, clearly a foreigner, when she noticed someone sitting beside her.

"Spying on people?" asked the recent newcomer in an ironic tone. "Let me remind you that now you're off-duty."

She turned to him. The same mirrored sunglasses, the same two-day stubble, never more; the same brilliantly white teeth, the same hands. The same individual whom she'd bumped into in the waiting room of a physiotherapy clinic and who, after watching her like a wolf over his newspaper, had said to her: "Massages bring out my tenderest part. Shall we meet downstairs in about an hour?" And she'd nodded, amused, thinking it was a joke.

"Crime never sleeps," replied Leire.

"Maybe not crime, but you should," he joked. He stood up. "My lungs need nicotine. And I need a beer. Did you come by motorbike?"

"Yes."

He gave her a quick kiss. Like her, he wasn't a fan of public displays of affection, but it left her a taste of his mouth, wanting more.

"Why don't we head toward the beach? I've spent a week suffocating in the heat of Madrid. I want to see the sea with you."

The beach bar was proclaiming the arrival of Friday night with disco music, and the customers, their bodies glistening with suntan lotion, allowed themselves to be seduced by that rhythm somewhere between smooth and monotonous, and the offer of mojitos prepared by a beautiful young Latin American woman in an annexed bar. Knees bent and feet resting on the seat opposite, Tomás lit his third cigarette and ordered his second beer. He'd finished the first in almost one swallow and was watching the beach, already half empty, and that tranquil city sea, almost waveless, a dull blue.

"You don't know how I've been longing for this . . ." he said, relaxing his shoulders and blowing out smoke slowly, as if he were expelling something within that was tiring him. He'd taken off his jacket and undone the top buttons of his shirt.

Leire smiled at him.

"You can have a dip if you want. They're not pure and crystalline waters, but they're not bad."

"I'm not wearing my trunks," he said. He yawned. "Also, right now I want to smoke and drink. Do you only want a Coca-Cola?"

"Yes." She tried not to have the smoke in her face. Why did smoke nearby make her feel nauseated though her own didn't?

"Well, what have you got to tell me? Any interesting cases?"

"The odd one or two. But let's not talk about work, please. I've had a horrible week."

"You're right. Although at least yours is interesting. Audits at times of crisis are depressing." He pulled her toward him and put his arm around her. "It's been a while since we've seen each other."

She didn't answer and he continued talking.

"I've thought of calling you a few times, but I didn't want to smother you. For a week it was rather intense."

Intense. That was the word. One of them. Just being at his side, feeling that strong arm, awoke all the impulses of her body. It was strange. Pure sexual chemistry, like they were each made to take pleasure in the other.

"But the other day I couldn't take it anymore." She didn't ask why. "I knew I had to see you. At least this weekend."

Leire kept her eyes on the sea, on some clouds moving at top speed on the horizon. She didn't want to see them.

"It's going to rain," she said.

"Don't you like being on the beach in the rain?"

"I'd prefer to be in bed. With you."

They barely waited to enter the house. The proximity on the motorbike, combined with the tense atmosphere of the storm, was raising their temperatures and he began to touch her while still on the stairs, shameless. She didn't resist at all. They kissed greedily on the threshold until she let go and dragged him inside by the hand. He didn't let go of her for a moment, not even when he searched for her underwear with his fingers while he brushed her lips with his tongue without fully kissing her, leaving her wanting more. Their hands, interwoven against the door, were descending as she became more and more excited. When they reached her hips, he kissed her for real, forcefully, and pulled out his playful fingers. Then he lifted her and carried her to the bed.

Tomás wasn't one of those that slept after making love, something that frankly was all the same to her. In fact, that day, she would have preferred it. Luckily, he wasn't one who talked either: lying by her side, he stayed in physical contact, enjoying the silence. Outside, an intense rain was battering the streets. She let herself be soothed by the sound, by the contact, while she thought that this was the time. Maybe he didn't have any right to know, as María had stressed the previous night, but she, in good conscience, should tell him. She wasn't planning to ask him for anything, or demand any responsibility of him. Just tell him the truth.

"Leire," he whispered. "I want to tell you something."

"Me too." He couldn't see her smile, in the dark. "You go first."

He turned her face toward him.

"I've done something crazy."

"You?"

"Don't get angry, OK? Promise me."

"Promise. And I say likewise."

"I've rented a boat. For next month. I want to go to the islands, Ibiza or Menorca, for a few days. And I'd like you to come with me."

For a moment she couldn't believe it. The idea of traveling with him, just the two of them, of entire nights of nonstop fucking in a cabin, of beaches with blue waters and romantic dinners on deck, left her speechless. She thought of María, carrying buckets of water to construct the surgery in the African village, and started laughing.

"What are you laughing at?"

She couldn't stop.

"Nothing . . ." she stammered, not able to avoid another giggle.

"Do you think I can't operate a boat or something?"

"It's not that . . . really . . ."

He started tickling her.

"You're laughing at me! Are you laughing at me? You'll . . . !"

"Stop, stop . . . Stop, please! Enough!"

The last order came out as definitive because he stopped, although he said in a threatening tone: "Tell me you'll come . . . or I'll tickle you to death."

Leire exhaled. Now. She couldn't put it off any longer. The rain seemed to have eased off. A storm moving away, she thought.

She inhaled and began.

"Tomás, there's—"

A telephone interrupted her.

"It's yours," he said.

Leire jumped out of bed, relieved by the momentary breathing space. She took a few moments to find her mobile because she didn't know where she'd left her jacket. She found it on the dining room floor, beside the door, and managed to answer it before they hung up. The call was brief, barely seconds long, but enough to tell her the terrible news.

"Has something happened?" he asked. He was kneeling, naked, in the middle of the bed.

"I have to go," she answered. "I'm sorry."

She scooped up her clothes at top speed and ran toward the bathroom, still overwhelmed by what she'd just heard.

"I'll come back when I can," she said before leaving. "And we'll talk, OK?"

20

It had already started raining when Héctor arrived at the station. He went in hope of finding Martina Andreu, but her office was empty. He greeted a couple of acquaintances, feeling very uncomfortable, as if this were no longer his place and, unable to avoid it, he looked sideways at the door of his own office. Although technically he'd been on holiday, everyone knew what had happened. He'd spent many years in stations, and they were like every place of work: a hotbed of rumors and comments. Above all if they were about someone who up to then had distinguished himself with an unblemished record. With decisive steps he went toward Leire Castro's desk and then he saw the report, placed on the computer keyboard in a file. Leaning against the desk, he looked through the report on Aleix Rovira's calls. This kid was turning out to be an inexhaustible source of surprises, he thought on seeing the names Rubén Ramos García and Regina Ballester. However, the first name was more a suspicion confirmed than a true surprise, he said to himself, remembering the conversation he'd just had with Óscar Vaquero.

He'd arranged to meet him at the door of a gym in the city center, and while he waited for him he thought the boy must have taken the idea of losing weight seriously. However, when a young man, not very tall but with broad shoulders, bulging arms threatening to rip his T-shirt sleeves and not fat at all, approached him he had to look twice to recognize him from the description he'd been given of Óscar Vaquero. Of course, two years had passed since that video, which had ended in Marc Castells' suspension and Óscar's changing schools. And judging by the results, he'd made good use of the time. Then, sitting on a street terrace despite the clouds beginning to cover the sky, he could see that the change in Óscar wasn't only physical. Héctor ordered a black coffee and Óscar, after a little thought, opted for a Diet Coke.

"Did you hear about what happened to Marc Castells?" asked Héctor.

"Yes." He shrugged slightly. "A shame."

"Oh? I didn't think you cared for him too much," the inspector hinted.

The boy smiled.

"Not for him, or for the majority of people at that school . . . But that doesn't mean them dying makes me happy." Something in his voice partly contradicted his words. "This isn't America. Here people on the margins don't go into the school with a shotgun and top everyone in their class."

"Through lack of guns or the desire to do it?" asked the inspector, keeping the tone light.

"I don't think I should have this conversation about homicidal angst with a cop . . ."

"We cops were also students once. But, seriously," he said, changing tone and taking a cigarette from the packet, "it's clear that this whole video affair must have damaged you."

"Well, that definitely damages you," replied the boy and pointed at the tobacco. "The truth is, I don't really like talking about it . . . It's like another time. Another Óscar. But, yes of course, it fucked me up a bit." He looked away, as if suddenly fascinated by the maneuvers of a minibus on the opposite corner trying to get into a parking space that was obviously too narrow. "I was the fatty gay boy." He had a faint, bitter smile. "Now I'm a gay stud. I try to forget the me of that time, but sometimes he comes back."

Héctor nodded.

"He comes back when you least expect it, doesn't he?"

"How'd you know?"

"I told you, we were all boys once."

"I kept some photos from then, so as not to forget. But tell me, what do you want?"

"I'm just trying to get an idea of what Marc Castells was like. When someone dies, everyone speaks well of them," and he surprised himself thinking that in this case it wasn't necessarily true.

"Yeah . . . And you've come looking for someone who might hate him? But why? Wasn't it an accident?"

"We're closing the case, and we can't rule out other possibilities."

Óscar nodded.

"Yeah. Well then, I'm afraid you've got the wrong person. I didn't hate Marc. Not then, not now. He was one of the few people I spoke to."

"Weren't you surprised that he put up that video?"

"Inspector, don't talk rubbish. Marc would never have done

that. The truth is, he didn't do it. Everyone knew that. That's why he was only suspended for a week."

"So he took the blame for someone else?"

"Of course. In exchange for academic help. Marc wasn't very clever, you know? And Aleix had him by the balls. He did all his exams."

"Hold on, are you telling me that it was Aleix Rovira who made the video and put it on the internet, and Marc took the blame for him?"

"Yes. That's why I left. That school made me sick. Aleix was number one, the clever boy, the untouchable. Marc as well, but less so."

"I understand," said the inspector.

"But in the end that imbecile Aleix did me a favor. And I think things are better for me than for him, going by what I've heard."

"What have you heard?"

"Let's just say Aleix is taking a walk on the wild side. And he's enough of an idiot to think he's a hard ass. You get me?"

"No. Hard in what sense?"

"Look, everyone knows that if you want something for the weekend, something to enjoy yourself, you only have to call Aleix."

"Are you telling me he's a dealer?"

"He was an amateur but I think recently he's been taking it more seriously. Dealing and taking. Or that's what they say. And that he's hanging out with bad people as well."

So now, seeing the name of another kid of a similar age and with a history of cocaine possession, Héctor knew that Óscar hadn't lied to him. He didn't know if this had anything to do with Marc's death, but it was clear that Aleix Rovira had a lot of explaining to do: about fights, about drugs, about blame being put on someone else . . . He longed to put the pressure on this brat, he thought. And now he had what he needed to do it.

"Inspector?"

The voice startled him. He was so absorbed in his thoughts that he hadn't heard anyone come in.

"Señora Vidal. Were you looking for me?"

"Yes. But please call me Joana. Señora Vidal makes me think of my mother."

She was wearing the same clothes as before and looked tired.

"Would you like to sit down?"

She hesitated.

"I'd prefer . . . Would you mind if we went for a drink?"

"No, of course not. I can offer you a coffee if you want."

"I was thinking a gin and tonic, Inspector, not a coffee."

He looked at his watch and smiled.

"Héctor. And you're right. After six coffee gives you insomnia."

It was bucketing down with rain when they emerged, so they went into the first bar they found, one of those lunchtime places that only survived in the evenings thanks to locals who didn't move from the bar, where they discussed football and consumed beer after beer. The tables were free, so despite the waiter's reproachful gaze Héctor directed Joana to the one furthest from the bar, where they could talk in peace. The waiter reluctantly wiped it, more attentive to the conversation continuing at the bar about Barça's new signings than to the customers. However, he was quick to bring them two strong gin and tonics, more so that they would leave him to his discussion than out of generosity.

"Do you smoke?" said Héctor.

She shook her head.

"I gave up years ago. In Paris you can't smoke anywhere."

"Well, it won't be long here. But for the moment we're resisting. Does it bother you?"

"Not at all. I like it actually."

Suddenly they both felt uncomfortable, like a couple of strangers who kiss in a seedy bar and ask themselves what the hell they are doing. Héctor cleared his throat and drank a gulp of gin and tonic. He couldn't help a grimace of disgust.

"That is terrible."

"It won't kill us," she replied. And she took a long and brave gulp.

"Why did you come to the station? There's something you didn't tell us before, isn't there?"

"I knew you'd noticed."

"Look . . ." He felt uncomfortable talking to her in such a familiar way, but he continued. "I'm going to be completely honest with you, although it may seem cruel: this may be one of those cases that is never resolved. I haven't had many in my career, but in all of them doubt remains, hovering in the air. Did he fall? Did he jump? Was he pushed? Without witnesses, and with very little evidence suggesting a crime has been committed, they end up being classified as 'accidental death,' through lack of evidence. And the doubt is always there."

"I know. That's exactly what I want to avoid. I have to know the truth. I already know that it may seem contradictory to you, and as my ex delights in reminding me every time he sees me, it's a belated interest. But I'm not going to leave without knowing what happened."

"Maybe it was an accident. You should count on that."

"When you can assure me that it was an accident, I'll believe you. Really."

They both drank at the same time. The ice was melting, and

the gin and tonic flowed better, as did the conversation. Joana inhaled and decided to trust in this inspector with the melancholy expression and kindly eyes.

"The other day I received another email." She searched in her bag and took out the printed piece of paper. "Read it."

From: alwaysiris@hotmail.com
To: joanavidal@gmail.net
Subject:

Hello . . . I'm sorry to email you, but I didn't know who to turn to. I heard about what happened and I think we should see each other. It's important that you don't say anything to anyone until you and I speak in person. Please, do it for Marc, I know you'd begun to write to each other and I hope I'll be able to trust you.

I'm flying back to Barcelona from Dublin next Sunday morning. I'd like to see you straight away and tell you some things about Marc . . . and about me.

Many thanks,

Alwaysiris

Héctor lifted his head from the piece of paper.

"I don't understand it." The threads of this case seemed to be multiplying, pointing in different directions, nothing definite. If half an hour before he'd been relatively certain that the fight between Aleix and Marc had something to do with drugs, now this new name had appeared, Iris. There'd been an Iris in Marc's phone. "Alwaysiris. It's a strange way to sign an email, isn't it? As if it weren't her name. As if it were a form of homage."

Joana picked up her gin and tonic, her hand shaking a little. She brought it to her lips, but didn't manage to drink. The group at the bar was reaching the level of passionate discussion.

"I was on the point of telling my ex-husband yesterday. Of asking him if he knew anything about this Iris, if the name sounded familiar. He was so cruel, I thought it was better not to. Also, this girl asked me not to tell anyone, as if there were danger, as if she were hiding something . . ."

"You've done the right thing in telling me," Héctor reassured her.

"I hope so," she smiled. "I barely recognize Enric. Want to know something? When we were boyfriend and girlfriend I thought I would be with him all my life."

"Doesn't everyone think that?"

"I suppose so. But everything changed so much when we got married . . ."

"Is that why you left?"

"That, and the idea of being a mother terrified me."

Joana finished off her gin and tonic and put it back on the table.

"It sounds awful, doesn't it?"

"Fear is human. Only idiots are immune to it."

She laughed.

"Nice try, Inspector Salgado." She looked toward the door. "Would you mind if we took a walk? I think it's stopped raining. I need some air."

The rain had left a shiny layer over a city preparing for the weekend. There was a slight breeze, not much, but between that and the drenched streets they breathed a freshness welcome after days of intensely muggy weather. Héctor and Joana began to wander aimlessly, walking toward Plaça Espanya and once there they heard animated ethnic music coming from the Montjuïc Palace area, where it appeared one of those summer parties was being celebrated. Maybe they felt comfortable with one another, maybe neither of them felt like returning to an empty house; what is certain is that both, with a tacit accord, walked toward the music. Night was falling, and the illuminated stage attracted them. En route stalls with empanadas, tacos and mojitos by the jug offered their produce between colored flags and puddles of water. Those in charge of the stalls had tried to put a brave face on the bad weather, but it was obvious that the rain had spoiled part of the party.

"May I ask if you're married?"

"I was."

"Another victim of falling out of love?"

"And who isn't?"

She laughed. It had been a while since she felt so at ease with someone. He stopped in front of one of the stalls and ordered a pair of mojitos.

"You shouldn't have, Inspector. One shouldn't buy a single woman more than one drink."

"Shhh, lower your voice." Going to pay, he took his mobile from his pocket and saw he had three missed calls that had gone unheard in the Caribbean beat. "Excuse me a moment," he said, and moved a few steps away. "What? Sorry, I'm on a street and there's a lot of noise. That's why I didn't hear the mobile. What? When? In her house? I'm coming."

Joana watched the stage, with the two mojitos in her hands. At the bottom, the fountains of Montjuïc were throwing out their streams of color and the street began to fill with people who, like them, had decided to join the party after the rain. The mojito was good. She took a long drink and held out the other glass to Héctor with an almost coquettish gesture, but her smile evaporated on seeing the expression on his face.

21

The Martís' house seemed to have been invaded by a troop of wary soldiers, who spoke in hushed tones and carried out the pertinent tasks with serious faces. In the lounge, a severe Lluís Savall gave succinct orders to his men, out of the corner of his eye watching Salvador Martí and his wife, who, despite being seated beside each other on the dark sofa, gave the impression of finding themselves kilometers apart. His gaze was fixed on the door; she was tense, braced by an inner force, and her dry, reddened eyes betrayed a mixture of pain and incredulity. In that closed space the horror was only in their minds, in images they would manage to erase only with difficulty. In the bathroom, however, the tragedy lay unfolded in all its macabre splendor: scattered strokes on the white walls of the bathtub, a razor blade on the ledge, the water dyed red, and Gina's inert body, with the tranquil appearance of a sleeping child. Opposite the door, Héctor listened attentively to what a serious Agent Castro was telling him while a colleague from forensics finished collecting evidence of the tragedy. It wasn't a long tale; no need for it to be so. Regina Ballester had gone to collect her husband at the airport around six, but the plane was delayed. During the wait, which was over an hour, she called her daughter a number of times, but Gina didn't pick up the phone. Salvador Martí's plane finally landed, and they both arrived home around a quarter past nine, after negotiating a huge traffic jam caused by the rain and the weekend rush. Regina had immediately gone up to her daughter's room, and not finding her there thought she'd maybe gone out, but when she passed the bathroom she saw that the door was ajar and the light was on. Her screams on seeing Gina in the bathtub, submerged in a sea of blood, alerted her husband. It was he who called the emergency services, although he already knew that there was nothing medical science could do to revive his only daughter. The apparent conclusion, from lack of any other evidence, was that Gina Martí had slit her wrists in the bathtub.

"Was there a note?"

Leire nodded.

"On the computer, barely two lines." She consulted her notes. "It said something like: 'Cant take it any more. I have 2 do this . . . I cant live with the remorse.'"

"Remorse?" Héctor imagined Gina, a bit drunk, indignant, looking at Marc sitting on the window ledge. Walking toward him, possessed by a grudge, pushing him before he could turn around and make her waver in her decision. That he could picture. What he couldn't believe was that this same girl, temperamental enough not to accept no for an answer, could then go downstairs to sleep in the bed of the boy she loved and had just killed and stay there, asleep or not, as if nothing had happened. He didn't believe that Gina Martí would have been capable of acting with such coldness.

"Inspector Salgado, they told me you were on holiday." The forensic scientist, a slight and lively woman, famous for her efficiency and her sharp tongue, turned toward them and interrupted their thoughts.

"I missed you, Celia."

"Well, for someone missing me so much you're late arriving. We were waiting in case you wanted to see it." She looked inside with the lack of expression of someone who'd spent years examining cadavers, young, old, healthy, sick. "I heard there was a suicide note?"

"Yes."

"Well, then I don't have much to add." But her tone, her furrowed brow, said otherwise.

Héctor went into the bathroom and looked at poor Gina's lifeless body. He suddenly remembered her outburst on the sofa, when she shouted that she and Marc loved each other, under the condescending gaze of her mother. He'd detected a flash of triumph in her voice at that moment: Marc was no longer here to contradict her; she could cling to that love, real or not. With time, with people unfamiliar with this affair, she would even have changed her story: removed Marc's rejection of her on his last night, transformed him into the young man in love who gave her a kiss, told her affectionately to 'Stay awake, I won't be long,' and then fell into the void in an unexplained accident.

"Agent Castro tells me you questioned her yesterday. Did she seem like a decisive person? Sure of herself?"

Decisive? Héctor hesitated only for an instant. Leire's voice was more unequivocal.

"No. Not at all."

"Well, in that case she had a good pulse. Look." Celia Ruiz turned to the bathtub and without thinking twice she took the right hand out of the water. "One cut, deep and firm. The other one is the same. Teenage suicides usually make a few cuts before daring to make the definitive one. Not her: she knew what she wanted and her hand didn't shake. Neither of them."

"Can we remove the body?" asked an agent.

"I'm done. Inspector Salgado?"

He nodded and moved away from the bathtub to let the others past.

"Thanks, Celia."

"No problem." Héctor and Leire were going out of the door when Celia added: "You'll have the full report Monday, OK?"

"Yes, sir." Héctor smiled at her. "Let's go to her room. I want to see this note."

Leire accompanied the inspector. The box of teddy bears was in the same corner that the agent had seen it in the previous evening. On the table, beside the computer, there was a glass with the remains of some juice.

"Now I'll tell the boys to take it to the lab, in case they find something." Hands protected by gloves, Leire moved the mouse and the computer screen came back to life. There was a brief message, written in large letters: "I cant take it any more. I have 2 do this . . . I cant live with the remorse." There was something else.

Leire minimized the message and brought up another page. The first thing Héctor saw was a blurred photo of a little girl and just below it another, in black and white, of a young woman with blonde hair blown by the wind. Leire scrolled up with the cursor until she reached the top of the page. A simple heading, typical blog format, said: "My stuff (above all because I don't think anyone will be interested!)" At the side, a small photo revealed that this was Marc Castells' blog. But what most caught Héctor Salgado's attention was the blog entry Gina was reading before she died, dated June 20. The last one Marc had written before dying. It was very short, just a few lines: "Everything's ready. The hour of truth is approaching. If the end justifies the means, justice will back up what we're going to do. For Iris."

"The name is familiar from the list of Marc's calls, and the text is very strange."

Héctor thought of Joana's email. Alwaysiris . . .

"We'll take it." Before closing it, he saw that Marc's blog didn't have many followers; in fact, just two: ginaM and Alwaysiris. "We need to speak to the Martís. Then we'll take care of this." While they went downstairs, he brought Leire up to date on his conversation with Joana Vidal. "This Iris who signed the message asked her not to mention her to anybody until they could see each other in person. I think it's best to follow her instructions for the moment. I hope that Sunday will tell us something important."

Leire nodded.

"Inspector, what do you think of all this?"

Héctor had a lost look on his face for a few moments.

"I think that too many young people are dying." He turned his head toward the room they'd just left. "And I think there are a lot of things we don't know."

"To tell you the truth, Gina Martí didn't strike me as the suicidal type. Yes, she was sad, but at the same time I got the impression she was enjoying her role. Like Marc's death had elevated her into the main-character category."

"Main characters sometimes die too," he replied. "And maybe Gina's problem wasn't depression, but the feeling of guilt."

Leire shook her head.

"I don't see her pushing him just because he didn't love her back. They'd been friends since they were kids . . . Anyone could have typed that note."

"Friendships can sometimes become twisted in unexpected ways."

"Do you think she killed him out of love?" she asked with a touch of irony.

Just then, a hysterical sob followed by a murmur of footsteps rose toward them. Regina, who hadn't said a word all night, broke into loud and uncontrollable weeping when the agents took Gina from the bathtub, on a stretcher and completely covered by a white sheet.

Savall was waiting for them at the bottom of the stairs, beside the door leading to the lounge. It was obvious that he was longing to leave.

"Salgado, will you take care of this? I don't think you'll be able to speak to the Martís tonight."

Regina's tense, hoarse voice reached them.

"I don't want a tranquilizer. I don't want to be tranquil! I want to go with Gina. Where are they taking her?" Regina escaped her husband's arms and walked toward the door. They saw her almost run in pursuit of the agents. But at the door she stopped, as if an invisible barrier prevented her crossing. Her knees buckled and she would have fallen to the floor if not for Héctor, who was behind her.

Her husband approached her with the hesitant step of an old man and looked at the agents with deep-rooted hostility. For once, words failed Salvador Martí and he just demanded: "Can you leave us in peace for today? My wife needs to rest."

It seemed unbelievable that the streets could be so calm, so alien to the drama unfolding just meters away. If on summer weekends the *barrio* was empty, this one, after days of hellish heat, had provoked an almost total exodus. Not even the rain in the evening had managed to dissuade anyone. A middle-aged man was walking a dog of undetermined pedigree in the center of Via Augusta; closed shops, dark cafés, parking spaces on both sides of the street. A panorama of peace broken only by the blue lights of the police cars that were moving away without making a sound, silent sparkles that took with them the last remains of the tragedy.

Héctor and Leire strolled toward the Diagonal almost without intending to. Unconsciously, they sought light, traffic, a feeling of life. She knew that Tomás was waiting for her but she didn't feel like talking to him. Héctor was putting off calling Joana to tell her what had happened, because he didn't really know what to say to her and needed to clarify his thoughts. Returning to his flat didn't appeal to him either: he felt as if appalling surprises might await him in that once welcoming space. The vision of him mercilessly hitting that bastard was neither easy to forget nor pleasant to remember.

"I saw what you left me about Aleix Rovira's calls," he said. And he went on to tell her about his chat with Óscar Vaquero: the suspicion that Aleix could be passing cocaine was a strong link to his calls to this small-time dealer, this Rubén. The calls to Regina Ballester were more curious, thought Héctor. He went on, not giving her time to say anything, speaking to himself as well as to her. "I think that I'm starting to have an idea of what happened that night. It was San Juan, a good day for Aleix's business. Gina told us he arrived later, so he must have sold something, but he definitely had more. He was receiving calls, and if we assume he was making a living from this, they had to be possible customers. But he didn't answer any of them. And if what his brother says is true, he returned home as soon as he left Marc's. If there was a fight, and the blood on Marc's T-shirt makes it more than likely, it's possible that the coke was the reason for the argument. Or at least part of it."

Leire followed his reasoning.

"You mean they fought and Marc destroyed the coke? That would explain why Aleix didn't answer his customers' calls. But, why would they fight? Gina told us about an argument: she said Marc had come back changed from Ireland, he wasn't the same . . . But there has to be a more important reason, something motivating Marc to confront Aleix and take revenge on him by destroying the cocaine."

"Aleix dominated both of them. And Marc rebelled."

"Are you suggesting that Aleix could have returned to Marc's house to settle the score with him? And then killed Gina, faking a suicide so she wouldn't give him away?"

"I suggest we shouldn't come to any conclusion until we interrogate this boy as God wishes. I also suggest we set a little trap for his friend Rubén. I want to have them both by the balls." He paused, and went on: "And then we have Iris. In Joana's email, in Marc's mobile, now in his blog. She's like a ghost."

"A ghost that will appear the day after tomorrow." Leire exhaled. She was exhausted. She noticed that her muscles were beginning to relax after the tension accumulated in the Martís' house.

"Yes. It's late, and tomorrow a hard day awaits us." He looked at her fondly. "You should rest."

He was right, she thought, but she guessed it was going to be hard for her to sleep that night. Not knowing why, she was starting to feel at home with this calm guy, somewhat taciturn but solid at the same time. His chestnut eyes hinted at a well of sadness, but not bitterness. Healthy melancholy, if that meant anything.

"Yes. I have to go and get the motorbike."

"Of course. See you tomorrow." He moved a few steps away, but suddenly he turned around to call her, as if he'd remembered something important. "Leire, earlier you asked me if I thought Gina had killed Marc out of love. No one has ever been killed out of love; that's a fallacy from tango. One only kills out of greed, spite or jealousy, believe me. Love has nothing to do with it."

22

Héctor entered his office as if he were an intruder. He'd had no desire to go home and had decided to return to the station to read Marc Castells' blog. He tried to shake off the feeling that he was doing something he shouldn't, but wasn't entirely successful. He started up his computer, remembered his password—kubrick7—and typed Marc Castells' blog address in the browser, while he pondered the lack of decency these twenty-first-century diaries betrayed. The old ones, paper ones, were a private thing, something read only by the person themselves and therefore they could pour all their secrets into them. Now private lives were exhibited on the Web, which he was sure imposed a certain censure at the time of writing. If one couldn't be absolutely honest, why bother writing it? Was it a cry to the world for attention? Hey, listen, my life is full of interesting things! Do me a favor and read about them . . . Maybe what was happening was that he was getting old, he thought. Nowadays people got involved on the internet; some, like Martina Andreu, even married people they'd met in that hazy world that was cyberspace, people who sometimes lived in different cities and whose paths might never have crossed had they not been seated in front of the computer one evening. You're definitely old-fashioned, Salgado, he concluded while the page was opening. *My stuff (above all because I don't think anyone else will be interested!).* It was a good name, although it was ironic that Marc's stuff was interesting to someone after he'd died.

From what he could see, Marc had started in the blogosphere when he went to Dublin, probably as a way of communicating with the girl who'd been his best friend, who commented profusely on almost all his entries. It included photos of his room in a Dublin students' residence, the campus, streets drenched by rain, colorful doors in austere Georgian buildings, immense parks, jugs of beer, colleagues holding the jugs. Marc didn't spend much time writing: the majority of his entries were short and discussed subjects as enthralling as the weather—always rainy; classes—always boring; and parties—always overflowing with alcohol. As he became bored with his commentaries himself, they became less frequent. Héctor scrolled down until he found a photo that caught his attention: a young woman, blonde hair being blown by the wind, standing on a cliff. Her face couldn't be seen because of the wind. Involuntarily, he thought of *The French Lieutenant's Woman,* who wandered through her sorrow over other sea-battered cliffs. Caption: "Excursion to Moher, February 12th." Gina hadn't commented at all. The following entry was dated six days later, and it was the longest blog entry by far. The heading read: "In memory of Iris."

It's been a long time since I thought of Iris or the summer she died. I suppose I tried to forget it all, in the

same way I overcame nightmares and childhood fears.
And now, when I want to remember her, all that comes
to mind is the last day, as if these images have erased
all the previous ones. I close my eyes and bring myself
to that big old house, the dormitory of deserted beds
awaiting the arrival of the next group of children. I'm
six years old, I'm at camp and I can't sleep because
I'm scared. No, I lie. That very early morning I behaved like a brave boy: I disobeyed my uncle's rules
and faced the darkness just to see Iris. But I found her
drowned, floating in the pool, surrounded by a cortège
of dead dolls.

Héctor couldn't help shuddering and his eyes went to the
black-and-white photo of that little blonde girl. Sitting in an
empty office that had become alien to him, in a half-lit station,
he forgot about everything and became absorbed in Marc's
tale. In the story of Iris.

I remember the floor was cold. I noticed when I got out
of bed barefoot and ran quickly to the door. I'd waited
for daybreak because I didn't dare leave that big deserted room in the night, but I'd already been awake
for a while and I couldn't put it off any longer. I took
a few seconds to close the door carefully without making a sound. I had to take advantage of this moment,
when everyone was asleep, to achieve my goal. I knew
there was no time to waste, so I went quickly; however, before walking the long corridor I stopped and
took a deep breath before daring to go forwards. The
downstairs blinds let a weak line of light in, but the
upstairs corridor was still dark. How I hated that part

of the big house! Actually, I hated the whole house.
Above all on days like this, when it was almost empty
until the next group of kids with whom I'd have to
share the next ten days would arrive. Luckily this was
the last one: then I could go back to the city, to that
familiar room just for me, to new furniture that didn't
creak in the night, and white walls that protected
rather than scared me. I exhaled without noticing and
had to breathe in once again. It was something Iris
had taught me: "Breathe in and breathe it out as you
run, so you blow out the fear." But it didn't help me
much: maybe because my lungs didn't hold enough air,
although I never told her because I was embarrassed.
I tried to move ahead clinging to the wooden railing
placed along the length of the corridor so no one would
fall down and keeping my eyes fixed straight ahead
to avoid seeing the stiff, big, ugly bird who, from the
little table against the wall, seemed to be watching my
steps. By day it wasn't so horrible, sometimes I managed to forget about it, but in the shadows that owl
with glass eyes was terrifying. I must have clung even
tighter to the banister because it creaked and I let go
immediately: I didn't want to make a sound. I walked
straight ahead, following the pattern of the cold tiles,
and I clearly remember the feeling of treading on
something rough when I stepped on a broken one. Not
much further: Iris's room was the last one, at the end
of the corridor. I had to see her before everyone else
got up because if not, they wouldn't let me. Iris was
being punished, and although deep down I thought she
deserved it, I didn't want another day to go by without
talking to her. I'd barely had time to the evening be-

fore, when one of the monitors found her after she had
run away and spent a whole night in the wood. Just
thinking about the idea of it, that wood peopled with
shadows and immobile owls, gave me goosebumps. But
at the same time I was dying with curiosity for Iris to
tell me what she'd seen there. Maybe she'd behaved
badly, but she was brave and that was something I
couldn't help admiring. Of course it was precisely for
that reason she was being punished; her sister and
her mother had told me so. So she wouldn't run away
again. Frighten them like that.

At last I got to the door and although I'd always
been taught to knock before entering, I told myself it
wasn't necessary: Iris was sleeping and also the main
thing was to not make a noise. She was sharing the
room with her sister instead of with the other children
because they weren't at camp: they were the cook's
daughters. And that night her sister was sleeping with
her mother. I'd heard Uncle Fèlix say so. Iris had to
spend two days locked in her room, alone, to learn her
lesson. Opening the door I saw that the windows were
completely closed: they were strange, different to the
ones in my house in Barcelona. They had glass, then a
wooden board that didn't let even a tiny bit of light in.
"Iris," I whispered, feeling my way. "Iris, wake up."
As I couldn't find the light switch, I moved closer to
the bed and felt it blindly, from the foot up. Suddenly
my hands brushed against something soft and woolly.
I jumped back and in doing so I stumbled into the
nightstand, which shook a little. Then I remembered
that there was a lamp on that nightstand, which Iris
usually had on until the early hours of the morning to

read. She read too much, her mother said. She threatened to take away her books if she didn't finish her dinner. The little lamp was there. I followed the cable up with my hand until I found the switch that lit the light bulb. It wasn't a very strong light, but enough to see that the room was almost empty: the dolls weren't on the shelves, or Iris in the bed, of course. Only the teddy bear, the same one Iris had lent me for the first few nights so I wouldn't be afraid, but I returned to her when one of the kids laughed at me. He was there, on the pillow, disemboweled: his stomach was open as if he'd had an operation and a green stuffing was showing.

I breathed in again and knelt down to check if there was someone underneath the bed: there was only dust. And suddenly I was also annoyed with Iris, like everyone. Why did she do these things? Run away, disobey. That summer her mother was scolding her every minute: for not eating, for answering back, for not studying, for continually pestering her sister Inés. If she'd run away again while she was being punished, Uncle Fèlix was going to be really angry. I remember for a moment I thought of telling him, but I told myself that wouldn't be good: we were friends, Iris and I, and in spite of her being older than me she never minded playing with me. Then I spotted the window and thought maybe she had gone down to the patio at first light, like I had, while everyone was asleep. It was hard, but I managed to move the metal latch which held the wood in place. It was already day. Before my eyes the wood rose, lines of very tall trees reaching up the slopes of the mountains. By day it didn't scare

me; it was even pretty, with different shades of green.
I didn't see anyone on the patio and I was already
closing the window when it occurred to me to look in
the direction of the swimming pool. I could only see
a little piece, so I leaned a little further out to have
a wider view. I remember as if it were right now the
happiness I felt on seeing her: that intense, childhood
happiness that soars with things as simple as an ice-
cream or a visit to a fairground. Iris was there, in the
water. She hadn't run away, she'd just gone for a swim!
I had to stop myself shouting and I limited myself to
waving to get her attention, although I realized it was
silly since from where she was she couldn't see me. I'd
have to wait until she got to the opposite side of the
pool, the part where the water was shallower, where
the little kids swam and those not daring to get in at
the deep end.

And now, years later, thinking of all this, reliv-
ing every detail of that early morning, the same cold
astonishment as then overcomes me. Because barely
seconds later, I realized that Iris wasn't moving, that
she was still in the water, as if she was playing dead
but the reverse. I know suddenly I didn't care if they
heard me and I ran down to the pool, but I didn't dare
go into the water. Even at six years old I knew Iris had
drowned. And then I saw the dolls: they were floating,
face down, like little dead Irises.

The image was so powerful, so disturbing that Héctor minimized the screen automatically. He looked for his packet of
cigarettes and lit one, contravening all the rules. He took a
deep drag and slowly exhaled. While he calmed down, blessed

nicotine, his brain began to put this new piece in a puzzle becoming ever more macabre. And he knew, with the certainty given by years in the job, that until he learned exactly how this Iris had died, he wouldn't understand what had happened to Marc at the window or Gina in the bathtub. Too many dead, he said to himself again. Too many accidents. Too many young people who'd lost their lives.

The telephone interrupted his musings and he looked at the screen, somewhere between annoyed and relieved.

"Joana?" he answered.

"Is it very late? Sorry . . ."

"No. I was working."

"Fèlix called me." She paused. "He told me about the girl."

"Oh?"

"Is it true? This girl left a note saying she killed Marc?" There was a note of disbelief and hope in her voice.

Héctor delayed a few seconds before responding, and spoke with extreme caution.

"So it seems. Although I wouldn't be too sure. There are . . . there are still lots of questions."

Silence. As if Joana was going through that vague response, as if she was thinking about what to say next.

"I don't want to be alone tonight," she said finally.

He looked at the screen; he thought of his hostile flat, the absence of Ruth, Joana's mature and beautiful face. Why not? Two loners keeping each other company on a summer night. There couldn't be anything wrong with that.

"Me neither," he replied. "I'm coming over."

SATURDAY

23

Deep in his mind Héctor knows he's dreaming, but he dismisses the idea and dives into this landscape of lively colors, this childish drawing supposed to be a wood: green, almost round splotches, blue rays dotted with lovely white bits of cotton, a yellow sun with an unfinished smile. A naïf set designed by Tim Burton and colored with Crayola. However, as soon as he steps on the brown stones forming the path, the whole space changes, as if his human presence transforms the environment all of a sudden. The green splotches become trees with high branches, thick with leaves; the clouds become fine threads and the sun really is warming. He hears the crunch of his steps on the gravel and moves decisively, as if he knows where he's going. He is surprised on looking and seeing that the birds are still fake: two curved lines joined at the center suspended in the air. This is the proof he needs to reinforce his belief that it's all a dream and keep going forward, as if he's suddenly become the main character in an animated film.

It's then the wind begins to blow: at the beginning it is a dull murmur that grows little by little, until it forms a grayish gale that sweeps these false birds away and shakes the branches from the trees without the least mercy. He can barely keep going; every step is a struggle against this unexpected whirlwind which has darkened the painting: leaves come shooting off the trees and form a green blanket that obscures the light. He must go on, he can't stop and suddenly he knows why: he has to find Guillermo before this hurricane carries him off forever. Damn it . . . He told him not to wander off, not to go into the forest alone, but as usual his son took no notice. This mixture of worry and irritation gives him strength to keep moving forward in spite of this unexpected whirlwind and a road that is now rising in the form of a steep slope. He surprises himself thinking of how his son must be punished. He has never raised his hand to him, but this time he's gone too far. He shouts his name, although he knows with this whirlwind of leaves shouting is useless. He ascends with difficulty, on his knees when the intensity of the gale prevents him continuing on foot. For some reason, he knows that he just has to reach the summit of this rocky road and everything will be different. Finally he manages to stand up again and, after a momentary stagger, he manages to get going and keep ascending. The wind has ceased to be an enemy and has become his ally: it pushes him upwards and his feet barely graze the ground. He can make out the end of the road and mentally prepares himself for what might be ahead. He wants to see his son safe and sound, but at the same time he doesn't want the relief to stifle his irritation completely, as always happens. No, not this time. One last push precipitates him to the other side of the road and he gathers all his strength to remain standing. As soon as he goes past the summit the wind dies down and the scene changes.

The sun shines. Yes! He was right. There he is. The figure of Guillermo, standing in a meadow with his back to him, innocently unaware of all his father has gone through to find him. He can't help a sigh seeing his son is there perfectly well. He rests for a second or two. He realizes, without the least surprise, that the rage that has carried him here is beginning to evaporate: it seems to leave with each breath, melt in the air. And then he tightens his jaw and tenses his shoulders. He closes his fists. He focuses on his anger to revive himself. He walks rapidly and decidedly, crushing the soft tufts of grass, and approaches the boy, who remains immobile, distracted. This time he's going to teach him a good lesson, whatever the cost. It's what he must do, what his father would have done in his place. He grabs him by the shoulder and Guillermo turns around. To his surprise, he sees his face is soaked with tears. The boy points silently ahead. And then Héctor sees what his son sees: the swimming pool of blue water, and a little blonde girl floating among dead dolls. "It's Iris, Papa," whispers his son. And then, as they slowly approach the edge of that pool dug out of the plain, the dolls turn over, slowly. They look at them with wide eyes and their plastic lips murmur: "Alwaysiris, alwaysiris."

He wakes with a start. The image was so real he has to make an effort to erase it from his mind. To return to the present and remember that his son isn't a little boy anymore and never knew Iris. To be sure that dolls don't speak. He finds it difficult to breathe. It's still night, he thinks, annoyed, knowing he won't get back to sleep. Although maybe it's better, maybe not sleeping isn't so bad after all. He stays lying on his back, trying to calm down, attempting to make sense of this strange, disturbing dream. Unlike most other nightmares, which fade when one opens one's eyes, this one persists in clinging to his mind. He relives the rage, the firm decision to give this disobedient boy a slap, and is grateful for not having done it, even in a dream, although he knows that if not for the terrible vision of the pool that is exactly what would have happened. Enough. It's not fair to torment yourself about what you dream. He is sure his psychologist would agree with him on that. It's then, thinking about the boy and his genius face, that he hears a sound which seems to be music. It's four in the morning—who puts on music at this time? He pricks up his ears: strictly speaking it's not music, more a drone, a chorus of voices. Not able to help it, the dolls come back to his mind, but he knows that was a dream. This is real: the voices stammer something he doesn't quite catch, in spite of its becoming more intense. He would say it is a sentence, a rhythmic plea in a language he doesn't recognize, and seems to be coming from the walls of his room. Unnerved, he stands up. Another noise has joined the chorus: a sort of whistling, nothing to do with the rest. Putting his bare legs to the floor his glance falls on the half-open suitcase, still abandoned next to the wall. Yes. There's no doubt: the whistling is coming from there. For an instant he thinks of the lost valise, the broken lock, and his eyes open as wide as saucers when he makes out a whistling shadow emerging slowly from it. It's a snake, slippery, repugnant, which drags itself over the floor in his direction. The whistle intensifies, the chorus goes up a scale. And he watches, terrified, how this slithery being inexorably approaches, head upright and tongue flickering in the air, while the voices murmur something that finally he can understand. They say his name, again and again: Héctor, Héctor, Héctor, Héctor . . .

"Héctor!" Joana's voice ended it. "Are you OK? You scared me."

For a moment he didn't know where he was. He didn't recognize the walls, or the sheets, or the light on at an unfamiliar angle. He only noticed the cold sweat soaking his body.

"Fuck," he whispered at last.

"You've had a nightmare."

Two, he thought. In style.

"I'm sorry," he stammered.

"No problem." She caressed his forehead. "You're freezing."

"Sorry." He rubbed his face. "What time is it?"

"Eight. Early for a Saturday."

"Did I wake you up?"

"No." She smiled at him. "I think I'm out of practice at sleeping beside someone. I've been tossing and turning for a while. What the hell were you dreaming?"

He didn't feel like talking about it. In fact, he didn't feel like talking.

"Do you mind if I grab a shower?"

She shook her head.

"I'll be good and make coffee."

Héctor forced himself to smile.

They'd made love with a tenderness uncharacteristic of two strangers. Slowly, carried more by a need for contact, the touch of skin, than by an unbridled passion. And now, as they had breakfast together, Héctor realized that the sex had strengthened bonds of something that resembled camaraderie. They weren't kids, they'd had their share of disappointments and hopes, and they accepted the pleasant moments without projecting hopes or desires onto them. There wasn't the least sensuality in this breakfast together: the light of day had returned to put them back in their places, without any pressure. He was partly grateful and partly saddened by the thought. Maybe that was the best he could hope for now: pleasant, friendly encounters which had a nice aftertaste. As comforting as this hot coffee.

"Is the shirt your size?" asked Joana. "Philippe left it here."

The comment wasn't wholly casual, thought Héctor. He smiled.

"I'll give it back to you," he told her, with a meaningful wink. "Now I must go. I have to see Gina Martí's parents."

She nodded.

"This isn't over, is it?"

Héctor looked at her fondly. Would he could tell her it was. Case closed. But the image of Iris in the pool, heightened by the dream, suggested otherwise.

"There's something I think you should read."

24

That morning, more than ever, Aleix wanted to turn back time. Gina's death had been an unexpected calamity, a harder blow than all the others he'd taken in the last few days, and lying in bed, with no energy to get up, he let his mind roll back toward a recent past that seemed almost remote now. Gina alive, insecure, easy to sway, and at the same time affectionate, fragile. All this was Marc's fault, he thought bitterly, although deep down he knew it wasn't wholly true. Marc, his most faithful follower, the one who'd even taken the blame for something he didn't do just because he'd asked him to, had come back changed from Dublin. No longer a boy he could bend to his will. He had his own ideas—ideas that were becoming an obsession, ideas that could get them all into serious trouble. The end justifies the means, that was his motto. And since he'd learned at a good master's side, he'd devised a plan that bordered on the absurd, and in itself could have unforeseen consequences. Luckily Aleix had managed to thwart it before it went too far, before one thing led to another and the truth came out. Not knowing his true motives, Gina had helped him in it: she'd been reluctant, but in the end she'd given in. Gina . . . They said she'd left a note. He imagined her alone, writing on her computer like a little girl, all full stops, careful grammar and accents, haunted by having betrayed Marc. Worn out by what he'd made her do.

Explosions that sounded like thunder had kept him company all evening. On the eve of San Juan, Barcelona became an explosive city. Dangerous fireworks lurked on every corner as everyone prepared for the all-night party that marked the luminous beginning of summer: sparklers, bonfires and cava toasting the shortest night of the year. Arriving at Marc's house, the first thing that struck him was how pretty Gina looked and he felt a stab of jealousy thinking she hadn't dressed and made herself up like that for him. Anyway, she looked uneasy, uncomfortable in those high heels, that tight black dress. In fact, the outfit clashed with theirs: plain T-shirts with faded jeans and trainers. Gina was playing princess with two scruffy dandies, thought Aleix. Marc was nervous, but that wasn't unusual: he'd been like that for weeks, trying to fake a decisiveness he didn't possess. For Iris. Damn Iris.

He'd arrived calling for beer, trying to give the get-together a party vibe. He'd done a couple of lines before leaving because he sensed he'd need them, and just then he felt euphoric, full of energy, insatiable. Dinner, some pizzas Marc and Gina had seasoned and put in the oven, was ready, and for a while, as they emptied their glasses faster than their plates, it seemed like one of the parties they used to have before. When Marc went down to the kitchen for more beer, Aleix turned up the volume and danced with Gina. Fuck, that night the girl looked good enough to eat. And coke, whatever they say, was a fantastic aphrodisiac. Just ask his friend's mother, he thought, refraining from feeling her up. As he danced with her, he almost forgot about Marc: that was the good thing about coke: it eliminated problems, made them fade away. Made you concentrate solely on what's important: Gina's thighs, her neck. He nibbled it jokingly, like one of those seductive vampires she liked so much would do, but Gina moved away from him a little. Of course, now she was saving herself for Marc. Poor little fool. Hadn't she seen that her beloved Marc was hung up on another girl? He was about to come out with it, but held back: he needed Gina as an ally that night and wasn't planning on saying anything that might turn her against him.

"Have you done what I asked?" he whispered in her ear.

"Yes. But I don't know—"

He put a finger on her lips.

"It's decided, Gi."

Gina exhaled.

"OK."

"Listen, this whole thing is mad." He'd said it a thousand times the afternoon before, and having to do so again was driving him crazy. He mustered all his patience, like a modern father with a stubborn child. "Madness that could have enormous consequences, for you and for Marc above all. Can you imagine what people would think if they found out the truth? How were you going to explain what was on that USB stick?"

She nodded. Actually she was fairly sure Aleix was right. Now they just had to convince Marc.

"And also, what's it for? Are we going to get into trouble to help out this girl from Dublin? Fuck, as soon as her hold on him passes even Marc will be grateful to us." He paused. "He'll be grateful to you. I'm sure of it."

"What will I be grateful for?"

Aleix noticed then that he'd raised his voice. Well, whatever. They had to tell him, and the sooner, the better.

The usual sounds of the house in the mornings didn't change at all on Saturdays. His father had breakfast at half past eight, and his brother had followed this routine since he came home during the summer. Someone knocked at his bedroom door.

"What?"

"Aleix." It was Eduard. He opened the door and stuck his head in. "You should get up. We have to go to the Martís'."

He was tempted to cover his head with the sheet, to hide from it all.

"I'm not going. I can't."

"But Papa—"

"Fuck, Edu! I'm not going! Get it?"

His brother stared at him and nodded.

"Fine. I'll tell Papa that you'll go later."

Aleix turned over in bed and stared at the wall. Papa, Papa. Fuck, his brother would still be taking his father's word as gospel when he was forty. Eduard hovered on the threshold for a few seconds, but seeing that the figure was staying still, he closed the door without making a sound and went. Good. He didn't want to see Edu, or his parents, and definitely not Regina. He preferred to look at that blank wall like a screen where his mind could project other images.

"What will I thank you for?" repeated Marc, this time with a note of suspicion in his voice.

Gina hung her head. A bang from outside startled all three of them. She let out a scream.

"I'm sick of the fireworks!" She went toward the table and poured herself another vodka and orange. It was her third that night. Plastic cup in hand, she watched her friends, who face to face looked like two gunmen poised to fire.

"Marc," said Aleix at last. "Gina and I have been talking."

"What about?"

"You know." Aleix fell silent, then walked over to the table to join Gina. He got there and stood at her side. "We're not going ahead with this."

"What?"

"Think about it, Marc," Aleix went on. "It's too risky. You could get into trouble, you could destroy us all. And you're not even sure if it's going to work."

"It worked before." It was Marc's retort, his constant refrain of recent days.

"Fuck, man, this isn't school! We're not talking about playing a prank on a silly teacher here. Don't you see that?"

Marc didn't move. Between him and the others, the open window showed a bit of sky that from time to time lit up with vividly colored fire.

"No, I don't see that."

Aleix sighed.

"You say that now. In a few days you'll thank us."

"Oh really? I thought it was you who had something to thank me for. You owe me one! And you know it."

"I'm doing you a favor, man. You don't see it, but that's how it is."

For an instant Marc seemed to hesitate. He lowered his head, as if he'd run out of arguments, as if he were tired of fighting. Gina had remained quiet throughout the whole conversation, and she chose that moment to take a step toward Marc.

"Aleix is right. It's not worth—"

"Fuck off!" His answer startled her as much as the firework. "I don't understand why you're so worried. You don't have to do anything else. Give me the USB and I'll take care of everything."

She went back to Aleix. Not knowing what to say, she finished off her drink so greedily she almost choked.

"There's no USB, Marc. It's gone," he said.

Marc looked at Gina, disbelieving. But seeing her hang her head, not denying it, he exploded:

"You're a bastard! A real bastard. I had it all ready!" And he continued in a lower voice, "Don't you know how important this is to me? We're supposed to be friends!"

"And we are, Marc. That's why we're doing it," repeated Aleix.

"Wow, great favor! I could do you one too." Marc's voice sounded different, bitter, as if it were coming from his stomach. "Stop doing this shit that's turning you into an idiot. Or did you think we haven't noticed?"

It took Aleix a few seconds to understand what he was referring to. Long enough for Marc to have a head start in rushing to his backpack.

"What the fuck are you doing?"

"I'm doing it for you, Aleix. It's a favor." He'd taken out the little bags, meticulously prepared in the amounts he usually sold, and he ran toward the door with a triumphant smile.

Aleix leapt after him, but Marc pushed him and ran downstairs toward his bedroom. Gina, astonished, watched as Aleix followed him, grabbed him by the collar of his T-shirt and forced him to turn around. She screamed when the first blow rang out: a slap which Marc took full on the mouth. The two friends were still. Marc noticed that his lip was bleeding, ran his hand over the cut and dried it on the front of his T-shirt.

"Man, I'm sorry. I didn't want to hit you . . . Come on, let's forget this."

The knee in his groin left him breathless. Aleix doubled over and squeezed his eyes shut while a thousand miniature fireworks went off in his head. When he opened them, Marc had disappeared. He could only hear the sound of flushing in the bathroom. An insolent, definitive stream of water.

Asshole, he thought, but when he tried to say it out loud the pain in his crotch became unbearable and he had to lean against the wall so as not to fall to the floor.

He heard the front door and guessed that his parents and brother had already left. Knowing he had the house to himself gave him a momentary sense of relief, which faded little by little when he realized that, of that reunion of three friends who ended up falling out, two were dead. Dead. Aleix hadn't ever thought about death. He'd never had to. Sometimes he remembered the long months of his illness; he tried to recall if, while he was in the hospital bed subjected to the tortures of the men in white, he'd ever been scared of dying, and the answer was no. It was afterward, with the passing of the years, that he became aware that others, affected by the same disease, hadn't managed to survive. And realizing that had made him feel powerful, as if life had put him to the test and he with his strength had managed to overcome. He'd shown he was brave. Edu had said it over and over: you're very brave; just bear it a little longer; it's over now.

He got out of bed, with no desire to shower. His room was a disaster: clothes everywhere, trainers scattered on the floor. Without wanting to, he thought of Gina's room, the rows of teddies on the shelves which she'd resisted discarding and which formed part of the charm of a room that still kept a certain trace of innocence. Gina . . . An alarm bell went off in his head. What shorts was he wearing the last day he saw her? He rummaged around in the three pairs thrown any which way on the chair. He sighed with relief. Yes, the damn USB was there. He connected the USB to the computer out of habit, not because he felt like looking at what it contained. That was for certain. In fact, he wanted to do himself what he'd asked Gina not to do, simply because he didn't trust her in anything to do with Marc: delete it, so those images would disappear without trace forever.

When the screen began to display its contents he was stunned, and that quick irritation toward others, the disappointment that overcame him on realizing, again and again, that he was surrounded by idiots, seized him. He reproached himself for being angry with Gina now the poor thing was gone, but . . . Fuck, she had to be stupid to get the devices mixed up and give him her Art History notes. Annoyance gave way to another even more intense alarm. Damn. The USB was still in Gina's bedroom, within reach of her parents and the police: that stern *sudaca* and the agent who'd be a good lay. It took him five minutes to be dressed and running out for his bike. Well, he thought maliciously, at least his father would be happy.

25

Standing before the stately, black-grilled door that led up to the Martís', Héctor consulted his watch. He had fifteen minutes before meeting Castro, whom he'd called on leaving Joana's house, and he told himself another coffee wouldn't be a bad idea before facing what awaited him upstairs. It seemed he wasn't the only one who thought so, since as soon as he entered the café, out of the corner of his eye he saw Fèlix Castells at the end of the bar, paper open, absorbed in his reading. He was someone he wanted to speak to one to one, so he didn't hesitate for a moment. He went over to him and greeted him, using the ecclesiastical address almost without thinking.

"Call me Fèlix, please," he said, affably. "No one calls us father these days."

"Would you mind if we took a seat at this table?" Héctor indicated one at the back, relatively isolated.

"Of course not. In fact, I'm waiting for my brother and Glòria. Given the situation, we thought it best to arrive all together, and stay only as long as is necessary."

Very considerate, thought Héctor. The Castells, en masse, offering condolences to Salvador and Regina on the death of a daughter who might have killed their son and nephew. Of course, if there was something for which he should be grateful to all those involved, it was that, up to then, they had behaved with the greatest delicacy. Even Salvador Martí's outburst the previous night had sounded more tired than insulting.

Once seated, cups of coffee in front of them—Fèlix had ordered another to join the inspector—Héctor hastened to bring up the subject before the others arrived.

"Does the name Iris mean anything to you?"

"Iris?"

Stalling, thought Héctor. Eyes lowered, spoon stirring the sugar: more stalling. A sigh.

"I suppose you're referring to Iris Alonso."

"I'm referring to the Iris who drowned in the pool during a summer camp years ago."

Fèlix nodded. He drank his coffee. He moved his cup and rested both hands on the table under Héctor's penetrating gaze.

"It's been a long time since I heard that name, Inspector."

It's been a long time since I thought about Iris, remembered Felix.

"What do you want to know? And," he hesitated, "why?"

"I'll tell you in a moment. First tell me what happened."

"What happened? I wish I knew, Inspector." He was recovering, his voice was gaining strength. "As you said, Iris Alonso drowned in the pool of the house for summer camps we rented every summer."

"Was she one of the little girls in your care?" He already knew the answer, but he had to extract more information: he wanted to get to Marc, the six-year-old who saw that macabre image.

"No. Her mother was the cook, a widow. For a little over a month, she would move into the house with us."

"Us?"

"The monitors, the children and me. The kids arrived in groups and stayed for ten days."

"But Marc stayed all summer?"

"Yes. My brother has always worked a lot. Summers were a problem, so yes, I took him with me." He lifted both hands from the table with a slightly impatient gesture. "I still don't see—"

"I'll explain it all to you at the end, I promise you. Please continue."

Héctor told himself that the man before him was more accustomed to listening than to expressing himself. He held the priest's gaze without blinking.

"How exactly did Iris Alonso die?" he insisted.

"She drowned in the pool."

"Yeah. Was she alone? Did she have stomach cramp? Did she hit her head on the side?"

There was a pause. Maybe Fèlix Castells was determined not to be pressured; maybe he was simply organizing his thoughts.

"That was many years ago, Inspector. I don't—"

"Did many little girls drown while they were in your care?"

"No! Of course not!"

"Then permit me to say that I don't understand how you could have forgotten her."

The answer came from his soul, if souls exist.

"I haven't forgotten her, Inspector. I assure you. For months I couldn't think of anything else. It was me who took her out of the water. I tried to give her mouth to mouth, revive her, everything . . . But it was too late."

"What happened?" He changed his tone, perhaps softened by the pain in the face in front of him.

"Iris was a strange little girl." He looked to one side, beyond Héctor, beyond the café, the street, the city. "Or maybe she was at an especially difficult age. I don't know. I've lost the ability to understand young people."

The priest gave a faint smile and continued speaking without Héctor having to pressure him.

"She was twelve, if I'm not mistaken. Full pre-adolescence. That summer her mother didn't know what to do with her. The previous years she'd been a happy little girl, secure; she amused herself with the other kids. She even took care of Marc. But that summer it was all rows and sulky faces. And then there were mealtimes." He sighed. "In the end I had to speak to her mother and ask her to ease up a little."

"Iris didn't eat?"

"According to her mother, no, and it's true she was skin and bone." He remembered her soaked, fragile little body and shuddered. "Two days before her death she disappeared. God, it was awful. We searched for her everywhere, we scoured the wood for a whole night. The townspeople helped us. Believe me, I mobilized everyone to find her safe and sound. Finally we came across her in a cave in the wood we would usually go to on hikes."

"Was she all right?"

"Perfectly. She looked at us so coldly and told us she didn't want to go back. I must own that at that moment I got angry. I got very angry. We took her home. On the way, instead of being more docile and understanding the fright she'd given us, she was still indifferent. Insolent. And I was sick of it, Inspector; I told her to go into her room and not come out; she was being punished. I would have locked her in if there had been a key.

Maybe you think I'm exaggerating, but I assure you that during those hours of searching I prayed without stopping that nothing serious had happened to her." He paused. "She even refused to apologize to her mother. The poor woman was devastated."

"Nobody went in to see her?"

"Her mother tried to talk to her. But they ended up arguing again. That was the evening before she died."

This man's story in essential points coincided with the one on Marc's blog. But the end was missing, and Héctor hoped the priest could shed some light on it.

"What happened?"

Fèlix Castells lowered his eyes. Something that could be doubt, or guilt, or both, took over his appearance for a moment. It was a fleeting expression, but it was there. Héctor hadn't the least doubt of that.

"No one knows exactly what happened, Inspector." He looked him in the eyes again, in an attempt to ooze sincerity. "The following morning, very early, a little boy screaming woke me. It took me a minute to figure out that it was Marc and I went running from my room. Marc was still screaming, from the pool." He paused and swallowed. "I saw her as soon as I got there. I jumped into the water and tried to revive her, but it was too late."

"Was there anyone else at the pool?"

"No. Only my nephew and I. I told him to go away, but he didn't listen. I wanted to save him seeing the little girl's body laid out beside him, so I stayed in the water, with Iris in my arms. I still remember his frightened little face . . ."

"And the dolls."

"How did you know?" The priest stroked his beard. He seemed truly disturbed. "It was . . . sinister. There were half a dozen of them in the water."

Little dead Irises, recalled Héctor. He waited a few seconds before continuing.

"Who put them there?"

"Iris, I suppose . . ." He'd made a great effort to hold back, but the tears glinted in his tired eyes. "That little girl wasn't well, Inspector. I didn't know how to recognize it, despite what her mother said. I realized too late that she was disturbed . . . deeply disturbed."

"Are you telling me that this twelve-year-old girl committed suicide?"

"No!" The negative came out of the priest's rather than the man's mouth. "It must have been an accident. We guessed that she'd gone down to the pool by night, with the dolls, and at some point got dizzy and fell into the water."

"We guessed? Who else was in the house?"

"It was three days before the next group of children was to arrive, so we were alone: Marc, the cook and her daughters, Iris and Inés, and I. The monitors were to turn up that afternoon: some were on a summer-long contract and worked through all the camps, but others rotated all summer. However, even the summer-long ones had gone back to the city for a few days. You can't have young people in the country too long, Inspector. They get bored."

Héctor sensed the priest hadn't finished. That he had something else to tell him now his guard was down. He didn't have to wait long.

"Inspector, Iris's mother is a good woman, who'd already lost her husband. Thinking that her daughter had died of her own volition would have finished her."

"Tell me the truth, Father," said Salgado purposefully. "Forget your collar, your vows, that girl's mother and what she could or couldn't take."

Castells took a deep breath and half-closed his eyes. When he opened them again, he spoke with resolve, in a low voice and almost without stopping.

"The night before, while we scolded her for running away, Iris looked at me very gravely and said to me: 'I didn't ask you to come looking for me.' And when I insisted that we had suffered a lot because of her, that she'd done something very bad, she smiled at me and replied in a scornful voice: 'You can't imagine how bad I can be.'"

From where he was sitting, Héctor could see Leire Castro poking her head around the door of the café.

"Anything else you'd like to tell me, Father?"

"No. I'd just like to know where all this is coming from. Digging up old tragedies can't help anyone."

"Did you know your nephew Marc wrote a blog?"

"No. I don't even know exactly what that is, Inspector."

"A sort of diary. He talked about Iris in it, about the day he found her."

"Hmmm. I thought he'd forgotten about it. After that summer, he never mentioned it again."

"Well, he remembered it while he was in Dublin. And wrote about it."

Leire was still at the café door. Héctor was about to say good-bye when Fèlix said something else: "Inspector . . . if you have any more questions, you can ask Savall."

"Ask Savall?"

"He was an inspector then and stationed in Lleida. It was he who took care of everything."

If the news surprised Salgado, he did everything he could to hide it.

"I'll do that. Now I must go. Thank you for everything."

Fèlix Castells nodded.

"My brother should be about to arrive."

"We'll see each other upstairs then. See you soon."

As he walked toward Leire, he saw that her eyes were fixed on Father Castells. She looked at him distrustfully, harshly, without the least compassion. And Héctor knew she'd also read Marc's blog, and that the same dark thoughts that had seized him were crossing Agent Castro's mind, be they just or unjust.

26

Leire had read Marc's blog that morning, before meeting the inspector and after getting through a fresh bout of morning sickness. Though she didn't know why, Marc's tale had moved her more than she would ever have imagined. She was definitely more sensitive in front of her computer at home, she told herself as soon as she'd finished reading. For once she wished she had someone at her side to share this worry, this feeling that she—both in body and mind—was changing at an alarming rate. The image of that little girl—the same one as in the black-and-white photo—submerged in the water turned her stomach and filled her with a mixture of rage and sadness that lasted long enough to make her wonder if there was any other cause of the intertwined emotions. Of course there was. She was grateful to be obliged to go to work, even though in theory it was her Saturday off. Anything except hanging around waiting for Tomás to call.

She'd seen his note when she arrived home the night before.

"You've been ages . . . some colleagues called and I'm going for a drink with them. See you tomorrow. T." T.? As if that afternoon she'd been fucking a Tomás, a Tristan and a Toby . . . Tomás's way of leaving his stamp on everything he did was beginning to irritate her. And spending half an hour wondering how to break the news to him only to come back to an empty flat irritated her even more. Knowing that wasn't entirely fair didn't help calm her down.

So, at the café door, when the inspector came toward her, leaving Father Castells sitting at the table looking as if he'd seen a ghost, Leire thought exactly as Salgado suspected. That she didn't like stories of little girls and priests at all.

"Let's go," Héctor said to her. "Did you sleep OK? You don't look well."

"It's the heat," she lied. "Shall we go up?"

"Yes."

"Nice shirt," she said as they crossed the street, and was surprised to see him blush a little.

Salvador Martí opened the door to them and for a moment Leire thought he was going to throw them out again. However, he stood to one side and let them in without saying a word. They could hear voices in the lounge, but Gina's father didn't take them there but to the stairs that led to the upper floor, where the bedrooms were. They followed him, and waited while he went to his wife's room and entered after knocking softly at the door. He came out shortly afterward.

"My wife wishes to speak to you, Inspector. Alone."

Héctor nodded.

"Agent Castro will go through Gina's room, in case we missed anything last night."

Salvador Martí shrugged his shoulders.

"You know where it is. If anyone needs me I'll be downstairs." He stopped for a moment on the stairs and turned his head. "People keep calling. Some have already come. Regina doesn't want to see anyone and I don't know what to say to them." He was the epitome of a defeated man, hunched shoulders and a weary expression. He shook his head, almost to himself, and began to descend slowly.

Regina received the inspector dressed in black and sitting in front of the window, next to a little table where a tray with an untouched breakfast lay. The contrast with the dazzling, boisterous, summery Regina of two days before was absolute. She seemed, none the less, possessed of a strange calm. The effect of the tranquilizers, Héctor said to himself.

"Señora Ballester, I am truly sorry to bother you under these circumstances."

She looked at him as if she didn't understand him and pointed to an empty chair, situated on the other side of the table.

"Your husband told me you wished to speak to me."

"Yes. I have something I must tell you." She spoke slowly, as if it were difficult for her to find the words. "They think Gina killed Marc," she said, with a note of questioning in her tone.

"It's very early to say something like that."

Regina moved her head, in a gesture that could express anything. Fatigue, incredulity, acceptance.

"My Gina would never have killed anyone." The phrase was adequate but it was absent of any emotion. "Whatever they say, I know it."

"Who says so?"

"Everyone . . . I'm certain."

"People talk for the sake of talking." Héctor leaned toward her. "I'm interested in what you think."

"My Gina didn't kill anyone," Regina repeated.

"Not even herself?" The question would have been brusque had it been formed in a less friendly tone.

Regina Ballester seemed to ponder her answer seriously.

"I don't know," she said finally. She closed her eyes and Héctor thought that he couldn't continue pressuring her, so he made as if to get up. "Don't go. I have something to tell you. And I must do it here, just the two of us. I don't want to cause him any more pain."

"Who?"

"Salvador," she answered.

And then, with a trembling voice that Héctor remembered Gina using to answer his questions, Regina began to confess, as if he were a priest, everything that had happened between her and Aleix Rovira.

Aleix had arrived a few minutes after Leire and Héctor, and he now found himself in the lounge, under his father's severe gaze. Salvador Martí was sitting on the sofa and silence, scarcely broken by Señora Rovira's whispered questions, reigned over the gathering. There was no sign of Regina, thank God, and Aleix, who didn't know the police were in the house, told himself she must be resting. When the bell rang again, Gina's father's expression was one of such intense irritation that it was Señora Rovira who went to open the door. Her husband took the opportunity to signal to his sons that it was time to go and stood up. Just then Enric Castells and his brother came into the room. Glòria was still at the door, whispering to Señora Rovira. It was clear she was asking about Regina, whom she'd come to see. Aleix said to himself that it was his last chance, and while Enric approached Gina's father and Fèlix greeted his brother Edu, he slipped between his mother and Glòria, murmuring that he had to go to the bathroom.

He went upstairs and walked rapidly toward Gina's bedroom. The door was closed and he opened it without thinking. He came to a standstill with surprise on seeing Agent Castro there.

"I'm sorry," stammered Aleix. "I was looking for the bathroom . . ."

Leire's stare rooted him to the floor.

"Come on, Aleix." Her tone showed that she didn't believe a single word. "You've been here a million times . . . What are you looking for?"

"Nothing." He smiled at her. He assumed his sad smile, the one he saved for his mother, the nurses at the hospital and for any female in general who might have some authority. Cops are women too, aren't they? "Well, I wanted to see Gina's room. Remember her here."

Sure, thought Leire. But since he was there, she had no intention of letting him go without a bit more.

"When did you last see her?"

"The afternoon you came."

"You didn't talk with her again?"

"On Messenger. The same night, I think."

"Did she seem depressed to you? Sad?"

"Of course she was sad. But I never thought it would come to . . . this."

"No?"

"No."

"She was really in love with Marc, wasn't she?"

He looked behind him and closed the door. He sat down on the bed and, involuntarily, his eyes fell on the box of teddies.

"Poor Gina, she kept the stuffed animals in the end."

His smile hadn't fooled Leire, but she told herself Aleix's affectionate expression couldn't be a pose. And if it was, the boy deserved an Oscar.

"Yes," he finally answered. "She was very much in love with Marc. Since forever." His smile was genuine this time.

"But he didn't feel the same?"

Aleix shook his head. She persisted: "He'd met another girl in Dublin, hadn't he?"

"Yes. A Spanish girl studying there. Gina took it very badly."

"Badly enough to push him out of the window?"

He shot her an impatient look.

"Gina was drunk that night, Agent. She'd have fallen herself first . . . It's ridiculous to think so."

The certainty with which he said it disarmed her. It was exactly what Leire thought.

"Then what do you think she was referring to when she wrote this on the computer?" Leire took out her notes and read aloud the last words Gina had left on the screen. She watched Aleix out of the corner of her eye as she read and made out a shadow of guilt in his expression.

"I have no idea," he said. He rose from the bed and came over to her. "Can I see it?"

Leire showed him the transcript. Aleix's expression went from surprise to disbelief, and from there to something like fear.

"She wrote it like this? Just as it is here?" he murmured.

"Yes. I took it down exactly as it was written."

He was about to say something, but stayed silent. And then Dr. Rovira's voice could be heard, calling him from downstairs.

"I must go." He stopped at the door. "Do you still want to see me at the station? On Monday?" There was a challenge in his posture.

"Yes."

"In that case, until Monday."

He went out quickly, and Leire re-read the note, thoughtfully. Something was eluding them, she was sure. And she was dying to see Salgado to compare impressions.

27

After the previous day's rain, the sun was taking revenge, beating down mercilessly on the city since the early morning. Even with the window and balcony open it's too much, thought Carmen, as she wiped the sweat from her forehead with a paper towel. And this from someone who had liked summer since she was a girl, but not this: this fiery sun blazing onto the streets that kept her sweaty and bad-tempered all day long. She poured herself a glass of cold water from the jug and drank it in little sips, carefully, and then turned off the radio that was always in the kitchen. Even music made her feel hot. She should have paid attention to that friendly young man who turned up at her door a few weeks ago to convince her to install air conditioning. Carmen had listened attentively and even arranged another appointment with him, but in the end she hadn't decided. Modern apparatuses worried her, but just then she scolded herself for not having taken his advice.

The cold water calmed her a little and revived her enough to finish preparing the gazpacho. It was all she could have in

summer: a cold glass of gazpacho. When she finished, she put it
in the fridge and tidied the kitchen. That's it, she thought with
a touch of apathy. It's all done. A long, long, muggy day lay before her. She moved to the balcony, but at this hour it was fully
exposed to the sun and she held back from leaning out onto
the street. How this *barrio* had changed . . . For good, she told
herself. She'd never been prone to false nostalgia. No past time
was better, although of course it had indeed been more enter-
taining. That was the worst of old age: these eternal hours not
filled by television or magazines. Before she'd at least had Ruth
and Guillermo upstairs. That child was an angel. Whenever
she thought of him, that little one for whom she'd been a grandmother, Carmen recalled her son. How long had it been since
she'd heard from him? Four years? Five? At least he hadn't
come back asking for money: Héctor had taken care of that.
Héctor . . . Poor Héctor! And it's not that she thought badly of
Ruth, no. Every couple knew what went on inside their marriage and if that girl had left after so many years it was for a
reason. But men didn't know how to be alone. An honest-to-
God truth, the same everywhere. In the twentieth century, and
in the twenty-first. They didn't even feed themselves as they
should.

Then the idea came to her, and although it was something
she wasn't altogether comfortable with, she decided to carry
it out. Surely Héctor wouldn't mind her going into his home?
She went to the kitchen, emptied half of the gazpacho into a
clean jug, grabbed the keys of her neighbor's flat and went to
the door. Seeing the stairs she was tempted to turn back, but
spurred on by goodwill, and partly out of boredom, she em-
barked on her journey with the jug in her hand. This staircase
smelled strange, she told herself as she passed the next landing. Closed up, or rotten. She'd been losing her sense of smell
for years, but something definitely smelled foul nearby. It had

happened before: some little creature crept into the empty apartment and died there. She kept going up, slowly, because she wasn't in a hurry, and arrived at the third-floor door. A second later, feeling a little like a nosy neighbor, she was inside the flat.

The layout was basically identical to that of her own flat, so although the blinds were lowered she moved in the direction of the kitchen without turning on the light. The fridge, empty as a brothel in Lent, received the jug with a purr of satisfaction. Carmen closed it and was already leaving the kitchen when she heard a noise coming from the master bedroom. As if the door had slammed due to the wind. But there was no draught, she told herself. There wasn't the slightest breeze in this flat of closed windows. Out of curiosity, she crossed the dining room and stood in front of the large bedroom. The door was indeed closed. She turned the knob slowly and then pushed the door lightly. It opened wide.

She stumbled over something she couldn't identify, a hard edge. Through the cracks in the blind a little light was coming in, so she pushed the switch to turn on the overhead light, but on touching it her fingers didn't encounter the plastic expected, but a hand leaning on hers. She jumped backward, suddenly aware that someone was there, but at the same time frightened enough that the fear impeded her reactions. She remained still, seeing a dark silhouette emerge from the shadows. She would have screamed, however useless it might have been, if her voice would come out, but her vocal cords were paralyzed. Like her.

A second later Carmen closed her eyes and raised her arm in a childish attempt to protect herself from that black figure brandishing some kind of long stick. The first blow fell on her shoulder and forced her to lower her arm with a groan of pain. The second plunged her into a bottomless abyss.

28

Héctor and Leire had left the Martís' flat and were now facing the intense midday heat punishing the center of Barcelona. There was no shade: it was a clear, stifling day. One of those days in which the city shone with untinted brilliance, like a Technicolor set inhabited almost exclusively by tourists in shorts and caps, armed with digital cameras and street maps. While they walked slowly down Rambla Catalunya, Héctor thought about the last moments in the Vía Augusta flat: the Roviras, including Aleix, had left before them and the Castells delayed very little before doing the same. It was clear no one felt comfortable. Salvador Martí was the only person who appeared not to understand the suspicions underlying every expression of condolence, every "I'm sorry," the apprehension with which Enric Castells gave his hand, the sidelong glances between Glòria and Señora Rovira. Regina, for her part, had refused to come out of her room or receive anyone in it, despite the other two women knocking at her door.

The avenue's terraces invited them to sit down, although

deep inside they both knew air conditioning, at that time, was the only refuge from the heat. However, the street gave them privacy in which to discuss the latest details of the case. Once seated at a table, and with two iced coffees in front of them, Héctor brought Leire up to speed on his conversations with Fèlix Castells and Regina Ballester, although out of caution he kept to himself the fact that Savall's name had come up again. She, for her part, recounted to Salgado her chat with Aleix Rovira and her renewed impression that this boy, like Gina before, was hiding something important from them.

"Notice how every thread in this case comes back to two names?" asked Héctor when she'd finished. "As if we were moving along parallel lines. On one hand Aleix, friend of everyone, Regina's lover, born manipulator; and on the other this Iris . . . even though she's dead."

Leire nodded. Despite the heat, her brain was working at top speed.

"There's something weird. Marc remembered all this while he was in Dublin. Why? And who sent this email to Joana Vidal?"

Héctor was starting to have vague suspicions relating to those questions.

"Iris Alonso had a younger sister. Inés, I think she's called." He let out an exasperated snort. "Tomorrow we'll get rid of doubts. Today we must concentrate on the other lead."

"Aleix." Leire took a few seconds before continuing. "One thing is clear: if Regina was with him yesterday afternoon, according to what she told you herself just now, Aleix couldn't have gone to Gina's house."

The inspector nodded.

"You know what? The worst thing about all this is that I can't imagine anyone in this case as a killer. They're all too educated, too proper, too worried about appearances. If one of them killed Marc and then Gina, it had to have been with a very powerful motive. A very deep hatred or an uncontrollable terror."

"Which brings us back to Iris . . . If she simply drowned in the pool, if her death was an accident, none of this makes sense." Leire remembered Father Castells' face in the café. "But we only have the priest's word on that."

Héctor looked her in the eyes.

"I know what you're thinking, but I think we shouldn't get ahead of ourselves."

"Have you read the rest of the blog, Inspector? In his last entries Marc keeps talking about justice, the end justifying the means, it not being long before the truth comes out."

"And in his last email to his mother he commented that he had to take care of an important matter in Barcelona. Something he had to resolve. Something certainly linked to Iris's death."

"When you spoke of parallel lines, I think you forgot one, Inspector. The exact one which crosses in the middle. The only name that appears in both cases." Leire's voice took on a hard tone, devoid of any sympathy. "Father Fèlix Castells."

No doubt she was right, thought Héctor. And his impression that the priest was hiding something came back even more forcefully.

"If that's what we're dealing with, the matter might take a very ugly turn."

"Think about it. All the details about Iris, the anorexia, the sudden personality change, totally fit the profile of a victim of sexual abuse. Marc was only a child that summer, but maybe in Dublin he began to remember, for whatever reason, and came to the same conclusion as we have now."

Héctor finished the reasoning.

"And returned to Barcelona ready to untangle the truth. But how? Did he openly accuse his uncle?"

"Maybe he did. Maybe he went to see him. Maybe Father Castells got frightened and decided to do away with his nephew."

The argument had an overwhelming logic. But logic, as always, left feelings to one side.

"Let's not forget they loved each other," replied Salgado. "Marc had lived with a distant father—and believe me when I tell you I know what that is—and then found himself in a new family in which he was relegated to second place. His uncle had been a kind of 'substitute mother.' He must have been very sure of what he suspected to dare to betray him. And on the other hand, this man loved his nephew as a son. I'm sure of that. He'd cared for him, raised him . . . You can't kill a son, whatever you do."

"Not even to save yourself?"

"Not even for that."

For an instant they were immersed in their own thoughts. Héctor knew he had to get rid of Agent Castro and speak to Savall. However, Leire's mind was far away from the case just then. Distant father, the love between children and their parents . . . All this was starting to affect her too much and she felt a sudden need to see Tomás.

"Now I need to take care of a few personal matters," said Héctor and she breathed a sigh of relief.

"Perfect. Me too," she murmured, almost to herself.

"There's something I'd like you to do this afternoon." And, lowering his voice a little, Héctor explained his plan.

Sergeant Andreu wasn't enjoying this bright summer Saturday afternoon in the least. In fact, she'd already woken up in bad form after spending half the night going over her meeting with that jumpy woman in the Ciutadella. But her doubts hadn't dissipated, and on waking they assaulted her even more vigorously. In the end she'd argued with her husband, something she detested and which usually didn't occur, and, despite the pouts, she decided she had to resolve these questions as soon as possible. Although she was more fond of Héctor than of any other colleague, or perhaps precisely because of that, she needed to get to the bottom of the matter.

She had only one lead to follow before confronting her friend and asking point-blank if he'd seen Omar the afternoon of his disappearance, as this Rosa was alleging. It was a shot in the dark, but it was worth a try. The damned pig's head had been delivered by a nearby butcher's which usually supplied similar delights to the sinister doctor. Maybe in this case he'd ordered it himself, as usual. Or maybe not . . . And when she pushed the door of the establishment, not far from the doctor's clinic, she hoped with all her heart that on this occasion it had been Omar himself who had placed the repugnant order.

The shop was empty, and Martina wasn't surprised. Saturday noon, too hot to go shopping, and the type of place her mother would judge second-rate without the slightest hesitation. On the other side of the counter a fat guy, equipped with an apron that would never again be white, looked at her with a smile on his lips, a gesture of welcome which faded as soon as she revealed that the reason for her visit wasn't exactly to stock up her fridge with chops.

"They already came to see me about this," replied the shopkeeper, ill-tempered. "What do you want me to say? If they ask me for a pig's head, I sell them one. It's none of my business what they do with it afterward."

"Of course. But you're not asked for them a lot, are you? I mean you wouldn't usually have them in the shop, for sale . . ."

"Not the whole head, of course. Although you know, we make use of the whole pig," the man pointed out proudly.

"Would the doctor order them in person? Or by phone?"

"At first he came in person. Then by phone."

Just then a kid of around fifteen, a scaled-down version of the shopkeeper, came out of the warehouse. "My son took the orders to his house, didn't you, Jordi? We're a small shop, Señora, you have to look after the customers."

And clean the windows, thought Martina.

"Who took the call this time? You or your son?"

"I did," said the kid.

"Do you remember when he called?"

"Two or three days before, I don't know." The boy didn't have the appearance of a genius and he didn't seem very interested in the conversation. However, suddenly he seemed to remember something. "Although this time he didn't call."

"No?" The sergeant tried to disguise the nervousness in her voice. "Who was it?"

The boy shrugged his shoulders. His mouth was half open. Martina was tempted to shake that stupid expression off his face. However, she smiled at him and asked again.

"Was it his assistant?" She didn't know if Omar had an assistant, but it was all she could think of.

"No idea." Jordi made a slight effort to remember, which made his mouth hang open a few millimeters more.

"What did they say? It's important, you know."

"Just that."

Martina bit her lip, but something in her gesture must have inspired the junior butcher to keep talking.

"It was a man. He said he was calling on behalf of Dr. Omar for us to bring a pig's head to his house, last thing Tuesday evening."

"And you did?"

"Of course. I took it myself."

"Did you see Omar?"

The boy shook his head.

"No, the same guy told me the doctor was busy. That he had a visit."

"How do you know it was the same guy?"

Jordi seemed surprised by the question.

"Who else would it be?" He saw that the answer didn't satisfy this demanding woman and he remembered another detail. "Also, they had the same accent."

"What accent?"

"South American. Well, not exactly."

Martina Andreu had to make a superhuman effort not to beat a clear answer out of him.

"Think hard," she persisted in a soft voice. She tried to find a point of reference this kid might understand. "Did he speak like Ronaldinho? Or more like Messi?"

That completely clarified the apprentice butcher's memory. He smiled like a happy child.

"Exactly! Like Messi." He would have shouted "*Visca el Barça*" had Sergeant Andreu's stare not warned him, with no room for doubt, to shut his mouth.

29

A surprised Lluís Savall opened the door of his home, a comfortable flat on Ausiàs March, near Estació del Nord. Receiving inspectors at his home at lunchtime on a Saturday wasn't exactly the superintendent's favorite pastime, but Héctor's tone of voice had awoken not a little curiosity in him. On the other hand, his daughters weren't at home, for a change, and his wife had gone to the beach with a friend and wouldn't be back until the evening. So the superintendent had the flat to himself and had spent part of the morning on his five-thousand-piece jigsaw, which still had over a thousand pieces missing. It was his favorite pastime, as innocuous as it was relaxing, and his wife encouraged it as much as his daughters did, giving him one puzzle after another, the more complicated the better. This one would end up forming an image of the Sagrada Família, but at the moment was as unfinished as the temple itself.

"Do you want a drink? A beer?" asked Savall.

"No, thanks. Lluís, I'm truly sorry to bother you today."

"Well, it's not as if I have much to do," replied the super, thinking wistfully of his puzzle. "But sit down, don't stay standing. I'm going to get a beer for myself. Sure you don't want one?"

"I'm sure."

Héctor sat down in one of the armchairs while he thought of how to bring up the subject. Savall came back immediately, with two cans and a glass each. Opposite him, after finally accepting the damned beer, Salgado said to himself that no one in a position of authority should ever wear shorts.

"What brings you here?" asked the super. "Something new in the case of that girl?"

"Gina Martí?" Héctor shook his head. "No news. At least until we get the forensic report."

"Right. So?"

"I wanted to speak to you today, away from the station." Héctor got annoyed at himself for beating about the bush and decided to take the bull by the horns. "Why didn't you tell me you already knew the Castells?"

The question sounded like an accusation. And Savall's mood changed instantly.

"I told you I was a friend of his mother's."

"Yes. But you didn't mention that you'd been on another case relating to them." He asked himself whether he needed to say the name or if the super already knew to what he was referring. Just in case, he continued: "Years ago a little girl drowned during camp. The camp director, or whatever you call the role, was Fèlix Castells."

Savall could have pretended, made believe that he'd forgotten it, that he hadn't put the two names together, the two deaths separated by almost thirteen years. And perhaps Héctor would have believed him. But his eyes betrayed him, revealing what they both knew: the Iris Alonso case, the girl drowned among dolls, was one of those that persisted in the memory for years.

"I don't remember that little girl's name—"

"Iris."

"Yes. It wasn't a very common name then." The super left his glass on the coffee table. "Do you have a cigarette?"

"Of course. I thought you didn't smoke."

"Only sometimes."

Héctor passed him a cigarette and offered him a light, lit another for himself and waited. The smoke from the two cigarettes formed a little white cloud.

"I'll have to open the window afterward," said Savall. "Or Elena will be telling me off forever."

"What do you remember about that case?" persisted Salgado.

"Not much, Héctor. Not much." His eyes showed that although they were few, the memories weren't at all pleasant. "Where is this coming from? Does it have something to do with what happened to Joana's son?"

"I don't know. Maybe you can tell me."

"I remember him. Marc. He was just a kid and he was badly affected. Shaken."

"He found her, didn't he?"

Savall nodded, not asking how he knew that.

"So they told me." He shook his head. "Children shouldn't see things like that."

"No. They shouldn't drown either."

The super gave Héctor a sidelong glance, and his expression, which a few seconds before had been uncomfortable, even apprehensive, was now one of hard impatience.

"I don't like that tone. Why don't you ask me what you want to know?"

Because I don't really know what to ask, thought Héctor.

"Lluís, we've known each other for years. You're not just my boss, you've treated me like a friend. But right now I have to know if there was something strange about that girl's case. Something that could pose a threat to someone now, almost fifteen years later."

"I don't think I understand you." Lluís put out his cigarette.

"You understand me." He took a deep breath before continuing. "You know perfectly well what I'm talking about. There are details that must have come out in the investigation: Iris wasn't eating, she'd run away from that house two days before, she was behaving badly, and she'd changed greatly in the last year. Her mother couldn't control her. Doesn't all this make you think of something?"

"You're talking about many years ago, Héctor."

"Abuse of minors isn't a new thing, Lluís. It's always been around. And it's been covered up for many years."

"I hope you're not insinuating what I think you are."

"I'm not insinuating anything. I'm just asking."

"There was no proof of that."

"Oh no? His behavior wasn't proof enough? Or is it that you trusted what Father Castells told you? A priest from a good family, why doubt someone like that?"

"That's enough! I won't tolerate you speaking to me like this."

"I'll say it another way, then. Was the death of Iris Alonso an accident?"

"Believe it or not, yes." Savall looked him in the eyes, trying to inject the assertion with all his authority.

Héctor had no choice but to accept it, but he wasn't going to give up easily:

"And the dolls? What were those dolls doing floating in the water?"

"I said enough!" There was a pause, loaded with as many

threats as questions. "If you want to look over the case, you can find the file. There's nothing to hide."

"I'd like to believe you."

Savall looked at him severely.

"I don't have to give you an explanation. That little girl drowned in the pool. It was an accident. It's terrible, but it happens every summer."

"Do you really have nothing else to say?"

Savall shook his head and Héctor rose from the armchair. He was about to say good-bye, but the super spoke first.

"Héctor. You said we're friends. As such, can I ask you to accept my word on this case? I could order you to leave it alone, but I prefer to trust in your friendship. I've shown my affection for you. Perhaps it's time you do the same."

"Are you asking me for a favor? If you are just say so. Say it, and then I'll know what I should do."

Savall kept his eyes on the floor.

"Justice is a two-way mirror." He raised his head slowly and kept speaking. "On one side it reflects the dead and on the other the living. Which of the two seems more important to you?"

Héctor shook his head. Standing there, facing his superior, he looked at this man who had helped him at times of need, and searched within himself for the gratitude he owed him, the trust he'd always inspired in him.

"Justice is a vague concept, Lluís, we agree on that. I prefer to talk of truth because of that. There's only one truth, for the living and the dead. And that's all I came looking for, but I see I'm not going to get it."

Standing in front of the lift, Héctor realized he'd left that house with a bad taste in his mouth and he seriously considered knocking on the door, entering and starting the conversation all over again. His hand was on the doorbell when his mobile rang and his priorities changed immediately. It was Martina Andreu and she was ringing to inform him that his landlady, Carmen, had been assaulted in her home. The lift had come, but he hadn't waited for it: he ran downstairs and took a taxi to Hospital del Mar.

30

If the way to a man's heart is through his stomach, it was clear that the four ready-made dishes Leire had bought from a deli weren't going to make Tomás fall at her feet in devotion. While she watched him chew the reheated croquettes half-heartedly, Leire almost took pity on him. He'd answered the phone with a deep voice that indicated that the drinks with colleagues had lasted until the early hours, and he'd reluctantly agreed to come to her house to eat. Now he was forcing himself to appear awake and hungry, not realizing that the dessert awaiting him was going to be more difficult to swallow than anything that had gone before.

"How was last night?" asked Tomás, while he wavered between taking another croquette or an *empanadilla* glistening with oil. He opted to drink some water.

"Rather hard. A dead girl. In the bathtub of her house."

"Suicide?"

"We don't know yet," she said in a tone that hoped to close

the subject. "Listen, I'm sorry to have woken you before . . . but we have to talk."

"OK, this sounds ominous." He smiled at her. He moved the plate off the table with a face of disgust. "I'm not very hungry."

She was, but it didn't matter. She wouldn't be able to swallow a bite until she had got the weight oppressing her off her chest. For the last time she recalled María's advice. What would she gain by telling him? She could end it with him, here and now, tell him she'd met someone else, and this guy would happily get on with his life, not knowing that she was carrying his child. He'd find someone to take on a cruise and he'd soon forget those half-dozen wild fucks. Maybe he'd call her again someday, but she wouldn't answer. She let out a sigh. Why the hell did she need to be so honest? She'd never been able to lie, not to herself, nor anyone. Lies came to her, but when the moment to speak them arrived, something inside her turned them back into the truth.

And after all, she told herself, she wasn't asking anything of him: no money or responsibility. The baby had been created by both of them, but it was she, and only she, who had decided that the pregnancy should continue. He could leave and never come looking for her again. That idea, the feasibility that this might happen, pained her a little more than she was willing to admit. Then she realized he was saying something to her, and she came back to reality.

". . . let's drop it. I know you hate commitment, you made that very clear. But I thought it would be fun."

"What?"

"The boat thing." He looked at her strangely and smiled. "I thought I was the one who was hungover!"

"Of course it would be fun."

He spread his arms in a gesture of surrender.

"There's no understanding you. I thought that the idea of spending ten days with me was too much for you. That you felt pressured or something."

"I'm pregnant."

It took him a few seconds to process the information. And a few more seconds to work out that if she was telling him this, it was probably because he had something to do with it.

"Preg . . . nant?"

"I have to go to the doctor on Monday, but I'm sure, Tomás."

"And . . . ?" He took a deep breath before asking. She saved him the effort.

"It's yours. I'm sure of that too." She hushed him with her hand. "Stay calm. Take your time. You don't have to say anything just now."

Of course he seemed at a loss for words. He cleared his throat. He shifted in his seat. She couldn't say what his face showed: surprise, perplexity, distrust?

"Listen to me," Leire went on. "I'm telling you because I think you have a right to know. But if you get up from your chair and leave right now, I'll understand completely. It's not like we have to be together or anything like that. I won't feel disappointed, or cheated, or—"

"Fuck." He leaned back against the chair and looked at her as if he couldn't believe it. "I couldn't get up even if I wanted to."

She couldn't help smiling.

"I'm sorry," she whispered. "I know it's not what you were expecting to hear."

"Definitely not. But thanks for telling me." He was beginning to react. He spoke slowly. "Are you sure?"

"That it's yours?"

"That you're pregnant! If you haven't seen the doctor yet—"

"Tomás."

"OK. And what are you intending to do?"

"You mean am I going to have it?" It was the logical question. "Yes."

"Yeah." He nodded slowly. "So you're just telling me, aren't you?"

Leire was going to contradict him, but realized that, in the end, he was right.

"Yes."

"And the alternatives you leave me with are . . . ?"

"Well, you can go out to buy cigarettes and never come back," she said. "Or stay and be a father to the baby."

"I think the cigarettes option is outdated."

"Classics never go out of fashion."

He smiled, despite himself.

"You're unbelievable!"

"Tomás." She looked at him gravely, and tried to make what she was going to say reflect exactly what she wanted to say, not sound like a threat, coercion or self-sufficiency. "The truth is I like you. I like you a lot. But we're not in a relationship, we're not a couple, or anything like it. I don't know if I'm in love with you, and I don't think you're in love with me. Not that I really know what being in love is, if I'm honest . . . But if I weren't pregnant, I would go on a cruise with you and see what happened. Given the circumstances," she continued, pointing to her belly, "everything has changed."

He nodded, and inhaled deeply. It was clear that a great many ideas, questions and possibilities were thronging in his mind.

"Don't be angry," he finally replied. "But I need time to get used to the idea."

"You're not the only one. We have approximately seven months for that."

He stood up and she knew he was leaving.

"I'll call you," he said.

"Of course." She wasn't looking at him. Her eyes were on the table.

"Hey . . ." He came over to her and stroked her cheek. "I'm not running away. I'm just asking for some time out."

She turned to him, and couldn't help the irony in her voice.

"Are you out of cigarettes?"

Tomás took a packet out of his shirt pocket.

"No."

Leire said nothing. She felt the hand move away from her cheek and Tomás taking a step back. She closed her eyes and the next thing she heard was the front door. When she opened them he was gone.

31

Hospital del Mar's brand-new waiting room was as full as might be expected on a July Saturday, and it took Héctor a moment to locate Sergeant Andreu. In fact, she saw him first and made her way toward him. She put a hand on his shoulder and Héctor turned, startled.

"Martina! What happened?"

"I don't know. It appears someone broke into her house and attacked her. It's serious, Héctor. They've taken her to the ICU. She hasn't regained consciousness."

"Shit." His expression was so intense the sergeant feared he might lose control. "Héctor, let's go out for a minute. Right now, we can't do anything here and . . . I have to talk to you."

She thought he'd refuse, demand to speak to the doctor, but what he did was ask the inevitable question she'd expected.

"How come you found her?"

The sergeant looked at him intently, trying to discern in that altered expression a sign that might let her decide, know. She didn't find it, so she merely answered in a low voice, "That's what I want to talk to you about. Let's go outside."

The sun was making the mirrors of the cars sparkle. It was half past three in the afternoon and the thermometer was hitting thirty degrees centigrade. Sweaty, Héctor lit a cigarette and smoked hungrily, but he felt sick and the nicotine tasted foul. He threw the remains of the fag on the ground and stubbed it out.

"Calm down a little, Héctor. Please."

He put his head back and breathed deeply.

"How did you find her?"

"Wait a minute. There're a couple of things you should know. There's news in the Omar case." She was hoping to see some reaction in her colleague's face, but all she could make out was interest, a desire to know. "Héctor, I asked you this Wednesday when we had lunch, but just so we're clear. Did you see Omar on Tuesday?"

"Where is this going?"

"Fuck, just answer! Do you think I'd insist if it wasn't important?"

He looked at her with a mixture of frustration and rage.

"I'll say this for the last time. I didn't see Omar on Tuesday. I didn't see him again after that day. Got that?"

"What did you do on Tuesday evening?"

"Nothing. I went home."

"You didn't speak to your ex or your son?"

Héctor looked away.

"What the fuck did you do?"

"I sat down to wait for someone to remember to call me. It was my birthday."

Martina couldn't suppress a guffaw.

"Fuck, Héctor! Hard man of the month, going around whacking suspects, and then sitting down at home to cry that nobody remembers him . . ."

Despite himself, he smiled.

"Well, getting older makes you sensitive."

"The worst thing is, I believe you, but a witness saw you outside his house on Tuesday evening, around half past eight."

"What are you saying?" he almost shouted.

"Héctor, I'm just telling you what I've found out. I don't even have to, so do me a favor and don't raise your voice." She went on to tell him Rosa's testimony, not omitting a single detail, as well as the information obtained at midday in the butcher's. "That's why I went to your house. The front door was open and I went up. When I passed the first floor I noticed that the door there wasn't closed either and it seemed strange. I pushed it and . . . I found that poor woman unconscious on the floor."

Salgado heard his colleague's story without interrupting her once. While he was listening to her, his brain tried to fit the other pieces into it: those disturbing recordings of him beating Omar and of Ruth on the beach. He didn't manage to do it, but he thought Andreu deserved to know. He didn't want to hide anything else from her, so he told her everything as soon as she'd finished. Then they both stayed quiet, thinking, each absorbed in their own doubts and fears. Héctor reacted first and took out his mobile. Nervously, he looked for his son's number in his contacts and hit the call button. Luckily, Guill-ermo answered immediately this time. Salgado spoke to him for a couple of minutes, trying to seem normal. Then, without thinking, he called Ruth. The only reply was a cold voice announcing that the phone was turned off or out of signal.

Meanwhile Martina Andreu was watching him attentively. He was aware of it, but told himself she was within her rights. There were reasons for her suspicions, and suddenly he realized—the irony of fate—that he would have to put forward the same argument he'd heard from Savall an hour before. Appeal to her friendship, trust, the years of working together.

"Ruth not answering?" she asked when he put away his mobile.

"No. She's away. At her parents' apartment in Sitges. I'll call her again later. She didn't find the thing with the DVD very amusing, as you can imagine." He turned to Sergeant Andreu. "I'm scared, Martina. I feel like my whole world is under threat: me, my house, my family . . . And now Carmen. It can't be a coincidence. Someone is destroying my life."

"You're not taking Dr. Omar's curses seriously, are you?"

He stifled a bitter laugh.

"Right now I could believe anything." He remembered what the faculty professor had said to him. "But I suppose I must force myself not to fall into that. I'm going to see if there's any news about Carmen. You needn't stay."

She looked at her watch. Ten past four.

"Sure you don't mind?"

"Of course not. Martina, do you believe me? I know all this seems very strange and all I can ask of you right now is blind trust. But it's important to me. I didn't go to see Omar, I didn't order a pig's head and I have no clue to his whereabouts. I promise you."

She took a little while to answer, perhaps more than he hoped and less than she might have needed to give a completely honest answer.

"I believe you. But you're in a real mess, Salgado. That I will say. And I don't know if anyone can help you out of it this time."

"Thanks." Héctor relaxed his shoulders and looked toward the door of the hospital. "I'm going inside."

"Keep me posted on any news."

"Likewise."

Martina Andreu stayed still a moment, watching Héctor disappear through the entrance to the hospital. Then, slowly, she went to the taxi rank, got into the first cab and gave the driver Salgado's address.

Sitting on a plastic chair in a corridor near the ICU, Héctor watched the comings and goings of the staff and visitors. At first, he looked at them, but as time passed he half-closed his eyes and focused on their footsteps: fast, slow, firm, anxious. And little by little even that faded from his consciousness, immersed in the memories of what had happened to him over the last five days. The flight, the lost suitcase, the meeting with Savall and the visit to Omar's clinic were mixed up with the statements of the suspects in the Marc Castells case, the image of Gina bleeding to death in the bath and that macabre vision of the drowned girl in the pool in a film as surreal as it was shocking. He didn't make the least attempt to put the sequences in order: he let them flow freely in his mind, battle each other to impose themselves on the screen of his memory for a few seconds. Little by little, like the noise surrounding him, these stills began to fade. The chattering calmed, and his brain focused on one particular blurry and poor-quality image, starring him, a violent and brutal Héctor Salgado, beating a defenseless guy with rage. An off-camera voice was added to the image, that of the psychologist, the kid who deep down reminded him of his son. "Think of other moments when you've been carried away by rage." Something he'd refused to do, not just in the past few days but always. But now, waiting for the doctor to give him news of Carmen, that woman who'd treated him almost as a son, he was able to break down the barriers and think of the other moment in his life when rage possessed him: that other day in which everything turned black and all that remained was a bitter taste like bile. His last memory of the first part of his life, the violent end of a phase. Nineteen years putting up with routine beatings at the hands of a "model" father, outwardly a perfect gentleman, every inch an asshole who never hesitated to impose discipline. Why he was normally the target of his rages and not his brother was something the young Héctor had asked himself many times in those nineteen years. That didn't mean his brother escaped, or anything like it, but as he grew up Héctor noticed a deeper cruelty in the beatings that fell to him. Maybe because his father knew by then that he hated him with all his heart. What he never suspected, not even in the bitterest moments of his childhood, was that there was another victim of these blows, someone who received them behind closed doors, in the intimacy of a bedroom conveniently situated at the other end of a long corridor. How his mother had managed to hide the bruises all those years could be explained only in the context of a home where secrets were the rule and the best thing to do was say little and keep quiet a lot.

He discovered it by accident, one Friday afternoon when he returned early from hockey training because he'd twisted his ankle. He thought no one would be home, since his brother also had training that day, and his mother had said she and his father would be visiting one of his aunts, who was old and unwell. Because of that, he arrived at what he thought was an empty flat, ready to enjoy the solitude that all teenagers long for. He made no noise—that was one of his father's rules—and that let him hear, with absolute clarity, the rhythmic blows followed by muffled screams. And then something exploded in his brain. Everything around him disappeared except the door in front of him, which he pushed decisively, and his father's face, going from surprise to panic when his younger son without a second's hesitation swung the stick into his chest and kept hitting him on the back, again and again, until his mother's screams brought him back to himself. The following day, still recovering from the beating, his father arranged for this outcast son to continue his schooling in Barcelona, a city in which he had relatives. Héctor understood that this was the best solution: starting again, not looking back. The only thing that he regretted was abandoning his mother, but she convinced him that there was no danger, that what had happened that day was in no way a regular occurrence. He left and forced himself to forget; but this afternoon, sitting on a plastic chair while the memory unfolded clearly in his mind, the anguish vanished to be replaced by a strange feeling of peace, bittersweet but true, that he hadn't felt since then. And he told himself, calmly, that if injustice and helplessness were the only things that had triggered his rage, in his youth just the same as a few months ago, he didn't give a damn about the consequences. Let the world say what it will.

He didn't know how much time had passed, but he noticed a hand jogging his shoulder. Opening his eyes, he saw a figure in white who told him, with an expression designed for giving bad news, that Carmen Reyes González was out of danger, although they were keeping her under observation for at least another twenty-four hours and, of course, it would take a while for her to recover completely. He added, in a routine voice that sounded to Héctor like malicious admonition, that while there didn't seem to be serious lesions apart from the contusion, they couldn't rule out complications in the next few hours, due to the patient's age. He could go in to see her, but only for a moment.

And before allowing him in, the doctor with the undertaker's face commented, in an admiring tone that was hardly professional, that the tenacity with which the older generation clung to life never ceased to amaze him. "They're cut from a different cloth," he said, shaking his head as if, in view of what the world was, this was incomprehensible.

32

Leire looked at her watch and couldn't help an irritated gesture. Why did all men disappear when you needed them? I'm starting to talk like María, she thought. But what was certain was that, despite Tomás's hardly dignified exit, he wasn't the target of her criticisms at that moment. The inspector had said he would call her mid-afternoon to finalize details. Well, fine; even though "mid-afternoon" wasn't a precise term, she thought that at least he might have bothered to show signs of life. She resisted calling him; after all, Salgado was her superior and the last thing she wanted to do was fall out with a boss.

In any case, she had done her duties that afternoon, she told herself, satisfied. In order, she'd cleared the table and thrown out the croquettes; cried for a while—something she put down to this state of sensitive foolishness and not to anything else; and then, after showering and dressing informally, as she had agreed with the inspector, she'd gone to the station to carry out the first part of her orders. Task number one was done in a moment: one Inés Alonso Valls was flying from Dublin to Barcelona the following day on a flight that was arriving at 09.25 a.m., local time. She'd run her details without finding anything that seemed important. The girl was twenty-one, she had spent a year studying in Ireland and was the daughter of Matías Alonso and Isabel Valls. Her father had died eighteen years previously, when Inés was very small, but her mother was still alive. Leire had noted the address, just as Salgado had said. As for task number two . . . Leire looked at her watch again, as if her eyes could speed it up. She wanted to make this call, but it was early.

There was little movement in the station that Saturday, so she didn't have anything to distract her and it left her time free to think. Inevitably her mind went back to Tomás and the conversation with him that afternoon, but also, and for the first time, she realized he wasn't the only person to whom she should communicate the news: there were her parents, of course, and, all going well, sooner or later her bosses too. After the summer, she said to herself. First she had to get used to the idea herself and she didn't feel like listening to reproaches or advice. Also, she'd heard thousands of times that it was best to wait until after three months had passed before announcing it. And for the first time she began to think of that being, who up until now had just brought on morning sickness, as someone who in less than a year would be lying beside her in a hospital bed. She saw herself alone with a crying baby and the image, although fleeting, was more terrifying than comforting. She didn't want to keep going over it, so, in view of the fact that the inspector still hadn't called, she picked up the landline and dialled her friend María's number. Right now Santi and the villagers of Africa seemed a fascinating topic of conversation.

By one of life's coincidences, Leire wasn't the only one thinking of Africa that afternoon. And not just because the heat be-
sieging Barcelona that day was closer to that continent than to
moderate Europe, even in its south.

The sun was still punishing when the taxi left Martina Andreu at the door of the block of flats where Héctor Salgado
lived. A pair of agents were guarding the door on the first
floor, anxious to leave: there was nothing else to do there and
they were happy to go. When they emerged, one of them commented that the stairwell smelled awful, and she merely nodded. She'd noticed it before, although perhaps not so strongly,
but she didn't want to keep them, nor did they want to stay.
The sergeant wanted to be alone, without witnesses in uni-
form, to explore on her own. Something told her the assault on
Carmen wasn't a random incident. Héctor was right: too many
things were happening around him, none of them good. On
the other hand, the statements of the witnesses—Rosa and the
butcher—were still fresh in her mind. Héctor could ask blind
faith of her and she gave it, as a friend. But the part of her that
was a cop demanded proof. Tangible proof that might counter
the effect of these testimonies, which in all honesty she had no
reason to doubt.

Once alone, she closed the door of Carmen's flat and took a
quick look around. She'd found her in the short passage separating the hall from the kitchen. The attack had been face-
on, so it stood to reason that the poor woman had opened the
door to a stranger who had attacked her after entering. But for
what? They hadn't searched the house—nothing seemed to be
missing; there were no drawers on the floor or open cupboards.

Maybe the guy had got scared after the assault and opted to get out of there? No, she didn't like that explanation at all. Carmen had been hit twice with a metallic object. There was no trace of the weapon in the flat. Fuck, there was no trace of anything in this flat, cursed the sergeant. She looked toward the cupboard that hid the electricity meter. If she wasn't mistaken, there were the keys to Héctor Salgado's flat. Someone else might have felt a pang of conscience, but not her. It was what she had to do.

Keys in hand, she went up the stairs. The foul smell became more intense for a moment, then faded. Martina was in a hurry to search the inspector's flat before he decided to return. The qualms hit her when chance awarded her first prize and the key chosen turned in the lock, but she rejected them without banishing them completely, as if putting them in a recycling bin. Once inside, however, she considered what she was doing there and what she hoped to find. The blinds were lowered and she switched on the light. She scanned the flat. Nothing seemed out of place. She went to the kitchen and opened the fridge, where she just saw some beers and a jug of what looked like gazpacho. She couldn't imagine Héctor making it, in all honesty, and it seemed homemade. From the kitchen she returned to the dining room and from there she walked to the bedroom. Unmade bed, suitcase open in a corner . . . The typical state of a single man's room. Or a separated one.

She was about to leave, feeling like a hypocritical intruder, but, crossing the dining room again she made out a flicker on the television. Héctor had left it on. No—it wasn't the television. It was the DVD screensaver that was moving. If Salgado hadn't mentioned the recordings to her, it would never have occurred to her to press the play button.

When the first few images hit the screen, she was overcome

by an instinctive, visceral repulsion and a suspicion that now there was no going back. Despite herself, she had to watch the recording twice more to take it all in. Luckily it wasn't very long, lasting only a few minutes, but within that time one could clearly see the bruised face of an old black man bleeding profusely, on the verge of slipping into unconsciousness. His parched lips could barely emit a slight moan and his eyes didn't succeed in focusing on whoever was being forced to record his agony. On the blurry screen, Dr. Omar tried to open his eyes for the last time, but the effort was too much for his battered body. Martina Andreu heard his last breath clearly and witnessed death overcoming his face. The recording ended there, giving way to a dark gray cloud. And then, with the coldness that comes with years of service, the sergeant knew what the next step was. The separate pieces came together to form an unpleasant but logical whole. The witness statements, Omar's disappearance, that horrendous film—and yes, the stench on the stairwell—fell magically into place and showed her the road to follow.

Taking the next step, however, wasn't easy. She had to call it in, but first she wanted to be sure. It took her an eternity to leave Héctor's flat. She descended a flight of stairs to the second floor, walking with the rigidity of an automaton. Carmen's keyring had all the keys and she had to try a couple before finding the right one. The stench hit her full-blast on simply pushing the door open. She felt her way forward, as the flat wasn't connected to the electricity mains. She followed her nose until she came to a small room in which she thought she could make out a little window. When she raised the blind, light invaded the space. Although she knew what she'd come looking for, the sight of Omar's body made her jump backward. And she ran, ran to the front door, went through it and leaned against the

door frame, eyes squeezed shut, blocking the space as if someone were pursuing her. As if the soul of that dead body could
abandon its casing of flesh and seek to possess her. Seconds,
maybe minutes had to pass before she was calm, before she
was sure he was inside and couldn't hurt her. Finally she managed to open her eyes, and she suppressed a scream of surprise
and fear on seeing before her, with a serious expression, the
friend she now feared with all her heart.

There's nothing less bearable than waiting for a phone call
with nothing to do. Agent Castro had many virtues, but patience wasn't one of them. So, after forty minutes of chatting
to María, during which she never stopped checking her mobile,
she reluctantly decided to take the initiative and contact Inspector Salgado. The only response was his voicemail, offering
as usual the opportunity to leave a message after the tone. She
hesitated before doing so, but finally opted to cover her back
and inform him of her plans.

"Inspector, Castro here. I've been waiting for your call and
it's after seven. With your permission, I'm going ahead on
the Rubén Ramos thing. If you have anything to say to me,
call me."

She didn't know if that was what Salgado would want, but
that day Leire Castro wasn't inclined to take the feelings of
the other sex into consideration. Because of that, and although
she knew she was taking a risk, she looked in her notes for
Rubén's number and dialed. A young voice answered with an
insecure "Yes?" She took on a similar, slightly nervous tone as
she explained to her listener that Aleix had given her his number, tonight was her birthday and she wanted to celebrate in
style with her boyfriend. Yes, one would do, she assured him,
trying to sound like the silly girl from a good family who could

be a customer of Aleix's. They agreed a time and place for the meeting without saying anything else, and she signed off with a quick "See you later."

When she hung up, Leire asked herself if what she'd just done would make things awkward with the inspector, and, just in case, she rang him again. Sick of the neverending voice, she hung up without leaving a message.

33

Martina didn't move even a millimeter from the door. She looked intently at Salgado, trying to read her colleague's mind through his eyes. She didn't succeed, but this gaze did at least manage to alleviate the panic that had overwhelmed her minutes before.

"Don't come any closer, Héctor," she warned him, in a firm, neutral voice. "This is a crime scene. You can't go in."

He obediently took a step back on the landing. With the door open, the stench from inside the flat was spilling out onto the landing, completely undiluted.

"What did you find in there?"

"You don't know?"

"No."

"Omar's in there, Héctor. Dead. Beaten to death."

Héctor Salgado had learned to keep calm in tense situations, to control his emotions so they didn't surface on his face. They remained face to face for a few seconds, like two expectant duelists, while she tried to work out what she should do next.

She had a murder suspect before her: someone who'd been seen with the victim the afternoon he disappeared, someone who had a score to settle with the dead man lying inside, in whose home there was evidence linking him to the case. And above all, someone who lived in the flat above the place she'd just found the body. She knew there was only one option. If he were in her place, Salgado would do exactly the same.

"Héctor, I have to arrest you on suspicion of the murder of Dr. Omar. Don't make it any more difficult for me, please."

"Are you going to cuff me?"

"I hope I won't need to."

"Does it make any difference if I tell you I had nothing to do with it?"

"At this moment in time, no."

"Yeah." He hung his head, like someone accepting the inevitable. The gesture made the sergeant take a step toward him.

"I'm sure it will all be cleared up, but right now it's best for you to come with me. For your own good."

He nodded slowly; then he lifted his head and the sergeant was shocked to see a smile on his face.

"You know what? The only thing I care about right now is that Carmen is going to be all right. That old lady is tougher than you and I put together!"

"You're very fond of her, aren't you?"

Héctor didn't answer. There was no need. And that peaceful expression, more grateful than afraid, made the two Martinas struggling within the sergeant suddenly establish a truce, a nonaggression pact.

"Héctor, I'm the only one who has seen the body." She silenced the start of a protest. "Shut up and listen for once in your life! Nothing can be done for Omar, so it's all the same if I find him today or tomorrow."

"What do you mean by that?"

"That I can take a few hours to investigate this case without any pressure. Not even from you."

He still didn't fully understand.

"Give me the keys to your house and get out of here. Disappear for a few hours until I call you. And promise me two things: first, that you won't come near here or Omar's flat under any circumstances."

"And second?"

"Second, you turn up at the station as soon as I ask you to. No questions."

Very slowly, he took the keys from his pocket and passed them to the sergeant. She snatched them roughly.

"Now get out of here."

"Are you sure about this?" asked Héctor.

"No. But I am sure that as soon as I call in the discovery of the body the entire investigation will center on you, Inspector Salgado. And no one, not me, not anyone, will be able to prevent it."

He began to go down the stairs, but turned around mid-flight.

"Martina . . . Thanks."

"I hope I won't live to regret it."

Héctor went out into the street and began to walk toward the seafront where he usually went running. He walked slowly, not looking at anyone, carried by inertia. A while later, sitting in front of the twinkling Agbar Tower, that blue-and-red monolith that seemed to have been plucked from a Tokyo street, he realized he had nowhere to go. He felt like an accidental tourist, a poor Buenos Aires imitation of Bill Murray who didn't even have the excuse of being "Lost in Translation." No, he was alone in the city where he'd lived for nearly twenty years. He took out his mobile, an act as instinctive as it was useless:

What the fuck was the point of it if he had no one to call? To make him even more fucked, he thought, smiling bitterly. He was checking his missed calls when it rang again, curbing that incipient melancholy for an instant. It wasn't Scarlett Johansson, of course, but an excited and satisfied Leire Castro.

Hours before, Leire had parked the car she'd borrowed from the station on the kerb in an unloading bay, ten minutes before the time fixed for the meeting with Rubén. It was one of the unofficial cars, of course, those the *Mossos* used for trips when they didn't want to attract attention. Nervous, she waited to see the boy in the photo appear, and once more she told herself she'd have been much more calm if someone, Salgado for example, had been ready as they'd planned, ready to intervene if things got ugly. She exhaled slowly: it was no big deal. She was only going to arrest a small-time dealer, to ensure his cooperation in putting pressure on the Rovira brat. And she could do that alone, fuck it.

She saw him arrive, on foot, his hands in his pockets and with the slick air of a third-rate delinquent. She was a little calmer. Leire considered herself a good judge of faces and this kid, barely twenty years old, didn't seem particularly dangerous. She didn't want to have to use her weapon, even to threaten him. He stood at the corner of Diputació and Balmes, and took a quick look around him. She flashed her lights, as if she were waiting for him. Rubén approached the car and, obeying the driver's gesture to get in, he opened the door and sat in the passenger's seat.

"I wasn't sure if it was you," she murmured in an apologetic tone.

"Yeah. Got the dough?"

She nodded and, while she pretended to search in her bag,

she activated the car's central locking. The kid gave a start which became a sigh of annoyance when Leire showed him her badge.

"Shit. I fucked up."

"Only a tiny bit. Nothing serious." She paused briefly, then started the car without taking her eyes off her new companion. "Calm down, kid. And put on your seatbelt. We're going to go for a spin and chat for a while."

He obeyed with a bad grace and hissed something between his teeth.

"Something you want to say?"

"I said chatting takes two . . ."

She laughed briefly.

"Well then, I talk and you listen. And if at the end you think it suits you to tell me anything, you do."

"And if not?"

She put the car in reverse and moved off.

"If not, I'll start up the monologue again to see if I can convince you. We girls are very tiresome, you know that. We like to hear ourselves talk."

Rubén nodded and looked away indifferently toward the window. She'd already joined the sliproad, relatively empty of cars this July Saturday.

"I want to talk to you about a friend of yours, pretty posh of course. You know who I'm referring to, don't you?"

Since there was no reaction from her companion, Leire continued her monologue without pausing, certain that he was listening to her attentively even though he pretended otherwise. When she mentioned the word "killer" he was tempted to turn toward her but resisted the impulse. However, as soon as she brought up Aleix's family's money, their contacts and the good lawyers they could hire to get their prodigal son out of this predicament—money, contacts and lawyers that he, a poor local fall guy, could only imagine—his survival instinct outweighed any other and Rubén told her what he knew and thought he'd seen on the eve of San Juan.

After making him promise to turn up at the station on Monday at the time she said, Leire let him go. She was sure the boy would keep his end of the deal. Then, for the third time that day, she grabbed her mobile and called Inspector Salgado.

34

When the old clock in her grandmother's flat struck nine with
the spirit of a chamber quartet, Joana realized she had been
in front of the computer for hours, immersed in Marc's texts
and photos. She'd read them again and again, she'd looked at
the photos, she'd seen him alive, drunk, smiling, playing the
fool, serious, or simply caught by surprise with an absurd expression. He was a stranger to her, and yet in some spontane-
ous gestures she clearly saw young Enric, he who cared about
nothing and lived to party, he who rejected his family's ideals
of effort and work. He who had won her over. And she understood with a mixture of relief and disappointment that the boy
in the photos had maybe missed a mother figure when he was a
child, but never her. Not Joana, with her faults, obsessions and
virtues. In these photos, this boy was happy. Unconsciously
happy. Happy as you can only be at nineteen, away from home
and with the future stretching before your eyes as an unending succession of exciting moments. Maybe she was partly to

blame for all that had happened to him, even the cursed chain of events that ended up throwing him out the window, but no more than Enric, no more than Fèlix, no more than these friends she didn't know, no more than this Iris. Everyone had played their part, more or less honorable, more or less dignified. Thinking that she, a stranger after all, could claim a prominent role in Marc's death was a sign of arrogance.

Night was falling, and she had to light the small table lamp, which blinked a couple of times, then went out completely. With a gesture of annoyance she rose to turn on the overhead light. It was a weak light which created a yellow, sad glow. Suddenly, she saw herself standing in that solitary, inherited flat, immersing herself in a past that she had left behind years before. She'd given up a lot then, but she'd managed to create a new life for herself since. Maybe not the one of her dreams, just one in which she could move without feeling trapped. And now, for the past few weeks, she'd fallen once again into a type of ridiculous self-imposed prison, that of a gray and defeated woman. Slowly, but without hesitation, she began to pack her bags. She didn't plan on leaving until she'd seen this Iris and listened to what she had to tell her; then she would do what she had to do. Return to Paris, pick up her here and now, perhaps more imperfect than before, but at least hers. She'd earned it. As she folded her clothes, she wondered if Enric would be reading that same blog. She'd called him in the morning to tell him about it, but he hadn't picked up the phone. She had left the message on his voicemail.

Enric started on hearing the creak of the study door.

"Did I frighten you?"

"No." At that moment he didn't feel like speaking to Glòria at all, but he forced himself to ask: "Is Natàlia in bed?"

"Yes." She came over to the table. "She was waiting for you for a while, but in the end she fell asleep."

Enric noticed the hint of reproach, so typical of his wife, who never complained directly. He usually pretended he hadn't picked up on it, but that night, after two hours in front of the screen looking at photos of his dead son, the words came out of his mouth without him doing anything to stop them.

"I'm sorry. I'm not in the mood for stories tonight. Can you understand that?"

Glòria looked away. She didn't answer. It was typical of her: never argue, look at him with that sort of condescending calm.

"You understand, don't you?" he insisted.

"I only came to ask you if you wanted dinner."

"Dinner?" The question seemed so trivial, so absurdly domestic, that he almost started laughing. "No. Don't worry. I'm not hungry."

"In that case I'll leave you alone. Good night."

Glòria went to the door without making a sound. Sometimes Enric thought he was married to a ghost, someone who could move without touching the ground. In fact, he thought his wife had already left when her serene voice, always in a tone lower than average, reached him.

"Unfortunately Marc is dead, Enric. You can't do anything for him. But Natàlia is alive. And she needs you."

She didn't wait for him to respond. She closed the door softly and left him deep in his helplessness, in a sea of worrying questions brought up by this blog of which he hadn't been aware until this evening. But the brief and thought-out appearance of Glòria had the virtue of adding another cross for him to bear. Another thing that was his fault. Because if there was anyone in this world who knew him, anyone who could read his mind with absolute clarity, that person was Glòria. And just as if he said it in words, his wife knew that he couldn't feel anything more than affection for the little girl she adored. However much he tried to hide it, however much she tried not to notice, however much Natàlia called him "Daddy" and put her arms around his neck. He'd had only one child, and that child had died, almost certainly at the hands of the girl who'd been his best friend.

Seconds later, with a clenched fist and tense jaw, he picked up the telephone and called his brother. No one answered.

Fèlix contemplated the telephone. It rang urgently, as insistent and inconsiderate as the person calling him. That night he, who'd always mustered patience before Enric's selfishness, hadn't the least intention of picking up. He knew what he wanted to ask him. Who was this Iris? What was the point of this macabre tale? Enric didn't remember anything, of course. Another father would, but not Enric. At most, he might vaguely remember that the camps finished early that summer due to an accident. Although, to tell the truth, he hadn't given him many details either. However, he had observed his nephew closely. But Marc hadn't suffered nightmares; in fact, as soon as he returned home, to his regular routine, he'd seemed to forget about Iris. Yes. Everyone had pretended to forget about Iris. It was best.

It was best, he repeated almost aloud, convinced that, given the circumstances, he'd done what was right. The poor little girl was past all help, in the hands of the Lord, but everyone else, those who were still living, were his responsibility. He had to decide and he'd done so. He'd spent all day telling himself that, but as soon as his eyes fell on the blurry photo of Iris on his nephew's blog, his self-assurance collapsed into a thousand pieces. Because he knew this claim of having done the right thing that summer was built on the unsound foundations of a lie. Iris's little face reminded him of that.

Tonight, opposite the image of that little blonde girl, Fèlix lowered his eyes and asked forgiveness. For his sins, his arrogance, his prejudices. While he prayed he recalled Joana's words a few days before, when she said that blame wasn't atoned for, it was carried. Maybe she was right. And maybe the moment had arrived to take a step back, to let justice take its course with all the consequences. Enough of playing God, he told himself. Let everyone take their share of the blame. Let the truth come to light. And may the Lord forgive my deeds and my omissions, and may the dead rest in peace.

"RIP" read the note that appeared on the saddle of his bike that evening, stuck to the lifeless body of a kitten. Aleix had to overcome all his disgust to take it off, and hours afterward he could feel the touch and smell of that tiny creature on his fingers. Time was running out and his problems, his problem, was ever further from being solved. He didn't have to be a genius to deduce who'd sent that message, or what it meant. There was little more than forty-eight hours left until Tuesday. He'd called Rubén several times with no answer. That in itself was another message, he thought. The rats were abandoning ship. He was facing the threat alone.

Holed up in his room, Aleix went over all the possibilities. Fortunately, his brain still functioned at times of great stress, although a teeny line would have helped him dispel his doubts. Finally, as he contemplated the darkening sky, he realized he had only one option. Although it would be the hardest thing he'd ever done, although his stomach churned at the very thought, there was only one person to turn to. Edu would lend him the money. For better or for worse. He didn't want to mull it over any more: he left his room and walked with quick, feverish steps toward his older brother's room.

35

Leire picked the inspector up at the foot of the tower without asking questions, and tried not to notice his tired appearance. He was still wearing the same shirt she'd seen on him that morning and he spoke slowly, as if he had to make an effort to pay attention. But as she was bringing him up to date on Rubén's statement, those tired eyes took on an interested gleam.

"I'm sorry I acted off my own bat," she said when she finished her tale.

"It's done now," he replied.

"See, Inspector? We have a witness, a stoned witness who believes he saw someone push Marc Castells. Not the testimony of the year, but I'd swear he was telling the truth."

Héctor tried to focus on the case, but it was difficult. Finally, when they reached the city center, it occurred to him, not without a certain shyness, to invite her to dinner. If it seemed odd to her, she said nothing, probably because she was dying of hunger and had nothing at home she felt like eating. The thought of some duck dim sum, the speciality of a Chinese restaurant she knew, overcame all other considerations.

"Do you like Chinese food?"

"Yes," he lied. "And don't be so formal. At least for a while." He smiled at her and continued in a low voice, thinking that by the following day he might no longer be an inspector but someone charged with murder. "Maybe forever."

She didn't fully understand the phrase, but sensed that questions were out of place, so she bit her tongue.

"Whatever you say. But, in that case, we split the bill."

"Never. My religion forbids it."

"I hope it doesn't forbid you eating duck as well."

"I'm not sure about that. I'll have to seek advice."

She laughed.

"Well, seek it tomorrow . . . just in case."

Héctor's decision to pay for dinner had been unyielding, so it was Leire who, in a fit of female equality, suggested going for a drink in a small bar nearby where they served "the best mojitos in Barcelona." REC was a small space, decorated in white, gray and red, which was usually full in winter, when the customers preferred cosy interiors to street terraces. That night there were only a couple of people at the bar, chatting to the owner, a muscular guy who greeted Leire with two kisses.

"From what I see you're well known here," commented Héctor, when they had sat down at a table.

"I come a lot," she replied. "With a friend."

"Leire, two mojitos?" asked the owner.

"No. Just one. A virgin San Francisco for me."

He winked at her, with no comment; if Leire wanted to abstain that night in front of this companion, that was her business. He brought them the two drinks and returned to the bar.

"Is it good?" she asked. She was actually dying to have one, but the image of a baby with three heads suppressed any temptation to try it.

"Yes. Are you sure you don't want one?"

"I'm driving," said Leire, grateful for once in her life for the hundreds of checkpoints scattered across the city on Saturday nights.

"Good girl." He stirred the sugar at the bottom of the glass and took another gulp. They'd been going over the case during dinner and come once again to a dead end: Iris, or, more accurately, Inés Alonso. They'd agreed that Leire would go to the airport to collect her and ensure that the young woman arrived safely at Joana Vidal's flat, or wherever she wanted to go first. Obviously, en route she would talk to her about Marc. Héctor had opted to stay on the margin, though Leire didn't know why. Nor could he tell her without getting Andreu into trouble. For the umpteenth time, he looked at his mobile, which remained insolently silent on the table. Not even Ruth had bothered to answer.

"Expecting a call?" asked Leire. She hadn't been drinking, but something in her impelled her to be forward. "A friend?"

He smiled.

"Something like that. And tell me, why is a girl like you free on a Saturday night?"

Leire shrugged.

"Mysteries of the city."

He looked at her with that old-dog irony, and all of a sudden she felt a huge wish to tell him everything: her conversation with Tomás, her fears.

"I don't think I can handle any more mysteries," he replied. She took another sip and lowered her voice.

"That's easily resolved, really." He was going to be the third person to know, after María and Tomás and before her parents.

But she couldn't take it anymore. "Can I give you an exclusive piece of news? Not to Inspector Salgado from the morning but to Héctor from tonight?"

"I love exclusives."

"I'm pregnant." She smiled as she said it, as if she were confessing a major indiscretion.

The words caught him mid-gulp. Smiling, he moved his glass to the San Francisco and touched it lightly.

"Congratulations." His smile was warm, and despite the wrinkles and the fatigue in his features, he seemed to be happy.

"Don't say anything, OK? I'm only a few weeks and everyone says not to announce it in case something happens, and—"

"Yeah, yeah," he interrupted her. "I know. And I'll be as silent as the grave. An Egyptian grave. I promise. I'm getting another mojito. Another old-lady fruit juice for you?"

"No. It's awful. It must have kilos of sugar."

While she waited for him to return from the bar, she felt disappointed. Stupid, she scolded herself. What did you expect? He's your boss, not a friend. And even as a boss you've known him for only four days. Héctor returned with his mojito and sat down again. The mobile remained silent.

"I told you a secret," she said. "It's your turn."

"When did we make that deal?"

"Never. But it's a craving . . ."

"Oh no. My wife harped on at me with that for months until I found out it was completely untrue. My ex-wife," he pointed out, before drinking.

"Do you have children?"

"Yes, one boy. They never become exes." Unless they're ashamed of a father convicted of murder, he told himself. He didn't want to think about it. "I warn you, and tell your boyfriend too."

He realized he'd put his foot in it when he saw her face.

"OK." He took refuge in his mojito, which was tart and strong. "Fuck, your friend's made this one strong." He stirred it vigorously. "You know what? You don't need him. I mean the father. I swear I could have lived without mine."

Leire watched him as he took another long drink. When he put the glass on the table and she could see his eyes she believed she understood the depth of the darkness glimmering in them and felt what her friend María called "the seductive power of sad childhoods." A mix of attraction and tenderness. She looked away so he wouldn't see while she cursed these turbulent hormones that seemed to be plotting against her. Luckily, just then some late customers took the table right beside them, so close that any confidence between them would have been an indiscretion. Both she and Héctor did everything they could to restore informal conversation, but their efforts resulted in a chat so forced that Leire was glad when he finished his drink and suggested that perhaps she might be tired.

"A little, to be honest. Do you want me to drop you somewhere?"

He shook his head.

"See you tomorrow." At least I hope so, he thought. "Drive carefully."

"I haven't been drinking, Inspector Salgado."

"Not Héctor anymore?" he asked, half smiling.

Leire didn't answer. She went to the bar and paid for the drinks, ignoring his protests. Héctor watched her from the table as she chatted to the owner. He heard her laugh, and he told himself that was exactly what he had been missing in his life lately: not someone to fuck, or walk with, or live with. Someone to laugh about this shitty life with.

He was in the bar, alone, until it closed, like a local drunk who
didn't want to go home. However, that night the mojitos had no
effect on him. He thought ironically that the heroes in the mov-
ies drink bourbon or whisky. Not even in this do you measure
up, Salgado. When the bar owner discreetly said it was closing
time, he went out into the street. He wandered aimlessly for a
while, trying not to think, to let his mind go blank. He didn't
succeed and, just as he was about to enter another joint to add
more alcohol to his body, his mobile took revenge for being so
long silent. He answered immediately.

"Martina!"

"Héctor, it's finished. It's finished! All over. Fuck, Inspector,
you owe me one. This time you really owe me one."

36

As soon as Héctor had left, Sergeant Andreu had gone back into the flat where Omar's mistreated corpse lay. She was by then mentally prepared for what she was going to find, so this time she observed the scene with the detachment required. If in life that man had caused pain, it was clear that he'd paid for it with a slow death, she said to herself as she knelt by the body. Abandoned like a dog. She wasn't an expert in forensic science, but she knew enough to see that the old doctor had died between twenty-four and forty-eight hours earlier. The large contusion visible on the nape of his neck, however, was older than that. Yes, the doctor had been given an almost fatal blow days before, the day of his disappearance, and they'd left him there, tied up, gagged, dying. In a show of sadism, she thought, remembering the disc in the DVD player, his killer had recorded the exact moment of his death for posterity.

She stood up slowly. However much she wanted to avoid it, all the evidence pointed to Héctor. A witness had seen him

with the victim the evening he disappeared; a man with an
Argentine accent had ordered then paid for the pig's head over
the phone. The call could have been made from anywhere. She
hadn't received a very trustworthy description from the boy at
the butcher's. Apart from the accent, the information contributed by the boy had been rather vague. Vague, yes, but not contrary to Salgado's physical appearance at all. And then there
was the corpse, just below Héctor's flat. And the discs in his
house. Martina closed her eyes and could visualize part of the
sequence of events, though not all. Of course it was hard for
her to imagine Héctor recording anyone's death, in an act of
perverse voyeurism, and much less attacking that poor neighbor of his. But what if Carmen's assault was a mere coincidence? Something that had happened that day and had nothing
to do with the Omar case?

Enough, she admonished herself. There was nothing more
to see. She left the room as she'd found it, and then did the
same with Carmen's keys. A strange uneasiness came over her
when she'd done so, the indefinable feeling that she was overlooking something. Or perhaps it was the fear that someone
might find out what she'd taken upon herself: those hours of a
head start she'd given to a possible murderer . . . She was playing for him, she thought, without the slightest guarantee she
could win the game.

She dismissed the idea of going back to Omar's flat and decided to go to the station, shut herself in her office with all the
material and find a crack, a thread to pull. She looked at her
watch. A long and possibly pointless night lay ahead of her, but
she wasn't ready to throw in the towel. Not yet.

Two hours later, however, with a crick in her neck and red
eyes, the feeling of being beaten was overwhelming her. She'd

re-read all the files, the ones from before the doctor's disappearance when he was under investigation for his connection with the network of pimps, as well as the most recent. She had produced a detailed outline using the witness statements: the lawyer who said he'd seen him on Monday night; the butcher; and above all that of Rosa, which placed the doctor in his office on Tuesday evening. She'd posed all the questions, and although she hadn't managed to answer them all completely, they all directed her thoughts to one name: Héctor Salgado.

For the last time, she went over the questions still unanswered. Some were circumstantial, along the lines of: How had Héctor moved Omar's body to the empty flat in Poblenou? He could have borrowed a friend's car, she told herself. Or his ex-wife's. What's more, she thought, he could even have taken one of the police vehicles. Not easy, but he could have done it. Question dismissed. Another point against the inspector.

She was exhausted. Her back, head, stomach all hurt. Hurt her to the point of irritability. But this same extreme fatigue forced her to keep going in an almost masochistic effort. She closed her eyes for a moment, breathed deeply and returned to the task, from the beginning. Another question dangled around the search of the house and the doctor's accounts. If she assumed, and she had no reason to doubt it, that this quack had collaborated with the women-trafficking ring, where was the money he got from it? Not in the bank, logically, but not in his house either. The question remained unanswered, but in no way did it exonerate Héctor. His motive, were he guilty, had never been robbery, but revenge. A distorted sense of justice. The same thing that had driven him to beat Omar.

"It's over," she said out loud. She couldn't take it anymore. She wasn't giving any more of herself. Maybe the best thing was to report the finding of the body with all the consequences and for Héctor to submit to the appropriate investigation. She'd done all she could . . . She took a few minutes before making the call that would set the whole process in motion, while she considered how to cover up her act, unprofessional from any perspective. She set the Omar papers aside and while she meditated on her own situation, she opened the file of battered women who had registered for the self-defense course she would be teaching in the autumn. If she wasn't put on checkpoints when all this came out, she thought. She went on leafing through pages, looking at photos. Unfortunately they couldn't accept them all, although she made an effort to take the maximum number of pre-registered women. Then some always dropped out, whether because they didn't feel able or they'd resigned themselves to putting up with these bastards. Poor women, she thought once again. Those who didn't deal with them didn't have a clue of the terror they were subjected to. They were all ages, from a variety of backgrounds, different nationalities, but they all had fear, shame, distrust written on their faces.

She stopped at the photo of a woman she instantly recognized. It was Rosa, no doubt about it. María del Rosario Álvarez, according to the form. Finding her there didn't surprise Marina all that much: Rosa had spoken of a husband she feared. She remembered her words in the park, her desperate plea to remain anonymous. Rosa must have forgiven her husband, since the report of assault was from February. But then another name caught the sergeant's eye. A name that chilled and unnerved her at once. The lawyer who'd represented Rosa was Damián Fernández, the same person who defended Omar's interests.

She had to force herself to stay calm, to think about this unexpected connection with a tranquility which had abandoned her hours earlier. She went back to Omar's file, but this time she studied it from a radically different perspective. Who had seen Omar on Tuesday? Rosa. Who had positively identified Héctor? Rosa. Only her, because an Argentine accent, the butcher's contribution, was easily imitated. Other than this woman's word, there was no proof that Omar was safe and sound on Tuesday evening. If this testimony was discounted, what was left? Damián Fernández's statement, which said he'd met Omar on Monday. And that was probably true. That Monday, the lawyer had gone to see his client, not to present the deal offered by Savall but to beat him. Yes, to beat him and steal the money he definitely had hidden in some corner of that fucking house! And then . . . then he'd calmly brought the badly injured body, in the middle of the night, to the empty flat, taking advantage of the fact that Héctor wasn't returning until the following day. The strange feeling she had had leaving the keys in Carmen's house, that game with all the keys of the building that the woman barely used, came back to her forcefully. She didn't know how Damián Fernández managed to get them, but she was sure he had. Keys he'd copied and used as he pleased, entering Héctor's house when he wasn't there, and the empty flat to imprison Omar's body and record his death. Even Carmen's assault fitted now. She must have surprised him at some point, probably while he was leaving the latest bits of evidence in Salgado's home, and he'd had no choice but to split her head and bring her down to the first floor. And, amidst all this, his accomplice Rosa had called her and played her part to perfection, putting Héctor at the scene.

Excited, with adrenaline pumping through her body, Martina Andreu knew that she didn't yet have all the answers, but she did have many questions to put to Rosa and Damián

Fernández. And she didn't plan to wait until the next day to start asking them.

Héctor listened, somewhat astonished and overwhelmed, to the tale that a sergeant seemingly possessed by an inexhaustible energy was telling him at four in the morning.

"We have them, Héctor! Maybe it would have been more difficult if we hadn't caught them in bed together in his house. Fernández was a tough nut to crack, but she went to pieces straight away. She told us everything, although obviously she denies knowing anything about the murder. And when we put Rosa's confession before him, he couldn't keep putting on an innocent face."

"Robbery was the motive?" After thinking about curses and dark rites, the explanation almost disappointed him.

"Well, a relatively meaty robbery for two wretches like Fernández and Rosa. We found more than a hundred thousand euros in the lawyer's house, which no doubt were stolen from Omar's office."

"How the hell did he get my house keys?"

"He didn't open his mouth, but Rosa told us when we leaned on her a little. He boasted to her, saying he'd passed himself off as an air-conditioning salesman. Poor Carmen showed him the house, had a nice long chat with him, and he took advantage of a moment of distraction to take those keys. He arranged a second visit for the following day and returned the originals."

She lowered her voice.

"He was spying on you the whole time, Héctor. He took advantage of your movements to go into your house and leave those discs."

"He did that too?"

Andreu frowned.

"It's strange. He recorded you beating Omar with the camera in his clinic and they were thinking of presenting it as evidence against you, so it occurred to him to use it to back up the other one, the one showing the doctor's death. With regard to your ex . . . I don't know what to think. Fernández says he found it among Omar's recordings." Andreu paused. "He added something about the doctor having been preparing something in the days before his death, one of his rituals."

"Against me?"

"It doesn't matter now, Héctor. He's dead. Forget all this. Just think that we have enough proof to charge them both. And to exonerate you . . ."

There was a brief silence, charged with complicity, with gratitude. With friendship.

"I don't know how to thank you. Really." It was true.

She raised her hand to her brow. The long night was catching up with her.

"Don't worry, I'll think of something. It's late . . . or early," she added, with a smile. "What are you going to do? Go home?"

"I suppose I'll have to go back tomorrow. But for tonight I'd prefer to sleep in my office, believe me. It wouldn't be the first time."

That night Héctor didn't sleep at all: he stayed awake, asking questions and setting out interrogations. It also helped, he knew deep down, to drive the memory of Leire Castro's laugh out of his mind.

SUNDAY

37

The airport was a seething mass of tourists pushing trolleys and suitcases on wheels. Some turned their heads for a last glimpse of that sun that had accompanied them, bronzed and hot on the beach and in front of the Pedrera; a star which, once they arrived at their northern destinations, would have disappeared or at best would appear timidly from behind a mass of clouds. Others moved toward the exits with excitement etched on their faces, although they stopped just after going through them and leaving behind the air-conditioned new terminal, with floors like black mirrors, to receive the first shock of heat.

Leire had picked Héctor up at his house, at his request. She had been surprised to receive his call, since they'd arranged that she would go to the airport alone to search for Inés. Having gone to his house first thing—just as long as was necessary to shower and change his clothes—he seemed to be in an excellent mood. The shadows under his eyes were still there, no doubt about that, but the spirit had changed. She hadn't slept much herself, and the bout of nausea that morning had been the worst yet. Worse than an awful Sunday hangover.

The flight was only slightly delayed, and it took even less time to recognize the girl from the photo, although the black-and-white had definitely flattered her. The young woman moving toward the door, not very tall, with curly hair and somewhat plumper than could be seen in the photograph, had little of the enigmatic about her. Héctor got there first.

"Inés Alonso?"

"Yes." She looked at the inspector apprehensively. "Is something wrong?"

He smiled at her.

"I'm Inspector Salgado and this is Agent Castro. We've come to collect you and take you to Joana Vidal's house. Marc's mother."

"But—"

"Relax. We just want to talk to you."

She lowered her head and nodded slowly, then followed them to the car without saying another word. She said nothing during the journey, although she answered a couple of trivial questions politely. She sat on the back seat, pensive. She was carrying only a type of rigid backpack and kept it firmly at her side.

She remained silent as they ascended the steep stairs leading to the flat where Joana lived. Héctor realized, with a pang of remorse, that he hadn't heard from her since the day before, when they had breakfast together. However, as soon as Joana received them, he noticed that something had changed in her in the last few hours. Her footsteps and her voice revealed a composure he'd only briefly glimpsed before.

She showed them to the dining room. The windows were open and the light streamed in.

"I had to inform the police of your arrival," said Joana, turning to this stranger, who had sat down, like the others, but with her back straight, as if she were about to undergo an oral exam.

"Maybe it's for the best," she murmured.

"Inés," Héctor interjected, "you met Marc in Dublin, didn't you?"

She smiled for the first time.

"I would never have recognized him. But he saw my name on the student residence's list. And one day he approached me to ask if I was the same Inés Alonso."

Héctor nodded, encouraging her to continue.

"He introduced himself and we went for a drink." She spoke tenderly, simply. "I think he fell in love with me. But . . . of course, though we avoided it at the start, in the end we had to talk about Iris. Always Iris . . ."

"What happened that summer, Inés? I know you were only a little girl and I understand it must be painful to think about her . . ."

"No. Not anymore." She was flushed, tears shone in her eyes. "I've spent years trying to forget that summer, that day. But not anymore. Marc was right about that, although he didn't know part of the truth. In fact, I didn't know it either until a little while ago, until last Christmas, when my mother moved apartments and we packed up everything from the old house. There, in one of the boxes, I found Iris's teddy bear. It was torn, the stuffing was coming out of a rip, but when I picked it up I noticed something inside."

She interrupted her story, opened her backpack and took out a folder.

"Here," she said, turning to the inspector. "Or would you prefer me to read it aloud? My sister Iris wrote it that summer.

I've read it hundreds of times since I found it. The first few times I couldn't finish but I can now. It's a little long . . ."

And, with a voice that wanted to be firm, Inés took out some pages and began to read.

My name is Iris and I'm twelve. I won't reach thirteen because before the summer is over I'll be dead.

I know what death is, or at least I think I do. You go to sleep and don't wake up. You stay like that, asleep but not dreaming, I suppose. Papa was sick for months when I was little. He was really strong, he could cut down big trees with the axe. I liked watching him, but he wouldn't let me because a splinter might come out and hurt me. While he was sick, before he went to sleep forever, his arms shrank, like something was eating him from inside. In the end he was only bones, ribs, shoulders, elbows, and a bit of skin, then he fell asleep. He wasn't strong enough to stay awake. I'm not very strong now either. Mama says it's because I don't eat, and she's right, but she thinks I want to be thin, like girls in magazines, and she's wrong. I don't want to be thin to be more beautiful. Before I did, but now it seems silly. I want to be thin to die like Papa. And I'm not hungry either, because not eating is easy. At least it was, before Mama focused on watching me during meals. Now it's much harder. I have to pretend that I'm eating everything on my plate so she doesn't get annoying, but there are tricks. Sometimes I have it in my mouth for a long time and then I spit it into a napkin. Or recently I've learned that the best thing is to eat it all and then vomit. You're clean after vomiting, all that dirty food is gone and you feel calm.

Inés stopped for a moment and Héctor was tempted to tell her not to continue, but before he could do so, the young woman took a deep breath and resumed her reading.

I live in a town in the Pyrenees, with my mother and my little sister. Inés is eight. Sometimes I talk to her about Papa and she says she remembers, but I think she's lying. I was eight when he died and she was only four. I think she only remembers him thin, like Jesus Christ, she says. She doesn't remember strong Papa who cut down trees and laughed and swung you round like you were a rag doll that weighed nothing at all. Then Mama laughed more. Later, when Papa fell asleep forever, she started praying a lot. Every day. I liked praying, and then Mama insisted on us making our First Communion, Inés and I, at the same time. It was nice: the catechist told us stories from the Bible and it wasn't hard for me to learn the prayers. But the hosts made me sick. They stuck to the roof of my mouth and I couldn't swallow them. Or chew them because it was a sin. Inés liked them though, she said they reminded her of the layer on the top of *turrón*. I have the photo of the communion. Inés and I were dressed in white, with ribbons in our hair. Hardly any of the girls in school did it but I liked it. And Mama was happy that day. She only cried a little in the church but I think it was because she was happy, not sad.

I already said I live in a small town so every day we have to catch a bus to go to school. We have to get up very early and it's very cold. Sometimes it snows so much the bus can't come to get us and we stay at

home. But now it's summer and it's hot. In summer
we move because Mama is in charge of cooking in a
house for camps. I liked it a lot because the summer
house is much bigger and it has a pool and is full of
children. They come in groups of twenty on a bus from
Barcelona. And they stay for two weeks. It's annoying, because sometimes you make friends and you
know that in a few days they will leave. Some come
back the next year and others don't. There is a boy
who stays all summer, like us. Mama told me it's because he has no mother and his father works a lot, so
he spends half the summer at camp. With his uncle,
who is in charge of everything. And the monitors who
help him. I have to help Mama too, but not much, just
a bit in the kitchen. Then I am free to swim or take
part in the games. Before I did but now I don't feel
like it. And Mama keeps telling me it's because I don't
eat. But she doesn't know anything. She lives in the
kitchen and doesn't know anything about what happens outside. She only thinks about food. Sometimes I
hate her.

It's the third summer we've spent here and I know
there won't be a fourth. I've seen him looking at Inés
out of the corner of his eye without anyone noticing.
Only me. I have to do something. He looks at her when
she is swimming in the pool and says things like: "You
look a lot like your sister." And it must be true because
everyone says so. Sometimes we both stand in front of
the mirror and look at ourselves, and we come to the
conclusion that we don't look so alike. But it doesn't
matter, I don't want her to be his new doll. Or at least
I don't want to be here to see it.

Joana got up and went toward the girl to sit by her side. She thanked her with a brief smile, but continued reading.

It started two summers ago, at the end of July, when there was only one group of kids left to arrive. We always have a few days alone between groups. Alone means Mama, Inés and I, and the priest and a monitor. For those days Inés and I have the whole pool to ourselves. It's like we're rich and live in a house like the ones on American programs. But Inés doesn't like the water very much, so that day I was swimming on my own. I liked swimming and I was good at it. Front crawl, backstroke, breaststroke . . . all the strokes except butterfly, which I couldn't do. Because of that, he offered to teach me. He came to the side of the pool and showed me how to move my arms and legs. He is quite good-looking and is very patient. He hardly ever gets angry, even when the kids are bad and don't listen to him. We were there for a while, me swimming and him at the side of the pool, until I got tired. Then he helped me out of the water even though he didn't need to. It was late and there was no sun, so he said it was better that he dry me straight away so I didn't catch cold. He stood behind me, wrapped me in a towel and began to dry me with pleasure. He was tickling me and I was laughing. He laughed at the beginning too. Then he didn't: he was drying me more slowly and breathing loudly, like when someone is asleep. I didn't dare move even though I was completely dry, but I started to feel strange. I was still wrapped in the towel and he was caressing me through the fabric. Then he put his hand underneath. And then I did try to get away but I couldn't. He didn't say anything: just shhh, shhh, even though I wasn't talking. Then he said: I won't hurt you. I was surprised because it hadn't occurred to me that he could. His finger was going up my leg, the inside of my thigh, higher and higher like a spider. He stopped where my thigh ended and breathed in. It was a few seconds: his finger went to the edge of my swimsuit. I squirmed. And then he breathed deeply and let me go.

"God!" exclaimed Joana, but Héctor's look silenced her. Leire remained quiet, watching this young woman sinking into a horrifying, brutally poignant story.

I didn't tell Mama. Or anyone. I felt like I'd done something very bad but I didn't know what. And he didn't say anything else. Except: go and get dressed, it's late, in a half-angry voice. As if I'd distracted him. As if suddenly he didn't want to see me anymore. The next day he didn't come to the pool. I saw him pass by from the water and I called him: I wanted to show him that I'd been practicing and I was doing it better. He looked at me, very serious, and left without saying anything. I didn't want to swim anymore and I got out of the pool. It was earlier than the day before and it was hot. I lay down on the towel, letting the sun dry me. I think I was hoping he would appear but he didn't. He must be angry with me. I said to myself that if he dried me again I wouldn't be so silly. But the next day the next group of kids arrived and the other monitors, and he didn't have time for swimming classes anymore. I kept practicing every evening, when the pool was empty, because the kids were doing other activities, and I told him one day that I was getting better at it. He smiled at me and said: I'll come and see you, I want to check your progress.

And he came: the last day, after the kids had left. And he clapped. I was proud: Mama didn't care if I swam well or not, she knows nothing about sports, so I was very happy. When I got out of the water I stayed still, hoping he would dry me. But he only gave me the towel. From a distance. And then he said I deserved a prize for having made such an effort in the pool. What prize? I asked him. He smiled. You'll see. It will be a surprise. Tomorrow go to the cave in the wood after lunch and I'll give it to you, OK? But don't tell Inés, or she'll want one too. It was true. Inés always complains on my birthday when I get presents. She complains so much that my mother and grandparents always end up buying her something even though it's not her party, it's mine. So I didn't tell her, and the next day I managed to go without her seeing me. I didn't tell Mama either because if I did I'd get stuck with Inés.

"You don't have to do this," murmured Joana, but Inés's glance was determined.

"I know. But I want to do it. I owe it to her."

That was two summers ago. Now I hardly ever go down to swim. I don't want to. I just want to sleep. Really sleep, without dreaming. I've asked everyone how to avoid dreams and no one has been able to explain how. No one knows anything really important. Anything really useful. Mama only knows how to cook

and watch me. She watches me every time we sit down
to eat. I can't bear her. I don't want her food. Every
time I vomit after eating I feel happy. Maybe this way
she'll learn to leave me alone.

The cave is twenty minutes from the house. You
have to walk a good bit uphill, through the wood, but
I know the way perfectly. Every group of kids hikes
there, so that summer alone I'd been there four times.
Sometimes a monitor goes ahead and hides in there to
frighten the little ones or things like that. So that day,
at siesta time, I went there as we'd planned. When I
arrived I couldn't see anyone. Caves don't frighten me,
but I didn't want to go in alone either and I sat waiting on a rock, in the shade. I like the wood: the light
slips in between the branches and makes designs on
the ground. And there's a silence that isn't complete
silence, as if it has music. There was a slight breeze
which was pleasant after the steep climb. I looked at
my watch, although I wasn't sure what time I had to
come. But he wasn't long. He arrived about ten minutes later. He was carrying a rucksack on his back
and I said to myself that my present must be inside.
He seemed nervous and he was looking behind him
the whole time. He was sweating, and I guessed he
must have run there. He let himself fall down beside
me and almost smiled. I asked him: Did you bring
my present? And then he really smiled. He opened
the rucksack and took out a bag. I hope you like it. It
wasn't wrapped so I looked inside the bag. Take it out!
he said. It was a pink bikini with little strawberries.
I loved it. Then he said: Put it on. Let's see if it's your
size. I must have hesitated because he insisted: Come

on, I want to see how you look in it. Change in the cave if you are embarrassed. His voice was hoarse. Then I didn't know if that voice came out when he wanted to play or when he was angry. Slower, slurring words. And when he has that voice he always looks away, like he's not talking to you. As if he's embarrassed.

I went to change and came out with the bikini on. I walked up and down like the models on a catwalk do. The way he looked at me made me feel pretty. Then he said: Come and sit beside me. I tried but I was uncomfortable: the earth and the pebbles stuck into my legs. He took out a towel from his rucksack and spread it out for both of us. And we lay down and watched the light coming through the trees for a while. I told him things and he really listened to me. You are very pretty, he whispered while he stroked my hair. And then I really felt like the prettiest girl in the world.

I hid the bikini, just like he told me to, so Inés wouldn't find it. My mother saw it, of course, and commented that one of the kids must have forgotten it. I smiled, thinking that just like he'd said, that present was our secret. I didn't put it on again until the next summer, the first day the monitors arrived, but he didn't notice. I swam in the pool, like I had the year before, but he was busy with the others and didn't pay me any attention. But afterward, when I met him in the corridor, he said very seriously: you have to wear a swimsuit in the pool. Then he winked at me and added: But you can put on the pink bikini when we see each other in the cave. After all, I gave it to you. I didn't understand, but I nodded.

Come tomorrow at four o' clock, he said to me quietly, and you can tell me how your year has been. I
was so happy because I had lots of things to tell him,
things about school, my friends, but the truth is we
hardly spoke at all. When I arrived he was already
there, sitting on the same towel as last summer.
You're late, he scolded me, although it wasn't true.
I'm wearing the bikini underneath my clothes, I told
him, so he wouldn't get angry. Then he laughed, and
I realized he was joking with me, but he kept talking
in an angry voice. Oh, really? I don't believe you, as
well as coming late you're a liar . . . and laughing he
took me by the shoulders, laid me down on the towel
and started tickling me. Let's see if it's true, he said
again, and he put his hands under my clothes to see
if he touched the bikini. OK, yes, it's there. I laughed
too, although his hands were warm. Very warm. Then
he lay down on top of me and stroked my face, and
told me again that I was very pretty. You're prettier
than last year. I was a little ashamed and he noticed
my red cheeks. Are you hot? he asked. I'm going to
undress you as if you were a doll, he said smiling. He
was speaking in that funny voice. And I let him take
off my T-shirt and pull down my trousers. You're my
doll, he whispered again and again. I could hardly
hear him. With one hand he stroked my hair, my arms,
tickled my neck. I closed my eyes. I didn't see anything else, but after a while I felt a warm liquid on
my tummy. I opened my eyes, afraid, and saw a sticky
white stain. I tried to move because it made me feel
sick but he didn't let me. Shhhh, he repeated, shh . . .
dolls don't talk.

Leire had to force herself not to grab the pages from her. At her side, Héctor took her hand. She closed her eyes and kept listening.

> That summer I learned to be his doll. Dolls close their eyes and let themselves be stroked. They also take their hand and put it where they're told to. And open their mouth and lick with their tongue even though it sometimes makes them want to vomit. Above all, good dolls don't tell anyone. They obey. They don't complain. Like real dolls, they must wait for their owner to pick them up and then get tired of playing with them. It's strange, you want them to play with you, although there are games you don't like at all. And above all, you can't bear the idea that your owner might forget about you, or replace you with another doll. At the end of last summer, the last day we played, he looked at me and said: You're growing up. And, unlike most people who smile when they say that, I felt that he didn't like it. Then in my bedroom I looked at myself in the mirror and saw he was right: my body was changing, my breasts were growing . . . only a little, but enough that the pink bikini was too small. That's when I decided to eat less.

"Bastard!" Joana couldn't stop the word coming out of her mouth. Inés looked at her, nodded and said: "There's not much more."

> This year everything's been different from the start. When he arrived he looked at me as if he didn't recognize me. I was proud: thanks to hardly eating a thing

I had barely put on any weight at all. But I was taller, that I couldn't prevent. And I saw that he noticed, though he said nothing. I tried to fit into the bikini but couldn't and I cried with rage. He didn't even mention it. He looked at me as if I didn't exist, as if he'd never played with me. And when one day I said we could go to the cave he looked at me strangely. He acted as if he didn't know what I was talking about. But my mother was useful for once and arranged everything. She told the monitors what a bad student I was and how worried she was about me, I think to embarrass me. And he nodded, and said, "Don't worry, we'll help her. I'll give her private classes in the evenings on the days I'm free." I loved the idea: the two of us together, in a closed room. I felt special again.

The first day I waited for him at the desk in my room, the one I share with Inés. The silly girl insisted on bringing all her dolls. While I prepared the notebooks and books, I looked at them and told them: Today it's my turn, today he'll play with me. But he didn't: he spent a while explaining some mathematical problems and then he gave me some exercises. Then he went over to the window and stayed there. When he came back I saw something was happening to him. His eyes were dark. And I said to myself: Now. I was waiting for him to speak to me in that hoarse voice, to touch me with those warm hands that at the beginning made me sick. But he just sat down and asked: What age is your sister?

I hated him. I hated him with all my heart. Before I'd hated him for what he did to me, and now I hated him because he'd stopped. And then, little by little,

I saw how he was getting closer to Inés. No one else
noticed, of course. Not even her. Inés can spend hours
playing with her dolls and not notice anything. She
doesn't like games outside, or sports. She doesn't much
like other kids: Mama always says she's too solitary. In
school she has only one friend and hardly plays with
anyone else. But he looked at her, I saw him while
I was pretending to read; while my mother's eyes
watched me to make sure I would eat, I had my eyes
on Inés. Then I decided to do something. I knew it was
in my hands, that the games last summer were bad;
in school they'd told us about it and we'd all put on re-
volted faces. Including me. Well, I wanted to end it all
but I didn't know how. And one afternoon, while the
monitors and the children were on an outing, I went
to speak to the priest. I meant to tell him everything:
talk to him about the bikini, the games in the cave, his
sweaty hands, even though I might die of shame.

"Fèlix!" exclaimed Joana.
"Yes," replied Inés. "Father Fèlix."

I knocked on his door and went into his office. And
almost without noticing I started crying. Really crying, with my whole body. I cried so much he couldn't
understand my words. He closed the door and said to
me: Calm down, calm down, first cry and then tell me
everything, all right? Crying is good. When your tears
are gone, we'll talk. I felt like my tears would never
end, like my stomach was a knot of black clouds that
kept raining. But after a long time the knot began to
unravel, the tears stopped and I could talk at last. I

told him everything, sitting on an old wooden chair
that creaked every time I moved a bit. He listened
without interrupting, only asking a question when I
hesitated. He asked if there was anything else, if he'd
put his "thing" inside me, and I said no. He seemed relieved. Suddenly I wasn't ashamed anymore, or weepy,
I just wanted to tell him everything. I wanted the
whole world to know I'd been his doll. When I finished
I felt like there was nothing left inside me, only the
sudden fear of what was going to happen from now on.

But nothing happened. Well, the priest told me I
should relax, that he would take care of everything,
to forget these things. Don't tell anyone else, he said.
They'll think you're making it up. Leave it to me.

That was three days ago. The private classes have
ended and when I meet him in the corridor he won't
even look at me. He is angry with me, I know. I know I
broke the rules of good dolls. The second-last group of
kids has gone. He's gone too, but he'll be back in a few
days. I don't want to be here to see him. I want to escape. Go where no one can find me and sleep forever.

The doorbell startled them all. Joana got up to answer it,
while Leire embraced Inés. She had left the pages on the table
and couldn't hold back the tears any longer.

The person who entered with Joana was the last person they
were expecting to see just then: Father Fèlix Castells.

38

Leire continued holding Inés. The young woman was sobbing almost silently, as if she were ashamed of it. When Fèlix came in, all eyes were on him. But it was Joana who said in a clear, loud voice:

"You felt relieved when she told you he hadn't penetrated her? Truly, Fèlix?"

He looked at her without answering.

"You did nothing?" she went on, accusing him in fury. "Nothing? This child told you what this bastard was doing to her and you thought since he hadn't raped her, none of it mattered? You didn't report him, even when this little girl drowned herself in the pool?"

Héctor grabbed the pages Inés had left on the table.

"You should read them, Father. And if indeed God does exist, I hope he forgives you."

Fèlix hung his head. He seemed incapable of defending himself, of saying a single word in his own defense. He didn't sit down. He remained on foot in front of this improvised tribunal.

"Don't put all the blame on him," murmured Inés. She moved softly away from Leire and looked at the priest. "What he did wasn't right, but he didn't do it just for himself. He was also protecting me."

"Inés—"

"No. I've spent years with all this. Feeling I was to blame. Thinking myself in debt to Iris, keeping her alive even if only in a symbolic way . . . Until last Christmas, when I found these pages and learned the whole story. I showed them to Marc in Dublin and he reacted in the same way you are now. Appalled, enraged, anxious to know the truth. But there's a part of that truth I didn't dare tell him. I let him hate his uncle, initiate a plan of revenge against him, to make him confess what he wanted to know." She took a breath before going on. "When the truth is that, very early that morning, I heard footsteps in the house. I couldn't sleep in Mama's bed; she kept moving. I went out to the corridor without making a sound and didn't see anyone, but I was sure someone had gone downstairs. One of my dolls was on the floor. I picked it up and went down to the garden."

Iris is sitting at the edge of the pool in a nightdress. Her eyes see only the dolls. She hasn't slept all night, staring at them intently. They belong to Inés and at this moment she hates them with all her heart. She's pulled the heads and arms off some of them before tossing them in the water; others she's submerged as if she could drown them. There's only one left in her hand, her sister's favorite, and before throwing it in with the others she contemplates her work, satisfied. The pool has become a pond full of little plastic bodies floating adrift. She doesn't notice Inés's presence until she hears her voice.

"What are you doing?"

She laughs like one possessed. Inés bends down and begins taking out the ones floating closest to the edge. The water is freezing, but they are her dolls. She loves them.

"Don't touch them!"

Iris tries to stop her. She grabs her with all her strength and wrestles her to the ground, but although Inés is smaller, Iris is very weak. Inés tries to free herself from her sister's arms and they struggle at the edge of the pool, they roll around fighting until they fall into the water. Inés notices how the pressure eases, how the cold penetrates her entire body. She barely manages to come to the surface and paddles like a puppy to the steps. Then she looks back. Iris is emerging from the bottom, like a big dead doll.

"That's how it was," Inés finished. "I ran away and hid. Mama found me a little later, with my hair still wet. She hugged me and told me not to worry. That Father Fèlix would take care of everything." Silence overwhelmed the room. Father Castells had sat down, although he kept his head lowered.

"God," said Joana. "And Marc?"

"Marc didn't know anything, Joana," answered Fèlix. "I took care of that. You can say I did wrong, but I swear that I tried to do the right thing."

"Oh really?" asked Héctor. "I doubt hiding the abuse of a minor was doing the right thing, Father. You knew the truth. You knew Iris was beside herself and you knew why."

"And what good would it have done?" shouted Fèlix. He stood up suddenly and his flushed face showed the torment escaping him. "Iris was dead, and this girl wasn't to blame!" He swallowed and continued, in a quieter but no less tense voice. "I doubted what Iris said. Perhaps I didn't realize the significance of it. I thought part of it was true and part the fruit of a problematic child's imagination. But then, when she died, I told myself that bringing all that filth to light would only serve to make this poor little girl face so much. Her mother begged me to protect her. And I opted for the living, Inspector. I confessed the truth to the inspector who took on the case," he said, not mentioning his name. "I asked him to stop investigating for this little girl's sake. And he agreed."

"But you didn't tell him you were letting a pedophile go free, did you? You just told him about a fight between sisters, an unfortunate accident. And what happened to the monitor?"

"I spoke to him as well." He knew it didn't matter, that by this point his excuses were falling on deaf ears, but he continued anyway. "He assured me he'd never do it again, that he would reform, it was just that one time, because—"

"Because Iris was looking for it, right?" Leire intervened.

Fèlix shook his head.

"He was a good boy from a good family. He believed in God and he promised it would never happen again. The Church preaches forgiveness."

"Justice, Father, preaches something else," interrupted Héctor. "But you all think you're above it, isn't that right?"

"No . . . I don't know." Fèlix lowered his eyes again. "I said the same thing to Marc when he came to see me after returning from Dublin. He wanted to know that boy's name. He barely remembered who the camp monitors were, he was only six. And I refused to tell him. I told him to forget the whole matter."

"But Marc didn't forget," continued Héctor. "He said so in his blog: he spoke of means and ends, revenge and justice, truth."

"I don't know what he was planning. I didn't discuss the subject with him again." He looked at Inés, as if she might have the answer.

"He didn't give me the details, but it was some plot against you. He didn't want to tell me what it was."

Héctor stood in front of Father Castells.

"Well, now the time has come to give this name, don't you think? The name of the monitor who abused this little girl and is, morally at least, responsible for her death? The name Marc was trying to discover?"

He nodded.

"I hadn't seen him for a while, but I met him yesterday at the Martís' house. His name is Eduard. Eduard Rovira."

39

"Pigs," said Leire as she drove toward the Rovira home. "They're all pigs. I'm sure that the friendship with the Roviras mattered more than what had happened to the cook's daughter. A good Christian boy from a good family who has made a mistake . . ."

Héctor looked at her and couldn't deny it.

"There was an element of that, I'm sure. And also hurt pride or fear. How could you justify all this happening under your nose without your seeing it? With Iris dead, the most 'practical' thing is to bury the matter."

Leire accelerated.

"I want to catch this fucker."

They caught him at home. The elder Roviras weren't there, so it was a surprised Aleix who opened the door to them, thinking they were looking for him.

"I thought it was tomorrow—"

Héctor grabbed him by the collar.

"We're going to talk then for a little while, you and I. But first we want to chat to your dear brother. Is he in his room?"

"Upstairs. But you have no right to—"

Héctor slapped him across the face. A red mark spread over the boy's cheek.

"Hey, this is police brutality!" he protested, seeking Leire's help with his eyes.

"What?" she asked. "You mean what's come up on your face? You've been bitten by a mosquito. There're lots in summer. Even in this neighborhood."

The uproar had brought Edu out of his room. Héctor released Aleix and focused all his attention on his brother. He forced himself to forget what Inés had read them barely half an hour before, to stifle the superhuman rage which threatened to cloud his vision once again. He remained tense for a few seconds, fists clenched. His face must have been frightening because Edu drew back.

"You know why we're here, don't you?" asked Leire, placing herself between the inspector and Eduard Rovira. "We'll all go to the station, and there we can talk more calmly."

Leire observed Aleix, who was sitting on the other side of the table in the interrogation room, not daring to look up. The red stain had almost disappeared from his cheek, but a slight scratch was still visible.

"We have to talk about Edu, Aleix." Her voice was cold, impartial. "You know your brother is sick."

He shrugged.

"All right. How long have you known? Did he abuse you too?"

"No! He doesn't—"

"He doesn't like boys. Just a detail! So he prefers girls. When did you find out?"

"I'm not going to say anything."

"Yes. Yes you're going to say. Because it could be that your brother killed Marc and Gina to hide all this. And maybe Marc mightn't matter to you, but you loved Gina . . ."

"Edu hasn't killed anybody! He didn't even know about this until yesterday."

Leire was treading carefully. Any error could be fatal.

"If that's true, talk to me, Aleix. Convince me. When did you realize Edu liked little girls?"

He looked her in the eyes; she knew he was calculating all the possibilities and mentally crossed her fingers until he finally answered.

"I don't know anything about that."

"Yes you do . . . You like knowing things about others, Aleix. And you're nobody's fool."

Aleix smiled at her.

"Well, let's say a couple of years ago, one summer that he came home, I found some things on his computer. I'm good at passwords. But you can't prove it because you won't find anything on it now." He kept smiling. "Not a trace."

Thanks to you, motherfucker, thought Leire. Aleix was bragging; he wanted to show that he was the cleverest. I'm going to get you for being cocky, asshole.

"And when Marc came back from Dublin determined to find the boy who had abused Iris, you ended up putting two and two together and thought it could be Edu, didn't you? You remembered he'd been a camp monitor with Fèlix, and it's obvious your family and the Castells got on well. Marc didn't even remember Edu, or know you when all this happened. And Edu's been away for years . . . In places where he does humanitarian work. And plays with little girls."

He held her gaze insolently.

"You said that, not me."

Leire paused. They were getting to the most important point in this whole matter, the point at which she stopped knowing and had to ask, the point at which she needed to be more adept than this conceited brat. She took a few seconds before forming the next question.

In the adjoining room, a silent and terrified Eduard was facing Inspector Salgado's harsh, tense voice. He'd told him, point by point, detail after detail, everything contained within Iris's diary.

"And what's more, you've been unlucky," he finished. "Because for some legal reason I can never understand, these cases of abuse expire after fifteen years. And that summer was only fourteen years ago. Have you heard what they do to pedophiles in prison?"

Edu paled, and gave the impression of cowering in his seat. Yes, everyone had heard of that.

"Well, in your case it will be worse, since I'll make sure the guards tell the reliable prisoners. And in passing let slip that you're a good boy who evaded justice for years because of Daddy's contacts." He laughed inwardly, seeing the face this worm was making. "If there are two things prisoners hate it's pedophiles and rich kids. I really wouldn't want to be in your shoes when three or four of them corral you in one of the rooms while the guards look the other way."

He seemed on the verge of breaking down. Good, that's how I like it, thought Salgado.

"Of course if you cooperate a little, maybe I'll do the opposite. Ask the screws to protect you, tell them you're a good boy who's made a few mistakes."

"What do you want to know?"

"What did your brother tell you?"

Leire was about to form the next question when a serious Héctor Salgado appeared in the room and, moving slowly toward Aleix, said to him very quietly:

"Edu's been explaining a few things to me. The idea of going to jail has made him very communicative."

Salgado sat on the edge of the table, very close to Aleix.

"And by the end I'd formed an opinion of you. Want to know what it is?"

The boy shrugged.

"Answer me when I speak to you."

"You're going to tell me anyway, aren't you?" replied Aleix.

"Yes. You're a clever guy. Very clever. At least in school. First in class, leader of the pack. A good-looking boy with a rich family behind him. But deep down you know there's lots of shit hidden in this family. The rest don't matter, but Edu is special. You've done a lot of things for Edu . . ."

Aleix looked up.

"Edu helped me a lot years ago."

"Yeah. Because of that you couldn't let Marc's plan proceed. It was a somewhat crazy plan, but it could have come off and your precious Edu would have had to face a very disagreeable time. You killed Marc for that? So it wouldn't go ahead?"

"No! I've told you a hundred times. I didn't kill Marc. Not me, not Edu—"

"Well, right now it's on you. It all adds up."

Aleix looked at Salgado, then at Leire. He didn't find even a hint of understanding. Finally he threw his head back, closed his eyes and inhaled. When he opened them again, he started speaking slowly, almost relieved.

"Marc got really angry with his uncle when he refused to tell him who that monitor was. And then that stupid idea occurred to him." He paused. "You know everything already, don't you? I suppose you found the USB at Gina's house."

Leire didn't know what he was talking about but nodded.

"I was lucky. I grabbed it when you left."

"Well, then you've seen it. The photos of Natàlia, ready to be downloaded onto his uncle's computer. In a way it would have been funny: seeing enormous Father Castells' face when he turned on the computer and found photos of a naked little girl on it, along with some others Marc had downloaded from the internet. Also, Marc worked on the photos. He took lots of the little one one night while she was asleep. Did you know that little Chinese girls are very popular with pedophiles?"

Leire tried not to let the emotion and disgust she felt show in her appearance. She was mentally putting two and two together, trying to anticipate and not put her foot in it. But then Salgado intervened.

"It would have been difficult for him to explain those photos if someone had seen them."

"Of course. And for once the cassock wouldn't protect him from the rumors. Rather the contrary."

"Rumors like the ones you spread in school about that teacher," said Héctor, remembering it at that moment.

Aleix smiled slightly.

"Yes. Stupid bitch. I found a profile of hers on the internet, all very decent, I swear. I stole the photos, played around with Photoshop to enhance certain charms, added other text and then sent the thing to her whole list of contacts. And not just private ones; I even included the principal of the school. It was brilliant!"

"And Marc thought to do the same with Father Castells' email account and the photos of Natàlia," added Héctor.

"More or less. Really Marc wanted to use it as a threat. Thanks to a few things I'd taught him, he'd deciphered his uncle's account password. His plan was simple. On one hand, upload the file with the photos onto Father Castells' computer, then after the San Juan long weekend call and corner him: either he gave him the name he wanted or those disgusting photos that Fèlix, horrified, was seeing for the first time would be revealed to all his contacts. Knowing his password and having the USB with the photos, Marc could do it from home. Enric, Glòria, the priest's colleagues, the clerical associations—can you imagine their faces if suddenly an email arrived from Castells containing photos of his naked niece?"

"It's sick," Leire pointed out. "He was going to do that to a man who raised him, who'd almost been a father to him?"

Aleix shrugged.

"Marc's theory was that Fèlix would have talked. In the moment of desperation he'd reveal the name he wanted. And then he wouldn't have to carry out his threat. Anyway, he didn't feel too bad about giving him a fright: at the end of the day he was an accessory."

"And you thought he'd get his way?"

The boy nodded.

"The plan could have failed spectacularly and Fèlix could have refused, but . . . It's a bad time for priests regarding this subject. He wouldn't have risked his reputation to protect Edu . . . I tried to dissuade Marc, point out the risks. I insisted that this wasn't a school joke anymore, it was a much more serious thing. If the truth came out he and Gina could have had a bad time of it. I managed to convince him to postpone the whole thing for a few days, at least. I told him we should think about it so as not to put our foot in it and I persuaded him to leave it until after the exams. He didn't bring up the subject again, but through Gina I knew he'd gone ahead with the plan behind my back."

"And you couldn't allow that . . ." Héctor continued interrogating him. "So you convinced Gina to keep the USB."

"It was easy. She was hugely jealous of the girl from Dublin and she was really frightened. Also, Gina was a sensitive girl." He smiled. "Too sensitive. Seeing those photos horrified her. Marc saved them on the USB to delete them from his computer. At my request, Gina convinced him that it was better that she kept it in her house until he had the opportunity to access Fèlix's computer."

"And the opportunity arose over San Juan weekend," said Leire, recalling that Fèlix was staying with the rest of his family in Collbató. "But Gina didn't bring the USB to the party and Marc got angry," she continued, sure of herself thanks to Rubén's story. "He got angry with you and with her and ended up flushing the drugs you had to sell. The drugs you still had to pay for, incidentally. You tried to stop him and you hit him. The T-shirt he was wearing got stained with blood. Because of that, he then took it off and put on another."

"More or less . . ."

"You said you left, and your brother confirmed it, but your mutual alibi isn't very satisfactory now, would you say?"

He leaned toward the table.

"It's true! I went home. Edu was there. I didn't tell him any of this. God, I only told him last night because I need money to pay these guys. If not, I'd never have told him anything. He's . . . my brother."

Leire looked at Héctor. The boy seemed to be telling the truth. Salgado pretended to ignore his colleague and sat down at a corner of the table.

"Aleix, what I can't understand is how a boy as clever as you could make such a crude mistake. How did you let Gina keep the USB? You were in control of everything. And you knew you couldn't trust her—"

"I didn't!" he protested. "I asked her for it the same day you came to question her. But she got mixed up and gave me the wrong one. You know something? I am cleverer than you. Do you have the transcription of the suicide note that Gina wrote to hand? Do you remember it? Gina would never have written that! She was incapable of leaving off an accent or using abbreviations. Her father, the writer, hates them."

Héctor watched Aleix, not saying anything. But it was Agent Castro who caught his attention then, as, in a voice trying to be firm, she asked: "What was on the USB Gina gave you, Aleix?"

"Her Art History notes. What does that matter?"

Leire leaned on the back of the chair. Far away she could hear Héctor continuing to interrogate the witness, although she knew it was pointless. Aleix hadn't killed Marc, and of course Gina hadn't either. He was an idiot and he deserved to have his face smashed in by the dealers, but he wasn't a killer. Neither was his brother, the pious pedophile.

Without saying anything, she left the room and made a call. She didn't need anything else: just to confirm something with Regina Ballester, Gina Martí's mother.

40

Sitting on the white sofa of the Castells' house, while Glòria finished bathing the little one before coming down to join them, Héctor said to himself that in this lounge he was breathing in the same peace he'd noticed the last time they were there. But now, while he contemplated the elegant décor and heard the soft music floating in the air, Héctor knew that all this was nothing more than a set. A false calm.

He and Leire had argued a lot on how to approach the next part of the matter. Salgado had listened to Castro's reasoning and together they'd joined all the dots to arrive at the same conclusion. But when they got to the end of the process, when the name of the person who had killed Marc, and probably Gina as well, was clear to both of them, Héctor remembered something he'd said to Joana: "It's possible this case may never be resolved." Because, even with the truth before them, the proof was minimal. So minimal that he could only trust that the tension and fear combined would be stronger than endurance and cold blood. For that reason he'd imposed his will and gone alone. For what he was going to do, two was a crowd.

Enric Castells was tired, Héctor said to himself. Dark circles cast a shadow over his expression.

"I don't want to be rude, Inspector, but I hope you have a good excuse for turning up at my home on a Sunday evening. I don't know if you are aware that this weekend hasn't been exactly easy for us . . . Yesterday we had to give our condolences to good friends whose daughter committed suicide and maybe killed . . ." He was quiet for a moment. "And since then I can't stop going over everything in my mind. Everything . . ."

He rubbed his face with his hands and took a deep breath.

"I want all this to be over," he said then. "If Glòria ever comes down . . . Can't we begin without her?"

Héctor was going to repeat what he had said to him as he came in, that he needed both of them to cooperate because new and disturbing evidence had come to light in relation to his son's death, but just then Glòria came in alone.

"Finally!" exclaimed Enric. "Does it take so long to bathe that little girl?"

The hostility of the question surprised the inspector. "That little girl." Not "the little one" or "my daughter," or even "Natàlia." That little girl.

Glòria didn't bother to respond and took a seat beside her husband.

"Well, get on with it, Inspector. Are you going to tell us why you've come?" asked Castells.

Héctor stared at them. And then, before this couple who seemed to be living in a state of cold war, he said: "I have to tell you a story that goes back years, to the summer when Marc was six years old. The summer a little girl called Iris Alonso died."

By the expression on Enric's face, Héctor gathered that he too had read Marc's blog. He didn't know how he'd learned of its existence, but it was clear that the name Iris was familiar to him. Salgado continued with his tale: he outlined to them the story of abuse and death, without giving more than the necessary details. He then went on to speak to them about Inés and Marc in Dublin, of his decision to bring the truth to light, and came to the plan devised to coerce Fèlix, who'd refused to reveal to his nephew the name he was demanding. He recounted the perverse trick for which he'd used Natàlia, and graphically described photos he hadn't seen. Doing so, he watched the Castells' expressions and saw what he had expected: his was a mixture of apprehension and interest; hers of disgust, hatred and surprise. He finished by telling them of Aleix's intervention to prevent his brother's name coming out. It was a succinct but clear summary.

"Inspector," began Enric, who'd listened to Salgado attentively, "are you telling me my son was trying to blackmail my brother? He wouldn't have done it. I'm sure of that. In the end he would have backed out."

Héctor shook his head, with a doubtful air.

"That we'll never know. Marc and Gina are dead." He put his hand in his pocket and took out the USB Aleix had given him an hour before. "This is the USB that Gina took from here, the one she then gave to Aleix. But there are no photos on it. In fact, it's not even Gina's or Marc's. It's yours, isn't it, Glòria?"

She didn't answer. Her right hand was clenched on the arm of the sofa.

"It has your notes from university on it. Haven't you missed it?"

Enric raised his head slowly, not understanding.

"I haven't had much time for studying lately, Inspector," replied Glòria.

"I believe you. You've been fairly busy with other things."

"What are you suggesting?" Enric's voice had recovered some of its characteristic strength, that of the lord who doesn't allow anyone to attack his family in his own home.

Héctor continued. He spoke in a calm, almost friendly voice.

"I'm suggesting that fate has played a dirty trick on everyone. The USB with the photos was here for a few days before Gina took it. And Natàlia, innocent and playful, did something that's fun for her these days. You said it yourself to Agent Castro when we were here. Natàlia took the USB with the photos and left it beside her mother's computer, and took the one you had, with the notes of the correspondence-course degree you are studying for, to Marc's room. And he, not wanting to have those photos on the computer again, gave it to Gina without realizing the error. But you . . . you opened what you shouldn't have opened. And saw those photos of Natàlia: photos of your daughter naked, photos suggesting a whole world of horror. You knew Marc had confessed to having posted that video of a schoolmate on the internet. You didn't trust him, or love him. After all, you weren't his mother . . ."

Glòria went red. She said nothing; she tried her utmost to stay calm. Her hand had become a claw clinging to the arm of the sofa.

"You saw the photos?" asked Enric. "You didn't tell me—"

"No," Héctor intervened. "She didn't tell you anything. She decided to punish Marc on her own, isn't that right?"

Castells jumped up as if on a spring.

"I won't tolerate one more word, Inspector!" But his eyes showed doubt. He turned slowly toward his wife, who remained still, like a rabbit in the headlights. "That night you didn't sleep with me. You went to bed with Natàlia. You said the little one was afraid of the fireworks."

There was a moment of extreme tension. Glòria took a few seconds to answer, the time needed to stop her voice trembling.

"And that's how it was. I slept with Natàlia. Nobody can prove otherwise."

"You know what?" Héctor intervened. "In a way I understand you, Glòria. It must have been terrible. To see those photos without knowing what else they'd done to your daughter, fearing the worst. The same would have happened to any mother. There's something powerful in a mother's love. Powerful and implacable. Even less aggressive animals attack to protect their young."

Héctor saw the hesitation in her eyes. But Glòria wasn't easy prey.

"I'm not going to continue talking to you, Inspector. If my husband doesn't throw you out of our home, I will."

But Enric seemed not to have heard the last statement by his wife.

"The following day we had to stop for petrol. I didn't even remember. Fèlix was driving because I wasn't capable of taking the wheel. But the tank wasn't so empty when we went up . . . I haven't thought about it since . . ." He faced his wife and whispered to her, unable to raise his voice. "Glòria, did you kill . . . ? Did you kill my only child?"

"Your only child!" The bitterness exploded in a hoarse shout. "And what is Natàlia? What would you have done if I had told you about the photos? I'll tell you. Nothing! The excuses, the justifications would have started . . . The little one is fine, it was a joke, teenagers are like that . . .

"What did you say when he posted that video on the inter-

net? 'He's had a difficult life—his mother abandoned him . . .'"
Her words oozed rancor. "And Natàlia? The years she spent in
the orphanage? Don't they count? This daughter doesn't count
for you. She's never mattered to you at all!"

Glòria looked at the inspector. She was trying to make him
understand the truth. To justify herself somehow.

"I couldn't forgive him, Inspector. Not this time. Who knows
what else he would have done to my little girl?" She'd started
and now she couldn't stop. "Yes, the night before San Juan I
told you I would sleep with Natàlia, but I went down to Barcelona in the car as soon as I heard you sleeping. I'd made sure
you would sleep, believe me. I didn't know what I was planning to do. Accuse him of it all and force him to leave without
you knowing, I suppose. I wanted him out of Natàlia's life and
out of mine. I got home just as Aleix was leaving. I saw the
light go on in Marc's room and then go out. A little later, I saw
him leaning out of the window. I crossed the street quickly and
went up to the attic. He was still there, and at that moment I
couldn't help it. I ran toward him and pushed him . . . It was
an impulse . . ."

And you put the ashtray on the sill back in its spot, automatically, thought Héctor, not saying a word.

"But killing Gina wasn't an impulse, Glòria," said Héctor.
"It was a crime in cold blood, committed against an innocent
young girl—"

"Innocent? You haven't seen all the photos, Inspector! They
did them together, the two of them. They took advantage of
a night she came to babysit Natàlia. She was even in one, although I suppose they planned to delete it."

"They didn't hurt her," murmured Héctor. "They were mis-
takenly trying to hunt down an abuser of minors."

"But I didn't know that. God, I didn't know! And I told myself that if Marc had died, she had to die as well. Also—"

"Also, you didn't even know she'd stayed over that night and when you found out you panicked. Luckily for you, Gina was so drunk that she fell asleep immediately and heard nothing. But when we saw you here, and you realized the case was still open, you were frightened. And you decided that Gina's false suicide would put a full stop to it all. You went to her house that evening, spoke to her, you certainly drugged her a little, as you did your husband on San Juan. Afterward you brought her to the bathtub and with utmost cruelty you slit her wrists. Then you wrote a fake suicide note, trying to imitate the style of young people when they write."

"She was as evil as him," replied Glòria with hatred.

"No, Glòria, they weren't evil. They might have been young, mistaken, spoiled, but they weren't evil. The only evil person here is you. And your biggest punishment won't be jail but being separated from your daughter. But believe me, Natàlia deserves a better mother."

Enric Castells watched the scene dumbfounded. He couldn't even say a word when Héctor arrested his wife, read her her rights and steered her toward the door. If his heart could have moved at will, it would have stopped that very instant.

41

Héctor left the station at around half past ten that night and knew that, although he didn't feel like it at all, he should return to his flat. He'd gone more than thirty-six hours without sleep; he was conscious of the nicotine filling his lungs, his empty stomach and fuzzy head. He needed to wake up a little, then take a long shower: get rid of tension, regain strength.

The city seemed muffled that warm Sunday night. Even the few cars that were circulating appeared to be doing so slowly, lazily, as if the drivers wanted to prolong the last throes of the weekend. Little by little Héctor, who had started walking at a brisk pace, began to keep time with the slow rhythm ruling the streets. He would have given anything to stifle his mind as well, to stem the flow of unbidden images. He knew from experience that it was a question of time, that these faces which now seemed unforgettable would sooner or later fade through the drain of memory. There were some, however, he'd prefer not to forget for the moment: Eduard Rovira's shocked, miserable face, for example. Despite the threats of jail that he himself had made, he knew it would be difficult to make him answer for his actions before the courts. But at least, he told himself, he'd have to put up with the shame of having been found out and the contempt of those around him. Héctor planned to make sure of that personally and as soon as possible: guys like Edu didn't deserve even the slightest compassion.

He took a deep breath. He had other things to do the following day. Speak to Joana and say good-bye, drop in at the hospital to see Carmen . . . And apologize to Savall. Maybe his behavior in Iris's case years before hadn't been exemplary, but his motives hadn't been selfish; rather the contrary. In any case, he had no right to set himself up as judge and jury. That he left to people like Father Castells. Tomorrow, he thought, tomorrow I'll sort all that out. That night he could do no more. He'd made one call from the station: to Agent Castro to inform her that her intuition was correct. He owed her. After all, if it hadn't been for her, this case might never have been solved. She was good, he thought. Very good. He didn't spend a long time on the phone because he realized she wasn't alone. In the background he suddenly heard a masculine voice asking something.

"I won't bother you any longer—we'll talk tomorrow," he said as he wished her good-bye.

"OK. But we have to celebrate it, all right? And this time I'll pay."

There was a brief pause, one of those moments in which the silence seems to mean something. But, after the usual good-byes, both had hung up.

Standing before a red light he took his mobile out again to see if there was any message from Ruth. It was almost eleven; perhaps they were still en route. It was almost a month since he'd seen Guillermo, and as he crossed the street he told himself that this couldn't happen again. He didn't want to be an absent figure, as Enric Castells had been with his son. Responsibility can be delegated, but not affection. The ironies of fate, he thought. Enric was once again alone and with a child in his care, a little girl he didn't even consider his own daughter.

By now he was close to home, and the apprehension of the moment of going back into his house hit him again. The building he'd lived in for years felt like a sinister place, contaminated by Omar, by his killers. Enough, he ordered himself once again. Omar was dead and those who had killed him were locked up in jail. He couldn't have asked for a better result. Inspired by this thought, he put his key in the front door, and just as he crossed the threshold, his mobile rang. It was Guillermo.

"Guille! Brilliant! You're back then?"

"No . . . Papa, listen—have you heard from Mama?"

"No. I spoke to her on . . . Friday, I think." It seemed as if a century had passed, rather than a few days. "She told me she would come to pick you up."

"Yeah. Me too. We arranged for her to come around nine, half nine."

"And she still hasn't arrived?" He looked at his watch, uneasy.

"No. And I've called her and she's not answering. Carol doesn't know anything either." He paused and continued in a voice that wasn't that of a child but a worried adult. "Papa, Mama hasn't spoken to anyone since Friday morning."

Mobile still in his hand, facing the staircase which led to his home, Héctor suddenly remembered what Martina had said about Dr. Omar, about the rituals he was preparing, about the DVD Ruth had received. "Forget all this, he's dead—it doesn't matter now . . ." the sergeant had said.

His forehead broke out in a cold sweat.

TODAY

It's already been six months since Ruth disappeared. No one has heard from her since that Friday she decided to go to her parents' apartment. We're not even sure that she got there, because her car was found in Barcelona, near her house. We've published her photo, put up notices, searched her flat. I personally interrogated the good-for-nothing lawyer who killed Omar and I've come to the conclusion that he knows nothing apart from what he's already told me. The damn doctor told him, with a Machiavellian smile, that I would have to suffer the worst possible sentence. The lawyer thought it was just one of his phrases. I wouldn't have taken it seriously either. But now I know it's true. There is nothing worse than not knowing, living in a world of shadows and doubts. I roam around the city like a ghost, scanning faces, thinking I see Ruth in the most unlikely places. I know one day I'll find her, dead or alive. I'll have to explain to my son what happened to his mother. I owe him: if I have kept my sanity it is thanks to him. To him and my friends. They're not giving up either. They know I have to find out the truth and I won't rest until I do.

ABOUT THE AUTHOR

ANTONIO HILL lives in Barcelona. He is a professional translator of English-language fiction into Spanish.